LOVELY, DARK, AND DEEP

TJ TRISTAN

SILVER BRANCH PUBLISHING LLC

For my mom, who gave me the strength to move mountains.
For my dad, who gave me the courage to climb them.

KINGDOM OF ARASTYA

The woods are lovely, dark, and deep,
But I have promises to keep,
And miles to go before I sleep,
And miles to go before I sleep.

— ROBERT FROST

PREFACE

This book is a work of fantasy inspired by the myths, deities, and legends of various Celtic nations. It is not intended to be a historically accurate or representative depiction of Celtic lore but rather a personal interpretation woven into a new and unique narrative.

My journey in writing this book began as an act of healing. Having endured traumatic experiences that left me deeply disconnected from my ancestry and faith, I found solace in revisiting the ancient stories of the Celts. Their rich and powerful mythology became a refuge, a source of strength, and ultimately, an inspiration. Through this world, I reclaimed a part of myself that I once feared to acknowledge.

This story imagines a world where Celtic paganism was never lost, never erased, and never assimilated into other faiths. Instead, it envisions a reality where its traditions flourished and evolved into a society of Druids, beings who wield natural magic gifted to them by their patron deities. This is not a retelling of history but a vision of what might have been—an exploration of a world untouched by suppression, where the old ways thrive in their purest form. The deities in this world are inspired by their mythic origins but have been reinterpreted to fit the cosmology of Arastya. They are not intended as literal depictions of the gods of living Celtic faiths, but as archetypes honoring their spirit.

I invite you to journey through this world with an open heart, to embrace its magic and spirit as I have, and to experience the wonder that these myths continue to inspire.

1

$\mathcal{F}$rom the edge of the Mortal Lands, whispered tales of a Forest Primeval echoed through the hearts of men. Its branches clawed at the skies, its predators grinned with bloodied teeth, and its' very gaze was enough to shred sanity. The Forest was a fireside story kindled by elders and woven into the nightmares of children. To the humans, the Forest harbored unfathomable horrors within its depths, their fears manifested in some form they could not comprehend or define. For the last century, these humans failed to realize that the beast they feared the most was not a creature of fang or fur.

It was me.

I was the reason men stopped venturing into the Forest. Though, I did prefer to think of it as a mutual arrangement. They no longer wanted to enter, and I saw no reason to invite them. They were greedy, abusive, and had an odd vendetta against any living thing that touched them. They were also easy prey for my clawed, fanged, and blinding co-inhabitants. Every time a human was lost to the Forest, more humans decided it would be a *fabulous* idea to try and find them. One human became prey, then ten, then twenty. This cycle only ceased when a creature was murdered—often not even the true animal involved, but one they could justify as a possible culprit—and even then, for hunting on its own territory, no less. It was in their best interest to stay away, just as it was in mine to keep them away. And for the last century, I'd succeeded.

It seemed, however, my luck had run out.

Through the shadowed paths of the Forest, two men wandered through the ancient trees and moonlit glens. They meandered through labyrinthine limbs, lit only by dappled beams of silver. It was a wonder they were alive, to begin with. The cu sith hounds hunted the edge of the Mortal Lands. Even the fleet-footed wilde hares kept their warrens far from the hounds' hunting ground, where death awaited anything within reach. How had they managed to get past them?

I needed to get closer, to see what they were up to—why they were here—alone and at night. As the last of my kind, it was my duty.

I'd learned long ago that wielding fear was much more potent than any blade. A mere display of my powers had once sufficed. But if the humans had forgotten me, perhaps they needed a more *creative* reminder.

I leaned into my elk's neck, running my fingers through his fur. "Quiet and slow, Orion," I murmured. Orion was a massive male, with fourteen points on his rack and his shoulders standing almost as high as my head. I hadn't hated my century of relative solitude, largely due to his companionship. His opinionated nature, punctuated by antler jabs and grumpy chuffs whenever we disagreed, was a much-needed bandage over the gaping wound caused by my father's disappearance.

Orion inched forward, lowering his mighty head so it wouldn't get caught in the foliage. Silver moonlight brushed the tips of his antlers, casting a gossamer glow on his tawny coat. His hooves were silent as they swept across the moss, only interrupted by the gentle heave of breath clouding around his nose.

The men paused, their muffled conversation drifting through the stillness of the Forest. One, with raven hair and a blade at his side, leaned callously against a tree and tossed a crimson apple in his hand. The other, with long silver hair and skin as rich as earth, stood in his shadow. He stood a few inches below his dark-haired companion, who peered down at him with dark eyes.

I had never seen men like this before. The men I knew were grimy creatures, either rotund from gluttony or gaunt from starvation. These men were neither. Maybe they weren't men at all. Perhaps they were Druids, like me. It might explain how they were still alive if they came from the Arastyan edge of the Forest, but Druids weren't typically ignorant enough to wander through the Western Territories. They knew what the gods kept here. If they were, in fact, Druids, they had a chance of making it out alive. A slim chance, yes—but better than none.

How could I get them out without being seen?

I pulled my leg over Orion's back and slid quietly down his flank. I patted his shoulder, and he swung his massive head towards me. Big intelligent eyes peered into mine.

"Stay, friend. I'll be right back," I said. Orion appeared to scowl in protest. He didn't like it when I meddled. It was *my* Forest, though, so it was *my duty* to meddle. He heaved a sigh and let his massive head fall to the ground, grazing on the moss beneath our feet.

I crept over to a tree, cloaked in the darkness of night, only yards from where the males conversed nonchalantly as if they weren't in the deadliest forest in all of Arastya. This Forest was the blessed land of the goddess of life, but only because of the bodies of the dead.

"Why are you so content in believing them extinct?" the male with the dark hair asked, sinking his teeth into the apple.

"We've been walking through here for days, Your Highness, and have found nothing," his silver-haired companion replied. "Surely, if they still existed, we would've seen one by now, or at least a sign of their residence. We both know this excursion was more of a formality than a necessity. The last Forest Druid died decades ago. Just change the competition's code."

A pause, a glance. "We should return to Kalys before we end up like that messenger. Something killed him before he even reached the thicket."

"Someone, Kyro. Not something," the dark one corrected, taking another bite of his apple.

The silver one snorted in disdain. "Because that's any better? Whoever killed him wasn't a Forest Druid. You know the history books, they practically worshiped all life. Terrifying creatures, perhaps, but they were far from the bloodthirsty savages your father believed them to be. If only we'd known that then."

I could now feel their magic from here—definitely not men. Both of them were blessed by the gods. Their power was palpable, a vibrant thread in the air. My own magic responded, a seething thrum beneath my skin. I shoved it down. I couldn't give myself away. My best chance at protecting the Forest and all of its inhabitants would be to remain unknown to the Druids and a monster to the humans.

My feet swept across the earth as I inched behind an oak, just several paces from where the Druids conversed. I crouched, balancing on the balls of my feet. Sharp moonlight speared through the leaves above me. I twisted myself to remain within the shadows. Shallow breaths clouded my lips as I peered around the trunk. The lichen-crusted bark crumbled beneath my fingertips, wet from the Western Territories' perpetual rain. The slightly sweet smell of pine sap filled the air.

"We should find a place to stay for the night," the dark-haired male spoke, eyes squinting through the thicket in my direction. I hadn't made a sound—there was no way he was looking directly at me. Not with the thick night and tree foliage. Still, he remained fixated, as if he could see my eyes through the underbrush. My breath lodged still, my heart slowing to a snail's pace.

"Regardless of what happened to the messenger, the monsters of the Wild are likely out hunting at this late hour, Your Highness," the silver-haired male cautioned with a shiver. "I suggest we either continue moving or return to the border where we can at least see our attackers. I'd rather not awaken to a beast's teeth around my neck."

The other one chuckled dryly. "I'm sure the beasts out here can find much easier prey than ourselves, Kyro."

His arrogance grated on me, my lips curling into a grimace. A bear or mountain lion might opt to leave them alone, but beasts borne of magic might welcome the challenge. The last thing I wanted to do was stand between one and its prey, but I couldn't allow any harm to befall them in the process. Hunting Druids was a messy business. Druids had the power to fight back, and I had no interest in cleaning up collateral damage.

"So you want us to continue then?" Kyro sighed in apparent frustration. "If we must keep going, sire, can we at least find a stream of some sort? Not all of us have constant access to our gods."

The dark one snickered. "You think Llyr would abandon you so easily? Leave you powerless the moment you're away from water sources?"

The male he'd called Kyro grimaced. "No amount of prayer to Llyr can summon water where there is none."

"Surely you can somehow utilize the obscene amount of water in the air," the dark one said. He rubbed his thumb and forefinger together. "This humidity is making my skin feel like a swamp."

Kyro shook his head. "That's beyond my power. Though, and

I must admit, sire, you *do* look like a drowned rat, it's hardly enough water for me to utilize." He paused, examining a leaf glittering with dew. "If we lived underwater, this would be an entirely different conversation. You always have access to darkness."

The dark one shook his head. "Arawn and Latobius hardly answer my prayers for magic in the South, where even shadows scarcely exist."

Kyro heaved a sigh. "I still think we should at least find a stream if something decides to have a go at us."

"We're already being followed, Kyro. If the creature following us wanted to attack, it would've done so already. We should set up camp. I want to rest." The dark one's gaze lingered back to the underbrush I'd entangled myself in. My heart stumbled.

"We're being followed?" Kyro immediately unsheathed his blade, steel ringing through the air and prickling my skin. "This is exactly why I wanted a stream."

I grabbed the shaft of the bow slung across my shoulder. A feral snarl coiled in the back of my throat as my muscles wound themselves taut, ready to pounce. I'd stop at nothing to keep my home safe.

"Kyro, I wouldn't—"

A haunting wail pierced the night air—high-pitched and gurgling. My stomach lurched, the snarl dying in my throat as quickly as it had risen. *Not good.*

I released the bow shaft and dug my fingers into the mossy earth—cool and damp and thrumming with life. Something was coming. I felt its hooves press into the soil across the glen, sure-footed and nimble. The Druids spun around; the blade gripped in Kyro's hand wavering as a skeletal creature emerged from the shadows. The smell of brine and rotten fish seeped through the breeze like fear down my spine.

Nuckelavee.

The horse demon's flesh clung to withering bones, a mane of wilted hair dripping with brackish water and seaweed. Its face was shrunk to the skull, eyes as pale as the moon and just as unyielding. From its spine, the skeleton of a human torso rose. Its jaw was unhinged as if in a never-ending scream, skinless arms dangling limply at either side. Another wail retched itself from the horse's teeth, frothing with seafoam. A heave of misting breath fumed from the creature's flared nostrils.

The dark-haired male grabbed his blade, and the nuckelavee tensed, baring its carnassial teeth. Shadows coiled around the male's feet like serpents drenched in smoke. Hairs on my neck rose.

A Dark Druid.

This could not end well.

I looked back at the creature, its heart beating unfathomably slow in its rotting chest. Its dilapidated veins pulsed with blood nonetheless, like any beast of the wild. Though it usually savored prey that put up a fight, this nuckelavee had a full belly and was returning to the sea to the north. Beneath the gruesome exterior, the horse demon was just another creature trying to find its way home. As if it saw me in the thicket, its head angled in my direction, looming eyes blank as they stared into mine. My own heart slowed, attempting to match its ungodly pace.

You see me.

This creature had done nothing wrong save for stumbling across two arrogant Druids who chose to judge the beast based on its appearance. Because they saw it and felt fear, they believed it deserved to die. How many had seen me and thought the same?

So much for remaining unseen. I would not let them harm the nuckelavee.

I sprinted through the thicket, the soles of my feet sweeping across moss and gnarled root. I broke into the clearing behind the nuckelavee. It didn't so much as tense as I pulled two arrows from my quiver and notched them against the shaft of my bow. The dark-haired male met my glare as my arrow tips aimed at him and his companion. The air was thick with the smell of brine.

The nuckelavee snorted in front of me, unfazed.

"Sheath your swords, or I fire," I said.

My eyes flicked to Kyro as he moved his blade back toward its sheath. He paused when his companion's hand clamped on his shoulder, stopping him.

"Forest Druid," the raven-haired male whispered, barely audible in the tension-wound air.

A grin crept onto my lips. "I won't miss."

2

*A*nother eerie wail loosed itself from the nuckelavee's bared teeth, the skinless torso atop its spine shuddering as it pawed the earth. Its breath smelled of rot and brackish seawater. The sword in Kyro's hand glittered in his trembling grip. His companion held his blade firm, outstretched in front of him.

"You'd risk your own life to defend this foul creature?" the dark-haired male challenged, his eyes glinting with the silvery edge of contempt.

I pulled my bowstring tighter—one arrow tip aimed at Kyro, the other at the arrogant male. "My life is not at risk, *ciarán*."

I tried to hold my bow steady, stifling my breaths. My knuckles blanched around the wooden shaft as my fingernails dug crescents into my palm. I waited for them to move, to lunge toward myself or the beast in front of me. Rage coiled in the nuckelavee's chest, a wordless vow to bleed the Druids dry should they so much as flinch. I couldn't say I disagreed with it; but engaging with a Dark Druid at night wouldn't leave the nuckelavee unmarred.

Kyro's brows knitted together as he stared at my bow. "Your

people were pacifists. Why do you choose to wield a weapon?" His eyes studied my stance. "Why do you *know* how to use it?"

My head tilted, bathing my cheek in the moonlight. "My people are not pacifists anymore."

The Dark Druid dropped his sword, the hilt dangling from his fingertips. "Your people? There's more of you?"

I looked between the two males, my blood stilling. "Sheath your swords. I will not ask again."

"I didn't realize *that* was asking," Kyro grumbled as his trembling blade slid into its sheath. The Dark Druid followed suit, sliding the steel back into its glimmering case.

A breath inched into my chest as I lowered my bow, allowing the bowstring to loosen beneath my arrows. I grimaced at the males' towering frames. They were larger than me, sure—but I was undoubtedly quicker.

The nuckelavee turned its milky, vacant gaze back to me and puffed a breath from its grimy nose. A sort of acknowledgment, I mused, so I bowed my head in response. It turned and walked past me, mere inches between us as it continued into the thicket behind me. Another bone-chilling wail from the nuckelavee pierced the air. Its footsteps vibrated through the soles of my feet, fading as the distance between us grew. The cries then disappeared altogether; the sudden silence interrupted only by the blood pounding in my ears. Though the beast was safe, I was still in the open.

"Are there more of you, *wildling?*" the Dark Druid pressed, taking a step closer.

I readied my bow once more, aiming at his left eye. "One more step and I'll fire."

Kyro intervened, hands raised in concession. "This is all a grave misunderstanding. I have read many books about your people. I can assure you we did not come to anger you or your goddess," he said, holding my stare despite his quaking fingertips. "Forest Druid, allow me to introduce the High King of

Arastya, Salem of the Kalystan bloodline, the Darkweaver, and Lord of Sky."

I snorted. "And?"

He appeared to choke. "And? And—and you should bow before the High King. Citizens of Arastya should always bow before their High King."

I remained standing.

The air around me seemed to grasp at my shoulders, tugging me to my knees as if the suspense was too much to bear alone. I forced my lungs open with a heave.

The supposed High King smirked in amusement, a chuckle reverberating from his chest. "It's all right, Kyro. She doesn't know any better. We can't exactly fault her for that."

I frowned, teeth grinding. "I bow to no one. I suggest you leave before the Forest decides to keep you."

I turned away, meeting Orion's gaze through the branches. His ears perked forward at my attention. He was undoubtedly annoyed, particularly because I didn't stay hidden. Most of the time, I yielded to his concerns and played out my role from the shadows. But I couldn't have sacrificed the nuckelavee's well-being in exchange for my secrecy.

"I'm afraid we can't let you leave, *wildling*," Salem's voice called from behind me. I paused, glancing over my shoulder.

I scoffed, irritation simmering just beneath my skin. "*Let* me leave? As if *you* could stop me?"

The Dark Druid hesitated, lips parted as if the words dangling there couldn't bear to part with them. A frown wrinkled between his brows, though the corners of his lips curled in a grin. It seemed he could not decide whether to laugh or scowl.

"Your presence is requested in Kalys," Kyro explained, rushed. "We require a Forest Druid to compete for the High King's hand per the Royal Decree for Arastyan Bloodline Mediation. Every Realm must send a representative, lest it is construed as disapproval of the High King's rule and therefore treason."

My teeth ground together as I spun back around, facing the two arrogant beasts that had wandered into my trees. Blood echoed in my ears as I spoke. "There's no High King here, only gods and monsters. I only yield to one of those three."

I stared pointedly at the High King and the sharp lip curling in amusement. My grip tightened around my weapon.

"Even if you're the last Forest Druid, having no representative from the Western Territories when there is a surviving and eligible Druid is effectively treason. If you refuse, you're voicing your lack of support for High King Salem's reign and, by proxy, the remainder of your Realm," he continued, his voice quieting to a desperate whisper. "We'd be forced to execute you, then search the Western Territories to determine if you truly were the last of your kind."

These threats, wrapped in the guise of royal decrees, only tightened the knotted rage in my chest. They dared to enter the Forest, threaten its inhabitants, and expected me to then comply with their demands or face death. My vision ran red.

I reached through the earth to the thrumming hearts standing before me. Kyro, though impassive, was bathed in fear's firelight. He desperately wanted to return home without a fight. Images of the nuckelavee hunting him down still swirled in his chest like a ship around a whirlpool. His companion, the supposed High King, was not nearly as afraid as his friend. He was either arrogant or stupid—perhaps both. Curiosity had sunk its talons into his chest, ever the cautious beast.

I grinned and clenched my fists.

Gnarled roots broke the soil, encircling the writhing Druids and knotting around their throats. Their eyes went wide, bulging white as they struggled to breathe. Kyro was pulled to his knees first, gasping as veins throbbed in his neck. Salem fell next. I held my breath for a moment, waiting to see if the Dark

Druid's shadows would come out to play. To my disappointment, the grass around his knees and feet remained moonlit. I'd expected more of a fight from the supposed High King.

Through gritted teeth, I said, "Let's get something clear. While I am mildly insulted that you think you could kill me so easily, I'll let that transgression slide. As your king put it so plainly before, *you don't know any better.* But if you threaten the Forest again, *I will end you.*"

I unwound my fists and the roots recoiled, slithering back into the earth. Kyro fell to all fours, heaving. Much to my frustration, his companion merely coughed as if my roots were nothing more than pests. The supposed High King glared at me with eyes as dark as the sky above. I stared back in challenge.

A lock of hair fell between his eyes as he spoke. "Killing me would only bring more war to your doorstep. Though you may not be the pacifist your people once were, the best way to keep your Western Territories safe is to come with me. I offer you a crown, *wildling.*"

Kyro coughed. "A *chance* at a crown," he corrected with a wheeze.

I chuckled dryly. "A crown? *Danu,* perhaps the Forest has gotten to you after all."

Salem began to pull himself to his feet. His tunic shifted from his chest, revealing tanned skin and a glimmering silver branch strung on a piece of thread around his neck. In the night, it glowed like a beckoning star.

My heart plummeted into my stomach. I could've sworn the Forest went silent. That time slowed at that very moment. Because I knew that necklace. I knew that branch.

My father had never once removed it from his neck. He'd never let me touch it.

How did the supposed High King get a hold of it? This arrogant Dark Druid—he *had* to have come across my father. Perhaps he knew what happened to him—if he was still alive.

Perhaps... perhaps my father was wherever these Druids had come from... wherever they were so intent on taking me.

"Where did you get that?" I demanded.

The Dark Druid glanced down at the necklace and then back at me. "Well, that's none of your concern, now is it?"

My eyes narrowed. "I'll decide what's of my concern and what isn't."

"Just as I will decide what information I believe you're privy to," he replied. He held my stare, a silent challenge.

The High King did not look away as he continued. "If you do not come, it will be treason, and I will have to send forces. If you kill me, the High Queen Regent will do the same as I would've. If you then kill her, my sister will follow the same path, and on and on. You'd have to kill my entire kingdom before you win. Are you willing to risk your Forest against my kingdom? The only way to avoid violence is to compete—if only for a little while. Then you can return to your desolate Western Territories as if none of it had ever happened."

I grimaced. I'd sworn an oath to Danu that I would protect the Forest. Though it had been a century of standing guard amongst the trees, waiting for someone to breach the thicket, I still felt apprehension at the idea of leaving. What if something happened the moment I left? What if the mortals began to hunt the Forest again? Even one life lost would weigh on me eternally. These creatures and I were the same.

But still . . . the Druid wore my father's necklace. He knew something. He had to. I'd waited a century to find out what happened to my father. This could be my only chance.

I knelt to the earth, bow at my side, and pressed my fingers into the damp soil. My eyelids pinched shut. Deep beneath the ground, something ancient watched me with unreadable eyes. I waited, holding my breath. She gave a single nod. My very soul thrummed as she spoke in a melodic whisper.

Find the one behind the necklace. She paused. *Do not allow your quest to be thwarted.*

The earth shifted as she returned to her slumber. My heart stuttered in my chest.

Even with Danu's approval, every moment away from the Forest was a risk. If one human ignored the stories and ventured in while I was gone, how many would follow in his footsteps? I guarded the Forest for a reason. It could not remain unprotected for long.

I swallowed thickly, rising to my feet and meeting the High King's stare. "If I must go, I will take my steed."

"Not if it's that thing," Kyro objected, waving in the direction the nuckelavee had gone. He rubbed his throat absentmindedly.

I nearly laughed at the thought of trying to tame such a creature. I'd been lucky enough to get them to tolerate me—I scarcely think they'd let me on their back. Though, it was amusing that Kyro thought I might heed his opinion.

I raised two fingers to my lips and let out a whistle. The ground shook beneath the soles of my feet as Orion thundered through the thicket toward us. Branches snapped beneath his hooves, leaves grabbing at his pale antlers as he charged through the underbrush. With a snort, he pushed through the bushes and into the open.

Kyro staggered back, eyes wide and hand flying to the hilt of his sword. "That is no horse," he whispered.

3

The two Druids in front of me walked gracefully through the Forest, never so much as tripping over the roots that reached from the earth like arms from a grave. Kyro's long, lithe limbs glided across the ground as if even gravity hesitated to tether his grace. Despite this, his posture was tense. He glanced back at me repeatedly, and his hand never lingered from the hilt of his sheathed blade. To say his apprehension did not bring me joy would be a lie. Perhaps the human fables of the Forest had somehow made it into Arastya.

Kyro did seem to be the more rational of the two, his fear not paralyzing but instead sharpening his senses. Every rustle in the bushes or twig snap nearby made him flinch, but not in cowardice—rather, in the direction of the nearest defensible position; a tree, a boulder, a downed log. Perhaps that was why the supposed High King lugged him along, for his strategy and logic despite his reactivity. The marine kelpies did something similar with their young. When the parents left to hunt, they would occasionally leave their defenseless offspring near a resting herd of deer. If the deer alerted to something, the young knew to hide.

In stark contrast, the Dark Druid, embodying the expected arrogance of a royal, walked with his chin aloft, surveying the surroundings as if daring the Forest itself to confront him. He was much more at ease than any other Druid would reasonably be in the Forest—except me. His fingers absentmindedly fiddled with the clunky silver ring on his right hand, seemingly oblivious to the creatures all around us—creatures that could and *would* attack if I wanted them to. Without Kyro's tactical acumen, I was certain the High King would've become prey the moment he entered the Forest. With his careless attitude, he probably would've walked straight into a dobhar chu's den, unaware the cave floor was covered in dried bones.

Orion's ears frequently flicked towards me on his back as if expecting me to turn us around. His heart was a few beats faster than usual, and I felt the wariness gnawing at his mind. His feelings mirrored my own.

"The castle is half a day's ride away," Kyro explained, keeping his eyes trained ahead as he spoke. "Our horses are tied at the edge of the Forest. We will move faster from there." Though I felt no malevolence from the male, the obvious disdain radiated off him like the waves of power from the High King. Given what I'd heard from him earlier, it seemed he was perturbed with me existing at all.

"And how long until I can return?" I asked, my eyes narrowing at the back of Salem's head. As if he had felt it, his head turned and dark grey eyes met mine.

I decided not to press the issue of the necklace. It was clear the Dark Druid would not reveal anything to me straight away. I'd have to glean whatever information I could as I went along, and hopefully, I'd stay long enough to find out Salem's involvement with my father. But they might suspect something if I was too eager and willing to please. If they believed me an unwilling participant, they'd be less likely to suppose I had ulterior motives. Acting as someone with nothing to lose was much less incriminating than someone with everything at stake. I could gather information about what happened to my father without censorship. If they didn't know what I was looking for, they wouldn't be able to stop me.

"As long as His Majesty decides. We uh—you probably are aware of our names by now, but we do not know yours," Kyro said, a pregnant pause following as he waited for me to respond.

"You didn't say you needed to know my name," I retorted. Orion let out a heavy sigh, a chuckle in agreement with my defiance.

"Well, what are we supposed to call you?" Kyro urged, keeping his eyes forward.

"You seem fond of calling me 'Forest Druid' and 'wildling,'" I said. "Let's stick with that."

Kyro shook his head, silver hair glimmering like waves in the rising sun. "I'm afraid that simply won't do."

He was a Water Druid—I could see that now. My father told me how they moved through time and space as if suspended in the ocean. Their powers were given by the sea god Llyr, king of travelers and tides. He had supposedly included time as a realm to travel through, giving his patrons a minute power over it. I wondered if that was why Kyro's hair moved as if it were in water, suspended in midair. If my hair attempted such a feat, the curls might strangle me.

At Kyro's words, Salem stopped dead in his tracks. Orion stomped his feet. I patted his shoulder and he heaved another breath of air, turning his head to the side and glowering at the High King. I did the same as I waited for him to speak, but his lips remained sealed in an arrogant grin.

"Do you *know* your own name?" Salem taunted.

Something vile writhed inside of me and bared its fangs. "Of course I do," I snapped in response.

"Then do you believe that being uncooperative will help you, *wildling?* That it'll make me send you home sooner? I can assure you, it won't. I'm rather fond of a challenge," Salem said, the words rolling off his tongue in a purr.

I frowned, wanting nothing more than to have the earth swallow him whole.

"My name is Quinn," I relented with a hiss. "You can find your *challenge* elsewhere."

"*Quinn,*" Salem said, a lazy grin tugging up the corners of his mouth.

I glared down at him. My name was strong. It was something to be screamed as a curse or a plea. The way he spoke diminished it to something whispered between sleepless dreams and satin sheets.

"Keep walking, *Your Highness.* You're making Orion impatient," I grumbled as Orion shook his head with a snort. Salem eyed my massive elk as if sizing him up, then spun around and continued on.

"You didn't answer my question earlier, *Quinn.* Are there more of you?" the High King asked. My blood stilled, breath lodging in my throat.

I swallowed. "I have not seen another of my kind in a century."

Both males turned back and looked at me, expressions unreadable. I couldn't tell if they pitied me or feared me. I couldn't be sure, and I didn't care to find out.

Kyro cleared his throat, his hair catching the silver moonlight between the leaves. "You are not to tell the other representatives that you met His Highness prior to the Announcement Ceremony to be held tomorrow night. It will be suggested that you had an unfair advantage, and we can't have that being thrown around the courts."

I scoffed. "You're not going to every Realm and demanding they offer a sacrifice?"

"On the contrary," Kyro replied. "We sent word to each Realm, and they sent their daughters. One from each as a representative. We'd been waiting for almost a week for the Western Territories' representative only to discover that the messenger had been killed and no one had been notified."

"And you two just thought it'd be a great idea to come out here—*alone*—and give the message yourselves?"

"There is very little that could harm either of us, *wildling*," Salem chuckled in response. Kyro shifted uncomfortably under the weight of my stare.

Was it the nuckelavee he feared the most? Or was it me? Was it a combination of both? Perhaps the fact he had no access to his god's magic?

I pursed my lips. "It seemed pretty easy to me."

Kyro glanced back over his shoulder at me, eyes glinting in the daylight like sea glass. "We needed you alive. This would be a different conversation if you were wanted dead." He turned away. "Or if we were underwater," he added under his breath.

"Whatever helps you sleep at night," I said. Amusement swelled in Orion's chest.

This would be the first time I'd left my forest home in a century, and I didn't know what awaited me on the other side. A tight fist in the pit of my stomach had my insides squirming, but I knew better than to show my fear in front of males who could likely smell it. Their power saturated the air around them like the silence. I didn't know if they could sense my power as well or if they could feel me trying to keep it at bay. I hoped they couldn't feel it. I didn't want them to know what monsters crawled beneath my skin. Not yet, at least.

The rest of the journey through the Forest was silent, but I sensed the woods watching us leave. Tree limbs appeared to reach towards me, the arms of a sluagh desperate for a soul to devour. As if my soul didn't already belong to the Forest. As if every part of me didn't ache to leave it behind.

Hidden beasts continued to follow us, curious eyes lingering on me as if to ask why I would leave them—what these males could offer me that they could not. Part of me wanted to usher them out of the shadows and tell them I had little choice in the matter. The need to uncover what happened to my father just barely eclipsed the need to protect my homeland. Was it selfish of me? Absolutely. But Danu knew how my father's disappearance ravaged me on the inside. I would be a better Forest Druid without this need—this pain. So regardless of how leaving my home behind gutted me, I did not call for my fellow beasts. If the High King and his bodyguard discovered what else lurked just beyond their sight, creatures that made the nuckelavee look like a doe . . . they might have my home destroyed regardless of my perceived obedience. Most things in the Forest lived here for a reason—including me.

After hours of stiff silence, the trees began to thin, and the beasts wandered back to their caves, leaving me to the ones marching several paces ahead. The sky above us warmed in the rising sun, skimming the rim of the plains that spanned out in front of us. Faintly, I could see rolling hills at the base of the Arastyan mountains past the prairie to my left. To my right, the plains continued to the horizon. Eventually, they would meet the sea.

Orion stomped his foot anxiously on the ground, wanting to run back to the comfort of the woods. I patted his neck, and he calmed a little, turning to face the two horses tied to a pair of elm trees at the Forest's edge. They perked their heads up, ears pointed toward us. One was a palomino, golden like the sunlight, with a silvery mane much like the male I suspected she belonged to. The other was dark and stood a few inches above the other, with long hair that fell across his eyes. He shook his head and whinnied, daring us closer.

Orion followed Salem and Kyro towards their steeds but stayed a few meters back as they climbed into their saddles. I didn't think Orion had seen horses before, aside from when their riders killed his mother. He had a right to be anxious around them. But he, just like I, knew they weren't responsible for the loss of our kin. It was the men that rode them who were to blame.

Salem swung into the saddle of his horse, the beast prancing around the palomino that continued to graze as Kyro mounted her. The High King trotted over to Orion's side. My elk raised his massive antlers high, warning off the dark horse.

"Kalys is hardly a place for a deer. I'd strongly recommend you leave the beast here," Salem said.

I scowled. "It's perfectly well that he's not a deer, then," I replied. "I will not abandon my friend. If you demand my presence in Kalys, then you will accommodate for my *elk*."

"Hmm," he hummed in response, eyes twinkling under the dusky light above us. Kyro trotted up behind Salem's horse and glanced between us both. Though he looked accustomed to being atop the mare, his pinched expression revealed some discomfort. Whether that was my doing or he wasn't that adept a rider, I couldn't tell.

"Shall we?" the Water Druid asked, motioning towards the foothills that hugged the base of the Arastyan Mountains.

Salem eyed me one last time before nudging his horse onwards, starting at a canter towards the sharp peaks in the distance. I pressed my knees into Orion's flank and he shook his head, galloping off after Salem with only a moment of protest.

BLADES OF TALLGRASS clipped at the bottoms of my feet as we rode through the rolling prairie lands. The region between the Northern and Southern Territories appeared sparsely populated, with meandering trails that eventually faded into wheat fields and a few cottages dotted across hills lined with sprouting plants. The heat of the sun beat down on my face. My forehead muscles ached from hours of squinted eyes and pinched brows.

We had slowed to a walk, partially because of the thick grass and partly because Orion and the horses seemed to be tiring. In particular, Salem's gigantic steed breathed heavily, his dark coat gleaming with sweat. The creature seemed more suited to cooler climates than where we were currently traversing. Only Kyro's mare seemed relatively unaffected by the heat.

Kyro's voice broke the sweltering silence. "My Lord, we should be nearing the Southern Road soon if you'd like to follow that north to Kalys."

The High King swiped his sleeve across his brow. "I was hoping we'd have crossed it by now. I wasn't aware how far east the Road traveled, I suppose. It seemed much less of a distance on our way here."

"*Or* we could just head north," I said.

"I wasn't aware it went this far east, either, Your Highness," came Kyro's clipped response. "But our way here was angled southwest from where we branched off the Southern Road, sire. Perhaps that was a shorter distance than heading directly west from the Road. It could explain why it now feels so much further. It's been quite some time since I've been this far south."

"For me as well. And I can't say I've ever tried to intercept the Road from the Western Territories before," Salem chuckled.

Clearly, my opinion was held in little regard.

The two Druids continued debating how much further east the Southern Road sat, making my current circumstance seem all the more unbearable. The Western Territories were never hot by any standards. The sun rarely shone through the perpetual blanket of clouds lingering just above the treetops. Wherever we were now, I was not accustomed to the climate, which changed rapidly between Realms. The patron god of the Druids often laid claim to the land they resided on, as well.

My head was beginning to throb. My skin burned. Orion's

fatigue gnawed at the inside of my chest, leaving me feeling rather hollow inside. It seemed he was as well suited to the plains as I was. I patted his shoulder gently, giving what little encouragement I could muster.

I needed to figure out how Salem had gotten hold of that necklace. Now that I'd been given Danu's blessing, I could find out what happened to my father. No amount of blistering heat or unyielding sunlight could stop me. I'd waited too long for this. Far too long.

We crested another undulating hill, this one slightly higher than the others. Kyro reached the top first. Salem's panting steed followed behind Orion and me. Orion hated that he couldn't see the creature or its master, and his ears kept flicking backward in attempts to locate them. Suddenly, Kyro jerked back on his reins.

"What is it, Kyro?" Salem called ahead.

The Water Druid shielded his eyes from the sun and squinted down the valley. Sweat glistened on the back of his neck. "Well, we've found the Southern Road, Your Highness, but a carriage seems to have been ransacked."

Orion jerked to the side as Salem and his steed trotted past us. His horse chuffed as Salem yanked on the reins, halting next to Kyro. "That's a Southern carriage," he said.

Kyro's eyes widened. "You don't think—"

Salem kicked his horse in the side and galloped down the hill toward the toppled carriage. It looked to be entirely made of gold and bronze, down to the very wheels. I'd never seen anything like it. When I was younger, my father told me how other Druids, and occasionally even Mortals, would travel the landscape. He'd drawn a carriage for me in the sand by a river with a twig. This was far more than I could've ever imagined one would look like. The thing practically glowed in the sun.

Two horses grazed nearby, still attached to ropes that trailed behind them as they walked. Both were chestnuts with coats that gleamed like amber tree sap. Snapped leather bridles hung from their heads.

Kyro urged his horse after Salem, clouds of dust billowing in their wake. I coughed, fanning the air in front of my face, then patted Orion's neck. "Slowly, my friend," I murmured.

Orion snorted in response and began cautiously making his way down the hill. Though he was adept at maneuvering over rock and root, he was about as well-versed in this landscape as I was. The soil was thin and slid beneath his hooves with every step.

Salem and Kyro dismounted their steeds next to the carriage. Kyro started shaking his head while Salem paced around it, trying to look inside. I stopped Orion a few meters away, then slid down his back. The moment my bare feet touched the arid soil, unease slithered into my body.

I took one step forward and Salem's head shot up, showing me only the obsidian of his eyes. "Don't come any closer. You won't want to see this, Forest Druid."

My lips parted in a retort, but the moment the air brushed my lips, I could taste it. Metallic. Bitter. There was blood.

A lot of it.

A raging flame sputtered into life in my chest, blooming into my muscles and flaring my senses. I marched towards the carriage, heart pounding.

Kyro began walking towards me, hands held in front of him as if trying to calm a wild animal. "Lady Quinn, I insist that—"

At the last moment, I sidestepped him and kicked my foot out in front of him. He tripped over me, landing on all fours in a cloud of dust.

I approached the High King, who now watched me with a stone-cold stare. His expression gave nothing away, but his frustration rumbled as clearly through the earth as a footstep. Frustration and . . . was that grief?

I swallowed bitterly and stood next to Salem, looking down

into the carriage through the open window. Immediately, I winced and turned away. I kept my eyes pinched shut, holding my breath and gritting my teeth.

This was an atrocity. A complete disregard for the sanctity of life. Not only had this poor Druid female been mercilessly slaughtered, but her body had been left to rot in the sun. A monstrous act in of itself, and one done without respect for the continuity of the soul to the Otherworld. Whoever did this wanted this poor creature to pay not only in this life but for all that followed.

A Druid buried without homage to their gods became a sluagh, a restless soul that haunted the Western Territories in search of a body to call their own once more. They could steal souls from living bodies and take the host form. It was a vile act to disrespect a living thing in such a manner and an even viler one to create such a creature. My father told me that even the God of the Dead, Arawn, despised the things. They were products of the most wretched acts, so they knew nothing else but to continue what they'd been borne of.

"What type of Druid is she?" I asked through gritted teeth, not daring to look back at the bloodied carriage.

Salem cleared his throat. "Light Druid."

"Her body will need to be returned to the Southern Territories for her burial rights. Otherwise, she will become a sluagh," I replied.

The High King didn't respond immediately. He merely pinched his brows together and continued to stare at me. "Did you hear a word I said?" I grunted.

Kyro cleared his throat from behind me and I whirled around. He brushed off his satin pants as he stood upright. "This is no ordinary Light Druid, Lady Quinn. This is Lady Vara, the matriarch of the Southern Territories. I believe the High King may be a little—well, a little in shock. I know I am."

When a footstep resounded through the earth nearby—one

that was not present before—I swung the bow from my shoulders and notched an arrow against the shaft. Salem and Kyro flinched at my sudden movement.

"Lady Quinn, what are you—"

I cut Kyro off. "Someone else is here."

he parched soil shifted beneath Salem's feet and a sigh heaved from his chest. "I see no one, *wildling*."

I held up a hand to silence him. It was just a single footstep, but far too light to be either Kyro's or Salem's, let alone the horses or Orion's. I stretched my senses through the earth like fingertips grazing a surface in the dark, looking for the source. I couldn't see them. But I felt them. *I know* I'd felt them. I quieted my breath, listening through the earth. A steady heart beating behind me, an undulating one to my side... just behind the carriage, there was something, a faint beating that nearly seemed to hum through the ground.

I stalked around the side of the carriage, arrow poised. No— I know I felt it. I could still feel it—the singing of a gentle heart through the arid soil. But the only thing living on this side of the carriage appeared to be the horses in the field a hundred yards away.

"Forest Druid," Salem said sternly, but I paid the supposed High King no mind. She was here. I could feel her.

"Lady Quinn, perhaps we should continue with the problem at hand?" Kyro asked.

I pulled my bowstring back, ready to fire. Though I couldn't see her, I could feel where she was. "Reveal yourself, or I will shoot," I warned in a voice so low I doubted the others could hear me.

But she did.

Slowly, the light in front of me began to distort. It formed fractures in the air as if I were underwater—gilded seams suspended in midair that glowed with colors I'd scarcely seen in the most vibrant of wildflowers. The light came into focus, and a female came into view.

Her skin was a warm golden brown, her hair just as metallic as the carriage and spun into tight ringlets around her face. Eyes like bronze glared back at me. She rose from her crouched position and my aimed arrow followed her, following her bloodshot eyes. Waves of grief and fury slammed into me with searing rage.

"Lady Quinn! Put down your weapon at once!" Kyro yelled now, approaching us. The female raised her hand towards him and he paused.

"How did you know where I was?" the female asked. Tear-stained lines glistened in the sunlight on her cheeks.

My arrow still remained pointed at her eyes. "You moved."

"And you, what? Saw my Illusion waver?"

"Something like that."

She glanced down at my attire, then met my stare again. "You're covered in filth. You know that, yes?"

The corner of my lips curled upwards involuntarily. "You're covered in blood."

Her attention shifted to her gown, a dry laugh escaping her lips. "I suppose I am." She turned toward the carriage and flinched, her chest pausing as if she were holding her breath. "I tried to save her when it first—but she was already gone, and I thought they would kill me too."

I lowered my bow. I hadn't seen another female Druid

before. She was vastly different from me with her doe eyes and rounded cheeks, yet vaguely similar. She was shorter than me, but the way she stared at me with bloodshot eyes and irises like molten gold made the height difference seem insignificant.

She outstretched her hand in a swift movement. "My name is Rhea."

I glanced down at it, then back up at her. "Quinn."

Salem cleared his throat from beside us and I narrowed my eyes at him. His attention was focused solely on Rhea, however. "Lady Rhea, my sincerest condolences for your loss. Perhaps we'd have intercepted whoever committed this tragedy if we'd only arrived sooner."

She pressed her lips together and swept her skirt aside into a curtsy. "High King Salem, it's an honor to see you again. Though I wish it were under better circumstances. Please do not place any blame on yourself, my lord. This—this happened last night."

The muscles in Salem's jaw flexed. "If you'd like to see your mother's body returned to Hera, I will not stop you. I must insist, however, that you ride with us to Kalys so I can arrange for armed guards to accompany you and your mother on the journey."

She smiled, but it never met her eyes. "That is most generous of you. Thank you, Your Highness."

"You're more than welcome to ride with my right hand, Kyro, or me." He bowed his head slightly. His hair seemed nearly blue in the brilliant daylight.

"Oh, it's no matter. I'll ride one of our horses." She sniffled, wiping her cheeks and waving her hand dismissively. We looked over to the chestnut steeds grazing in the field, their backs bare and reins snapped.

Kyro cleared his throat. "My apologies, Lady Rhea, but are you sure you wouldn't be more comfortable in a saddle?"

She gave another hollow smile. "I've always ridden bareback, Lord Kyro."

When she turned back to look at me, her eyes widened slightly as her gaze fixed over my shoulder. "Is that a deer?"

I spun around and saw Orion watching us curiously. He raised his head, sniffing the air. "Elk," I corrected.

Her attention flicked to me, eyes still wide. "When I heard the High King say Forest Druid, I didn't think he was referring to someone directly."

"Yes, he's particularly fond of referring to me as anything other than my actual name." I send a snide glare toward the High King. He hardly seemed to notice. "My sincerest condolences for your loss," I repeated the words I'd heard Salem say, given it appeared to be received well. She gave me a knowing smile.

"Thank you, Lady Quinn." She bowed her head a little. "Is it alright if I ride beside you on the Road north? I must confess, I know very little about Forest Druids."

I gave a single nod. Rhea pulled her lips into a tight-lipped smile and turned towards the High King and his lackey. "I'll be just a moment," she said, then lifted her skirts to wade through the tallgrass towards the horses.

I walked back over to Salem and Kyro. "If you do not hurry in sending someone down here to escort the body to the South, her soul will be trapped in this realm," I said in a hushed voice.

The High King's eyes flared with starlight. "Do you believe me completely uneducated, *wildling*? I am well aware we have till nightfall on the third day. The moment we get to Kalys and Lady Rhea decides whether or not she will accompany the entourage, it will be done. My people worship Arawn. I am fully aware of what could become of Lady Vara should I leave her to rot. It's just odd. First, the messenger to the Western Territories, and now this? Perhaps I should postpone the competition."

Kyro stepped closer, clearing his throat. "Your Highness, you know that is no longer an option. We've delayed as long as we can. The Realms are unsettled with an unmarried High King.

But may I suggest we not bring this up with Lady Rhea in earshot?"

"Lady Rhea! Would you—shall we give you a moment?" Salem glanced to my left and my gaze followed. Rhea sat atop one of her steeds, her fists wound around its bronzed mane.

Rhea turned her head once more towards the fallen carriage. The sunlight glimmered at the rim of her eyes, then down her cheek as a tear fell. Her chest rose in a trembling inhale. "No. The sooner we leave, the sooner we can ensure my mother gets a—gets a proper burial." She seemed to force the words out.

"My apologies, Lady Rhea, but we will need to discuss what happened to your mother at some point so we can carry out a full investigation," Kyro said.

Rhea's bottom lip quivered as she inclined her head. "Of course."

My eyes lingered on her, on how she continued to stare into the carriage. Her mother's blood, though dried, stained her golden dress like patches of night sewn into the day. It was still caked across her arms and hands as if she'd tried to stop the bleeding when her mother was first hit. From the brief moment I'd seen the contents of the carriage, it looked as if Lady Vara was first shot by an arrow in the stomach. It *was* odd. To fire an arrow, you need a clean line of sight. There were curtains covering the windows of the carriage. The one on Lady Vara's side had a frayed hole right through its center. Almost as if whoever had shot her had known *precisely* where she was.

I whistled for Orion, who trotted to my side and blew a heave of hot air into my neck. I patted his nose and walked to his side, gripping his withers and swinging myself onto his back. When I looked back up, Rhea was watching me curiously. Perhaps she'd never seen an elk before, given she first thought Orion was a deer.

Salem and Kyro mounted their steeds and waved us onward. From here, the Southern Road seemed to slither between hills and valleys northward. The sun was just beginning to descend, but the midday heat clung stubbornly to the dry air. Rhea trotted up alongside me.

"I'd been alone there since yesterday. If I'd known it was the High King approaching the carriage, I wouldn't have kept my Illusion up," she said. "Bends all the light around me and I can't really see that well through it. My mom, though, was amazing at it. She said I just had to adjust to looking through it, like when you're underwater. I think she was just a prodigy. Even my father couldn't best her at Illusions. If she'd known we would be attacked, she'd probably still be alive."

I glanced over at her, a little unnerved. When my father was taken, I teetered between inconsolable and entirely numb. I was filled with rage and grief and a thirst for vengeance that my goddess never allowed me to quench. But this Light Druid, who had apparently just watched her mother's violent murder, seemed more mentally sound than I'd ever been.

Perhaps she had a different relationship with death than I did. Though her reaction was unsettling, I had to reason that she was undoubtedly still mourning. I had no practice in comforting other Druids, but with animals, food seemed to work well.

"Here," I said, unlacing the little sack from my hip and tossing it to her. "It's dried fruit."

She caught it in her lap. "Thanks."

She popped a few dried berries in her mouth. "Can I ask why you're going to Kalys? Like I said, I don't know much about Forest Druids, but I thought your people hated leaving the Western Territories. I also wasn't aware there were any of you left."

My eyes immediately flicked toward Salem. I didn't know Rhea, so I wasn't about to confess to her the real reason for leaving my Forest. It was best if no one knew about Salem's necklace—my father's necklace. Anyone who knew what I was after might try to stop me.

"I have to, or else they'll see it as treason," I replied. I didn't mention the multiple threats they'd also laid against my Forest.

Rhea gave a little smile. "You're a part of the competition, aren't you? I thought they'd scrap the whole 'all six Realms require a representative' part this time, given no one has seen a Forest Druid in quite a while."

She heaved a sigh after it was clear I wouldn't respond to her speculation. It seemed like she was trying to distract herself from her trauma by indulging in her curiosities about me.

"I'm also a part of the competition. My mother was accompanying me on my journey to Kalys. That's—well, I don't know if I'll forgive myself for that," she said as if trying to shrug it off.

I met her stare. "I understand. My father was taken from me when I was younger, and I felt I could've stopped it." My breath caught in hesitation, but not quickly enough. "If you find a way to forgive yourself, I'd appreciate your advice."

The muscles in her jaw flexed for a moment, then she nodded and looked down at the satchel still in her lap. She popped a few more berries in her mouth. At least she was eating. When I was in her situation, I didn't have an appetite for days.

She swallowed and looked ahead again. "My people have an understanding with death—with Arawn. It's why we do not mourn. We know that he will deliver our souls to the Other-world after we pay Rites to Lugh. We know that even when someone is gone, he allows their love to stay. My dad always said that grief was just love with nowhere to go. And I can still feel her love. I just wish I still had her here. I feel like I have so much left of my life to live, and I wanted her to be there for it. I know that she will be safe and happy once she's had her Rites. But I suppose I'm just—I'm more selfish than my people are. I want her with me."

"It's not selfish to miss the people you love," I replied.

She sighed. "I've had a lot of time, alone, since she passed. Sitting there with just my thoughts for company. I'm not really great at being alone. It's one reason my mother came with me in the first place." She turned her head to the side, squinting at me through the daylight. "Thank you for letting me ride with you. I'm not sure what relationship your people had with death, so I don't intend to make you uneasy talking about it. I just need someone."

I gave her a small smile. "My people believe that life and death are just two names to encompass one idea, like the push and pull of the tide. You can speak as much as you want. I didn't want to be alone after I lost my father, either."

She chuckled and popped another berry in her mouth.

5

*A*t first, I'd thought the castle was an oddly shaped mesa. Made of dark stone, it jutted up from the rolling hills like a forest's edge. At its center stood an oddly shaped peak, far smaller than those behind it. As we grew closer, I realized what we approached was not entirely earth-made. What I believed to be a mesa became a stone wall. The odd-shaped peak morphed into a perfectly symmetrical castle.

I rode in silence as we drew closer. The wall stood as tall as redwoods and appeared to encompass the entirety of a village as well as the castle positioned at its center. The imposing structure appeared to have been built atop a granite butte, guarded on all sides by jagged snowcapped peaks. It sat far above the rest of the village, watching us approach from the undulating plains. My stomach twisted uneasily at the thought.

We approached a massive stone archway gated with iron. Atop the arch stood several armored Druids with obsidian breastplates and glittering blue tunics. Some odd symbol at the center of the breastplate glinted in the wavering daylight. My gaze fixated upon the weapons slung by their sides and across their shoulders. Immediately, my hand went to the bow around my chest. From down here, I could quickly disarm them with a well-aimed shot. The one on the left side was the most exposed. I readied myself should they make the slightest offensive movement.

Upon seeing the High King, however, the armed Druids all swooped low in bows and the gate swung open with a creak. I tried to calm my racing heart, a breath still lodged in my throat. Once we had passed through, Salem tugged a dark hood over his head. He slouched, and his power withdrew from the air around us, allowing me to breathe freely once more. Perhaps he didn't want his people to know their High King was in their midst. I would've thought the opposite given how he seemed to flaunt his title.

The structures that huddled against the outer wall were a picture of neglect, their wooden frames splintered and stone facades weathered. The roofs were scarcely cloaked in thatch. Some had Druids perched atop the skeletal frames, threading in more straw. Each home, despite its dilapidation, had a plot of land where animals grazed, corralled by rickety fences. There weren't many of these houses, and upon reaching into the earth, I could understand why. The soil beneath Orion's hooves was parched and barren. It groaned beneath every clop of Orion's hooves. I imagined farming atop one of the frigid Arastyan peaks would be easier than here. No amount of prayer to Dagda could make grain grow from poor soil.

The Northern Territories received only a few hours of daylight. As we'd trekked north, the night had seemed to hasten its approach. Still, I would've thought they'd receive more rain. Aside from the Seas and Eastern Territories, the Western Territories were among the wettest places in Arastya. Given its relative proximity to the Northern Territories, I had assumed their climate would be somewhat similar, even if their day and night cycles were shifted.

As we passed through a smaller inner wall, the run-down

cottages morphed into manicured stone houses lined side-by-side down the street. Several Druids meandered along the road, some with young children clinging to their arms. Others hauled tote bags of grain and meat or tools and wood. I'd only seen this many of a species once before, and they'd been humans in the mortal Realm. My gut swirled painfully in remembrance.

The Druids who passed us paid the High King little attention. Their eyes would linger on Kyro momentarily, then fixate on Orion and me. Despite Rhea's blood-soaked garments, they seemed to pay her little mind. I wondered if they had ever seen a Forest Druid before. Likely not. Whenever my eyes met theirs, they turned away quickly and scattered. If they knew what I was, then they did not like it.

Orion was skittish around the Druid masses, his ears flicking back and forth as if waiting to be attacked. His apprehension mirrored my own—my stomach lurching at every sudden movement, every loud noise. There were so many Druids, I found my mind scattering as I tried to keep track of each one. We could be attacked at any moment, and I wasn't sure I could stop it. There were far too many of them. It was overwhelming. Suffocating, even.

My mind swirled with sensory chaos. The thrumming of hundreds of heartbeats had my head throbbing. I could hardly feel through the earth. Every time I stretched my mind downwards, through Orion's sturdy legs and cloven hooves, past the friable soil and into the deep earth—I expected quiet. But I got hundreds of different footsteps, vibrating hearts, and unfiltered emotions. I tried covering my ears, to no avail. It was all in my head. I couldn't escape.

"Lady Quinn?" a faint feminine voice spoke. I blinked, her voice seeming to blend with the pulsing heartbeats ringing in my ears. "Lady Quinn, are you alright?" A hand touched my leg and I flinched, gripping the bow around my chest. I turned to the source of the voice. *Rhea.* She stared at me with amber eyes, her brows pinched together. "Are you all right?" she asked again.

I loosened my grip on my bow shaft. I focused on her. Her heart hummed quietly in her chest, a bottomless pit of emotion just past the surface. I felt myself teetering on its edge, then slowly backing away. "We're almost through the worst of it. There are fewer Druids near the center," she said.

I nodded and narrowed my senses on Orion. His muscles ached from the long trek, and his anxiety was nearly corporeal. I patted his shoulder and he heaved a breath, calming slightly. We ascended several wide flights of stone stairs, Orion leaning forward with his massive head to keep our momentum. The horses easily climbed them, and I whispered words of encouragement to Orion upon noticing his struggle.

Once atop the stairs, we passed through another stone archway into a large circular stone courtyard with various runic symbols carved into the slabs beneath Orion's hooves. Armed Druids stood a few feet apart from each other around the yard, eyes lingering on me—waiting for me to lunge. But I kept my senses trained on Orion and allowed my gaze to trail upwards.

My father had explained castles to me, but I'd never imagined anything like this. From its base, only the Arastyan mountains seemed to compare in size. Dark slabs of stone comprised its imposing exterior, with massive archways lined with intricate sculptures and towers grasping at the twilight stars. Its design was elaborate and regal—almost otherworldly. The Forest had nothing this oddly *symmetrical*. Whereas nature's chaos was comforting, the predictable grandiose patterns of the castle were unsettling. From within, brightness poured through the windows into the dark like scattered troves of gilded light. It was as if they'd entrapped stars and bound them inside the castle's halls.

Salem flung back his hood as we approached the castle. The

armed Druids immediately dropped to a knee, bowing their heads as we rode by.

"Welcome to the capital of Arastya, Lady Quinn and Lady Rhea," Kyro spoke from behind me. "We call this city Kalys, after the first King of Arastya. He was King Salem's great-great-grandfather and conquered the mortals who had kept us hidden from their Realm for millennia. This was his home, and now it is ours."

"It will be your home as well for the next few months," Salem said. He began ordering around two armed Druid females. One went to Rhea's side, helped her from her steed's back, and led her inside the castle. Oddly enough, they seemed happy to oblige his strict requests. I'd never seen anyone command another creature in such a manner. Unease settled in my stomach. Surely he wouldn't expect me to follow his commands with the same tenacity.

"Captain Granger, would you please attend to Lady Quinn and her steed? I'll have staff assigned to her within the next hour or so," Salem called to a male with fiery hair, clad in black armor. His dark skin was only interrupted by a jagged scar stretching down his neck and cheek. Aureate eyes flicked to mine as he strode up to Salem's flank in front of me.

"Your Majesty, I am a soldier—not a handmaiden," the captain protested.

"She doesn't need a handmaiden. She needs a soldier. Make sure she doesn't leave her room." Salem glanced back over his shoulder at me, undoubtedly expecting a rebuttal.

"I don't need either. You threatened to raid my Forest if I left. Why would I leave?" I asked.

"Because I'm sure some part of you thinks you can protect the Wild all by yourself. And I don't need you lurking around my castle in places you don't belong," Salem tossed over his shoulder, nudging his horse onwards with a kick to its flank.

Granger glowered and turned abruptly on his heels towards

me. "Dismount, *Lady* Quinn. We will place your—your *steed* in the stables."

The male and female behind him eyed each other. The female had the same dark skin as Granger, but her eyes were like tree sap, and her lips had pulled back in a smile. The male to Granger's left held the same expression as Granger, but his pale skin glowed lavender in the dusk, and his eyes tapered like the blade sheathed at his side.

"Orion will not be placed in a stable. He doesn't like confined spaces. Do you have a field? A woodland grove?"

"No," Granger countered with a glare.

"Then leave him in this courtyard."

"I can't do that, *my lady*," came his response, those last two words appearing to taste bitter on his tongue.

"Granger—just take the steed to the Royal Gardens," Kyro interjected from behind me. "I will let the landscapers know."

Granger's jaw flexed, the pale scar rippling at his jaw, then inclined his head. "Yes, sir."

My lips twitched as I fought the urge to bare my teeth. Such a mannerism was commonplace in the Forest, easily understood by my fellow creatures. I didn't know if it would be as easily received here. Granger may not understand the expression at all. But I didn't trust that he would keep my companion safe. I didn't trust a single person here. I knew Orion could defend himself, but I prayed he wouldn't have to. I'd tear the world apart before I allowed any harm to befall him.

I leaned forward on Orion's back, promising I'd see him soon—that he'd be safe. He was frustrated with me, though, and it was well-deserved. My impulsivity had landed us in an unfamiliar place where neither of us was safe. But he wouldn't have stayed behind, even if I'd asked him to.

"I'm sorry," I whispered.

He merely let out a puff of air and shook his stalwart head as I slid down his flank and landed on cool, unfeeling marble slabs.

I turned just in time to see Rhea disappear through a massive set of wooden doors. Despite not knowing me at all, she'd tried to provide comfort. I wondered briefly when I'd see her again.

"While Granger is seeing to your steed, I will show you to your quarters," Kyro said from behind me, dismounting his golden mare. His boots clicked against the hard stone as he strode up to my side, outstretching his bent arm for me to take. I eyed it and raised a wry brow.

He grimaced. "As you wish. Follow me." His silver hair flushed in starlight as we approached the imposing wooden doors at the castle's base. Dozens of eyes seared into my back as I followed Kyro, no doubt watching my hands and ensuring they remained at my side rather than on the bow slung around my back.

"Lord Kyro." Two males lowered their heads as they pushed the mighty doors open.

We entered a grand hallway lined with stone bricks and ornate sterling chandeliers dangling from the lofty arched ceiling. Painted tapestries and canvases lined the hallway; some battle scenes, others mountainous landscapes with dark skies. Occasionally, my eyes lingered on portraits of dark-eyed, dark-haired Druids. A blue rug stretched down the length of the hallway, glittering silver in tallow candlelight. Tinsel appeared to be threaded into the carpet, swirling like the limbs of a galaxy.

I wrung my hands together, cracking the knuckles. With as out of place as I already felt, it didn't appear that blending in would be much of an option. Somehow, I'd have to remain inconspicuous while I gathered information about Salem's involvement with my father.

"Why is everything so *shiny?*" I asked with a grimace.

Kyro glanced at me from the corner of his eye. "Silver is held in high value here."

Dirt crumbled from the soles of my feet as we followed the carpet. I glanced back at the trail I'd left, leading back toward the massive doors. "So, do you all wear fancy jewelry, or is that just your High King?"

Kyro shook his head in obvious annoyance. "If you're curious about Kalystan fashion, you'll need to ask the High King himself or his relatives. My Realm does not value material wealth."

I glanced at his luxurious clothes, sewn with a reflective fabric that seemed to ripple beneath the candlelight. If his people didn't care for material wealth, why was he cloaked in it? Perhaps that was Kalystan influence as well. Given the state of this mere hallway, luxury appeared to be synonymous with the Kalystan name.

Growing up, I'd been told stories of castles like this—with intricacy and wealth woven into the floor, the ceilings, and the walls. My father had said that only Druids with shallow souls found pleasure in things made by other Druids. Only those with deep souls found pleasure in the things created by the deities to whom we were bound. However, I couldn't help but feel a little mesmerized by these beautiful objects around me, that someone could use their hands to create something so wondrous. I didn't know what that said about my soul.

The hallway opened into a vast ballroom with more grandiose chandeliers and paned windows overlooking Kalys and the Arastyan mountains looming over the city. Father told me about kings and queens that would hold balls for their subjects—that many used it as an opportunity to flaunt their fortune and success. He explained that they would wear bizarre contraptions under the guise of 'fashion'. I hoped I wouldn't be expected to attend one of those. I had no fortune, no success to flaunt other than my survival, and my fashion consisted of old cloth and armor made from woven tree bark. Perhaps that's what the Druids were staring at as we walked through the streets. My attire was a far cry from the artisan pieces worn by the townsfolk, let alone the luxurious fabrics adorning the armed Druids. But it was no matter—I was not one of them, and I wouldn't pretend to be.

We ascended an imposing marble staircase that broke into a left and a right wing, banisters tangled in budding vines. We climbed the right, but my wandering eyes lingered over my shoulder at the left. I hurried to Kyro's side when I noticed I'd fallen back.

"You are not to venture outside of your wing, Lady Quinn," Kyro said, leading me through another resplendent hallway. "His Highness would prefer it if you remained in your room, as a matter of fact."

"You make it sound like I'm being held prisoner here," I scoffed, the tapestries appearing to glare at me as I walked by.

"You're here on duty to your Realm," came his curt response. "I would act as such. Keep that spiteful tongue of yours in check unless you'd prefer to see your home ablaze."

"It will take more than a mere fire to kill the nuckelavee you're so afraid of."

He didn't respond.

We continued down the hall, making several turns until we stopped outside another hulking door. I tried to take note in the event I needed to escape, but with every corridor, I realized just how labyrinthine the castle truly was.

Kyro turned to me, arms folded across his teal tunic, eyes cold and impassive. "There will be two guards stationed outside your door at all times. They will not be permitted to engage in conversation, so do not try. Furthermore, His Highness will appoint some staff to your care, hopefully within the next hour. Until then, Granger will be stationed outside your door as well, should you need anything. Tomorrow morning, you will be served breakfast and lunch, and then at approximately 2 o'clock, we will begin the Announcement Ceremony. Your staff will brief you on what is required of you. Any questions?"

"Yes. When do I get to leave?"

Kyro frowned. "When His Highness decides you can."

"You all are lucky I've decided to play nice," I hissed, the Water Druid's expression souring as he turned away from me and marched down the hall.

The Druids scurrying around the corridor flinched as he passed them. Almost as if they, too, felt his power. He was right to be afraid of the nuckelavee. I once was. But now, I wasn't entirely sure the nuckelavee would win against him. But a battle with the beast *would* ruin his fancy clothes. I swiveled back towards the towering door and turned the gilded knob, shoving it open.

The ornate room was unlike anything I'd ever imagined. The walls were covered in an elaborate sterling design that glistened in the candlelight. A bed with lavender sheets had its headboard pressed against the wall to my right. On my left sat a pair of armchairs positioned next to a set of windows overlooking the garden. Beside the windows stood an archway leading into a washroom with a sterling mirror. When I met my own gaze, I almost jumped. No wonder the citizens of Kalys had been wary of me. The thick layer of grime coating my skin and the twigs littering my troublesome mane made me look positively feral. I'd bathed in the river yesterday; I didn't know how I'd gotten so filthy.

I leaned closer to the mirror. I'd never seen myself in something other than a muddied lake's reflection. Gone was the girl with round cheeks, bright eyes, and dimples. The female who stood before me now was as wild as the Forest she came from. Her cheekbones were high and angular, her eyebrows arched like a bowstring ready to fire, with lips as sharp as her tongue. How much I had changed since I saw myself last. I wondered if my father would recognize me now if he were still alive. I didn't resemble him in the slightest, so I often wondered if I looked more like my mother. My father, however, refused to speak about her. I'd been an infant when she left us. I'd given up on uncovering that facet of myself long ago. It seemed to be something my father was determined to keep hidden.

I scowled at my reflection, turned on my heel, and walked back into the bedroom. I'd spent the last however many years sleeping in trees—it'd been so long since I'd slept in an actual bed. My father had built us a cottage when I was a toddler, and I'd had my own bed then. But the earth wanted us underneath her skies, not a roof. Lightning had struck the cottage, and it burnt down a few days after he'd built it. We'd slept in the branches of trees ever since. I never minded it. The stars were beautiful in the Forest, and my father used to tell the ancient stories behind their names.

I walked over to the paned glass, looking down into the gardens. Relief flooded my veins when I saw Orion grazing on some shrubbery and seeming relatively content. I wanted to get him back home where he belonged. He didn't belong here. But then again, neither did I. Once I figured out what happened to my father and why Salem had his necklace, we would be on our way home.

6

100 YEARS AGO . . .

*A*nother arrow sunk into the mossy earth beside the gnarled root of the oak tree. I'd been at this for weeks now and still couldn't hit the tree, let alone the circle of red pigment brushed into its swirling bark. I groaned in frustration and glanced over to my father, who seemed more than amused at my failures.

"I'm doing everything you told me to," I hissed in annoyance.

"No, you're not." My father beamed back at me, sending my blood boiling. He offered no further instruction. As per usual.

This was usually how his teachings went—me failing miserably and him sitting back as he let it happen. He never corrected me and never offered any guidance. According to him, Druids learned best by figuring it out themselves. Teaching could skew the learning process and prevent one from garnering everything they can about any given topic. I thought he was ridiculous.

"Then tell me what I'm doing wrong so I can fix it!" I tightened my grip on the shaft of the bow. The wood tensed beneath my fingertips as if bracing to be snapped in half.

"That is not the Forest Druid way, Quinn. You know that," he chided with a downward tilt of his head. I rolled my eyes and ground my teeth together.

Forest Druid this, Forest Druid that. Despite being alive for nearly two decades, I still hadn't seen another Forest Druid. I'd begun to doubt they even existed. My father claimed he was one and claimed I was as well, but I'd begun to doubt his word. He worshipped the mother earth goddess Danu and the horned god of the wild, Cernunnos, inexplicably believing they somehow granted us power through prayer. I'd never heard so much as a breath from the earth or the Forest. I didn't understand the point of worshipping two deities that had allowed my entire race to die off. After two decades of prayer, neither god had made themselves known to me and the fabled magic of the Forest remained a myth touted by my father. All I felt towards this forest was sentimentality—it was my home.

"No wonder there's hardly any of us left," I mumbled.

My father's sharp intake of breath pierced the brisk air, undoubtedly withholding a fierce rebuttal to my statement. Unlike me, my father showed restraint. He often said that our kind was not meant to cause pain or take it away, only meant to live alongside it. According to him, words were perhaps the greatest weapon of them all. I disagreed, which was why I insisted on learning archery.

"Again," he said, eyes glimmering like the leaves of the tree my arrows avoided. "You will never learn a single thing if you allow the process of doing so to stop you."

I grunted. More esoteric wisdom was *not* what I needed.

We were further north than normal, and the vegetation was dense here. Branches reached and grasped at other trees, forming dark knotted limbs that blotted out the gilded light bleeding through their canopies. Their treacherous roots tangled across the forest floor, sometimes visible, sometimes covered in the same dark moss that blanketed the earth. I'd tripped over those roots more times than I cared to admit. My father often told me that I wasn't listening to the world around me, allowing it to guide me through its maze, but no meditation or ritual elicited a single sound.

I huffed and pulled yet another from my quiver, gripping the shaft of the bow steady as I drew the arrow taut against the bowstring. My grip tightened on the bow as I closed my right eyelid, aiming the tip of the arrow slightly above the mark on the tree. Breathe *in, breathe out, release.*

The dart flew up into the shadow-drenched leaves of the tree, hidden from view.

Great. Another one lost.

These arrows weren't exactly easy to make. When I'd told my father a year ago that I wanted to learn archery, he'd furrowed his brow and said that if I wanted to use a weapon, I'd need to make it myself. So, that'd been my project for the last year. I'd spent months grinding down river slate into arrow points, binding them to the arrow shafts using rope I'd threaded from tweed, and aligning the feathers along the end after collecting them from around the Forest. It'd taken ages, and I'd only made seven. One I'd lost last week to the glacial creek that meandered several paces behind the oak tree and another just now to its branches.

I'm sure my father was perfectly fine with it. He'd been reluctant to teach me archery in the first place. We didn't exactly have a purpose for it, given that we only ate plants and the occasional migrating salmon. My father only knew how because he'd learned it from another Druid when he was younger. They had taught him precisely where to aim to disarm someone but not kill them.

The act of killing another Druid violated our god's principal tenant, the only rule given to Forest Druids in utilizing Danu's powers. Of course, I didn't know the explicit wording of this tenant, given the goddess had never spoken so much as a word to me. My father refused to reveal it aloud. He insisted the goddess would come to me when I was ready. Regardless, he'd only ever heard Danu speak to him when he was a child after earning her magic. He hadn't heard her since. But to him, the noise of the life around us seemed to fill her silence.

He did say that Forest Druids used to kill animals here and there for sustenance, but they would always thank the creature's spirit for its sacrifice. For whatever reason, Danu's no-killing rule was more complex than simply refraining from the act. It was *conditional*. Still, my father and I did not kill, except for an occasional fish. It was perhaps the only Forest Druid custom that made some sense to me, so I would not fight him on it. I'd seen enough creatures in the Forest to know that they were as intelligent as I, if not more so. Even the terrifying beasts wandering through the trees at night looked at me with the same eyes my father did.

"I don't understand what I'm doing wrong. I'm aiming slightly above the mark, so the arrow can fall through the air; I'm holding the bow sturdy—I can't think of anything else!" I said in exasperation.

My father snickered and stepped towards me, clapping his hand down on my shoulder. Verdant eyes, so different from my own, twinkled as he looked at my quiver. He told me my eyes were the silver of salmon scales and my wild hair the crimson that flowed through their veins. But I wished I had something of his. He looked like the Forest had blessed him—with his lush eyes and oak-colored hair. I looked like I didn't belong, and I felt like it.

"It will come to you. I urge you to think about it and ask the Forest for guidance. If the Forest wills you to wield a bow, then you will. But for now, you can defend yourself, and I am content with that. You should be as well." He gingerly took my bow and quiver, then meandered towards the tree, plucking misfired arrows from the earth and sliding them into their pouch.

He was right, as painful as it was to admit. He'd trained me in hand-to-hand combat, as well as with a staff and a blade. According to him, most mortal men wielded blades, so it was best that I be trained in swordsmanship. I, however, preferred to stay high in the trees where the mortals couldn't see me, never interacting with them. Being able to hit them before they knew of my existence seemed much more logical than praying I could best them one-on-one.

My father slung the bow across his chest and glanced at the sky. "Let's head home, shall we?"

The sun was setting, painting the skies with gold and rose streaks. When darkness came, usually the cu sith did too. I'd even come across a dobhar-chu before, and I was lucky it hadn't seen me. The half-canine half-otter beast pulled itself from the river caverns at nightfall and spent its time hunting for mortals or Druids to feast on. Its taste for animals was negligible. If it had seen me, I feared that might've been it. Cu siths, the massive hounds that roamed the forest in the night, hunted everything that moved and tended to scare off easily. According to my father, the dobhar-chu, ellen trechend, and sluagh were the beasts to run from. Though the sluagh weren't truly beasts. They weren't even alive.

I wrestled my mind from the haunting images of sinewy beasts and gave my father a quick nod. He turned and began bounded off through the trees. I sprinted after him. Moving casually through the Forest put a target on your back, so my father and I had always opted to run whenever we went anywhere. The easiest prey to catch was the slowest—we were anything but that.

The murky trees blurred around me as I urged my muscles forward, the familiar burning in my legs reminding me to pace myself. We had several miles to go until we reached our current home, a large deciduous tree by the banks of a shallow stream in the southern part of the Forest. The trees were much sparser there, and you could easily see the beasts roaming below in the dark. Only in the summer would we would head north, following the migrating salmon.

I ran alongside my father, his steady breathing helping me pace myself. With the light turning bronze in the sky, we didn't have time for any delays.

We'd soon arrived back at our tree, just in time to scramble up the thirty feet into its massive branches before the sun hit the horizon. It's taken years of my father helping me through pull-ups in order to reach the top branches. When I was younger, we would stay on the lower limbs because I couldn't pull myself up higher.

We were, after all, only up here to survive. While darkness reigned, so did the beasts. We could only hope to remain unseen, unheard, and unnoticed until morning, when they slithered back to their dens.

I nestled into a crook between burly boughs, pulling two woven blankets from the supply bag we'd hoisted up earlier in the day. My father, curled against a stout branch just below mine, reached towards me and took a blanket. He bunched the stiff fabric around himself and reclined against the trunk, looking through the leaves to the darkening sky.

I followed his gaze toward the blossoming night. From its depths peered little pinpricks of silver light, flickering in the deep like a thousand candles wavering in a breeze. They'd all once had names, long since forgotten to time's unyielding current.

A rustle of underbrush beneath a neighboring tree sent cool adrenaline surging through my veins in a rising tide. My heart racing, I glanced down between the thick leaves encasing my father and me, searching for the source. My father was doing the same. It was a fawn munching on a bush at the base of a nearby maple tree. I sighed in relief.

Safe.

Only when the fawn paused, alerting to something nearby, did nauseating fear crawl back under my skin. As my father had taught me, I covered my mouth and nose with my hand, tensing all my muscles to hold myself taut against the tree. The blankets covering us were drenched in tree oil, masking our scent. We were effectively blind to any beast on the ground, but I pitied the poor creature who had wandered from her herd. That was a death sentence here.

My stomach lurched into my throat when a shadow flinched behind the sapling. The fawn saw it all too late, and blood splattered the earth before she could so much as scream. It was an ellen trechend—a three-headed raptor with greasy black feathers, an emaciated body, and white eyes. Despite its wings, the beast preferred to hunt on the ground due to its poor vision. I pinched my eyes, hoping to erase the image of the beast snapping the fawn's neck in two before swallowing the head whole. The sound of bones crunching and blood splattering echoed across the otherwise silent forest. The metallic tang of her blood was thick in the air. If I could smell it, other beasts would too. With the kill made only a few meters from the base of our tree, the monsters of the Forest would be lingering about, waiting to see if the ellen trechend left any decent scraps.

Another sleepless night.

7

My handmaidens and I were off to a rough start. I was asleep when they knocked on the door this morning, prompting me to fly from the sheets and aim my bow at the door. I'd forgotten I was to be assigned staff. They hesitantly came in, a Light Druid called Eyla and a Dark Druid, Ryz. Eyla looked similar to Rhea, albeit older and with less delicate features. Ryz, although telling me she was a Dark Druid, had silver hair like Kyro. Given that our power was gifted to us by our patron gods in combination with our heritage, she must've had some Dark Druid lineage. I wondered why she'd forsake the god of the sea, Llyr, in favor of the darker gods, Arawn and Latobius. But I didn't press.

They'd given me various fruits and odd breads filled with sweet jams before forcing me into a bathtub. I'd prepared myself for the water to be frigid, as it always was in glacial rivers, and nearly screamed when it was the temperature of a hot spring. For whatever reason, they'd found that amusing.

After drowning the perfectly good water with floral-smelling oils and scrubbing my skin raw, my handmaidens spent an inordinate amount of time trying to tame my hair.

Every tug had me lunging at them, partially out of instinct and partly because I couldn't understand what was so important about untangled manes. The first few lunges startled Ryz and Eyla, but they seemed to figure out I wasn't aiming to hurt them, just stop them. My groans and hisses of pain were dismissed (as this was apparently 'essential') and they continued ripping at my scalp. Once they'd put me in a robe, they asked some off-duty guards to hold me down. Including my hand-maidens, it took five of them.

After the torture, they'd proceeded to paint my skin with odd pigments. I kept my eyes closed for what felt like forever. When I opened them, I didn't recognize my own reflection. Black ink stained my eyelids and fanned out into an arrow point at either side of my eyes. My immediate thought was that it was war paint. They quickly informed it otherwise, that it was common in Kalys to wear pigments casually. Nonetheless, I still felt that I was heading into battle.

After they'd ushered the guards out, they'd stripped my robe and began to lace something rigid around my waist. It pressed in at my sides and chest, making it impossible to take a full breath. Despite lashing out at them, they didn't stop. A gown made of deep green silks was pulled up my legs and arms, then tied at my back.

By the end, I couldn't decide if I looked more like a predator or prey. My muscular legs were easily seen through the slits rising to my hips, and the delicate, draping sleeves made me appear like someone of high esteem. The bodice, however, appeared to be shaped like plates of armor made entirely of leaves and vines. At my feet, the gown's hem was laden with what appeared to be moss. My exasperated handmaidens had left my hair in its natural curls—bushy and wild around my face. Regardless, I didn't look at all the *wildling* Salem had found in the shadows of the Arastyan forest. I admired how the gown made me feel—like I was worthy of representing what my people once were. However, the dress was so revealing and constricting that I wondered if that was its purpose at all.

A knock resounded at my door, and I spun to face Kyro, clad in his teal waistcoat and trousers, as he stomped in the room. Silver tinsel swirled across the satin fabric, glittering in the gilded daylight seeping through the paned glass behind me. Kyro had insisted the Seas and Eastern Territories did not value material wealth, but my father explained that they were a land of luxury and scholarship. Pearls and gemstones found beneath briny waves were traded for research funding, and research was then exchanged for luxury goods. *Blasphemous*, he'd called it, *to use your god's blessings for wealth.*

"I've come to retrieve you for the Announcement Ceremony, Lady Quinn." Kyro's lips twisted into a frown as he examined my gown. It almost looked like he was inspecting it for any mistakes made in the stitch work, the way an artist might look at a painting.

"Fine," I relented, the gown straining as I bent to grab my bow and quiver. Kyro let out a loose chuckle, and I scowled. "What?"

"You are not permitted to bring your weapons," he said. "Not only do you have little need for them, but they'd give you an even poorer reputation, and you could, theoretically, use them against His Highness. They must stay here."

"Like *ifreann* they will," I snarled, snatching them and stringing them across my shoulder. I marched to him and glared down my nose, waiting for him to let me pass.

"Lady Quinn, please be obedient. I will *personally* assure your safety."

Like that made me feel any better.

"No. I don't trust you, *and* I don't like you," I replied.

He paused briefly as if weighing my argument. "That is fair. But if I permitted injury to you, High King Salem would have my head. So it *is* in my best interest to keep you safe."

I grimaced in reluctance. Despite saying I wanted to be sent home, I needed to be kept here to find out what happened to my father. I had to play nice.

I glowered at him and reluctantly set my bow and quiver aside. "If you let someone so much as *touch* me, *water boy*, we're gonna have issues."

He nodded, then moved to the side to let me through the doorway.

Little did he know I'd strapped throwing knives to the inside of my sleeves.

He led me down the tapestry-lined corridor, air heavy with must and candleflame yet cool with the early dusk. Kyro made several turns, landing us atop a grand staircase that swept down to a vast ballroom. It appeared to be the same one I'd ascended the day prior. The stone was so polished it reflected the tallow candlelight hung from the walls and the chandeliers above us.

The ballroom below was filled with Druids—male and female alike. They were all dressed in muted tones, aside from three females already positioned at the room's center. The Druids in grey gave them a wide circumference of at least several yards. An aisle at the base of the stairs remained vacant to where the females stood. I assumed that was where I was supposed to be going.

"I will announce you last, following Lady Zora and Lady Rhea," Kyro said. "You will walk *slowly* down the staircase. Do not respond to anyone speaking to you. Simply stroll down and take your place next to the females down there." He motioned to the females in the ballroom. "If you would like to, most of the females tonight have demonstrated a little bit of their power as they descended the staircase in honor of their heritage. You're welcome to do so, but please—don't kill anyone or damage anything. Everything in the castle is extremely historic. And expensive."

"Do you say that to all of us?"

"No. I'm not frightened by the others or their impulses," Kyro replied. "With you, I have very little idea of what to expect save for reckless impulse and animalistic behavior."

I snorted. The creatures of the Forest were far more well-mannered than what I'd seen of Druids thus far.

"I'll return shortly. I will retrieve Lady Rhea now and gather Lady Zora after her. Please—*please* stay put," he said, swiveling and hurrying back down the corridor.

I sighed and examined the room from this hidden corner. The staircase was covered in budding white roses and dark vines stretching down the length of the banister. My eyes swept down it and across the crowd. There were so many types of Druids here, and many of them, I couldn't readily identify. Many of them appeared to be like Ryz—half something, half another. My heart hammered within my chest at the thought of them all watching me, at being amongst them. Would they batter my mind again? I could hardly breathe as it was with this wretched gown. If I focused on one person, perhaps I'd be okay.

"Well, well, well," a deep voice purred from behind me, and I whirled around. "*Wildling*, I thought for sure you'd have ripped off the gown by now and gone with your tattered rags. I'm pleased to see I was wrong."

I hadn't even felt him approach. Perhaps my senses were already too muddled by the crowd.

High King Salem leaned nonchalantly against a wall, starlit eyes unabashedly studying me. His hair was set into disheveled waves with a rather plain obsidian ring poised atop his head—a crown. In contrast to everything in this castle, striking in its opulence, the crown was almost anticlimactic.

"I tried. It won't come off," I replied, regarding him for a moment before turning back to face the crowd.

"Yes, I hear corsets are very restricting in that manner. They usually require assistance to remove."

"Rather convenient for you. I'm assuming you picked this out, then?" I said, eyeing him.

"I had it fashioned for you, yes. But it seems you're a particularly difficult female to please."

"It's rather presumptuous to assume you know a single thing about me, *Your Grace*." The title tasted bitter on my tongue.

He took a step towards me. "I could say the same for you, yet you've judged me just the same."

I grimaced. "I've only judged what information I've been given—you *stole* me from my home and *demanded* I compete for your hand. You used my love for my homeland to manipulate me and refuse to let me leave. If you don't like how I've judged your character, perhaps you should try to change it."

A moment of silence followed my accusation. I wondered for a moment if I'd gone too far. My quest for my father's fate could be over before it started—all because of my spiteful tongue. My gut coiled in apprehension.

"I don't blame you for that," he said.

My brows shot up in surprise. "You don't?"

"No. Not at all." He turned as if to leave, then paused to look at me again. "You look divine, Lady Quinn. I apologize about the corset. I'll have that amended in your future gowns."

At that, he turned and sauntered off down the hallway. I hardly had time to process our conversation when Kyro's hushed whisper echoed down the hall, footsteps tapping against polished marble. He approached with a female adorned in gold. *Rhea.*

Her curly hair had been styled straight, appearing as lustrous as a metal. The aureate gown clung to her skin as if it were wet. My eyes traced along her skin, a shimmering bronze in the chandelier light as if embedded with tourmaline. Her gold-dusted lips parted in a slight smile.

She came closer to me, scrutinizing my dress. "This is *much* better than those rags. But are you able to breathe?"

I coughed. "No."

A laugh bubbled up from her glittering chest. "Welcome to the world of modern fashion. You can only get away with no corset if you wear something like this." She motioned to her gown, loosely hanging from her skin. It seemed that one quick movement would release it from her shoulders and send it tumbling to the floor.

"I hate both options," I replied.

She nodded. "Yes, well, the endless joys of being a Lady, I suppose." Her head swiveled towards the crowd below. "Are you going to be alright? I'm sure it's overwhelming to be around this many of us when you've—well, when you're a Forest Druid."

I swallowed. "I'll be fine. I'd be more concerned for their safety than mine if I were you."

Amber eyes narrowed on me before she smiled. "That's the spirit."

"I'm a little surprised you're here at all." I paused. "Let alone smiling."

She loosed a deep sigh, her expression souring. "I've no other choice but to be. My mother is gone. Nothing I do will bring her back. But this competition was important to her and my people, so I feel it's best I stay."

I nodded slowly. "You're not alone. Or you don't have to be. I'll make sure my guards let you in should you need company."

A dimple creased on her cheek. "Thank you, Lady Quinn." She turned again towards the crowd as Kyro stared at her impatiently. "I'll see you down there," she said, gliding over to the center of the staircase.

Kyro clapped once, and the room went silent, all attention focused solely on Rhea. "May I announce Lady Rhea of the Southern Territories, daughter of Lord Hellas and Lady Vara," his voice boomed.

Rhea winced at her mother's name. Still, she lifted her chin and pinched the skirt of her dress as she glided down the stairway. Her skin began to glow brighter and brighter until I couldn't hardly look at her without being blinded. I held my hand across my eyes, glancing to the side down the ballroom. The other females shielded their eyes as well.

One had Kyro's sterling hair and dark skin adorned in a periwinkle gown swirling with silver thread. She must've been from the Seas and Eastern Territories. Given how her braided hair floated around her face, it was evident she also worshipped Llyr.

The one next to her wore a deep red gown with skin like embers and hair the color of a dying rose. Flames licked the underside of her skin in a near-silent hum. I could smell the ash that clung to her breath. She was most definitely a Fire Druid, which meant she prayed to Brighid.

The third wore white. Curled blonde ringlets kissed the fluttering pale eyelashes of her azure eyes. Given the color of her gown and her icy-toned skin, she was most likely a worshipper of Cailleach. That made her an Air Druid, an ethereal people found in the Arastyan Highlands to the north.

Rhea's glow faded as she reached the bottom of the staircase, striding across the ballroom floor to take her place among the other females.

I turned back around, and my stomach lurched. I was met with the glare of a female cloaked in a dark, glittering gown. She had tanned skin, dark eyes like Salem, and midnight hair that fell sharply to her collarbone. This one was a Dark Druid— there was no doubt about that. I hadn't heard her approach, let alone felt her footsteps through the stone floor.

"I don't know what they were thinking, bringing a feral animal into the castle," she said. My instincts flared, and I fought the urge to whip out my throwing knives. I had to remind myself that this wasn't the Forest, that she likely wouldn't kill me at the first opportunity. Druids here were *civilized*. She would at least wait until we were alone to try.

I gave her a venomous smile. "I'd rather be a feral animal than a tame Lady."

Her nose scrunched at the insult, and her gaze wandered up my gown in judgment. "Your body is rather masculine," she replied.

"Strength and masculinity are far from synonymous."

"A Lady never needs to flaunt her strength with something so superficial as muscles. She demonstrates it with her manner of being," she chuckled, sticking her downturned nose high in the air. "Something you should've learned from your parents, but I suppose being an orphan is a sufficient excuse."

"I'd watch your tongue if you intend on keeping it. I might not have trained in how to be a Lady, but I've trained in how to paralyze one," I retorted without hesitation. I broke my glare when Kyro cleared his throat beside me. We both turned to scowl at the imposing Water Druid.

"That escalated rather quickly, don't you think?" he suggested, eyeing me as if it were *my fault* she decided to insult my pride. Still, perhaps I needed to temper my tongue lest I be sent home because of it.

"Rather unbefitting of a High Queen, if you ask me," the Dark Druid replied, marching towards the edge of the grand staircase.

I fought back the bitter hiss that burned in my throat as Kyro approached her side and spoke. "May I announce Lady Zora of the Northern Territories, daughter of Lord Alastair and Lady Kalla."

Zora glanced over her shoulder, giving me a wink as she started down the stairs. It took a moment to realize her powers were working. Then, darkness began to gather at her feet and trail behind her as she walked. In looking out amongst the crowd, it was apparent something was missing.

Shadows.

She'd stolen their shadows and now used them as her

personal carpet. The inky tendrils swirled and coiled at her feet like vipers, sizzling in the air like frost in the sun. The moment she reached the bottom of the stairs, she sent the shadows back to their masters, darkness soaring out from her feet in an explosion of black light.

"It's your turn, Lady Quinn." I whirled around to look at Kyro.

"What exactly are my limitations on this entrance?" I asked, still riding the fury from my encounter with Zora.

"Don't kill anyone. And I'd prefer if you didn't break anything either."

Prefer sounded more like a suggestion.

"Fine. I'm ready," I said and walked over to the top of the staircase. The crowd regarded me with gasps and whispers.

"That's the Forest Druid."

"I heard she tried to kill her handmaidens."

"I heard she has fangs. And claws."

"I heard she drinks the blood of children."

My stomach bottomed out. Is this truly what they thought of my people? Of me?

"May I announce Lady Quinn of the Wild and Western Territories," Kyro spoke, his voice echoing across the ballroom. "No known lineage."

I swallowed, blood roaring in my ears as my heart raged in my chest. The violent creature inside me frothed at the mouth, baring its teeth. My breath hitched as I lowered my foot to the first step.

And the world shook.

Beneath the pointed tip of my shoe, cracks emanated across the marble step like the delicate veins of a hatching egg. A collective gasp erupted from the crowd as I took my next step, the earth shuddering beneath my feet. With a mere flick of my wrist, the dormant vines laced around the bannisters stirred to life. Verdant buds laden with thorns and ivory blooms broke from the hardened stems, unfurling and slithering across the staircase behind me. The chandeliers dangling from the ceiling shivered as the castle trembled beneath my feet. I didn't have to feign the smile that now pulled at my lips. It did not matter that the castle bore his name. It was made of stone, and so it was mine to command.

These Druids had decided who I was when I walked through the Kalystan gates—a feral beast, caged and tamed by their prolific High King. But now, they saw me clearly.

I was no helpless creature. This castle was not my cage. Perhaps I was the monster they whispered about, but who was truly to blame when *they* had invited me inside?

The stairs crumbled underneath my feet in shockwaves, liquefying into pebbles and radiating outwards on each step before solidifying again. Some of the Druids clamped their hands over their mouths in surprise and horror, though I couldn't tell one from the other. It did not matter. I relished in both.

I could hear and feel every heartbeat—every pulse—of every Druid in this room. If I wanted to, I could make their hearts stutter, even stop. I could even break their knees and make them bow.

They were lucky I didn't want to. They were lucky I wasn't here to take a throne. Because if I wanted to, I so easily could.

8

$\mathcal{W}$hen I reached the bottom of the steps, I lulled the
earth back to her slumber and released the
blanket of thorns from behind me. The vines cracked and
curled in reluctance as they returned to the banisters. My eyes
surveyed the ballroom, daring someone to speak—to challenge
me.

It was silent. *Deafeningly* silent. They watched me, waiting to
see if I'd attack them and cause the hysteria they now knew I
held within my bones. I turned my attention to my fellow
competitors. Half of them watched me like fawns in the Forest,
ready to flee at any sudden movement. The other half looked
more like wolves, curious about the strange beast that had
wandered into their den. Rhea was among those, but so was
Zora.

I stalked over to them, taking my place beside Rhea, then
swiveled and faced the staircase as they were.

I could still feel their eyes on me—the Druids of Kalys. The
fools focused on me even as another beast lurked at the top of
the stairs. Only when he sent out a shockwave of power did
they turn to look at the High King.

He radiated darkness and magic. It swept off him in volatile waves, crashing around me like a furious sea against a cliff face. The obsidian ring was a dark halo atop his head, his hair cascading in flowing waves around it. His jaw tightened as his gaze bore down into mine, a sign that he'd seen—*oh yes*—he'd seen my entrance. He knew I was no common Druid. I'd held my power at bay when I'd first met him, but after that little display, *oh*, how those galaxies swirled as they glared at me. Little did he know that to me, that *was* a little display of my power.

However, it was evident that he now questioned ever obliging to that silly law in the first place. Had he put his people in danger? Was I here to steal his throne? Had he fallen into my trap?

Salem gave me far too much credit. Though he would be right in assuming I was not here for his hand.

"Druids of Arastya." Kyro's voice disoriented me from my staring contest with the High King. "His Highness, High King Salem of the royal Kalystan bloodline, first of his name."

The ground shook as hundreds of Druids fell to their knees before him. Only I and the other females remained standing.

High King Salem strolled down the staircase, his posture and gait nonchalant. He did not need to demonstrate his power, as we all felt it leaden on our chests, but he did so anyway. It felt like a response to me, and me alone.

Darkness flowed out from his fingertips like ink through water, sinking to the ground around him and flowing outwards in a cloud composed entirely of night. Those eyes glowed as his power ebbed and flowed, the darkness cascading from the stairs in a slow waterfall. His power shuddered once, making my heart lurch like he'd swung a tree branch into my gut. All of the lights in the room began to dim as if he were suffocating them. Audible gasps erupted from around me as the crowd's eyes inched upwards. The ceiling had been replaced with swirling galaxies and millions of stars, each twinkling with a life of its own.

He was showing off, and he damn well knew it, given the smug smirk. His eyes were still on mine, a voice nudging at the edge of my mind—*I've got the power here, wildling.*

A snarl bubbled in the back of my throat, knuckles bloodless as I wound my hands into fists. I scowled, and his irises flared steel in a sick delight at my irritation.

Salem outstretched his hands, voice echoing as if we were in a cavern. "People of Arastya, please join me in welcoming the Ladies of the six Realms to our city, to my home."

The applause ricocheted off the walls, echoing much like his voice. My stomach twisted.

Why was it so *loud*?

I fought the urge to clap my hands over my ears, to crouch down and make myself small, and find something to hide behind until it stopped. The sound was—it was *everywhere*. The air thrummed with energy, thick in my throat. How was I supposed to breathe? I could hardly hear my thoughts, let alone anything else in the room. It was as if a banshee had wailed in my ear.

I glanced around, wide-eyed. Despite the obscene volume, nobody else seemed to take issue with the noise. Apparently, this was *normal*. I felt an elbow nudge my ribcage.

Rhea.

Amber irises slid to the corners of her eyes, dimmed like a sinking sun in a slow blink. Her chest rose in a deep inhale, then gently fell as her eyelids opened again. The tip of her chin tilted towards her collarbone ever so slightly—a barely noticeable nod. I swallowed and stole a deep breath from the humming air, trying to focus solely on Rhea. Her slow breaths. Her humming heart. Her unwavering calm.

Finally, the High King's attention shifted from me to the other females. His gaze lingered on each of them, studying them like a dobhar-chu poised to strike. Their heartbeats thumped in my eardrums, each becoming faster when his eyes landed on them. Those hearts almost burst when his hand would take theirs and again when his lips would press to their bony knuckles. The beats would then slow as he moved on to the next. It almost seemed like he could hear them, too, given the way his gaze twinkled with every crescendo of a heartbeat.

My lips twisted in disdain. *Sadist.*

Then his attention was back on me, irises a starless sky as he waited for my heart to falter—to cower in fear. But it didn't. My steady heart thumped proudly in my chest, even as gentle claws trailed across the edges of my mind. Darkness curled around my fingers before his hand took mine. When it did, starlight skidded through my veins. Goosebumps blossomed on my skin like wildflowers through a blanket of ice. Those eyes remained stoic as his lips brushed against my knuckles. My knees threatened to buckle beneath his power. It grasped at my shoulders as if shoving me to the ground.

I remained still. My heart held steady. I would not yield.

A barely-noticeable curl of his lips was the only response I got. Then he circled back to stand in front of all of us.

"It is a pleasure to finally meet all of you," Salem said. "I've waited a very long time for this moment, when I at last, meet my High Queen. Though we were concerned we'd be unable to find a representative from each Realm, as is required, we've succeeded in yet another generation of kingdom-wide support. Your loyalty to the Kalystan crown is acknowledged and will be rewarded, potentially, with representation in my court. For those of you who are unacquainted with the traditions of Arastyan Royal Selection, and for the females in front of me—the contest will proceed as follows. I will formally court each of you for the next several moons, and when I decide against you, I will send you home. For now, you will remain guests of my castle and Kalys. In the end, I will select my High Queen, who will rule by my side so long as the gods allow it."

"However, there are a few limitations," he continued. "First, you are in no position to reject my requests. If I desire a meeting, an occasion with you, you will oblige. Second, you are not permitted to leave unless I request you do so. And third, you will not sabotage any of the other relationships. If I discover a ploy to do so, the perpetrator will be rightfully punished."

As if on cue, all of the Ladies curled their bodies into curtsies, bowing their necks in submission. I remained still. Salem's eyes flicked to mine, flaring in warning.

"Yes, Your Grace," they spoke simultaneously as if they'd been trained. However, the snide smile Rhea sported seemed rather supportive of my decision to stand tall. Or perhaps she just found it amusing that I refused to conform to what appeared to be a social standard. Either, I was okay with.

"Lady Quinn?" Salem's staccato voice was laced with venom. Right below his cavernous eyes, a tanned pigment attempted to conceal skin stained indigo. It was as if he'd tried to hide his exhaustion with the same pigments the handmaidens had used on me.

He paused, holding his breath in his chest as he waited for me to respond—to oblige in royal protocol as the other Ladies had. But as I said before, I was no Lady.

I bared my teeth in a snarl. *"Your Highness."*

An audible gasp erupted from the room. Perhaps they were surprised I could speak at all, given the rumors they'd spread about me thus far.

Salem's jaw twitched. "Do you agree to the terms of the competition, Lady Quinn?"

I nearly laughed. *"Now* you're giving me a choice?"

The High King's impassive face winced so quickly, I wouldn't have caught it if I weren't in a deadlocked stare with him. "Lady Quinn," he said, his voice as taut as a bowstring.

The *appearance* of a choice is what I was given. Nothing more than a facade. My only consolation was that I *had* made my choice, regardless of what he'd provided me. He could continue to see me as the wild beast, a creature at mercy to his whims. He could believe he'd trapped me in a gilded cage, placed me on a boat of his command, and set us to sail on a vast river. But he would not know that it was *I* who carved the river—that regardless of how he pulled at the rudders, we would end at the same shore.

My lips spread in a feral grin. "Fine."

"Fine?" Salem took a calculating step towards me, the first step of a dobhar-chu towards his prey.

"Fine, *Your Highness*," I bit out with a slight curtsy but refused to bow my head to him.

Those dark eyes glittered with amusement as I stood straight again.

I do not kneel before anyone, ciarán, let alone a Druid I just met claiming to be High King.

The darkness slithering at the edge of my mind retreated as Salem turned to face his people. My gaze flicked upwards to Kyro, sterling hair framing his slack-jawed expression. Kyro's eyes met mine, and I opened my jaw slightly in imitation, then tucked my thumb underneath my chin and pressed it upwards, closed. His jaw snapped shut and quickly diverted his attention with a grimace. The Water Druid seemed less amused with me than I was with him.

Salem continued to address his people, speaking on the decreasing poverty rate in the Southern Territories, other fancy words I didn't recognize but that others applauded him for, and a looming threat to the North that he dismissed rather quickly. I wasn't entirely sure what the Forbidden North had to do with Arastya, as it technically wasn't a part of the kingdom. Other Druids seemed content with this, though.

"Now that we have all of that out of the way, I suggest we do what we came here for," Salem said. "Kyro, my friend." He motioned to the Water Druid.

Kyro flicked his wrist, and a symphony of instruments played by string erupted through the room. The Druids playing them were positioned around the ballroom, all swinging into a crescendo simultaneously. I hadn't even noticed them until now. Again, the volume startled me.

The Druids around me rose to their feet, chattering and laughing as they embraced their partners and began to dance. The Ladies of the six Realms and I stood still, unsure of what to do. I had never danced before. Not really, anyways. When I was young, my father had let me step on his toes as he twirled me around to the rhythm of his humming. That was the extent of my experience.

High King Salem turned to face us, his eyes trailing from one Lady to the next. "As this is a celebration of my people, you are all free to dance with whomever you'd like," he said. "However, unless you'd like to throw away your shot at a crown, I'd keep the dancing platonic."

A wave of his power shuddered out from him. Heartbeats skyrocketed. Rhea's seemed almost as steady as mine, however. It was encouraging that I seemed to have found a strong ally in a castle full of monsters.

At that, the females broke apart, each off to find their own partner. Rhea turned to me and smiled, amber eyes glowing.

She beamed. "You've got power."

"So do you."

"Perhaps. But I've never made knees tremble," she chuckled. "I suppose Lugh is to blame for that. Glowing only does so much. However, the artisan god has made me rather adept at painting." Her head tilted as she watched Salem saunter over to the Air Druid and ask for a dance. "That poor girl, she looks about ready to faint."

He wrapped an arm around the Air Druid's waist and guided her gracefully into a dance. "Who is she?"

"Lady Aria of the Arastyan Highlands. Daughter of Lord Typhon and Lady Thetis. Rumor has it this is the first time she's left her palace since she was a child. Her Aavali parents have reared her entirely for this purpose—they've chosen her sister as heir to their mountain."

My stomach curdled. "Heir to a mountain? Mountains are not *owned*. They are to be revered. *Honored.*"

Rhea shrugged. "The Aavali do honor the mountains, but in their own way. Air Druids are notoriously fond of jewels and pure metals. The oldest lineages in the Air Realm each claimed a mountain for their bloodlines long ago, and now those lineages are called the Aavali. They guard their mountain, and any wealth found within it is inherited by their family. The Guardian role is typically passed down to the firstborn, but Aria's claim was renounced at birth."

"So they're scavenging mountains for their own selfish gain?"

"I suppose." Rhea shrugged. "Her parents probably decided she was too frail upon birth to guard their stores and decided she'd be better off wooing the future High King instead. She'll be devastated when His Highness discovers the wilting flower beneath all that tulle. I mean, *Lugh above*, what were her hand-maidens thinking with that gown? She's positively drowning in it."

Rhea seemed to be correct. Aria's heart rate resembled a hummingbird's. Salem seemed content, however, as content as a spider who'd woken to find a fly trapped in its web. An impassive smile seemed carved onto his lips as if he were stone.

I broke my gaze from them and motioned to the Water Druid, dancing with another female. "And who's she?"

It was difficult not to stare as the two Druid females danced across the floor—one clearly guided by a force of grace that the other was not. Her eyes were as blue as a daytime sky, but her skin was equal in shade to the night. Her silver hair shimmered like an insect's wing beneath the lights, floating around her head as they spun.

"Lady Xandria of the Seas and Eastern Territories," Rhea replied. "Daughter of Lord Kirin and Lady Aella, cousin of Salem's right hand, Lord Kyro. She's as intelligent as they come, I hear. But I suppose being raised in the Land of Scholars will do that to you. From what I've seen of her at prior events, she is close with Lady Ingrid and, at one time, with Lady Zora as well. Though I can't imagine why."

"And the Fire Druid?" I searched the crowd for the dark-haired female in the fiery gown.

"That's Lady Ingrid of the Wastelands. I've heard terrible rumors about her, but she's been very kind since I've known her. I've wondered for a while now if it's all a ploy by her parents to maintain their fierce reputation. Brighid didn't bless the Fire Druids with flame and hearth for them to become bakers, after all," she chuckled. When I didn't respond immediately, Rhea continued. "The Wastelands are the home of blacksmiths and warriors, Lady Quinn."

I shifted in my uncomfortable gown. "How do you know all of them?"

"I was raised on these sorts of events. My—" Rhea paused, swallowing, "my mother spent each one whispering the names and stories of pertinent Druids in my ear as I saw them. She said one day it'd be an asset in court. But now? Now, I'm little more than a gossip," she replied dryly. Her eyes narrowed at the High King and his partner, clearly keen to change the subject. "What do you think of him?"

"I hardly know him."

"You know him enough to refuse to bow before him," she

mused. She wanted to know what I knew that she did not—if I'd somehow figured out something about the High King he didn't want others to know.

My response was far too quick. "I don't bow for anyone."

"Yes, I noticed. I'm quite surprised he was able to get you here at all. With power like you have, I don't think I'd let a single person command me if I were in your position. But I suppose having treason levied against you will force your hand." Her lips curled in an understanding smile.

"Lady Rhea." I heard a soft, feminine voice behind me and spun to face the Fire Druid. *Ingrid*. The smell of smoke saturated the air around her as if she had a hearth within her skin. I could clearly hear the roaring flames that called her body home. Her power was monstrous. There was no mistaking it.

"Lady Ingrid." Rhea bowed her head in greeting, and Ingrid did the same.

The Fire Druid studied me for a moment. "I don't believe we've met."

She, too, was absurdly beautiful, the deep color of her skin appearing to glow red from within. Her cheekbones were high-set like my own, but her angular features were offset by generous lips and a delicate nose. Eyes like embers held my stare. When she glanced at my dress, I did the same. Her gown was as revealing as my own, if not more so. But whereas my body was lithe and lean, hers was generous and muscular—obviously that of a warrior.

"Quinn."

"Ingrid. I liked your entrance." Her lips twisted in what could've been a smile.

"I wish I'd seen yours. I bet it would've been just as intriguing."

Another tight-lipped smile. Or grimace. "It's been quite some time since I've seen a Forest Druid, Quinn of the Wild," Ingrid said. "Have you been hiding all this time?"

My brows settled into a scowl. "What would I be hiding from?"

Ingrid's molten stare seared into mine. "You tell me, *Forest Druid.*"

"It's no secret that Forest Druids were not well-liked across the Realms at the time they—well, when they went missing," Rhea explained, offering a gentle smile. "I'm sure some Druids still hold resentment towards them, and that may translate to resentment for you. Despite the fact you're far more civilized than your people were believed to be."

"Hardly," a shrill voice spoke to my left. "I'm surprised she hasn't been eliminated already. Having such a beast here *stinks* up the place. Pollutes the air, if you will."

I ground my teeth together. I didn't need to look to know who the voice belonged to.

Lady Zora stood, arms folded over her chest and eyes narrowed as she eavesdropped on our conversation.

"Lady Zora. Forgive me, but aren't you two related? You and the High King?" Rhea asked. I didn't stop the grin that followed her remark.

"You dare accuse me of such a thing, Lady Rhea? When we all know Lord Hellas is Lady Vara's fourth cousin? Or, should I say *was?*"

Rhea's responding glare was equal in fury to a banshee— equal in damnation and in the promise of absolute devastation. "If you're looking for a battle, Lady Zora, you will not find one with me. The fact that I stand here at all speaks volumes about my strength. The fact that you stand here trying to weaken me speaks volumes about yours."

Zora's jaw flexed. Her lips were the color of blood, parting to reveal brilliant white teeth. But before she could speak, her mouth was sealed once more by a looming shadow over my shoulder. Her dark eyes trailed behind me.

"Lady Quinn." A shiver crawled up my spine. I hesitated, gritting my teeth as I swiveled around.

"May I?"

Salem's hand was held before me, darkness swirling around his fingertips like tendrils of smoke.

9

*D*ance? With him?

My eyes met his, and I watched for any sign of amusement—any indication that this was merely a joke. Surely he wouldn't endanger himself like this.

"Your Highness, I would be happy to oblige." Zora's shrill tone came from my right, and I instantly made my decision, his calloused palm sliding against my own.

A brief twinkle of satisfaction flitted through his eyes, and he squeezed my hand, tugging me away from Rhea and Ingrid. I briefly glanced back at them, only to receive looks of confusion and bewilderment. It seems they were wondering the same thing as I was.

"You put on quite a show." His voice dropped into a low baritone purr as his arm wrapped around my waist, thumb against the base of my rib cage. His pressure against the bodice did not help. I could hardly breathe as it was through the boning of the gown.

I glared back at him. "As did you, *ciarán*."

He started to move, and I mirrored the step. Amusement

illuminated his dazzling eyes, and he grinned. I cursed myself for giving away my lack of experience.

"Have you ever danced before, Lady Quinn?" he asked, brows arching downwards in condescension.

"Oh yes, often. Death makes a wonderful partner."

"My people were correct. You *do* have sharp teeth. But do you drink the blood of children?" he teased, glancing around the room.

Before I could protest, his grip tightened on my waist, and he lifted me, setting my toes down on top of his feet. I felt a cold breeze of a solemn memory curl up my spine and quickly broke eye contact with him before he could see it.

"Does this not hurt you?" I snapped, hoping to conceal my brief moment of sentimentality with dry condescension. My heels were undoubtedly digging into his toes. I couldn't say I abhorred the idea of that.

"If you think that stilettos on my toes are enough to cause me tangible pain, Lady Quinn, you've got more to learn about me than I thought."

"You assume I want to know anything about you at all," I said.

His grip tightened on my waist as he dipped me downwards, exposing my neck. Cool breath grazed the exposed skin, a chill threatening to escape through my steel willpower.

"Do you truly have no interest in the crown? The title? The riches?"

I glanced at the obsidian halo sitting so righteously atop his head. Then, at the dangling silver piece around his neck—at the fate I needed to uncover.

"None," I replied. "I just want to protect my home. Which you threatened to get me here. Do not forget that, *Your Highness.*"

He yanked me upright, pulling my body taut against his. He

was as solid as the marble staircase I'd descended—the dark stones that built the walls of this castle.

"Interesting. Then, what would be the purpose of flaunting your power like that earlier?" he asked.

His breath was dizzying. Or perhaps it was the gown. Regardless, the room began to swirl.

"Showing you who you invited inside." A feral grin tugged on my lips, and Salem watched it grow—watched my eyes with intrigue.

"Who are your parents?" he asked, swinging me gracefully into the next step of the dance.

"Well, I don't think that's any of your business, is it, *Your Majesty?*"

He flinched as he dipped me again. The world blurred, and I swung a leg around his thigh to steady myself, hooking it beneath my calf. My lungs strained against the corset.

"Caution, *wildling*. Your sharp tongue and reckless behavior might get you into trouble."

"I doubt a tempered tongue and docile behavior would do me any better, *ciarán.*"

"For someone who claims to have spent most of her life alone with a deer, you sure have a talent for snide remarks." His upper lip curled as he spoke, twirling me and pulling me back to his chest. The world spun. I gasped for air, gripping the lapels of his jacket. He was warm. I blinked, gathering myself.

"Elk. He's an Arastyan Mountain Elk. Not a deer, you ignorant arse."

"You realize I could have you beheaded for such a remark," he said, his thumb digging into my rib cage in warning. My side ached at the added pressure.

"Do you expect me to thank you for not doing so?"

"I'd be careful if I were you, Lady Quinn," he breathed against my neck. "Not too many Arastyans were fond of your kind, to begin with. The fact that you're here, competing for the title of High Queen—puts a target on your back. The messenger sent to retrieve you was murdered, as was Lady Vara. Someone out there is very capable of killing, and you're a very enticing target for much of Arastya. You do not have to make me into your enemy."

The music slowed, and we came to a halt.

"You are the one who painted the target on my back, *ciarán*. I'd hardly say I'm making you into something you're not."

"If I didn't find a Forest Druid to compete in the competition, despite your kind very possibly being extinct, the laws say that I would not be able to extend Arastyan protection to the Western Territories," he explained stiffly. "It would shrink Arastya considerably and bring the mortal border within reach of Kalys. I was not about to forfeit you. I was not about to forfeit your land."

I paused. "You do not have Arastyan protection of the Western Territories as it is. The border with the Mortal Lands is vacant. It has been for a while now."

Salem's brows pinched together. "No, that's not correct. A rotating group of patrol Druids is stationed just north in the Air Realm. They've been instructed to send word to Lord Typhon if anything was ever amiss. The Forest is a powerful deterrent to the humans, yes, but not nearly as powerful as our kind. They remember that when they see us."

I stepped off his feet. "I alone have guarded the Western Territories for the last century. And I hadn't seen another Druid until you," I replied. "Surely, if you had patrol guard, I might've seen them once every decade or so—if they truly traversed the entire Mortal border."

The High King took a step back from me, his eyes flaring with silver embers. "You must understand, *wildling*, that I will opt to trust in my forces. However, I will confer with my General." He turned slightly, then paused and looked back at me. "You're saying that you patrolled hundreds of miles of forest—alone—for a century? The entirety of the border?"

I nodded. "The Mortals stopped venturing into the Forest shortly after I began."

"Why?" he asked. "What could you possibly have to gain from holding the Western border?"

Danu had instructed me to protect the Forest, to act as her right hand in keeping it safe from greedy Mortals aiming to take what wasn't theirs. With her guidance and her power, I was able to scare the Mortals off. The ones that the Forest didn't devour ran back to the Mortal Lands with tales of the Forest—of trees come to life, of beasts far too intelligent to be mortal, of woods so dark not even a compass could see. I could hear them speak from the western edge, warning their kin to watch the tree line as they slept just outside the border. None had dared cross it in decades.

I parted my lips to respond but was cut off when Kyro hurried up to Salem's side. He whispered something in Salem's ear, something that sounded like 'breach'. Then, Salem looked to me, bowed his head, and stalked off into the shadows.

Footsteps approaching me vibrated through the floor, and I spun around.

Rhea. Her brows were furrowed in what looked like concern.

"What is it?" I asked.

"The guards are telling the Ladies to return to their rooms. I'm not sure why," she explained with a sigh. "I was hoping tonight would offer me some reprieve from my solitude, but it seems I'm overruled."

I frowned. Another pair of footsteps approached, and I turned in their direction. An armored guard with a black helmet and sword in hand marched towards us. Only their eyes were visible through the helmet—pale blue.

"I must ask that I accompany you to your rooms," the Druid said.

Rhea nodded and wound her arm through mine. I flinched at the contact, unsure what she was doing. The guard led us up the grand staircase with Rhea clinging to my arm. She glanced back down at the crowd, at everyone who continued dancing despite the Ladies being ushered off. Unease coiled tight in my gut.

Something was wrong.

It was apparent in Salem's eyes when Kyro whispered to him, and even more so with the Ladies being escorted by armed guards.

The boots of the guard leading us clicked against the marble stairs as we neared the top. We veered right down a tallow-lit corridor that I recognized. We continued walking in silence down more labyrinthine halls that seemed to progressively grow darker. The further we went, the less I felt like I knew where we were. Rhea's arm tugged on mine a little, down a hallway we passed by. But when I looked to where I knew she stood, nothing was there. I heard her heartbeat. I still felt her firm grip on my arm, tugging me away from the guard.

"Rhea?" I whispered. The moment I spoke, her grip on my arm vanished. I stretched my senses through the earth. Footsteps running away . . . footsteps running towards me?

I spun around just in time to dodge a blade. It swung horizontally above my head, mere inches from my nose. I fell back a few steps, realizing only then that the guard was attacking me. Was that why Rhea had tried to pull me away? Had she somehow known the guard wasn't who they said they were?

The guard swung the blade around their wrist, obviously comfortable with the weapon. I ground my teeth together. The twin throwing knives felt cool against the burning skin of my forearms. As far as they knew, I was weaponless. Which meant I had two chances at surprising them before I was out.

The guard advanced again, the steel singing as it arced through the air toward me. It'd been a century since I'd had a sparring partner, but my muscles leaped into action as if of their own accord. Where the guard stabbed, I dodged. Where they swung, I dove. But they were fast—much faster than my father had been. I mistimed my lunge, and the steel sliced through my shoulder. I hissed at the sharp pain, at the sensation of scalding blood dripping down my arm.

I couldn't keep this dance up forever, especially in this corseted nightmare of a gown. The boning of the contraption dug into my ribs even now, restricting my movement and breathing. I heaved a deep breath, forcing my chest muscles outward. Splinter by splinter, the boning of the corset began to fracture. Portions stabbed into my skin, drawing blood. Heat pooled at my waist. But I could breathe. And I could move.

"Well, let's go then," I sneered. "If you want me dead, you're not going to get it by standing there."

The guard charged, but this time I was ready. I flung a blade from my uninjured arm. It whirred through the air, sinking into a chink in the guards' armor between their breastplate and shoulder plate. The force of the impact had them reeling back, so I took the opportunity and went on the offensive.

They swung the blade, predictably, in their other hand, which was considerably weaker. The blade slammed onto my right forearm, clanging against the throwing knife I still had strapped there. My shoulder screamed with searing pain, and I fell back at the hit. I recollected myself and pulled my momentum into a kick, landing square in their gut. They reeled back, and I followed, grappling them for the sword.

But they were larger than I was and heavier too. Despite the wound, they easily flipped me on my back. I gripped their wrist as they pressed the blade to my neck. My heart pounded violently in my ears, roaring so loud I couldn't hear my own breath. I just had to wait for their legs to move. Then, I could place my other blade below their chest plate on their left side.

My arms strained to keep the blade from piercing my neck. My right arm was growing numb and noticeably weaker than my left. The sword's steel was already coated with my blood, dripping onto my skin as if marking its aim. The guard's hot breath fanned my face through the helmet. Pale blue eyes glared down at me, drowned in the darkness of their dilated pupils. My reflection stared back at me.

"I know what you're after," they seethed. "You will not find him."

My stomach plummeted. But I couldn't allow myself to be distracted. One moment too late, and I'd be finished. My lips curled in a feral grimace. I braced my left arm with as much strength as I could muster. The throwing knife slid down my right forearm into my hand. Beneath me, the marble hummed as they set their right knee onto the ground beside my waist, holding their weight as they leaned the sword against my neck. The knife slid past my fingertips and I gripped the hilt, stabbing it right above the guard's pelvis. Their body jolted above me in shock. I took the chance and used my remaining strength to push them off me.

I stood, panting. "I'd like to see you stop me."

he guard was still alive—for now. They wouldn't bleed out too quickly as long as they didn't remove the blades. As odd as that was, it brought me some relief. My hands were far too bloodstained already. I didn't need another death on my conscience, regardless of circumstance.

My heart roared in my ears, and my heavy breathing broke the otherwise deafening silence. I steadied myself, glancing down at the cut on my shoulder. It was only about an inch deep, but just enough to slice through my muscle. The skin around the wound was hot and inflamed. Red snaked down my arm towards my fingertips like sap from broken bark. I felt no pain aside from when I moved it. I doubted I'd be able to say the same in a minute or two. The waist of the intricate gown was soaked through with dark blood, though the cuts merely stung. I prayed the High King would keep his word and provide me no more corsets.

My gaze wandered around the vacant corridor to where Rhea had tugged me before the guard attacked. An adjacent hallway. My heart thrummed with adrenaline as I hurried towards it, glancing back every now and then to ensure the guard remained writhing on the floor. I peered around the corner. "Rhea?"

Gilded seams of light formed several feet from where I stood. The air appeared to fracture, and glimmer with hundreds of colors as Rhea's form came into view. She was shaking. I rushed over to her.

"I'm sorry I hid, I just—"

I shook my head vehemently. "Don't apologize. Are you okay —can you breathe?" Her wheezing breaths echoed down the hall. "Focus on your breathing, Rhea. You're safe. We're going to go find the High King."

Her eyes remained wide, and she continued to shake. I gently took her hands from where they gripped her sides. I winced at the sharp pain now echoing through my wounded arm.

"You—you're bleeding, Quinn. Oh, gods, you're bleeding. *Lugh above*, why can't I stop this from happening?"

Blinding streams of grief and rage tore into my chest. But they were not my own. The sheer strength of her emotions was staggering. My stomach hollowed. My throat tightened to the point of pain.

"Rhea." Her name came out as a gasp.

She paused, tears trembling in the corners of her eyes. "Are you—why can't you breathe? Were you poisoned?"

I shook my head. "Calm down." She looked furious for a moment before I added, "—please."

Her suffocating fury began to withdraw from the air, loosening the strain on my chest. Her lips parted as if she were going to say something, but I stopped her before she could. "We need to find the High King."

Rhea gave a shaky nod. She continued trembling as I led her down the hallway to the corridor where I'd faced off with the guard. I glanced at where I'd left them moments before, but only a pool of blood lay in their place. My heart began to race again. There should not have been a way for them to stand, let alone flee, after the last wound I'd inflicted.

But as I surveyed the entirety of the corridor, it was completely vacant. No heartbeats, no footsteps—nothing. It was almost as if it had never happened, save for the blood. I swallowed thickly.

Cool air whipped across the bare skin on my bleeding shoulder, stinging the scalding skin. Rhea and I spun to our left, where it had come from. At the end of the hall sat an open window. Night air swept in, billowing the velvet curtains on either side. Whoever that guard was, they were gone. The window had not been open when we'd entered the hall. They must've left through it. How they'd managed to escape through it without being able to stand, I hadn't the slightest clue.

I gritted my teeth. "They're gone."

The guard's voice rang in my ears—

I know what you're after. You will not find him.

I would not—*could not* let anyone stop me from finding out what happened to my father. I'd waited too long for this chance. But whoever wanted to stop me was apparently adamant enough to kill for it. Could this have been what Salem was warning me about? Perhaps he hadn't painted a target on my back at all. Perhaps I'd done that to myself the moment I'd left the Forest. But I wouldn't let them stop me. Whatever reason they had for wanting to keep his fate a secret, I'd discover it soon enough. I wouldn't let anything come between my father and me. Not again.

The air smelled like blood. Not even the night wind could clear it out.

"Let's go," I muttered.

As we walked down the hallway, light bent oddly around

her. It was as if her panic had made her powers hyperactive, ready to protect her at the slightest flinch. I tried not to look at her too often. It made me dizzy. The light appeared to spin around her, contorting her features and surroundings. Filaments of golden sun fractured into being every so often around me, splitting the hallway in two. I tried to stare at my feet. Watching her Illusions made me sick to my stomach.

Rhea tugged me back and forth down the winding corridors as if she somehow knew them. The ballroom below was empty by the time we reached the grand staircase. The room remained lit by its grandiose chandeliers, saturating the air with gilded light. My arm was beginning to throb. The adrenaline seemed to be wearing off.

Rhea jumped beside me, and my heart lurched again, the world around me exploding into brilliant white light. I nearly screamed, but by the time I opened my mouth, the light was gone. I blinked, everything coming into focus very slowly. My arm was throbbing, and now my head was as well.

"Lady Quinn! Lady Rhea—by the gods, are you all right?" I immediately recognized the brisk voice of Kyro long before his dark skin and magic silver hair came into view. My sight was still blurry, but I could faintly make out the Water Druid as he sprinted down the hall toward us. "Oh, *great Llyr below*."

Rhea was still shaking next to me. Her grip rivaled a python's. Thankfully, she held my unwounded arm. "Quinn— and then I—"

"We were attacked by someone dressed as a guard," I said, blinking as Kyro's features came into focus. His silver brows pinched together, creasing the skin between them.

"Dressed as a guard?" Kyro's usual smooth voice seemed to waver. "And did you . . . *take care of them?*"

My teeth ground together. "I thought I did, but they escaped through an open window."

Kyro's throat bobbed. "I see. Lady Rhea, did you have any part in this undertaking?"

She shook her head slowly, gripping my arm a little tighter. "I . . . but yesterday—and I just couldn't—"

Her voice came out weak and breathless, trembling in tandem with her body. Kyro nodded and outstretched a hand toward her. "If you come with me, Lady Rhea, I'll take you to your rooms now. We'll make sure you have triple the number of guards stationed by you tonight."

She reluctantly reached out and took his hand, the blood rushing to my fingertips the moment she released my arm. My body sagged the instant she let go. I stared blankly at Kyro. Was I supposed to go with them?

As if on cue, the Water Druid turned back to me. "Lady Quinn, if you follow us, I'll take you to the High King. I'm positive he would like to hear about your attacker."

I heaved a sigh, wincing as my shoulder fell. I begrudgingly followed, despite my throbbing shoulder and wandering thoughts. How could someone have known what I was after? I'd told no one. Was it possible someone was able to read my thoughts? A Druid with powers over thought could've potentially discovered my secret. For all I knew, no god had dominion over the mind, but what if one did?

My heart stuttered at the idea. How could I stop someone who could hear my every thought? How could I outmaneuver someone who knew my move before I made it?

We turned several corners, our shoes clicking against the stone floor and echoing down the corridors. These halls were much more alight than the ones the guard had led us down. That might've been how Rhea had known we were heading in the wrong direction. She was a Light Druid, after all. I suppose it made sense she'd notice something like that.

We arrived at a large wooden door across the hall from what looked like my room. Two guards were stationed at either side of the doorframe. Their postures straightened as we approached.

"Lieutenants, please see to it that four more guards are stationed at every entrance to Lady Rhea's rooms tonight," Kyro instructed. His voice seemed to have regained its usual tenacity.

The guards inclined their heads, one of them hurrying off down the hall. Rhea continued to tremble, her knuckles white as she gripped Kyro's hand. "I—I don't want to be left alone, Lord Kyro," she said.

Kyro gave a slight smile. "I'll call for your handmaidens to accompany you through the night, my Lady."

At this, she seemed to relax a little. Her shoulders slumped, though she still appeared to tremble.

"That would be—be most appreciated, Lord Kyro. Lady Quinn's . . . her, uh, shoulder." Rhea motioned with her chin towards my arm.

Kyro swallowed. "I will see to it that it's taken care of, Lady Rhea. Let your handmaidens or guards know should you require anything else this night. Rest assured, you are safe now. High King Salem will not let anything befall you during your time here."

I rolled my eyes. *By Danu*, how was she supposed to believe that after what happened tonight? Salem hadn't done a thing to protect her from that guard. All he'd done was flee a party at the word 'breach'. It was preposterous to think Rhea would feel anything but fear after tonight. After yesterday as well.

The remaining guard outside Rhea's door opened it for her with a creak. Rhea released Kyro's hand. Her golden eyes met mine once more before the door sealed shut behind her. I ground my teeth together as Kyro turned to me.

"Are you well, Lady Quinn?" His cerulean eyes wandered over my shoulder.

"Spectacular."

His eyes narrowed. "Would you like a healer for your shoulder before you see the High King?"

I glanced at the wound. "I can heal it on my own if you provide me with some yarrow and anise. Also, a mortar and pestle."

The corners of his lips tugged downwards. "The High King may not find such a practice sufficient, Lady Quinn."

"I did not ask if he'd find it sufficient."

His chest heaved in a sigh. "Very well, I suppose. We will stop at the healer's quarters on our way to the High King's reading room. Will you come with me?"

My jaw flexed, but I gave a stiff nod. As much as I'd tried to handle the attack alone without killing them, I'd come up short. They'd escaped. If I'd used a mere drop of my power, they might not have escaped, but they might not have lived through it either. High King Salem would probably demand to know why I didn't kill them on sight. Any other Druid would not have hesitated.

We continued on down the corridor. Sconces glowed gold, dripping with candle wax. The air smelled of must and flame. The flickering light danced across the satin back of Kyro's tunic and glittered in his hair. Though it was tied back, stubborn strands continued to float about the air as if carried on some unseeable current.

A right turn led us down an unreasonably long hallway. Halfway down, we'd stopped at a wooden door with a brass knob. Kyro walked inside, leaving me alone in the corridor. When he came back through the doorway, he held a mortar and pestle in his hands, as well as some yarrow leaves and a vial with what appeared to be ground anise.

"After I leave you with the High King, I'll take these to your room," he said.

My jaw flexed. "Thanks."

We continued, turning a corner and arriving at another

imposing wooden doorway. A pair of ornate silver doorknobs stood on its face. Kyro raised his free hand, embroidered cuff twinkling in the dim light. He knocked thrice, holding my stare. He cleared his throat.

"I apologize that you were . . . that you were placed in an uncomfortable position, Lady Quinn. Despite my reservations about you, I hope you realize I would not wish such a thing on you. From what I know of your people, I can understand that it was likely a difficult . . . *decision* to make."

I paused. "Thank you."

"Come in," a voice resounded through the doors.

Kyro leaned forward and twisted one of the doorknobs, pushing it open. "I'll set these on your bedside table, Lady Quinn."

I nodded and stepped through the threshold. The room was dimly lit by a dying fireplace. It smelled of dust and smoke. Books lined the walls on either side of me, stretched towards a paned window. An imposing desk sat at the center of the room, and behind it posed an even more imposing chair. The back of the seat was so absurdly high it blotted out some of the windows. In the odd chair sat the High King, scribbling away on parchment with a trembling quill.

His attention remained focused on the paper, only pausing to glance up when the door clicked shut behind me. His body jolted slightly as if he weren't expecting me at all.

"Lady Quinn," he said, brows furrowing. His gaze drifted from my eyes to the sliced fabric hanging from my wounded arm. "What—"

"I was attacked. As was Lady Rhea, but they came after me directly."

Salem pushed the seat back from his desk with a creak. He stood, slowly walking towards me as if I were a wounded animal. I eyed him warily. He paused before his desk, leaning back against its edge to face me. "Did you kill them? Or are they still here?"

I bit down. "They escaped."

He loosed a breath. "I see. And what makes you so sure they were after you?"

My lips parted in response, but I stopped myself. He couldn't know what they were after—what I was after. "I don't. But they came for me when Rhea hid."

His dark eyes were positively unyielding. "Why didn't you kill them, *wildling?*"

"Forest Druids do not kill if we can help it," I replied. "I believed them disarmed and incapable of escape. I clearly misjudged."

"Your shoulder needs medical care." He motioned towards my wounded arm with a tilt of his chin.

The flickering shadows from the fireplace seemed to drench half his face in darkness, the other in gilded light. One eye I could hardly see at all—the other I could see all too well.

"Kyro is taking supplies to my room. I can handle it myself," I said.

"I'm sure you can," he hummed. "But I would feel better if you would allow a healer to see to it."

"And I would feel better handling it myself," I shot back.

The corners of his lips curled in a barely noticeable smile. "Do you recall anything about your attacker, *wildling?*"

"Pale blue eyes. Larger than me."

"Skin color? Accent?"

"Not sure."

He grimaced. "So all you have is eye color? And body size?" he chuckled dryly. "That's hardly anything to go on."

I stiffened. "I wasn't paying attention to what they looked like. When I'm being attacked, looks are the least of my worries, *ciarán.*"

He stared back at me blankly. "Next time, get me more than an eye color."

"Next time?" I snapped. "I *expect* there will not be a *next time*, Your Highness. Unless that's a threat?"

Again, he smirked. "Not a threat, *wildling*. But as I said, Forest Druids were not well-liked amongst Arastyans. Whoever has decided to target you will likely not be the only one. And I do not have to be your enemy."

My lips curled in a savage snarl. "Prove it, *ciarán*."

11

*B*y the time I woke the next morning, my shoulder felt worlds better, as did my waist. Despite being sutured shut at my own unsteady hand, the cut on my arm was healing nicely. The skin around the wound remained red and inflamed but ached much less than it did yesterday. I suppose the yarrow and anise were to thank for that. My waist was littered with superficial cuts that were easy to mend, though I felt some remorse for destroying the gown.

I'd spent the morning interrogating my handmaidens about the gods and goddesses—if they knew of any Druid that had access to minds. They both had denied knowledge of such a deity, much to my disappointment. Whereas eye color wasn't necessarily indicative of a Druid race, having a power related to a specific deity all but proclaimed which one you worshipped. If I could narrow down the god or goddess the Druid that attacked me had worshipped, then perhaps I could intercept them before they came after me again. I wouldn't let anyone stop me from figuring out my father's fate. I couldn't.

I now had two tasks at hand. First, figure out how Salem is connected to my father—how he came by my father's necklace.

Second, and perhaps foremost, find my attacker before they, or anyone else, can stop me. And somehow refrain from taking lives in the process. It would be incredibly unfortunate if Danu and Cernunnos decided to forsake me and strip me of my power. Their utmost principle regarded the sanctity of life. I could not kill without their explicit permission. As far as I knew, each deity had a singular rule that, if not obeyed, would result in the stripping of your power. I did not know any other principle but my own. Clearly, other deities were far more lenient with their Druids than mine were with me. If all had abided by the sanctity of life rule, there would be no murder—even if it was because of little else than fear of losing one's power.

My handmaidens yanked at my curls until they managed to pull them into a braid that fell across my shoulder. Errant strands refused to remain in place and instead lingered across my cheeks and forehead. Despite this, Ryz and Eyla managed to disguise the *wildling* beneath an unassuming exterior. True to the High King's word, my gown today had no corset. The dress was ash-colored and entirely satin, with intricate vines and thorns embroidered across the hem and up the bodice. My eyes, framed with black pigment and ink, appeared the same color as the fabric.

A knock resounded at the door only a moment before it opened. Kyro strode in with Rhea on one arm. "Lady Quinn, Lady Rhea has insisted you accompany her to the first competition," he spoke with a slight bow of his head. Today, he wore an ice blue jacket embroidered with glittering seams of white and turquoise. The pale fabric was brilliant against his dark skin, like foaming waves on a volcanic beach.

I stood from the armchair I'd been sitting in, glancing down at Orion. He was napping in the sun. I turned back towards the door. "Kyro, do you know of any deities that have dominion over the mind?"

The Water Druid straightened his back, clearing his throat uncomfortably. "I . . . I am not aware of such a deity, no."

I did not have to reach through the earth to tell that he knew something—something he didn't want to say to me. Perhaps it was Llyr. The sea god had control over water and time, so why not minds as well? The Druid who had attacked me also had blue eyes, an atypical Water Druid feature. Maybe this was a secret of theirs, something their god didn't want others to know.

I stalked over to Kyro and Rhea. "Well?"

I glanced at Rhea, who gave me a slight smile. "Thank you for accompanying me, Lady Quinn. Your presence comforts me." She released Kyro's arm, then reached out and took hold of mine before I could protest. She turned to Kyro. "Whenever you're ready, Lord Kyro."

Kyro bowed his head slightly, then shuffled off into the corridor. We followed past the not two, but four guards stationed outside my door. They'd arrived in the middle of the night last night. It had woken me. Hearing two extra heartbeats outside my door in the dead of night was hardly calming. But I guessed this was Salem's attempt at proving himself 'not my enemy'.

"How is your shoulder, Lady Quinn?" Rhea asked beside me. Her metallic hair was coiled into tight ringlets that bounced as she walked.

I glanced down at my arm, forgetting that long sleeves covered the offensive wound. "Much better today."

I felt her tense. "Again, I must apologize for not—not fighting beside you. I just—"

"You don't have to explain yourself to me, Rhea. I understand. And I do not fault you for it."

A sigh heaved from her chest. "You're far more forgiving than I believed you'd be," she confessed.

I shook my head. "I am not. But you've done nothing to be forgiven for."

A moment of silence passed between us. Tense.

"There is something I'd like to ask you, Lady Quinn, when we're in private."

I swallowed. What could she possibly have to ask me that she didn't want Kyro to hear about?

"Alright," I said.

"Until then, have you any idea about the nature of today's competition, Lady Quinn?"

"I was hoping for sparring but seeing as we're in gowns yet again, I think I'm wrong."

She laughed—a bright, melodic sound. "I was hoping for painting. But I suppose we're both wrong for the same reasons," she said. "I'd hate to ruin this thing with paint, anyways. I mean, the craftsmanship on these gowns is quite admirable."

I glanced to the side at her dress. It was bronze and comprised of soft fabric, beaded with tiny crystals that glittered in the tallow light. Her sleeves, unlike mine, were sheer. Swirls of golden ink danced down her arms to her fingertips. I hadn't even noticed last night—perhaps her handmaidens had covered them up. Though, I couldn't understand why they'd do such a thing. It made her seem like she had sunlight bleeding through her skin.

"Is the ink on your arms permanent?" I asked.

She nodded. "It's optional once you complete Light Druid training in the Southern Territories. Most choose to get it, though. It marks mastership of light and craft."

"Sounds like quite an accomplishment."

We reached a lone door, and Kyro pushed it open with a creak. The room was sunlit, with indigo rugs and black sofas with furs strewn across them. A dusty fireplace stood against the wall, dividing two walls of paned windows. Four Ladies stood at the center of the room, three watching us as we entered. Ingrid was again in crimson, Xandria in blue, Aria in white, and the effervescent Lady Zora in pitch black. The Dark Druid stared off into space absentmindedly, drumming her fingers against her thigh.

Rhea and I took our place next to the line of Ladies, with me at the end. Rhea leaned in and whispered in my ear, "I'll tell you more about them later if you'd like."

I gave her a nod, then turned back to face the doorway. Perhaps I could ask Rhea if she knew anything about deities with control over the mind. She seemed to know quite a bit about everything—maybe she somehow knew about this. Though, if she had known, she might've answered when I'd asked Kyro.

Kyro stepped inside the doorway, then slightly to the side as the High King strode into the room. Everything about him screamed darkness, all except for the obsidian ring atop his head, glinting dark gold in the blinding sunlight. His jacket remained unbuttoned at the top, revealing a silver chain that swung in tandem with his steps. My jaw flexed. It did not belong to him.

Kyro stepped forward in front of the High King. "Good afternoon, esteemed Ladies of Arastya. The first set of events will assess your abilities regarding the duties of a High Queen," he explained. "A Queen must be able to keep her cool, even in the most emotionally taxing situations. She must think logically and quickly before acting. As such, today, you will each be placed in emotionally taxing situations. The High King's council and the King himself will assess your reactions to these situations. The winner will receive the first occasion with the King."

Salem stood a few steps back, arms folded. His eyes swept across us like a wave, crashing down on me and holding my glare.

"These situations are designed specifically for each of you. And are designed to induce an emotional response. If at any point it's too much—" Salem's glimmering eyes held mine, "—feel free to tap out."

My lips twisted in amusement.

Bring it on, ciarán.

"What will happen to us if we do?" Lady Aria spoke up, much to my surprise. Her voice was breathy and soft as if one slight sound would drown it out.

"You'll simply be disqualified from receiving the first occasion with the High King," Kyro replied gently, somehow knowing the wrong tone might make her wither. "Any more questions?"

"Who's first?" Zora's voice pierced the air like a blade.

"Lady Aria is, actually." Kyro's turquoise eyes straitened at Zora before flicking to Aria. The Air Druid wrung her hands together. Blonde hair tumbled in curls past her shoulders, where it met with a white dress trimmed with lace and crystals. Her heartbeat whirred like a hummingbird's as she curtsied, then took a few small steps and intertwined her arm with Salem's. Her heart fluttered at his touch, and her breathing quickened. If she kept on like that, she'd undoubtedly faint. She hadn't even gotten to the test yet.

"The rest of you, please remain in this drawing room," Kyro instructed. "We will come and retrieve you as necessary." His eyes slid to mine as he turned, trailing in Salem and Aria's wake.

The second they left, the Ladies scattered to different parts of the sunlit drawing room. The walls were the same dark stone, and the floor was the same polished marble, a prismatic glow reflecting from its face in the bronze rays of midday. I sat down next to Rhea on a loveseat, resting my elbows on my knees and holding my chin up.

"I give her five minutes," I said, and Rhea snorted, leaning forward.

"Two." She folded her hands in her lap. "What do you reckon

these emotional challenges are?" she asked in a hushed tone, even though the other Ladies could easily hear us.

"My guess? They'll insult and threaten us just to see how we respond."

"I didn't realize they would be *training* us to be Queens. Based on prior competitions, I believed it would be more of a beauty contest. Maybe a 'who's better in bed' contest." She snickered.

"I doubt I'd still be here if that were the case," I said. If it were, I might not have had the chance to discover my father's fate. I was not the elegant beauty the other females in the room were and placing me alone in a bedroom with Salem would likely result in regicide. After I got the information I needed, of course.

"It'll probably end up being that anyways, sunshine. I wouldn't worry about it," Zora snapped from across the room.

Rhea's irises glowed golden. "You're right. After all, he's probably already screwed you and didn't come back for seconds, so at least I know I wouldn't come in last," Rhea shot back, her voice a blade. My brows shot up.

"You bitch," Zora snarled, stomping toward us.

I stood abruptly, glaring down my nose at her. "*Watch it.*"

Zora's thundering heart wavered like a tempest raging against a cliff face. Her dark gaze flicked to Rhea, lounging on the loveseat as if she couldn't give a damn.

"No, you watch it. You all will have to bow to me when I'm High Queen. And I'll seek retribution for every wrong turn you've made," Zora hissed.

"I'm trembling."

"Zora, stop. You don't have to go for everyone's throat," Xandria interjected from the corner of the room. She appeared to be examining a wall of dust-coated books.

Zora spun and faced the Water Druid. "I don't recall including you in this conversation."

The Water Druid's eyes flared with frost. "You addressed all of us when you said we'd bow to you," she said. "Whichever one of us the High King selects—I'd expect better behavior of my High Queen. We are here for the future of our kingdom, not for spiteful threats and lust for power. If you're so intent on gaining a crown, Zora, I'd rein in your vice. At least disguise it, lest you have a full-blown mutiny demanding you be stripped of your title."

They held each other's gaze for a moment, a silent exchange of words perhaps, before Xandria returned to blowing dust from book spines.

Zora didn't respond after that. She heaved an irritated huff and stomped back to her sad little armchair to pout. At that, I sat back down.

Rhea nudged my ribs. "Thanks."

I nodded as a knock resounded on the doors. They swung open with a creak.

Kyro's attire glittered as he marched into the room and cleared his throat. "Lady Zora?"

She practically leaped from her armchair, sashaying over to the door. There, she took Kyro's arm and followed him out.

Thank the gods.

The room remained in a comfortable silence in Zora's absence. One by one, each of the Ladies was selected and taken to their trial. Rhea was the next to go, followed by Ingrid and then by Xandria, until I was the only one remaining. By then, the room became steeped in silver, casting eerie shadows over the tapestries and bookcases. A prickling sensation had goose-bumps blooming over the back of my neck. Almost as if someone was watching me. And yet no one was here. I heard no other heartbeat.

At last, the door opened, and my stomach soared into my throat. I stood upright, expecting to see Kyro at the door waiting for me, but instead, the High King himself stood beneath the archway.

"Lady Quinn," he murmured. His dark eyes reflected nothing at their surface.

I meandered over to him, still covered in goosebumps. "*Your Highness.*"

He outstretched his arm for me to take—a peace offering, perhaps. I eyed it for a moment, then walked through the doorway by myself. I almost snickered when rushed footsteps echoed behind me as he caught up to my side.

"I must say, I'm surprised you're still here. I saw your deer in the gardens this morning and thought I was hallucinating," Salem said.

"Elk."

"Whatever."

"Why are you making me go through this when you know you're going to send me on my way the first chance you get? Why test me?" I asked.

"Because I don't know that I'm going to send you home the first chance I get," came his swift response. I swiveled my head to face him, confused. The way we'd argued at the Announcement Ceremony made me believe that he despised me for being here. Last night's discussion did little to contradict that.

"Grown fond of me, have you?" I sneered as he picked up his pace. I followed him as we turned down another corridor bathed in moonlight. A few candles remained lit amongst the tapestries, but not enough to see clearly. I should've assumed as much—Dark Druids thrived in their element.

"In the three days I've known you, Lady Quinn, you have managed to become the most insufferable Druid I've ever come across," he replied. Silver thread embroidered the back of his waistcoat, swirling across the fabric like far-off galaxies.

I strode lazily behind him, examining the tapestries on the walls. "I could say the same for you, *Your Highness.*"

Salem turned, glowering at me. "How many times must I warn you to mind your tongue?"

"At least once more."

"You'd be wise to keep that to a minimum around others, or I might be forced to punish you for it," he snarled, his brows pinching together.

"Kinky," I hummed, strolling past him to examine one of the tapestries. It depicted what looked like a male and a female embracing each other whilst they lay on a forest floor. The male consisted of intricately woven dark fabrics swirling like the contents of a cauldron. The female was sewn with a myriad of colors, like rays of sunlight diffusing through mountain peaks at sunset. Flowers blossomed from the ground beneath the two figures, trees sprouted, and branches of rivers flowed from their touch.

"What's this?" I asked.

"It's thought that it depicts the story of our Creation. The earth goddess, Danu, and the father god, Dagda, meeting, creating our world and all life," Salem said from behind me, and I flinched. He was a little too close for my comfort. I turned, giving him a cool glare, then continued down the hall.

"It's been three days—was Lady Vara's body returned to the South?" I asked.

"I don't see how that's any of your concern," he replied, "but yes, she was. Lady Vara received her Rites in time."

"Rhea didn't want to go with her?"

"Would you?" he quipped. "Would you want to travel the same road your mother was brutally murdered on not two days ago? Relive an extremely traumatic experience and possibly put your own life at risk again?"

I scowled. "Where are you taking me? This is rather far."

"Here."

He held open a small wooden door. I fought to hold his dominating stare as I marched over to him.

"Thanks," I mumbled in passing, walking into the warmly lit room.

It was small, maybe half the size of the drawing room. A large wooden table sat at its center with several Druids positioned around it. Kyro sat at the chair closest to the door. Next to him was a female with tan skin and dark eyes like Salem. She shared his dark hair aside from the very tips, which were stained a pale pink. Her eyes narrowed at me upon noticing she had my attention.

The Druid beside her was large, obviously a warrior of sorts, given all the scars littering his exposed arms. His midnight skin glowed golden in the firelight, with amber-colored eyes trained on me like a hawk. The final Druid in the room was a female with greying hair and glacial eyes. She watched me with curiosity and judgment as I made my way over to a chair that had been pulled away from the table—I assumed, for me.

"Lady Quinn, I hope your accommodations thus far have been adequate," she spoke softly, but her hard gaze sang a different tune. Power radiated from her like ripples on a pond, bending around the others in the room as if they were rocks piercing the water's surface. It thrummed against my skin, and as it hit me, I knew—I knew who she was. Perhaps it was the hardened stare or the aura of power, but I knew.

"Yes, Your Grace." I bowed my head but held her gaze as I always held Salem's. Her lips quirked up in subtle surprise.

"Right then," Kyro said. "Let's get straight to it. Following the tests, you will be given a potion that will erase them from your memory. This is a precaution not only for His Highness's safety but also for your own. Do you agree to comply?"

"You're asking if I'm okay with you erasing my memory? What are you going to do to me exactly?" I chuckled dryly, glancing around the room. Nobody else laughed.

Kyro shifted uncomfortably. "That can't be explained until-—"

"I will be using my powers to enter your mind and conduct the trials within your own subconscious," Salem said, leaning back in his plush seat. "It allows me to get a better sense of your reactions."

I *knew* I'd felt a claw brush against my mind two nights ago. If he could enter minds, did he know all along what I was truly after?

Did *he* send that Druid after me?

But if I was wrong, if he didn't know why I was here, denying him access to my mind would only raise suspicion that I had something to hide. No—I could do this. It was *my* mind. He would only know what I allowed him to.

My lips curled in a snarl. "You tried to get in without my permission before. Why ask for it now?"

The silence was corporeal as Salem's throat bobbed. "You felt that, did you?"

"Enough. Will you consent to the potion?" the High Queen asked. Her eyes glared into mine, sizzling like melting ice.

"Do I have a choice?" I asked, earning a smirk from the current High Queen. *No, no, I did not.* "Fine."

"Sign here." Kyro pushed a piece of parchment across the table to me, along with a quill and ink. I sucked in a frustrated breath and dipped the quill, scribbling my name illegibly at the bottom. The last time I'd used a quill was when my father was with me. My signature could've easily passed as a different language entirely, but no one mentioned it.

"Thank you for your cooperation. Your Highness, it's all you, sir." Kyro bowed his head as he rolled the parchment.

I hesitated, turning to face the High King. My gut coiled and flipped as my eyes met his, the understanding of what he was about to do settling in.

I'd given him access to my mind. The only thing left was to show him why he should've stayed out.

His lips twisted into a sardonic grin, his eyes a dusky gold from the firelight. And then, it all went black.

12

*I*nky black fog surrounded me, coiling around my ankles like a serpent. The tendrils were frigid, like a midwinter breeze given form. I could see nothing else, hear nothing but the beat within my chest and the echo of my panting breath.

Where was I?

My eyes searched, almost frantically, for any sign of anything—but to no avail. Two dark shapes in the distance blurred into view as if obscured by fog. They stood still, unwavering. I rushed in their direction, eager to see who had joined me in the dark. That feeling faded as I realized who they were.

To the right stood Orion, an iron chain coiled around his muscular neck. The sight of his antlers nearly brought me to my knees. They'd been severed off his head like pruned branches from a tree. Blood matted the fur across his face. It was a wonder he remained standing. Next to Orion stood a faceless figure holding a sword to his throat. The figure multiplied into three, then nine—all facing me.

On the other side of those nine figures stood someone I hadn't seen in many years. My father, emerald eyes brimmed with tears, hadn't aged a bit. His dark hair was speckled with bits of grey, and the same smile lines creased around his eyes as his gaze met mine. An identical sword pressed to his throat.

"One lives. One dies," a voice boomed in the emptiness.

My heart echoed in my ears, breath shallow on my lips as my blood ran cold. "And if I don't?"

"They both die." *Great.*

"Me. I choose me," I said. All nine faceless figures turned to face me and tilted their heads to the side. A swallow lodged in my throat.

"You can't choose you," they said simultaneously, but it wasn't entirely convincing.

"Why not? You didn't say I couldn't."

"She's right. We didn't," one of them mumbled, wincing as the figure next to them shoved an elbow into their ribs.

"You're not supposed to say that out loud, dumbass," one of them hissed. Another one shook its head in disapproval.

"Let the girl have her choice," the figure to the far left spoke.

An arm wrapped around my chest, a thin blade held against my throat. I grappled with them for a moment, waiting for them to tense before the strike. When they did, I bit down on their arm with all my might. They screamed out, and I slammed my elbow back into their ribs. With their balance now off, I knelt, pulling them down with me until they leaned across my back. I reached back, gripping their arms, and flipped them over me. I readied to grapple for the sword as they fell, but nothing happened. There was no figure, no blade, not even a cloak.

My skin prickled. "That was rude," Salem's voice purred from behind me.

I whirled around. He was cloaked in the same black robes the faceless figures had worn. I'd almost forgotten he was in my head—that this wasn't real. This was a game. *His* game.

"And you're surprised?"

"I was—at that self-sacrificial bit. I didn't peg you for the hero type," he replied, taking a deliberative step toward me.

"You don't know me, *ciarán*. Don't pretend to."

"Why do you think I'm inside your head, *wildling*? I don't know you *yet*," he smirked, emphasizing the last word.

"Let's get on with it, shall we?"

He grimaced. "Fine."

The darkness dissipated into brown.

There they stood. My heart thundered, and my powers sang in my blood. They were dead. They were still dead. I'd killed them. I'd—

Red bloomed across my stomach. All I could see was blue sky. Pain.

No. Not this part of me. I would not give him this.

Shadows swam across my eyes until the world turned into night. And then it turned green.

I was in my Forest. I sucked in a deep breath, admiring the deep aromas of pine and grass and freshly blooming wildflowers. Dappled light seeped through the leaves above me, a brisk breeze trailing ghostly fingertips down my arms and throat. It pulled the curls from my neck, a shiver racing down my spine as it met with sweat and dimpled skin. I felt a brush against my shoulder and turned. Orion—antlers and all. His fawn fur glistened with morning dew, sparkling like gemstones in penumbral light.

A blast of heat curled against my face. My gut twisted.

Fire.

Druids were flinging fire into the Forest. There were hundreds of them charging towards us from the plains. Flames danced in their hands and eyes as they hurled them toward me—towards my home. Embers flew from outstretched palms to the bark of ancient trees, the winding limbs of elderflower bushes, and dense thicket, setting them ablaze in gilded flame. Sulfur clouded my throat as smoke singed my nose, my eyes stinging with tears.

This Forest was all I had left.

I swung onto Orion's back and nudged him forward. Dread coiled in his stomach, fisting his throat. He shook his head, refusing to approach the flames. I swallowed the acrid taste on my tongue and leaned down, patting his neck as the blaze raced toward us. Charred skeletal trees were left in its wake, glowing red from within.

"I will protect you, my friend," I said. "You are safe with me."

I nudged him again. Reluctantly, he listened and charged toward the edge of the forest. The earth rumbled underneath us as we ran, asking me if I wanted her help. *Yes. Yes, I do.*

The heat of the flames seared against my skin as we charged through the fire, Orion's heart racing in his throat as glowing ashes fell on his fur like snow. I swatted them away, hissing when they melted the skin on my hands.

I spread my arms to either side of me, reveling in the sheer force of the earth beneath us. It writhed and shook beneath my will, eager to be set free. My fists wound tight, and I pulled with my arms, muscles straining as I yanked her from the deep. Walls of rock shot upwards on the forest's edge, leaping into the sky like water from a geyser. Higher and higher they soared. A scream wrenched from my chest as I pulled more and more from her until I was sure we were safe.

Then, *darkness.*

I collapsed onto the cool ground, an inky fog swirling around me again. I panted, fanning the pesky clouds as I stood to face Salem. His arms were folded, brows pinched in deep thought. I waited to see if he'd question what he saw at first— what I'd yanked away from his grasp.

"Could you do that? Could you really?" he asked as if he didn't believe me. This was, as a matter of fact, all in my head.

Relief bloomed in my stomach. "Why do you care?"

I brushed the hair away from my face. It clung to the sweat on my face and neck, my skin still fevered from the blaze.

"You—" he paused in deliberation and sucked in a breath. "Final challenge, Quinn."

The pitch then faded into the city of Kalys. It was dark, embedded stars twinkling like far-off candles. I was alone in the cobblestone streets. The lights of all of the buildings were out. A dry wind billowed down from the peaks, ringing windchimes and shuffling flower boxes that hung on windowsills.

A little pitter-patter of feet against rock echoed down an adjacent alleyway. I turned to the source of the noise, furrowing my brows at the little boy racing towards me. He sprinted past me, barely offering me a second glance. Behind him were three burly male Druids, bounding after him like hunting dogs.

"Oi, where'd the boy go?" one of them grumbled as they slowed in front of me.

The one to his left cracked his knuckles and gave a sour grimace, clearly thinking they could intimidate me into revealing the truth. The boy was nothing to me, but the way these males looked at me was enough to set my mind in stone. If they found that boy, I wasn't sure he'd make it out alive. These were the kind of Druids my father had once warned me about— the kind that tortured the innocent, the weak, the unarmed—for sport.

I tilted my head to the side. "What boy?"

"I know you was standing here when he came by, don't play dumb with me," another one spat.

"I'm afraid I can't help you," I replied and began to walk away.

A tight grip wrapped around my wrist. I turned, lips peeled back. I reached downwards, feeling for the earth—but to my surprise, there was nothing.

Absolutely nothing. No power, no whisper, nothing. Only the aching soles of my feet stood beneath me. My eyes widened as I realized the nature of this challenge.

I had no power.

The male with his hand around my wrist leered and yanked me towards him. "Let's have some fun, doll." His voice could've curdled milk.

My stomach roiled. No—not again.

I swung my knee up into his groin, and he doubled over. I threw a right hook into his cheek, flinging his massive body backward. Perhaps the High King thought my identity was rooted solely in my connection to the earth. But it wasn't. I was more than my power.

I grinned, swinging my leg into the male's torso to knock him down. "Still want to have some fun?"

His rotund body fell to the cobblestone with a thud, his companions wincing at the sound. Blood pounded in my ears as I stalked in their direction. I did not need magic to remember every muscle of an ellen trechend as it approached its prey, every movement of a nuckelavee before it devoured a person whole. I'd feared the beasts for years before I'd recognized that I was one of them.

Unfortunately, they weren't nearly as wise as prey animals. They didn't run.

I nailed the first with a kick to the gut, which he predictably —caught. My other leg swung up around his shoulders, constricting his stout neck in a chokehold with my knee. I flung my body weight backward, landing him flat on his spine with my knee still around his neck. The other male was quickly approaching, so I slammed his head against the stone. His eyes rolled back as blood seeped from the wound. The smell of salt stung in my throat as I scrambled to my feet.

This one was tougher. Every punch I threw was countered, and every kick I swung was blocked. I was getting annoyed, so I grabbed a nearby flower pot and slammed it down on his head.

His eyes whirred. Before I could hesitate, I put as much strength as I could muster into a kick to the side of his head. He crumbled like sand.

Then, *darkness.*

My eyelids flung open as I gasped for air. I flew to my feet, frantically searching the room. My chest heaved, heart pounding in my throat—echoing in my head with every labored breath. Everyone else was standing, Kyro with his hands out in front of him as if trying to calm a wild animal. The female next to him simply stood, watching me. The gigantic male next to her had a crossbow aimed at my chest.

This was real.

I was out of my head.

I turned to face Salem, towering above me like a tree. His eyes resembled the sky I'd seen not a moment ago. With the crease between his brows and his taut jaw, he was the only one in the room who looked more confused than concerned.

"Well?" I demanded breathlessly.

There was a pregnant pause.

"Kyro, will you please escort Lady Quinn back to her room?" Salem asked, eyes never leaving mine.

"That's it?" I shot back. "You violate my mind and send me back to my room?"

The room itself seemed to hold its breath at my outburst.

"You're right. I'd almost forgotten. Kyro—the potion." Salem motioned for the Water Druid, who placed a cerulean flask on the table.

"I will not drink that *vile thing* after you pranced around in my head like that," I snarled at Salem.

He heaved a slow breath, the air curling around his lips like smoke. "The contract you signed was binding. If you don't, we will be forced to execute you."

I glanced briefly around the room, at all the stone-cold eyes staring blankly back at me. I loosed a deep growl and snatched the potion, downing the bitter liquid in a single swallow. My stomach lurched, but I kept it down with a painful gulp.

I shoved past Salem towards the door, where Kyro stood waiting. "Nice technique with the flower pot," Salem murmured.

"*Go dtachtar le d'anáil thú*," I cursed, not bothering to look back as I followed Kyro out of the room.

We were silent as we walked through dimmed corridors with stone walls reluctantly lit by tallow candles. Kyro's muscles were tense beneath his ornate jacket. Part of me wondered if that was my doing, with my violent outburst. Perhaps I didn't want to know. I'd forget it soon, regardless.

When we arrived at my room, he silently opened the door for me, and I entered. Just as he was about to leave, I stopped him.

"Do you know? What he did in my head?"

Kyro turned, his sharp features only more defined by the shadows cast across them. "Yes, Lady Quinn," he admitted with a swallow.

"How long until I forget?"

His eyes held a certain kindness I hadn't seen there before, as if he pitied me. "By the time you wake up, this will all be gone."

"Will I be going home now?"

I waited—waited to see if Salem had somehow seen past what I'd given him, if he knew why I was truly here. If he did, he would undoubtedly send me home at daybreak.

"I doubt it, Lady Quinn. You should get some rest," he replied, quietly closing the door behind him.

A part of me was relieved that I would be staying. But another, deeper part of me felt absolutely sick because he kept me despite everything I'd done, everything I'd said, everything he'd seen in my head. He wanted me here. And I didn't know why.

13

100 YEARS AGO . . .

Sweat beaded against my forehead as I dodged the fist my father sent flying toward my left cheekbone. I dove out of the way and jabbed my arm toward his gut. He deflected it off his forearm and swung his leg at my torso. I reeled back, earning a scowl from my father.

"I know what you're going to say," I said. "You'll say 'stay in close, don't give them a chance to breathe'—don't swing at my head, then."

My father's eyes lightened, and he chuckled, shaking his head dismissively. He stepped towards me, then gingerly brushed a wayward curl from my forehead.

"Any attacker is going to aim for your head repeatedly, Quinn," he replied. "I'm not going to patronize you. It's my job to make sure you can protect yourself. The world beyond the Forest isn't safe. Chances are, you'll experience that at some point or another, and I want you to be prepared."

I fought the urge to roll my eyes. The Forest wasn't safe, to begin with. Even the trees seemed to antagonize me. Thanks to his goddess, my father might see this place as a safe haven, but I was excluded from whatever protection she may have provided him. Animals fled from my presence. If I wasn't careful, the predators tended to recognize me as potential prey. I had no affinity for nature as my father did. The Forest had just as easily abandoned me as Danu had abandoned the Forest Druids, leaving them all to die. For whatever reason, she spared my father. Perhaps that's why he worshipped her so ardently.

"My attacker would never get the chance to aim for my head if I could figure out how to shoot a damned arrow," I grumbled.

"Language," he chided. "You can't base all of your trust in one fighting method. You may prefer to use your bow but will not get to it in every situation. You have to be prepared, regardless of the circumstance."

"I've been sleeping with blades in my sleeves since I was an infant, father," I said. "I know I have to be prepared."

"If you knew, you would try harder," he replied. "You're going through the motions with me until I allow you to return to archery. If you knew what evil lay in the hearts of mortals and Druids alike, you would take advantage of my training."

My chest tightened. I always wondered if his distrust of Druids and mortals was derived from whatever had happened to my mother. He hardly spoke of her, and when he did, his eyes turned a ghostly pale.

I relented. "I'll try harder."

"Good. Again." He widened his stance once more, and I followed suit.

This time, I used my speed to my advantage, keeping close proximity to my father. It forced him to make split-second decisions that weren't always wise. Every jab of his fist was blocked by my wrist, and every swing of his leg was dodged or blocked. It wasn't until I noticed his movements were getting sloppy that I began my assault, rapidly throwing punches toward his head, followed by a kick to his chest. It landed on his sternum, sending him flying onto his back. He held his chest with a pained expression.

"I—"

He held up his palm to silence me. "Do not apologize for your successes, Quinn," he coughed out, cradling his chest as he heaved himself to his feet. "No one else will."

I waited for the praise I hoped would one day come, but it never came. Sometimes, I'd begun to doubt it ever would. I suppose calling my kick a success was something. I took that sliver and held it close—as if it meant more than what it was.

"Does that mean we can go train with the bow now?"

My father's expression hardened, and he shook his head. "Blades."

I groaned.

We *always* trained with blades. It was the first weapon my father taught me to use. He rarely beat me in a sparring match nowadays, which I found quite boring. There were many other things that I could improve on that didn't involve the clumsy broadsword my father took from a mortal camp. He didn't seem to care and strolled to the nearby tree he'd propped two swords against. With a grunt, he sent one flying through the air toward me. I caught its hilt, swinging the blade around my wrist to test its balance. The swords we trained with were never even. Mortals tended to place more weight on the hilt than the blade itself.

"Ready?" my father asked with an up-kick of his brow. I grimaced and nodded.

A slash of my father's blade sang through the air as it arced toward my face. My heart jumped into my throat, adrenaline cooling my veins as I threw the sword up and blocked it with a metallic clang. He countered and sliced toward my gut. I jumped back in surprise.

"Can't we warm up a bit first?" I grunted. "You were just telling me to stay close, and now I have to back up."

"Your opponents will not give you a warm-up, Quinn," he replied. "You have to be able to flip between fighting styles as quickly as you breathe in and out."

"I understand, but it's just you and I right now. You're not an opponent trying to disembowel me," I said.

His eyes narrowed. "If you do not *practice* as if I am trying to kill you, you will never know how to defend yourself against someone who is. You will only know how to fight someone who is trying to spar with you. You will never be prepared with that mentality, and the world will devour you."

I swallowed, any amusement dying in the back of my throat.

"Can't we ever just take a break?" I asked, pleading a little. "Just a day. Just one."

I didn't realize how badly I wanted to do anything but fight until now, do anything but chart the stars, memorize healing herbs versus poisonous ones, and climb trees faster and faster until my hands were raw. It was all we'd ever done. My body was constantly bruised and sore, my mind never rested, and my hands had grown more calloused than my feet.

He shook his head in what appeared to be disappointment. "The world will take advantage of that day, Quinn."

A tight ache in my chest made my throat tighten to the point of pain, and I pinched my eyes shut, shoving the thought back into the depths of my mind. My father was right. I could not, *would not* be weak. The world would devour me whole. His teachings were the only chance I had at survival. Unlike the mortals, I had no clan of friends and family to help me. Unlike the Druids, I had no deity to gift me magic. All I had in this world was my father.

"Again," I whispered, hoping he'd ignore the little crack in my voice as I spoke.

He swung his blade again, the sound of steel ringing in the air until the night began to rise once more.

a knock resounded at my door, and I shot upright, my stomach lurching. "Come in," I said.

In strolled Ryz and Eyla, rolling in both a breakfast trolley and a rack of gowns. I rubbed my eyes, straining to ensure none of them were corseted. It seemed I was in luck—or the High King had kept his word.

"Good morning, Lady Quinn. You are to meet with the High King and the other Ladies in approximately an hour, so you may need to eat breakfast quickly." Ryz placed a few platters beside me on the bedspread.

My stomach churned. "Oh, I'm alright. I'm not hungry after—"

I paused. Last night. Dreams of cobblestone streets and flowerpots, of blood, matted fur and blades, of fire—*so much fire—*

I was not supposed to remember. I'd taken a potion that would make me forget. How on earth did I remember?

"After what, Lady Quinn?" Eyla's voice pulled me from my thoughts.

I swallowed, bile burning in my throat. "Nothing. Just didn't sleep well."

My handmaidens nodded and continued about their business, removing the trays from my bed. I felt sick. The High King had pranced around inside my mind, and *I'd let him.* Sure, I had little choice if I was to remain inconspicuous and a contestant in the competition. It hardly settled my stomach, though. Whatever was in that potion had me dizzyingly nauseous.

I yanked the sheets from my body. Goosebumps prickled my sweat-drenched skin as I hung my legs over the side of the mattress. The world spun. My stomach coiled.

"Lady Quinn?" Someone's voice.

"Bucket. I need—"

Someone shoved a ceramic pot beneath me just in time. I retched into the pot, my body shaking. Sweat pooled across my brow, trickling down my nose. The muscles in my belly ached as I sat upright once more, wiping the side of my mouth with my wrist.

I blinked. A confused-looking Eyla and Ryz came into view. "I just—I didn't sleep well. Do you have water?"

Eyla handed me a glass, and I downed it. "Should I tell the High King you're ill, Lady Quinn?"

I shook my head. The more I isolated myself from the others, the quicker he would be to suspect something of me. He would wonder why I was sick after last night, especially when I shouldn't have remembered the challenge at all.

I looked up at my handmaidens. "I just need to rinse off, and I'll be fine."

Ryz frowned. "We don't have time to dry your hair, Lady Quinn."

"Leave it. I'm more concerned about the sweat," I said dryly, motioning to myself.

Ryz and Eyla didn't argue. One hurried to the bath and began to run the hot water while the other pulled a gown from the clothing rack. I hobbled over to the tub, stripping my clothes as I went. Eyla scrubbed my skin and hair much more efficiently than I would've, then helped me from the tub and dried me off. Though my hair remained drenched and tangled, she coiled it above my head in thick cloth and began working away on my face. Ryz did her best to dry my hair by hand. My stubborn mane was having none of it, however, and promptly coiled into thick ringlets the moment she stopped touching it.

They dressed me in a dark blue gown with sleeves like scales. Eyla painted white ink across my eyelids. I tried to stop staring at my hair; how it looked like the fire burning my home to embers, the blood down Orion's neck—

"Lady Quinn?"

I flinched and spun around. Kyro stood in the doorway. He wore his usual cerulean satin today. Whatever pity had marred his features last night no longer remained.

"No Rhea today?" I asked, standing from the stool my hand-maidens had placed me in.

"No, Lady Quinn. Though, she did ask." His glacial eyes flicked to my handmaidens and then back to me. "I presume your handmaidens have informed you of today's events?"

I parted my lips to respond, but my confusion must have been evident because he continued on. "Last night's challenge will be addressed by the High King and you will be informed of the succeeding contestant, who will accompany His Highness on a date this afternoon."

I swallowed. "I see."

The thought of seeing the High King again was enough to make my stomach churn once more. Spending the rest of the day with him—I wondered if I could manage. I'd have to if I'd somehow succeeded last night. I needed to convince him to tell me how he'd gotten that necklace. Still, I couldn't fathom how I'd have done any better than the others last night, especially after cursing at him as I left the room. Definitely one of my best moments.

Kyro no longer offered his arm as I walked over to him. He merely held the door ajar for me to pass through. I followed him down the hall, fixated on the iridescent hair coiled at the back of his head. My eyes trailed down an adjacent corridor, falling on the tapestry I'd asked Salem about last night; a dark figure embracing a light one with a bed of wilderness flowing from beneath them. Kyro cleared his throat, and I hurried back up to his side.

We meandered down the corridor until we reached the grand staircase I'd descended two nights prior, the marble banisters still draped in stygian vines and blanched roses. The other Ladies were already here, standing side-by-side at the base of the staircase. A beam of light bled through the stained glass windows above the stairs, adorning the Ladies in a myriad of colors. My eyes fell on Rhea first, her expression impassive as she stared blankly at the ceiling. She wore a patterned turquoise gown adorned with filaments of amber and gold. Her swirling tattoos were on display, glittering in the sunlight.

Then there was Aria. Her eyes were puffy, and her lips and nose blushed scarlet. Perhaps she'd had a difficult night as well. Maybe we'd both received faulty memory potions. Despite her distraught appearance, she wore a crimson gown covered in tulle and flowers like a bouquet of poppies.

Zora's eyes met mine, and my jaw tightened. Her lips were pulled into a tight line as if biting back a venomous insult. She wore a white gown with a dangerously high leg slit to her right side, exposing her tanned, muscular leg. I scowled at her as I reached the base of the stairs and strode to Rhea's side. I looked back up the staircase. My eyes found his almost instantaneously, much to the frustration of my curdled stomach. He held my gaze for a moment, waiting for me to break, to flee—but I didn't. I would never waver. So he did.

Salem's lips curled into a wicked smile as he slowly descended the steps. "Good morning, Ladies of Arastya. I trust you slept well?"

Aside from the steel cuffs and trim on his jacket, he wore all black. The hair atop his head was neatly pulled back like a swelling ocean wave underneath a night sky.

There was a unanimous hum of agreement, and his gaze flicked to mine for a moment before returning to the rest of the Ladies.

"I know you all probably have some questions about last night. We had to erase your memory of the challenge for your own mental security and mine. I hope you understand—it was purely out of benevolence. That being said, the winner of last night's challenge was promised to have the first occasion with me."

There was a moment of silence as he appeared to deliberate his decision.

"The winner was Lady Quinn."

My blood ran cold. *Not possible.*

"How was this decided?" Lady Zora quipped in her shrill tone, arms folding across her chest.

Salem's cavernous eyes dragged lazily in her direction. "Unanimous decision by my council and I. And I'd suggest the use of my title when speaking to me directly, Lady Zora." He turned back to me. "Lady Quinn, shall we?" He offered an outstretched hand in beckoning.

How did I win? I'd essentially refused to make any of the decisions offered to me. How was *that* a royal quality? I was not High Queen material. I was made to survive. Winning this challenge placed an even greater target on my back. Whoever had attacked me before—once they discovered I'd not only remained in Kalys but won the first challenge—I'd have to expose them before they exposed me.

But was this not what I needed? The more time I spent with

him, the closer I'd be to figuring out what happened to my father; how exactly that necklace had come into Salem's possession.

I felt a gentle nudge against my ribs as Rhea shoved me forwards, my hand hesitantly taking his. Long fingers intertwined with mine, and I looked up at him, trying to keep my heart steady. His eyes swirled with galaxies, twinkling as if they saw my internal turmoil.

"If you would follow me," he said, hot breath fanning my lips.

I took stepped back. I hadn't realized we'd been standing so close.

He just about chuckled, instead tugging on my arm and leading me from the ballroom. Once I was sure we were out of earshot from the other Ladies, I pulled at his arm, yanking him back. Perhaps I could convince him to take a different contestant. I had to remain inconspicuous, and becoming a top contender did the opposite.

"Pushy," he murmured as he came to a halt before me.

"What are you playing at?"

The skin between his brows creased. "Not sure I follow."

"I should not have won that challenge," I replied in a hushed voice.

Salem's features contorted in something near suspicion. "How would you know?"

I fumbled for words. I hadn't thought about the memory potion when I brought it up. "You said you were looking for the quick, logical thinking of a Queen. I am positive I didn't react that way."

"And how are you positive, Quinn?" His voice went so dark, I could've sworn all the candles and windows in the hallway dimmed as well. He stalked towards me.

My spine hit cold stone. "I know myself, *ciarán*."

He looked down at me, his breath staining my lips like a red wine. "Apparently not. Your reactions were exactly what I had been looking for."

I glared up at him. "Ever heard of personal space?"

"Dark Druids don't believe in such a concept."

"Forest Druids embody the concept. Back. Off," I warned.

I didn't like how I could feel the dark heat radiating off his body, the waves of his power crashing into me and pushing me harder against the wall. He was a tumultuous, dark ocean poised to erode away at me until my cliffs became a soft sand. My only hope was to put more distance between us.

"Or what? Are you threatening me, *wildling?*"

My lips twisted. "Yes, I am."

With a flick of my wrist, a wave of rock rippled the ground underneath him and flung him back onto his knees. I dusted myself off as I pushed away from the wall and strode towards him. His eyes met mine as I stood above him.

I had to admit—it was a pretty sight. The High King on his knees.

His lips curled into a smirk as if he saw what I'd been thinking, and he stood again, towering over me. He stepped closer, and I held my ground this time, tilting my chin to maintain his glare. For a moment, I wondered if I'd gone too far—if I'd finally face the wrath he'd mentioned. But instead, his calloused hand slipped back into mine, thumb pressed over mine.

"We do have somewhere to be," he grumbled.

He tugged at my arm, leading us toward whatever torture he'd selected specifically for me.

15

I frowned. "You're joking."

His lips broke into a dazzling smile. A deep crease dimpled into his left cheek but not his right. For a moment, I wondered what he would look like if he had it on both sides, but I quickly decided against it. His face was already far too symmetrical. Any more so, and it would give me a headache.

"You're being difficult," he chuckled.

"I am not! I just—I figured you were going to take me to a tea party or some other ridiculously pretentious event."

I gripped the withers of the dapple-grey stallion and swung into the saddle. The leather groaned beneath my weight as I grabbed the reins and slid my feet into the stirrups. I was so used to riding Orion bareback; it was odd to feel comfortable sitting atop an animal.

He rolled his eyes. "The last time you were at a pretentious party, you made all my people shudder with fear. Why would I give you an opportunity to do that again?"

The dark stallion beneath him chewed on the metal piece between his teeth. Tufts of hair covered the beast's hooves, and his wild mane shook as he whinnied. An impatient creature.

I ran my fingers along the burly neck of the horse beneath me. His heartbeat was heavy and slow, beating only once for every two of my own. "What's his name?" I asked.

"Scáth. And this is Nuin." Salem patted the neck of his massive steed, who huffed in agreement.

"You're beautiful, Scáth," I whispered to my stallion.

He heaved a deep breath and shook his head in thanks. He liked me. None of his riders had complimented him before.

I could feel Salem's eyes on me as I grinned, running my hands up and down Scáth's neck. "You must not have had many great riders then," I replied. He whinnied in agreement.

I met Salem's stare. "You do realize by giving me a steed, you've given me the opportunity to run?"

Nuin swished his tail in impatience. "You wouldn't leave without your deer. And your forest's safety is still at stake," Salem said.

"Elk."

"Whatever," Salem replied. "Per the laws set forth during this competition, you must stay until I dismiss you. Otherwise, it would be seen as not only an act of treason but an act of war."

Scáth tightened beneath me. "Relax, your Majesty. You're so quick to bite," I said.

The High King didn't seem very fond of being toyed with. I already knew why I couldn't leave—he'd made that perfectly clear. He was completely oblivious that I didn't *want* to leave just yet, that I simply enjoyed getting underneath his skin.

"Can you talk to them?" He motioned to Scáth with an upwards tilt of his chin.

"No. I feel what they feel. They understand what I say, and I can feel how they respond. I can feel his heart, his pain if he had any," I explained, careful not to give too much of myself away.

"I wasn't aware that Forest Druids had connections to animals as well."

"I haven't met any other Forest Druids, so I can neither

confirm nor deny." I shrugged, eyeing the impatient stallion underneath the High King.

His eyes met mine for a moment. "It's a shame. What happened to your people."

"Yes. A plague is always unfortunate."

Salem's swirling eyes flashed with something for a moment, but dark tides swept it away before I could truly see it.

"We'd better be off," he said with finality. His knees nudged Nuin, who eagerly began to canter off towards the Arastyan mountains. I gently urged Scáth onwards, and he obliged, meeting Nuin's speed as we followed them toward the looming peaks ahead.

"Where are you taking me?" I called out after Salem. He swung his head back to face me, once immaculate hair now disheveled by the wind.

"You'll see, *wildling*," he yelled back, pushing Nuin faster. With a whinny, the horse obliged and surged forward, eager to please his rider.

"Want to show them how it's done?" I suggested to Scáth, his head flying up in a whinny as he raced onwards to catch the dark stallion and High King.

It was odd to imagine the same male racing his stallion in front of me as a foreboding dark king. With his jacket flying behind him and the wind-blown hair, laughter echoing as he went faster and faster—High King Salem seemed less like a High King and more like an ordinary Druid. Much less like somebody who'd stolen a poor Forest Druid's necklace. Even less like somebody who'd violated my mind only the night before.

Looming ahead of us, a dark oak forest stood at the base of the peaks. Verdant leaves blotted out the flaxen light, which seemed to all but disappear a few steps into its thicket. Nuin slowed to a trot in front of the trees, and Salem slid off his back, tying the reins to a branch. Scáth slowed, ears perked towards the dense underbrush for any sign of movement.

"Will you stay? I don't want to tie you up," I asked my steed.

Scáth shook his head and heaved a breath that misted around his nose. I dropped his reins, and he began to graze on the lush grass around us, a beautiful meadow that stood like an archway to the ominous greenwood. Perhaps ominous wasn't the right word. For many years now, the most dangerous thing in the Forest was me.

"Why did you take me to a forest?"

Salem stood with his back facing me as he stared into the woods. "It's where you're happiest. Am I wrong?"

I just about choked. "Why do you care where I'm happiest?"

His face eclipsed in gilded light as he turned towards me. "You're not a prisoner, *wildling*. This patch of woods is a short ride from the castle. I know it's not the same as your home Forest, but should you need an escape from the pretentiousness, this is here."

"You'd let me come here?"

"If you notify Kyro or me first, yes," he said. "I don't want to think you're running away when really you've just come here. But I realize the importance of having some of your element nearby. When I visited the Southern Territories as a child, I suffered greatly. It's only dark for an hour or so there, and then the sun rises again. I felt like I was being suffocated,"

His brows pinched together as if remembering the pain. Through the earth, I could feel it, too; a dull ache in his chest, like someone was sitting on it and refusing to let him breathe.

"Thank you," I replied, my voice wrenching him from the memory.

"I've only ever met a few Forest Druids." He changed the subject quickly as if realizing I had felt his pain—that he had unknowingly shared it with me.

My breath nearly caught. "How long ago?"

He turned to me, outstretching his hand. I glanced up at the few strands of darkness falling across his face and the sharp curve of his lips. My hand slid into his, and he tugged me into the woods.

"Quite a while. A century at least," he said.

My heart throbbed. He'd seen a Forest Druid in the last century. Given the pendant hanging on his neck... but I couldn't seem too eager. If I pressed too hard, too fast—he would undoubtedly grow suspicious. If I returned to the subject later, perhaps he'd be more receptive and think nothing of it. Playing this game with him, biding my time, required a patience I didn't know I possessed. But this was too important to risk. I had to play it safe.

"How old are you?" I asked. I paused as his features twisted. "Just curious."

His scowl loosened. "I'll be 300 this Elder Moon."

Druids could live seven or eight centuries comfortably. We aged very slowly after maturing around age twenty—the age we selected our patron deities. Up until that point, we were effectively as mortal as humans. But once we chose a deity to worship, one affiliated with our bloodlines, divine magic kept our bodies from withering with age. So long as we paid heed to their guidance and rules, godly magic moved through us. So long as the magic remained, so did we.

"Old guy, huh?" I teased, and he shot me a glare. "You're not that much older than I am. So temperamental."

"You're one to talk," he quipped. "Half the time, you're quick-witted as a scholar, and the other half, as temperamental as a wild creature."

"I prefer the term 'volatile'."

He paused, glancing at me. Shafts of aureate light bled onto his burnished skin, blotted out by the shadows cast by fringed leaves. "That doesn't surprise me at all." He turned to continue walking again but hesitated. "Why were you so convinced that you didn't win the challenge? Did you not want to?"

I mulled the words over in my mouth. A partial truth, I could give.

"I was conflicted. I miss my home terribly and do not feel like I belong in a castle. But I would not like to be eliminated, either."

He stared at me blankly. I was tempted to reach through the earth and feel what those cavernous eyes refused to reveal. But he spoke before I had the chance. "Your honesty is refreshing. I don't know a single Druid who would speak to me as plainly as you."

The air grew thick. Stifling, nearly. So I gripped his wrist and tugged him through the underbrush. "Is that why you haven't followed through on beheading me yet?"

"Contrary to popular belief, I don't *enjoy* hurting others. I don't enjoy cruelty—despite whatever rumors I'm sure you've heard."

I heaved a sigh. "And I don't drink the blood of children, despite the rumors you may have heard as well."

At that, he snickered. "Yes, that was the most interesting rumor about you that night. But more have followed in its wake that I find much more intriguing."

I stilled. "Such as?"

"You can strangle a room of Druids without so much as moving a muscle."

I snorted. "And you still decided to take me to a forest *alone*?"

"I didn't say I believed it. And I could always tell the darkness to strangle you back should you decide to have a go at me," he replied.

"Can darkness truly strangle?"

"It can do whatever I ask it to. It can soothe, it can kill. It can search and hide. Darkness is whatever I wish it to be. Similar to how you can make solid rock ripple like a pond," he explained.

I hesitated before speaking, but if he noticed, he said nothing. "Tell me about the Forest Druids you knew. Could they make rock ripple?"

"I only ever knew two," he said. "The first was my tutor as a child. He was old and blind but could feel all the life around him. You could hold your breath, and he'd still hear your heart beating across the courtyard. The second was a female rebel hiding in the Wastelands. She'd amassed quite a following in hopes of overthrowing my father. That was actually when I met Kyro, believe it or not. He believed she was the last of the Forest Druids. Clearly, he was incorrect."

My heart sank. My father fit neither of those descriptions. And he wasn't lying. But just because he didn't know him directly didn't mean he didn't know *something* about what happened to him. I knew that necklace. It was my father's. There was no doubt about that. He had to know something.

He tugged at my arm, and I stopped, glaring at him. "What?"

"This way," he chuckled, leading me to the right.

We ducked underneath some more branches, the thicket catching on my cloth tunic in attempts to pull me back. Up ahead, saffron light soaked the funnel-shaped leaves that sprouted from serpentine limbs. We pushed through the dense underbrush into a meadow teeming with pearled blossoms and clinquant dew. The gilded waves of a pond lapped against a muddy shore that budded with reeds and willowy grass. Birds sang from their branches, signaling our arrival to the creatures that scurried through the underbrush to their dens. Still, the frogs continued to croak, and the bees remained steadfast in their quest for pollen.

"It's beautiful," I breathed as my muscles uncoiled beneath the balmy setting sun. Vibrant waves of carnelian and amethyst rippled across the sky like gems sewn into satin, the stars embedded in the fiery clouds glittering like seeds of gold.

"We can stay for a bit if you'd like," Salem offered.

"Yes." I paused before adding, "—please."

I knelt down on the soft grass and laid back, savoring the dewy blades of grass tickling my bare skin. The earth thrummed with energy beneath me, burrowing its roots into my body and bestowing me with warmth. With breath. With power.

I felt alive again—*whole* again.

Salem laid down next to me, his chin pointed toward the sky. "What is it like?"

"What?"

"To feel all the life around you," he replied.

I sucked in a deep breath, trying to gather my thoughts. "Overwhelming at times. Walking into Kalys the first time was jarring, to say the least. As was the Announcement Ceremony. Everything is so eager to be heard, to be seen. The trees want to be appreciated, the flowers to be admired, and the grass to be free. I give as much as I can. They feel me as much as I feel them."

The infernal sky was doused in shades of blue and lilac, the stars turning silver in the dusk. A moment of silence passed between us. Perhaps I'd said too much.

Salem shifted in the grass. "Darkness isn't like that. It obeys without a second thought. No hesitation. It's always there, looming but never whispering, just waiting for me to tell it what to do." His fingers brushed mine as they slid across the grass. "Can you feel this?"

His hands combed through the blades. I closed my eyes and reached down into the earth. Roots, reaching into dark soil. I followed them. Freedom flooded my chest the moment I broke from the dirt. Each blade of grass bowed beneath calloused fingertips, scraping his skin with dew. It was as if he were touching my own skin. I swallowed hard.

"Yes," I said. "Can you feel the stars?"

"No." He snorted as if it were a ridiculous question. "I can't feel the darkness. It's just there. But I can do this."

My jaw fell slightly ajar as the lilac sky darkened to a shade of onyx. Millions of stars seemed to appear from the abyss, screaming that, *yes*, they were still there. The sky was bathed in a silver glow, glistening like the scales of a salmon beneath a frozen river.

I heard a gasp, flinching when I realized it was my own. How had I never seen these stars before? They were always there— were they not? How many nights had I perched on a tree, naming the stars and ignoring the darkness, completely unaware that the dark stared back?

"Darkness allows you to see what light tries to hide," he said. "Darkness is truth in its most raw state. I can see through the skies, if I wanted, to other worlds and galaxies. I can see through the shadows, see the creatures that lurk and watch us. Darkness doesn't allow me to feel, only to see past light's illusions."

The onyx sky yielded to sapphire.

"That's how you saw me. In the Forest. Behind that tree. I was in a shadow," I said. "Do they all know? The Ladies back at the castle; do they know what you can do with darkness?"

"No. They know I can bend it because that's what I chose to show them at the Announcement Ceremony. And I'd prefer if you kept it that way."

He did not know that I already knew another of his secrets— one he clearly went to great extents to protect. I'd keep them both for now. Until I found a use for them, that is.

16

I dismounted Scáth and handed his reins to the stable hand. Another took Nuin's reins from Salem, and the High King strode towards me, eyes brimmed with moon dust. The darkness of the night curled around him like a cloak, drifting out behind him in a nonexistent wind.

The air tonight was cool and damp. His breath curled on his lips in a silver cloud, dewing on his eyelashes. "Thank you for accompanying me today, *wildling*."

"Thank you for the unpretentiousness, *ciarán*."

He cleared his throat. "Tomorrow, I take Lady Rhea. You two are acquainted."

A statement, not a question.

We strolled towards the imposing castle doors. Its stonework glowed like walls of ice, blanched from the stars and pale moon above. High up in its towers, gilded light poured from the tiny windows dotted along its side. Guards bowed on either side of the castle entrance, then opened the imposing doors with a creak. I followed Salem down the corridor that opened into the ballroom, then up the stairs and down a hall I recognized. The Northern Territories had a much earlier sunset than elsewhere in Arastya, but perhaps my perception of time was off. I'd believed it to be only late afternoon, but the hallways were vacant.

"Rhea enjoys painting. If you needed any ideas," I said.

"I'm not interested in her hobbies. I'm interested in giving her a reprieve so she might fare better during the remainder of the competition."

I winced. "Her passions in life might give her reprieve. Who are you to judge that for her?"

"The High King. I'm not interested in any aspect of the Ladies other than their ability to rule in Kalys. Finding a way to satiate her need for sunlight is one of the issues I must address should she become my High Queen."

I scoffed. "You expect to spend centuries with a Druid you know little to nothing about? To trust her with your kingdom, despite knowing little more than her political aptitude?"

His jaw flexed. "There's no point in getting to know someone you're only marrying to appease the Realms. This is for peace, *wildling*. Representation in court. Nothing more."

"Representation in court doesn't count if you know nothing of the culture they come from," I hissed.

His body stiffened. Irritation bubbled within his chest. "I know plenty about the cultures of the Arastyan Realms. What I'm most concerned with is the ability of the individual to survive here—to act with rationale and grace in the face of chaos."

I snorted. "And that's why I won the challenge? Because I act with *rationale and grace*? I *am* chaos, Your Highness. According to your criteria, I am the farthest from a High Queen you could want."

When the words left my mouth, I cursed myself for saying them aloud. I needed to stay here. I needed to figure out what had happened to my father. But my impulsive tongue was becoming a potential threat to my goal.

The High King stilled. His face remained annoyingly impassive. Again, I wrestled with the urge to violate his feelings; to know what he truly believed. Then his lips parted with the slightest hesitation. "I disagree."

We passed a corridor, and I paused, staring back at a tapestry I recognized. A female and a male—Danu and Dagda were what he had said. That was the hall he'd taken me down. The challenge had been held down there. But I shouldn't remember that. Cursing myself for hesitating and letting my mind wander, I spun around to continue.

Salem, however, blocked my path.

His expression was unreadable. "What are you looking at?"

"Nothing."

His lips twisted as if he'd tasted something bitter. "I told you earlier I *appreciated* your honesty, and now you choose to *lie* to me?"

I gritted my teeth together. Stupid mistake. I should never have stopped. Was I *that* terrible a liar that he knew straight away? Of course, I'd never really had to lie before now.

"Am I not allowed to look down hallways?" I retorted.

By Danu, please let it go. Stupid, stupid—

His eyes narrowed. "Why did you look down *that* hallway, of the many, many halls in this castle?"

I glared up at him, his expression infuriatingly unreadable. Claws tapped at the corners of my mind, cold and vicious. My stomach lurched, and I instinctively recoiled from him. I felt like I was going to retch again. The blood drained from my face. And as I looked back up at him, his eyes burned with silver embers.

"You remember."

My mouth went dry. "No, that's not—"

"Your handmaidens reported that you were ill this morning as well. It's clearly a reaction to my intrusion."

My lips parted, another lie on the tip of my tongue.

He pressed on. "Do not lie to me again. How did you bypass the memory potion?"

"I didn't."

Shadows exploded beneath his feet. His fury bled into the air like ink on a page. Every breath was like swallowing lightning —charged.

My muscles wound themselves taut, preparing to fight. Inside of me, a beast frothed at the mouth, rattling against its chains. The stone beneath me tensed, awaiting instruction.

"I don't want to fight you," his whisper was sharp, bit out between gritted teeth.

A feral smile tugged at my lips. My powers raged inside of me, thrashing back and forth. Screaming. "Don't force my hand, *ciarán*. You'll regret it. I'm telling the truth. I did not bypass your ridiculous potion. *It. Didn't. Work.*"

The ground began to tremble. Blood raced through my veins. My eyes remained locked on his. *Do not make me do this, ciarán. I don't want to. But I will.*

He blinked at me, eyes wide as if he had seen something he hadn't seen there before. The shadows began to recoil from the air, withering. "That potion should have worked on any Druid, regardless of heritage or Realm," he said. "And I know it worked on the others. They would've been affected as you have been. But no one else was sick this morning. Just you."

I heaved a breath, trying to calm my still-raging power. "I don't know why it didn't work. But I had nothing to do with it."

He nodded, jaw flexed. "I believe you." He ran a hand through his disheveled hair in frustration. "I should have you executed for retaining that memory."

"So why don't you?" I sneered.

"I can't," he shook his head.

I knitted my brows together. For a moment, I'd been positive he'd try to kill me. Perhaps I still had a chance at achieving my goal. If he could trust me after this, he might reveal what he knew about my father—how that necklace came to be strung around his neck.

"Why?" I asked, holding my breath.

The High King stared at me for a moment, his eyes so dark it made me wonder if anything lay behind them at all. "I can't. Leave it at that. You keep my secret. I'll keep yours."

"My secret?" I recoiled. "I did nothing wrong."

"If anyone in my council discovers what you know about me, they will kill you," he said. "And if anyone outside the council thinks you know how to bypass a memory potion, they'll torture you for that information. It's in your best interest that I do not tell anyone, *wildling*."

I had no choice. I had to oblige. I didn't know why the potion hadn't worked on me. He was right. If Salem decided to tell anyone, I could be in big trouble—trouble even *I* couldn't work myself out of.

With a heavy sigh, I nodded in agreement. We continued walking in heavy silence. By the time we reached my bedroom door, neither of us had spoken. I reached out a hand to turn the doorknob, but Salem's sharp intake of breath gave me pause.

He hesitated for a moment, then spoke quietly. "A member of my council was intrigued by you last night and would like to meet with you."

"Even after I cursed at you?" I raised an eyebrow.

He chuckled, his eyes twinkling once again. "I think that was what sold her, actually."

"Her?"

Salem's lips pressed into a thin line. "My mother, the High Queen Regent."

My heart stuttered a little. His mother was intrigued by me?

Suddenly, my 'remaining inconspicuous' plan seemed like a far-off dream. With her attention, I'd have eyes on me constantly. Every move I made would be questioned. But what if *she* knew something about my father that Salem didn't? Sure,

Salem had the necklace, but maybe *she* knew where he got it. I could still do this. My plan would just have to adjust.

I gritted my teeth together. "Alright." I began to turn the knob again but paused. "Why did you violate our minds like that? And demand we forget it? Does that not seem incredibly immoral to you?"

His heart stumbled for a moment, a breath lodged in his throat. "It was the only way to measure a true response to an emotionally devastating situation. The child in the last challenge? That was me. When I was younger, I used to escape the castle to play with kids my age. One time, I left too late." His breath grew tight in his chest as his brows pinched, eyes glazing over. "You were the only one who protected me and defeated my attackers. You didn't ask questions. You saw someone who needed you, and you chose to protect him. *That* was why you won. And that is why I think you'd make an excellent High Queen."

My words died in my throat. That boy—the one running from those burly males—had been *him*? It was a memory? *What had happened to him?*

I swallowed. "I don't want to be High Queen."

"The only ones worthy of the crown are those who don't want it."

"Rhea doesn't want to be Queen. She'd be a great High Queen," I offered.

"I agree. That's why I'm taking her out tomorrow. And why tomorrow afternoon, you will be meeting my mother."

"*Tomorrow?*" All other words died in my throat.

"Don't forget—as far as she knows, you do not remember her at all. I'll find your guards. They must've gone off to dinner. Goodnight, *wildling*."

And with that, he sauntered off down the hall, leaving me in complete and utter disarray.

17

Spears of sunlight stained Rhea's skin. Her bronze curls lay strewn across the grass, eyes closed and lips pursed in thought. She combed her fingers through the blades; gingerly, as if through her own hair. I watched the movement—felt it as if it were against my skin, despite being perched in a tree a few meters away. Orion was curled beside her, munching away at the ground cover. He sniffed her face for a moment, and she giggled.

"I never knew such a wild creature could be so gentle," she hummed, reaching up and petting his nose. "The horses in the South are raised by hand, bred for their temperament, and bonded with their riders. I'd have never believed the same could be said for an elk, Lady Quinn."

I rested my head against the tree trunk, allowing my legs to dangle from the branch on which I'd come to rest. My hands were sticky with sap.

"Though I've known Orion since he was a calf, his personality is entirely his own. I have no claim towards how he chooses to act."

Orion continued grazing. "I suppose that makes him an even more remarkable creature then," Rhea said.

I felt Orion's chest swell at the compliment and chuckled. "If you continue to praise him, it'll go to his head, which is large enough as it is."

Rhea's eyes opened, blazing gold. "Can I ask you something, Lady Quinn? And please, do not judge me for asking. You by no means have to answer. It's just—it's been on my mind for some time."

I blinked. "You can ask."

"You feel what he feels, yes? And what others feel?" She stared openly at me in the moment of silence that followed. "When we entered Kalys, you were overwhelmed—that I could tell. I first thought it was because you'd never been around that many people before. But again, at the Announcement Ceremony, you seemed on the verge of a panic attack. And when we were attacked, and I was panicking, you seemed to be having as much difficulty as I was. And just now—you speak as if you can feel him. As if you truly know his heart."

My head rolled back, and I stared up at the verdant leaves. "It's not common knowledge, Rhea, and I hope you'll keep it that way."

To my surprise, she beamed up at me. "Of course, Lady Quinn. I wouldn't tell a soul. I was merely curious. Do you know if all Forest Druids had that ability?"

I shook my head. "I have no idea. I don't think my father could. He's the only other Forest Druid I knew."

Her smile faded. "Right. You mentioned him before. I'm sorry." She glanced down at her lap. "That question I wanted to ask you in private—again, I don't mean to pry, but I've been trying to find the right way to bring it up without sounding like I'm accusing you of something."

My throat clenched. "Accusing me of something?"

"That night we were attacked, I heard what the attacker said to you. That they knew what you were looking for, and you would not find him." My stomach dropped. "Who are you looking for, Quinn?"

The blood drained from my face.

"I cannot tell you, Rhea."

She stared at me. Unyielding. "It's your father, isn't it?"

My hands wound into bloodless knuckles.

"I can help, you know. You can trust me. I won't tell a soul."

Tears stung at my eyes as I met her stare. "Please. Don't."

She pressed her lips together, her expression softening in understanding. "I won't. I promise. I have no intention of putting you in more danger."

"More danger?"

Rhea twiddled her thumbs. "There are whisperings about you."

"There were always whisperings," I grumbled.

Rhea shook her head. "Not like these. People know the castle was infiltrated on the first night of the competition. They think you had something to do with it."

My face scrunched. "I was the one who was attacked, why would they—"

"No one knows what happened in that hallway aside from you, me, Kyro, and the High King. They're just spreading rumors. But given that your kind was held in low regard, they assume that you had something to do with it."

"All because of my heritage?" I asked.

Rhea shrugged. "Fear is a powerful weapon. It lasts long after the truth is gone. And, to be fair, you did make the castle shake."

I was fortunate Kyro and Salem believed Rhea and me, then. If they didn't corroborate our story and our innocence, my quest to find my father could be thwarted before it had even begun.

Rhea's head tilted to the side like a raptor watching a hare.

"We don't need to talk about it. I just wanted you to know," she said. "Did you want to hear about my tattoos?"

I nodded, thankful for the change of subject. "Mastership of light and crafts, yes?"

She outstretched them before her, the ink glittering in the sunlight. "Each arm represents the mastering of each tenant of Lugh, god of light and artisanship. My left arm—" she held it up for me to see, "—represents my craft, painting."

I leaned forward on the tree branch, examining the artwork. A paintbrush sat on the inside of her forearm, swirls of gold erupting from its tip and coiling up her arm and beneath the straps of her gown. In the whirls of ink were blades of wheat and horses cantering, all culminating in a rather artistic representation of what I believed to be the sun.

She raised her right arm. "And this one represents mastership of light and all of Lugh's beliefs."

This arm was much less intricate than the other; lines of golden ink, some thick, others thin, stretched down from her shoulder to the inside of her wrist. At this shoulder sat another sun, but this was a simple circle from which all lines radiated.

"Can I ask—what is Lugh's principal tenant? I don't know any but Danu's."

She stiffened. "It's not really a polite question to ask, Quinn."

I raised an eyebrow. "Because we're only asking polite questions of each other now?"

Her lips quirked. "Fair point. Lugh's principle tenant is 'there is to be no light without creation'. In other words, if we don't create, we will be stripped of our access to light. I got these tattoos to commemorate my mastership of the tenant, as most Light Druids do once they complete their artistry education and philosophical courses."

"How long did it take to have inked in?" I asked.

She chuckled. "Half a day for my right arm. A full day for my left, being that it's much more detailed than the right."

"Did it hurt?"

She grinned. "Terribly."

"I believe it. They're beautiful."

Her eyes glittered as if made of the same ink as her tattoos. "Thanks."

"Lady Rhea, are you—" an articulate, masculine voice called from behind a shrub, "—ah, there you are." Kyro approached, clad in his usual satin attire. Stubborn strands of silver hair floated around his face, iridescent in the sun.

Rhea huffed and pulled herself from the ground. "Is it that time already, Lord Kyro?"

"I'm afraid so, Lady Rhea," another voice said as it rounded the foliage. Salem.

He wore no jacket today, merely a black button-down and trousers. The first few buttons were undone, revealing tanned skin beneath and a certain pendant that I wanted to rip from his neck. He sauntered forward, standing next to Kyro. Orion shifted, pulling himself up to his feet at Salem's arrival. My friend raised his mighty head as if warning off the Dark Druid.

Rhea bent into a curtsy. "High King Salem, my apologies. I didn't mean—"

"No need for apologies, Lady Rhea. It's a beautiful day to spend in the garden." Salem outstretched an arm towards her. As she took it, his eyes ran the length of the tree I perched on, landing on me. "Lady Quinn."

Kyro flinched next to him, looking around frantically until his eyes also landed on me. "*Great Llyr below*, Lady Quinn! I didn't even realize you were there." His gaze fell toward the tree's base, then again to me. "*How* did you get up there?"

My lips twitched. "I climbed."

Kyro's lips parted in confusion, then closed silently. Salem's eyes lingered on me, even as he held Lady Rhea. I glared down at him. "You're needed in my reading room," he said stiffly.

By Danu, I'd nearly forgotten his mother wanted to meet with me today.

"I can provide assistance if you would like. In getting down," Kyro offered, stepping toward the tree.

Orion seemed to hate the idea of the Water Druid getting any closer to me and blocked his path, lowering his head to the ground in preparation for battle. A heavy snort heaved from the elk's nose as he leveled a glare at Kyro. Kyro took a slow step back, swallowing.

I chuckled at Orion and maneuvered to the midpoint of the branch. I gripped the limb, swinging myself down to a lower bough, then leaped to the ground. Wiping my hands on the gown, I looked up at Kyro, Rhea, and Salem.

Kyro's jaw was slightly ajar. "That was Heran silk."

"What?"

"You just wiped your sap-drenched hands on *Heran silk*, Lady Quinn."

Salem seemed slightly amused, however. "It's no matter, Kyro. I wasn't a fan of that gown on her anyways. We'll have a different one made. Blue, perhaps, instead of red."

Rhea's eyes glittered as she met my stare. "I'm rather fond of Lady Quinn in red, Your Highness. If I may, I think it makes her look rather fearsome."

Salem's jaw flexed. "Fearsome, indeed."

Kyro cleared his throat. "Well, Lady Quinn, perhaps we should take you back to your chambers so that you might have a change of gown prior to your arrangement."

My attention shifted to Kyro, and I could've sworn the Water Druid winced. I walked over to Orion and placed my hand on his flank. He curled his head in my direction, dark eyes watching me. He was frustrated. He didn't want to be here. This garden was hardly a place for a creature like him.

I rested my forehead against Orion's. "I know, my friend. Soon."

At that, I followed Kyro back into the castle. Rhea and Salem went an entirely different direction- I assume somewhere towards sunlight, given the reasoning he'd revealed to me yesterday. Kyro escorted me to my room, where Ryz was waiting with another gown made of a similar fabric to the one I wore now. When Kyro stepped outside, she helped me into this one—pitch black with a silver neckline. Not a moment later, Kyro knocked on the door again, asking if I was finished. Ryz replied for me, indicating that I was.

Kyro entered the room, hands clasped behind his back. "Excellent. Lady Quinn, please do try to refrain from clambering up trees in this one."

I stared openly at the Water Druid. "If I asked you to avoid all water for the sake of a silly garment, would you?"

His jaw flexed. "I suppose it depends on the garment."

My nose scrunched. "You care far more for clothes than I, then." I glanced down at the gown, then back at him. "I suppose *His Majesty* selected this one specifically for this occasion?"

The twitch of Kyro's lips told me all I needed to know. He beckoned for me to follow, holding open the door for me. Grinding my teeth, I obliged. We meandered down several hallways I'd been down before. Despite being midday, the corridors remained dimly lit by sconces. Though I'd begun to grow accustomed to its heaviness, the musty air still weighed on my chest. Could they not have designed this place with more windows?

We approached Salem's reading room, which I'd recognized only because of the four armed guards outside the double doors. It shouldn't have surprised me that the High Queen Regent kept guards, but for some reason, the female I'd met the night of the challenge seemed to hardly require the need of a shield, let alone protection.

Kyro knocked thrice on the door, paying no mind to the guards flanking him on either side. He turned back to me. *"For the love of Llyr*, Lady Quinn, please be respectful. The High Queen Regent will not tolerate—"

The creak of the door opening cut Kyro off mid-sentence. In the doorway stood the same imposing female I'd encountered the night my mind had been violated. She was shorter than me by nearly a foot, but the way her icy gaze stared down her nose at me made her seem much taller. Her peppered hair was pulled back into a tight bun. A delicate crown laden with dark crystals glittered atop her head in the tallow-lit hall.

"You are Lady Quinn of the Western Territories," she said. Her voice was crisp. Deep.

I bowed my head ever so slightly and held her stare. "I am, Your Highness."

She blinked. "Come in."

With a sweep of her hand, the guards pushed open the two doors, and I followed her inside. Glancing back over my shoulder, I realized Kyro remained in the hall. His pinched expression left very little of his feelings to the imagination. The doors creaked shut behind us. The reading room was just as I remembered it, though much more stifling than it had been with Salem sitting in his chair. Now, his mother sat elegantly across the desk from me, the high back of the chair making her presence seem all the more imposing.

She stared openly at me—examining, almost. "I am surprised you recognize me, Lady Quinn. Did Lord Kyro inform you of our meeting today? Or have you been paying mind to the tapestries and paintings? I do have several around the halls fashioned in my liking."

"You have a crown on your head, Your Majesty," I said. "But yes, I was informed."

The corners of her lips twitched. "Yes, of course. You must be wondering why you, of all the Ladies, are meeting with the High Queen Regent. Are you not?"

"I'm not entirely surprised. I won the first challenge."

She seemed to mull over her words for a moment before continuing. "You did. Though you do not remember, your performance during the challenge was most. . . intriguing to my son's court and me. Especially the harsh words you had to say afterward."

I fought the smirk that tugged at my lips. "I can't say I recall."

"You told him to 'choke on his own breath' in the old tongue."

Now, I smirked openly. "That does sound like me."

Her lips, stained the color of mulberries, pursed in thought. "I notice you hardly use titles in speaking to my son and me, as well as Lord Kyro. You also do not curtsy or bow correctly in our presence. Is that a result of your upbringing or lack thereof?"

Her hands clasped together atop Salem's desk. Silver rings decorated all but one of her fingers, glittering with dark gemstones. Her fingernails were painted black and filed into sharp points. Even if her power did not already sit as heavily in the air as the musty odor, it was clear the High Queen Regent was a predator, through and through. Sharp claws and a sharp tongue, not unlike myself.

I held her glare. "Though it may seem incorrect to you, Your Highness, what I've done thus far has come from respect. But I will not lower my gaze or act any less than what I am to make you or your son feel more esteemed."

At this, she leaned back into the high-seated chair. "Even if it's social protocol?"

"Even then." I leaned forward. "I am not a Lady, Your Highness. Do not mistake me for one."

Her jaw flexed. The glacial stare alone seemed to cool the room a few degrees. "Well, at least you're honest."

To my utter surprise, the High Queen Regent smiled. *Smiled.* As if I'd said something amusing.

She then stood from Salem's chair and walked around the desk to stand in front of me. She leaned back against the desk, eyeing the rings on her knuckles. "You are far more than I expected, Quinn of the Wild," she said. "I can see why my son is so intrigued by you. It's been quite some time since I've met a Druid who will hold my stare. Even the High King struggles sometimes. I must admit, these eyes are my finest weapon." She paused. "Now tell me, dear, how are you finding Kalys?"

I was at a loss for words. She had so quickly flipped from being a stifling presence, one that had my instincts flaring, to one that hardly felt like a presence at all. I couldn't feel her power in the air at all—almost as if it had never been there, to begin with.

"It's . . . different."

She snickered. "Yes, I imagine so. If there's anything I can do to make the change less drastic, dear, do let me know. It's my opinion that you will be here for a while."

Before I could stop myself, the words tumbled from my lips. "Do you know anything about Forest Druids?"

She paused, looking down at me. "I—well, I'm not very familiar with your culture, if that's what you mean."

I resolved myself to the path I'd started on. "No, I mean—did you ever know any of us? Do you know if there's any of us left?" Her narrowed gaze pushed me to explain, to give some excuse for why I wanted the answer to what so many believed to be a useless question. "I've been alone for so long. I just want to know if there's hope—if there's any more of us out there."

I prayed she'd find sympathy in my words, even if I hated having to play the whole 'my entire kind is extinct and I'm an orphan' card.

Her gaze softened, and she placed a hand on my shoulder. I tried not to flinch. "I will tell you what I know, dear." She heaved a sigh. "Centuries ago, the Earth Druids and their varying subsets began to die of a Plague. The Bog Druids and

Prairie Druids were the first to go, followed by the Tundra Druids. It was suspected that this was because they lived in nomadic groups rather than Forest Druids, who lived alone. But the Forest Druids eventually followed. I have not seen Bog Druids or Prairie Druids since I was a little more than a century old. I never came across a Tundra Druid. I saw the last Forest Druid a little less than a century ago. He went with the High King, and I never saw him again."

My heart thundered in my chest.

Less than a century ago. He. She might've seen my father. The timeline fit. If she had seen my father—here—that meant I was on the right path. Regardless of what Salem had said, my father had been here. I had been right.

My elation was swept away by the realization of the High Queen's last sentence. *He went with the High King.* Did that mean Salem had lied to me about the last time he'd seen a Forest Druid? Had he known what I was after all along and decided to tell a lie to send me off his trail?

The High Queen watched me, waiting for some reaction. So, I frowned. "Thank you for the information. Will you let me know if you hear anything about another Forest Druid? It would bring me comfort to know there's more of us."

Her lips widened in a gentle smile. "Of course, dear." She patted my shoulder. "I would like you to meet with the rest of my son's court at some point. Would that be amenable to you?"

My brows furrowed in confusion, but I nodded. "I suppose."

She motioned for me to stand and led me over to the doors. "Very well. I'll see to it that arrangements are made." She raised a hand and knocked thrice on the door. "Thank you for meeting with me, Quinn of the Wild. I understand this is likely very overwhelming for you. Do let me know if there is anything you need to ease your mind."

I nodded as the doors creaked open, revealing a pacing Kyro. His brows were pinched together, a thin line of sweat beading across his forehead. "Ah, thank you, Your Highness. I trust Lady Quinn was . . . respectful?" he asked, beckoning for me to join him in the hall.

The High Queen chuckled. "Relax, Lord Kyro. My son is not the only royal that finds Lady Quinn intriguing."

A dry laugh escaped Kyro's lips—most definitely forced. I eyed him momentarily, then returned my attention to the High Queen. "Thank you for your time, Your Highness."

She smiled. "Thank you for yours, Lady Quinn. I look forward to hearing what other curses you have lined up for my son. Your creativity is noted."

Kyro blanched. Luckily for him, the doors behind the High Queen Regent had already begun to close.

18

I returned to my room following the meeting with Salem's mother. Kyro informed me that the High King would want to speak with me after his *occasion* with Rhea. I assumed he wondered what his mother wanted to meet with me about, presuming she hadn't already told him that it would be a fairly meaningless conversation. She seemed was more interested in why I acted the way I did than anything else. Perhaps I'd just interested her, and she wanted to make herself known to me, as she assumed I remembered nothing of the challenge. Whatever her reasoning, I'd gotten more out of the conversation than I'd believed I would.

She might've seen my father. If it was slightly under a century ago, then the timeline fit. And she'd described the Forest Druid she'd seen as a male. I suppose I could just be getting my hopes up, but it seemed too coincidental to be anything else.

However, she had also said that he went with the High King. So, either *she* was lying to me, or *Salem* was. If she lied to me, it brought her entire account into question. Perhaps she hadn't seen a Forest Druid at all and merely said so to provide me some comfort. If Salem lied, it made me wonder what else he could be untruthful about—and why.

I gripped the ridge of stone just above the archway into the bathroom and pulled myself off the ground. My back muscles strained against the silk fabric of my gown as I pulled my chin to my knuckles, then dangled again. I would not allow myself to grow weak in the constraints of this castle. My father had me doing pull-ups from the time I could walk. Climbing up trees for the last century had kept my muscles in shape, but ever since I'd begun sleeping on a mattress instead of a branch, I felt my body start to settle into its new state of comfort.

I dropped to the floor only when the callouses on my fingers began to peel. A line of sweat beaded across my brow, and I wiped it with the back of my hand. A knock resounded at the door. I spun around just in time for the doors to open.

Salem strode into the room, as manicured as he was when he'd left this morning. Now, however, shadows hung beneath his eyes.

"You're lucky I didn't attack you," I mumbled, dusting off my hands. "Barging in unannounced like that."

He waited for the doors to close before speaking. "Tell me about your meeting with my mother."

"Straight to the point then, *ciarán?*" I mused. "When was the last time you saw a Forest Druid?"

His brows pinched together in a scowl. "I told you. More than a century ago." He stared at me in silence. "Why does it matter to you?"

I scoffed. "Because they were my people, *Your Highness*. Danu curse me if I don't have a right to know if I'm truly the last of my kind!"

A moment of silence passed between us before he spoke again. "Perhaps a better question would be '*why do you ask again*'?"

My lips pressed together. "Your mother told me the last time she saw one of my kind was *less* than a century ago." I paused. "She said the last time she saw one, it had been with *you*."

He blinked. "That's simply untrue, *wildling*. I did not lie to you. You would know if I did, wouldn't you?"

My breath caught in my throat. "What do you mean?"

Had Rhea told him I could feel his emotions as easily as any animal? I shouldn't have trusted her. I didn't know what I was thinking, admitting to something that could be used against me.

"I just assumed. But by your reaction, I'm guessing I was right." He smirked. "When you mentioned you could feel what your steed felt. I assumed that applied to all creatures."

The breath escaped through my lips. "Oh."

The High King raised an eyebrow. "So you know, then, that I was not lying to you."

I suppose he was right. But I hadn't noticed anything off about his mother either.

"One of you is a fantastic liar, then," I grunted.

"What exactly did my mother say?"

I rolled my eyes. "That the last time she saw a Forest Druid was less than a century ago. That he went with the High King."

Salem paled. His lips pressed together in a thin line as if he had immediately recognized a lie in his mother's words. But his hands wound themselves into white-knuckled fists, and the hollow sense of fear—of something he wished he could forget— coiled deep within his stomach. I had not sensed fear in him before. My instincts flared.

"My mother didn't lie to you. Neither of us did," he said as if it were a confession of guilt.

"I don't understand."

"She did not mean me, *wildling*. She meant my father. I was not the High King a century ago. I was not High King until a few decades ago. The High King she is speaking of is my father. If the last she saw of a Forest Druid was with him—I can guarantee that the Forest Druid she spoke of is no longer alive. My father detested your kind."

My throat burned. I fought against the pressure that swelled against my eyes, that thrashed inside my chest, screaming in agony.

If the male she had seen was my father, he was dead. And I was too late.

But my attacker—the guard after the Announcement Ceremony—they had known what I was after, and they had said I would not find him. Could that mean there was a chance he still lived, that perhaps he was being held captive somewhere? That, for some reason, *someone* wanted to keep me from him?

No, I would not give up. Not yet. Not if there was still a chance he was out there somewhere, alive. I would not give up on him.

"Are you alright?" Salem's voice ripped me from my thoughts.

I swallowed, all too eager to change the subject. "What was it you wanted to know about the conversation with your mother?"

If he noticed my shift in topic, he didn't pay it any mind. "Ah, yes—I wanted to know what she wanted from you."

"Nothing," I replied. "She asked why I refused to follow 'social protocol' and commended me for cursing at you during the competition. Asked if I would be 'amenable' to meeting with your court sometime."

The corners of his lips twitched. "Commended you?"

I nodded. "She said she looked forward to what else I could come up with."

He chuckled—a low, rich sound. "It seems you have my mother's favor, *wildling*." His gaze traveled down my gown to the shoulders, where it now hung loose. "You've stretched out your gown. Did you climb more trees while I was away?"

I heaved a sigh, rolling my eyes. "Is there anything else you need from me, *ciarán*? It has been a rather long day."

He straightened his shirt sleeves, tugging the cuffs down to his wrists. "Yes, actually. I wanted to inform you that I will discuss your immunity to memory potion with my Potions Master."

"Can I come?" I asked all too quickly.

He shook his head. "No. I will be posing it to her as a hypothetical. If you're there with me, she will most definitely see through the question. As much as I trust my sister, I made you a promise, and I aim to keep my word."

I narrowed my eyes. "Fine."

"Fine?"

"But you have to inform me of whatever she says," I added. "I have a right to know."

His jaw flexed, a harsh shadow rippling across his cheek. "A fair request, I suppose. I'll inform you what she says, then." He turned, heading towards the door, then halted. "Lady Rhea is concerned for your wellbeing, you know. She informed me of a... malicious rumor being spread around the townsfolk."

I tried my best to remain impassive. "People talk."

He cleared his throat, straightening his sleeves. "I would suggest you pay it no mind. You're easy for them to vilify because they fear you. This gossip will never amount to more than that."

"Anything else?" I asked.

His lips twitched in a wisp of amusement. "Your deer scared off half the kitchen staff today."

"You're insufferable."

He smirked knowingly. "He started licking the windows. I think he saw the apple cakes being cooked in there today. Regardless, half of my cooks looked out the glass and saw a massive tongue sliding across the panes."

A smile tugged at my lips. Of course, Orion would do something like that. "And did somebody bring him a cake?" I asked.

"I tried. He charged at me. Ran me out of my own garden, despite the fact I'd brought a peace offering."

"Bring more next time. And stop calling him a deer."

The High King smiled briefly, bowing his head in a single nod, before exiting through the bedroom door. I walked over to the windows, looking down into the moonlit gardens. Orion lay peacefully in the lush grass, fast asleep. His stomach rose and fell in slow breaths. And as I looked towards the garden entrance, an iron gate bordered by stone walls, I noticed a small cake sitting atop the ledge. Uneaten, but still there.

$\mathcal{I}$ held a blade to Rhea's throat. She swallowed, and the edge dimpled her bronze skin. Droplets of sweat beaded her brow, golden in the morning's rays like molten metal. She huffed in frustration and took a step back. "Again," she said.

"You can't learn knife combat in a day, Rhea. Give it time," I replied.

The moment the words left my lips, a memory slithered down my spine. I pushed the grief away before it could take hold.

She grimaced and widened her stance, gripping a small blade in each hand. "Fighting is nothing more than another craft for me to learn. I can do it. Again."

I flexed my jaw in frustration but relented. I was once this eager to learn how to defend myself. I couldn't say I didn't understand. I did, almost too well. But I had no intention of injuring Rhea, and the thought of Salem or Kyro walking in at any moment had me on guard. Catching me sparring with another Lady might make the High King send me home—or at least think twice about keeping me here.

Rhea charged me, swinging her blades in cross-body arcs. She was slower than I was but still strong. A small voice in the back of my mind, one I hadn't heard in quite some time, proposed that I go easier on her. But my father's voice was much more prominent. *The world will take advantage of that day, Quinn, and it will swallow you whole.*

Rhea had already been in a position where she could not save someone she loved. It would be unfair to her to make her go through that again.

So, I dodged left and right, countering her swings. Whenever I saw an opening, I jabbed her with the hilt of my blade, so she knew where she was unguarded. Her irritation was as thick as tree sap, making her attacks reckless. I forced her to stop when I pointed the tip of my right blade right over her heart.

"That's enough. You're not thinking clearly anymore."

My father's voice rang in my ears. *Coimét daur.*

Rhea groaned in frustration, dropping her knives to the floor. She stomped to the loveseat positioned beneath her windows and threw herself across it, a hand draping over her forehead.

"I don't know how you're so good at this," she said. "I thought your people valued life, but you're a total expert in taking it." My breath hitched. As if Rhea felt the air I'd sucked from the room, she paused, sitting upright. "I didn't mean that, Lady Quinn. I'm just surprised at your expertise in combat, is all."

She was right about me, though. And she had no idea.

My throat burned as I swallowed the air. "I know the boundaries, Rhea. Where I can hit and not kill."

"Of course," she replied hastily. "I didn't mean any offense, Lady Quinn. I just had assumed Forest Druids, since your people valued life so much, wouldn't spend time learning anything about fighting—about injuring anyone."

I sat on the edge of her bed, strapping my knives back to the insides of my wrists. "All I know is what my father taught me. I don't know if my people knew how to fight."

Rhea pursed her lips, watching me intently. "What was your favorite thing that your father taught you?"

I blinked. I hadn't ever thought about that before. "Once, I might've said archery. I begged him to teach me to shoot for the longest time. He called it 'a mortal form of weaponry' but taught me anyways to help me survive."

"And now?"

My chest hollowed. "How to see beyond my eyes."

Rhea's brows pinched together in confusion as she laid back on the loveseat. Her swirling tattoos glittered in the sunlight. Today, she wore a white gown threaded with bronze filament and gilded beads.

Her chest rose and fell as she heaved a deep sigh. "I'm afraid I don't quite follow."

My mind raced back to a meadow brimming with wildflowers, back to a creature with a mind like my own and eyes the color of a wasp. "It's hard to explain."

She was silent for a moment, clasping her hands together above her belly. "My mother taught me how to paint. She was a brilliant artist. Watercolor was her medium of choice. We would sit for hours at the cliffs, watching the ocean waves crash against the rocks below. Sunsets were her favorite. My father used to tell her that she painted the sky better than the sun himself. She used to laugh when he'd say that. I loved her laugh."

She rolled her head to the side and looked at me with wide amber eyes. "I won't let what happened to her happen again. Not to anyone I love."

I paused, meeting her stare. "I know, Rhea."

Her attention flicked to the gilded knives she'd abandoned on the floor. Her head lolled back into the sun. "I'd never used those knives before. My father gave them to me when I turned twenty. He wanted me to be able to protect myself. But he never taught me. Having twin blades doesn't matter if you don't know how to use them."

"You'll learn," I said. "Where did you end up going with the High King yesterday?"

Her lips curled in a smile. "South to the plains. We had a picnic and laid in the sun for a few hours. He asked me about my ambitions and what I would change about Arastya if I could. A difficult question to answer when it's asked by the High King," she said.

"And what did you say?"

A moment of silence passed between us. "The communication between our leaders and our people."

I parted my lips to respond but was cut off when a knock resounded at the door. I jumped to my feet and kicked Rhea's knives across the floor toward her. She grabbed them, concealing them beneath her gown.

"Come in," she said, flattening the tulle over her weapons.

Kyro strode into the room, his hair disheveled and soaring about his head. His jaw flexed as he ground his teeth together. Fury swirled around him in tumultuous waves, the sheer power making my stomach curdle. He glanced at me, fists wound tight at his sides.

"The High King wishes to see you, Lady Quinn," he said. "Now."

Rhea sat upright, ensuring her knives remained concealed. "May I ask why there's cause for such urgency, Lord Kyro? Lady Quinn and I were having a lovely morning." She blinked a few times. "I thought the High King was with Lady Xandria today."

Kyro's attention shifted to her. "He was."

"Has something happened?" Rhea's brows pinched in concern.

Kyro shifted uncomfortably. "I am not privy to all information at this time, Lady Rhea. Once I am, I will inform you of what I know." He glanced back at me. "Lady Quinn, it is urgent."

I looked back to Rhea, who had already returned to bask in the sunlight. Then I followed Kyro out the door. He closed it shut behind us, eyeing the guards at either side of the archway, then marching off down the hall. I lengthened my stride to keep up with him. The moment we were out of earshot from Rhea's guards, Kyro leaned towards me.

"There's been an attempt on Lady Xandria's life," he whispered through gritted teeth. "You mustn't say a word, Lady Quinn. At this point, everyone is a suspect."

My stomach leaped into my throat. "She's been attacked?"

"Not attacked, no. Someone tried to poison her." Kyro directed me down an adjacent hall. I realized we were heading toward Salem's reading room. "The High King will brief you. For whatever reason, His Majesty believes you have the potential to be an asset. I pray he is correct. Xandria is my cousin. If anything were to happen to her—"

"Why would she even be a target?" I asked.

He shook his head. "I haven't the faintest idea, Lady Quinn."

If Xandria was being targeted by the same person I was, that meant she had a connection to my father somehow. What a Water Druid would want with a Forest Druid; I had no idea. But perhaps it wasn't what she wanted—perhaps it was something she knew. Water Druids were supposedly the scholars of our kingdom. Perhaps she knew something that someone didn't want her to. Perhaps she was a threat to them.

And if she was a threat to them, she was an ally to me.

I had to figure out what she knew—if my hunch was even correct. The idea that Xandria was the lead I needed to uncover my father's fate had my heart racing. This wasn't over. I would find out what happened to him. Not even the gods themselves could stop me.

Kyro approached the reading room doors with me at his

heels. Guards stood on either side of the entrance, eyeing me through their helmets. Kyro knocked on the door, then stepped back.

Not a moment later, it swung open, revealing the High King in a state of disarray. His cornflower shirt was unbuttoned at the top and untucked at the bottom. The hair he always kept in a neat wave now hung loosely across his forehead. Grey shadows sagged beneath cavernous eyes.

He looked to Kyro. "Go tend to your cousin. I know that is where your heart lies. You would serve me best in helping her recover."

Kyro blinked. "Your Highness, I can assist you here if you would like me to."

Salem reached forward and placed a hand on Kyro's shoulder. "Go, my friend."

Without another word, Kyro bowed and shuffled down the hall. Salem's attention turned to me. His eyes were jarring. An otherworldly shade of black.

"Come in, *wildling*. We have much to discuss."

20

*M*y nose itched. My father sat cross-legged a few paces away, eyes closed and soul seemingly in another world entirely. I'd been attempting to follow his lead for the last few hours, to no success. Although I was six years past the age most Druids first heard their patron deity's call, my mind remained silent. That silence only amplified the quieter noises I once wouldn't have noticed—the buzzing of incessant insects near my ears, the singing of a bird in the far-off distance, the slight breeze ruffling the blades of thick green grass at the edge of the meadow. It seemed to distract me from 'clearing my mind' or whatever my father was somehow able to do during these sessions. Slowly, I peeled a single eyelid open, glancing at my father.

Oak-colored hair was braided back behind his ears. The frown lines that had taken hold over his forehead as of late were now nowhere to be seen. Every so often, his shoulders shifted as he inhaled, followed a few moments later by a deep exhale.

Insects buzzed around his face, their membranous wings glittering in the soft light. Still, he remained unaffected.

How could he just sit there? There was so much going on, to think about, and to *do*. I still hadn't mastered archery—not even close. We could have spent this time practicing. Instead, we were here, wasting time. My father insisted it strengthened his connection with our goddess, despite hearing nothing but silence from her since he selected Danu as his patron when he was my age. It seemed rather obvious to me that Danu had either died or given up on Forest Druids entirely. I couldn't fathom another reason for her ignoring my existence.

I huffed and closed my eye again, trying to focus on clearing my thoughts. My nose twitched as I got a whiff of something, and a sneeze pinched at my face. I held my breath, hoping to shove that reflex down, but it returned with a vengeance. I sneezed loudly, wincing as I opened my eyes again to look at my father. Eyes like leaves glared back at me.

"You're not focusing, Quinn," he said in a disappointed tone. The frown lines had carved themselves across his forehead once again.

"I'm trying, father, but I can't feel anything. I just keep hearing random things, realizing the grass is itching my legs or smelling something I don't really like." I shrugged. "I guess we'll have to try again another day."

With a sigh, I pulled myself up and stretched out my legs, which had begun to ache after sitting there for so long. I looked down at my father, who remained cross-legged in the grass.

"I didn't say we were done," he replied.

I groaned, rolling my eyes and lowering myself back to the ground with a huff.

"Channel your thoughts away from yourself," he said. "You must allow yourself to become one with the earth, Quinn. You are far too determined to remain separate."

He was right about that; I would admit it. I didn't want to

become dependent on something. And if I found something waiting for me in my mind, some doorway that once opened would forever remain that way, would I ever be just myself again? Would my thoughts remain my own, or would everything become so much larger, so much louder?

But that worrying could've just as well been for nothing, given all the proof I'd had of Danu thus far.

As if he could feel my apprehension, my father spoke again. "Becoming one with the world around you is the rite of passage for all Forest Druids. Being able to sense all life around you, feel their fear, their happiness, their anxieties—it is what makes us who we are. Some are blessed by the gods and are given powers beyond that. I promise you, my daughter, if you open yourself to the earth, she will listen."

But did I want her to?

Silently, crossed my legs and closed my eyes. With a deep breath, I pressed my fingertips into the cool soil between blades of grass. Insects buzzed around me, birds chirped in the distance, and infrequent breezes ruffled through the foliage. I loosed the air I'd trapped in my lungs, searching my mind for something in the soil. It was so dark—it just seemed empty to me. Another inhale followed by an exhale.

It went on like this for a while longer, to the point where I counted the seconds between each breath. The soil remained lifeless, and I was growing frustrated. Only when the insects, the birds, and the wind around me began to quiet did I feel the slightest bit of interest. This hadn't happened before.

My fingertips burrowed into the earth, searching for something, *anything*. For a moment, it felt like I was anchored to something—something unmoving. Then, I heard something, a voice. A screaming voice. Why would the grass be screaming? Why would it be screaming my name?

Then, there was something much louder, a deep *thud-thud* that reverberated in my chest, echoing in my ears. Soil bunched underneath my claws, the breeze brisk against my fur. I could smell her. She smelled like a tree but was far too warm to be a tree. She was breathing. I knew she was alive, but she sat so still in front of me. A curious little beast.

Hot air fanned my cheeks, and my eyes shot open.

Adrenaline skidded through my veins, my heart leaping into my throat as I met the flaxen eyes of a dobhar chu. A low snarl rumbled in its throat as it glared at me, centimeters from my face. I'd never seen one so close. I didn't think you could unless it was eating you alive.

It had a feline face reminiscent of the predatory cats that used to thrive in the mortal world. But this animal was positively massive. It stood on all fours at a height similar to my father's, and I imagine it was much taller on its hind legs alone. Its lips were pulled taut in a grimace, carnassial yellow teeth dripping with frothing drool. Its fur was the same shade as my father's hair, but white tufts of fur stood atop the pointed ears angled down at me. The dobhar chu's massive body extended several feet behind it, each of its sinewy muscles flexed and prepared to lunge. Its tail extended several feet past that, thick and reptilian. Its paws, spiked with five claws as long as my hand, startled me the most. It could shred me apart without a second thought.

It was then that I realized I could still hear the loud *thud-thud* echoing around in my head, so loud my own heartbeat seemed to slow in an effort to match its pace. I swallowed, warranting another snarl from the terrifying beast. Its putrid breath stung the back of my throat, and I fought the urge to recoil, knowing that any sudden movement would likely end my life.

"Quinn," there was a soft voice several paces behind me. *My father.*

I didn't dare turn to look at him. I kept my gaze glued to the yellow eyes before me, ensuring the creature's attention remained on me. It would not touch my father. I wouldn't allow it.

As I looked into those eyes, I realized I could see myself through them. Not only as a reflection across them, but I could see myself as it did. The wild hair crowned my face like a mane, and my narrowed eyes watched the creature's every move. I wanted to pull back, to yank my consciousness to where it belonged inside my head, but I feared that if I did that, the beast would yield to its predatory instincts. So, despite my wishes, I remained in the beast's head, watching myself.

Apprehension stung in my chest, and I inhaled at the shock of it. The apprehension was not mine. It was different in quality than my own emotions. This felt foreign—and older. Could it be the beast's? Was it afraid of something?

I watched my brows furrow through the beast's eyes, and its heart rate soared as I stood up off the earth, eye-to-eye with the creature. It growled low, a warning to me.

Too close. Too close. Protect.

Another growl from the beast's tightened chest.

"You have nothing to fear from us," I heard my voice in the beast's ears and watched my hand reach, gently resting between the beast's eyes. Its heart rate slowed again, muscles uncoiling.

A breath forced itself into my chest as my consciousness slammed back into my own mind. The beast watched me carefully, its eyes narrowing as if to determine if I had been telling the truth— as if it somehow understood me.

"You're protecting your home, aren't you? You thought we would take it from you," I whispered to the creature, pale eyes unmoving as they stared into mine.

My fingertips grazed the coarse, matted fur, stroking between those eyes and atop its forehead. The creature allowed it, even enjoyed it a little.

You see me.

I felt the words in my chest—like they had been spoken to

me, but without a voice. A gleeful chuckle escaped my lips. I couldn't help it.

I stepped back from the creature, fixating on me as I inclined my head respectfully. I heard nothing more as one of the most fearsome beasts of the forest meandered back into the depths of the forest, leaving imposing footprints in its wake. It was difficult to forget what those feet felt like beneath me, how it felt to have claws and sharp teeth. Back in my own mind, I felt weak—clawless, toothless, and utterly powerless. Something inside me began to grow, something that wasn't there before.

Something that felt an awful lot like hunger.

I looked at my father.

He blinked, then knelt back down on the grass. "Again," he muttered and closed his eyes.

21

Salem paced back and forth behind his desk, the clicking of his shoes mirroring the clock hanging just above one of the bookshelves. The sun had begun to set already, painting the paned glass behind him with shades of marigold and lilac. The waning light cast harsh shadows over the High King's pinched features.

He paused his incessant pacing and glanced at me. "Did Kyro brief you at all? As to why you're here?"

I shifted my weight. "No. I know Xandria was targeted, but that's all."

Salem heaved a breath through his nose. "Someone tried to poison her with apricots."

"*Apricots?*"

"It's a common allergy amongst Water Druids specifically," he replied. "Kyro always told me that Llyr had some personal vendetta against the fruit, and I hadn't thought much of it until the competition began—when I knew I'd have a Water Druid Lady competing for my hand. I ensured that all apricots were removed from the castle kitchens just to be safe. Clearly, someone managed to thwart that plan."

Salem's fury swirled through the air, clouding it like smoke. He ground his teeth together as he resumed pacing, gritting them so hard I was surprised they didn't shatter. Guilt, so much guilt, hollowed his chest. It was seemingly endless—a deep abyss the High King had begun to precariously lean into. The guilt tugged, no, *ripped* at him. If he fell, he would not climb out again.

"How is she?" I asked, pulling myself from his heart.

He raked his fingers through his hair. "Recovering. If we hadn't been close to the castle, my sister would not have been able to treat her in time."

"And you've questioned the kitchen staff?"

He nodded. "That was the first thing I did once I knew she was safe." He paused, staring out at the sunset. His back flexed as he rested his hands on the windowsill, straining the satin material covering his shoulders. "I even had them searched. No apricots. *Anywhere.*"

"So someone snuck them into your food for the occasion," I said. "Do you have any idea who would want to harm Xandria? It was under my impression that, given how close you are to Kyro, the Northern Territories had a similar relationship to the Seas and Eastern Territories as well."

I watched his back rise and fall in a heavy sigh. "We *are* close. I'm at a loss as to why someone would wish her harm," he replied. "The attack on you could've been politically motivated by a harbored hatred for your people. Xandria's attack is not so easily explained."

But he didn't know that my attack likely wasn't politically motivated. It was specifically aimed at my father and me. And that made me wonder if Xandria's also had something to do with me.

"Why did you call me here, *ciarán?*" I asked. "To remind me that my people are despised by yours?"

"No." He spun around, facing me. "No. I need your help."

"My help?" I shook my head incredulously. "How could I *possibly* help you?"

He stalked towards me, then planted his hands on the desk before me. "Your Forest Druid powers—to feel what animals feel—how adept are you at feeling what another Druid can feel? Are you able to isolate one person's feelings from another?"

I narrowed my eyes at him. "Why?"

"I believe you can help me find her attacker. By finding whoever harbors malevolent feelings towards her," he explained.

His eyes swirled with shadow as he stared down at me. The guilt he'd already placed on himself was immeasurable. We'd barely begun the competition, and not only had I been attacked, but Rhea had lost her mother on the way here, and now Xandria's life was at stake. The emotion sat heavily on his chest, a bitter taste staining my lips like I'd sunk my teeth into a belladonna berry. I swallowed, trying to push myself past his feelings. It'd have been much easier if they didn't cloud the air like smoke.

Of course, he did not know I was interested in finding Xandria's attacker for my own sake. That the attempt on her life could be connected to mine—to finding my father. I had to play this right; make him believe I was doing *him* a favor.

However, isolating emotions from a crowd could prove tricky. I'd been overwhelmed more than once by masses of Druids, even by one Druid's feelings alone. Trying to focus on one in a crowded room, let alone identify that specific Druid from the one next to them—I wasn't sure if I was capable of such a feat. But I could try. It could lead me toward my father if Xandria's attack and my own were somehow connected. It just seemed too soon after my attack to be a mere coincidence.

But I wouldn't let Salem in on my secret just yet. If he knew what I was after, then he had the chance to stop me. Better to let the High King remain in his beloved shadows.

I raised my chin. "And you believe I'll do this for you because I'm a Forest Druid? Because I value life above all else?"

He shook his head. "My mother wants you in my court, regardless of whether you win the competition. She was poised to offer you a position to represent your territory here in Kalys. That is why she wanted to introduce you to my court. I have proposed a better idea. You will act as a sort of advisor to me, informing me of those who wish me or any other Druid ill will. If you are able to feel the emotions of others, I suspect you will be able to help me protect my kingdom from those who wish to see it razed."

"You told your mother of my powers?" I asked, feeling slightly betrayed.

I hadn't exactly told him not to—unlike I'd asked Rhea to. Still, it made me feel rather exposed. Perhaps that was my own oversensitivity to others knowing anything about me. Going from an elk as my sole companion to residing in a castle where even the shadows have eyes was *a bit* of an adjustment.

To my surprise, he again shook his head. "She already knew. She said it's a commonality amongst all Forest Druids, inherent to your connection with life. She believed such a power would benefit my council, with you representing those without their own voices. I believe your powers could do that, *yes*, but you could do more, too. And you are uniquely suited to this circumstance."

This was news to me. I hadn't realized my people had all shared in the feelings of the world. Perhaps that was why we held life in such high regard. We could feel it all. Every blade of grass, every insect, up to every single Druid in Arastya. I knew from experience that it's nearly impossible to hurt another creature when you feel its pain as your own. It didn't take me long to learn that the perceived hierarchical value of a life was little more than a facade used to trivialize what it meant to kill another being.

Salem was asking me to utilize such a power for his own benefit. He also expected me to agree merely because he offered me a place in his council. The idea was laughable.

"Why in Danu would you think I desire a position in your court? To expose the hidden feelings of others, no less?" I asked.

"Because I will see to it that my own soldiers are stationed at the western border of Arastya. I will guard your homeland if you help me protect mine."

I pursed my lips. "I thought you didn't believe me when I told you the western borders were no longer being patrolled."

"Iryx, my War General, has informed me that he sent a scout to the border who confirmed your reports. No one guards the western border. But I will ensure it is guarded should you join my court," he explained. "I will also redesign my gardens with your deer in mind so that he may be more comfortable during your time here."

If I hadn't already wanted to investigate Xandria's attack, I did now. Despite Danu's blessing on my journey, I still worried about the safety of my homeland while I was away. With 75 days left, there was still a very real possibility of mortals breaching the border and wreaking havoc amongst my fellow creatures. Having guarded the Forest for a century made me rather protective of it. The idea of Mortals traipsing through it, hunting beasts for sport and hacking at trees that had seen kingdoms rise and fall, curdled my stomach. Though I was fully aware that his guarding of the border had specific political appeal to him as well, it didn't negate the sense of security it provided me in knowing my homeland was safe. Making Orion happier during our time here only sweetened the deal. I could ask that the High King refashion his gardens a meadow style, so Orion might have more space to graze and lay out in the minimal sunlight. Giving him more trees to wander through would also make him feel at ease.

I folded my arms across my chest. "Very well."

Salem stood upright, eyeing me. "That was easier than I'd anticipated."

"I want my homeland protected. And I want my friend happy."

The High King nodded, moonlight now glowing behind him. "I'll arrange for the meeting with my council this week. Have papers drawn up and an official title provided for you. But you mustn't tell the other Ladies of this agreement. It will not be looked upon favorably by the other territories."

"Not even Xandria? It is her attack I'm investigating," I asked.

"No. She'll see it as an unfair advantage you've been given at a cost to her. I don't want this being thrown around the courts. I can't offer every Lady a position on my council."

A moment of silence passed between us. "I'll need to speak with her tomorrow."

"I'll have it arranged."

22

*K*yro came to retrieve me the following morning. His usual stoic demeanor seemed dampened by recent events, given his slightly slumped posture, sagging eyes, and shuffling feet across the stone floor.

Of course, I didn't blame him. I'd be sleepless as well if anyone in my family was attacked. I didn't sleep for days after my father was taken, though that might've had more to do with the idea of a beast attacking me at night. I hadn't realized how well I connected with fearsome creatures then—and that I had as much to fear from them as they did from me. As I aged, my relationship with the animals roaming the Western Territories became one of kinship rather than predator and prey.

Kyro hadn't said a word as we walked down the corridors toward Xandria's room. Anxiety swirled in his chest like ink in water, clouding any other emotion that might've surfaced. His heart beat faster than normal—perhaps a sign of exhaustion. But every inch of the Water Druid looked tense, teetering on the edge of fight or flight.

We turned a corner, approaching a room with six armed guards positioned at a doorway. Their heads swiveled in sync as we approached. As Kyro came to face them, the guards bowed slightly in deference.

"Lord Kyro," one of them said quietly.

"Lady Quinn is to speak with Lady Xandria alone. She will knock thrice on the door when she is ready to leave. When she does so, have someone retrieve me. I'll be in the High King's reading room," Kyro replied stiffly.

The guards' armor clanked as they nodded in response. The one who had spoken before turned to the door and knocked. "Lady Quinn for Lady Xandria," they said.

A moment later, the door opened with a whispered creak. Xandria's iridescent hair floated around her head in gilded braids, glowing like liquid silver. She peered through the crack in the doorway, her sky-colored eyes narrowed as she stared back at me.

"The Forest Druid," she muttered.

My lips twitched. "Good morning to you, too."

As I started to walk towards the cracked doorway, Kyro gripped my wrist. I resisted the urge to snap his arm in half and instead leveled a steely glare in his direction. "Yes, Water boy?"

His jaw flexed. "Please, just—just be gentle with her, Lady Quinn. She's been through a lot," he said.

I yanked my wrist from his grip. "I'm only a monster when I *want* to be, Kyro."

Despite my venomous tone, his shoulders slumped in a sigh of relief. He gave a single nod, then swiveled and marched off. The clicking of his boots soon faded into silence. I returned to the partially opened doorway, where Xandria remained, staring blankly back at me.

"How do I know it wasn't *you* that tried to poison me, Lady Quinn?" Xandria asked.

I nearly laughed. "If I was going to poison you, Xandria, it wouldn't be with apricots." A moment of silence passed between us. "I thought you came from the 'Land of Scholars'. Shouldn't you know better? My people were pacifists."

Her nose scrunched. "I try not to generalize based on cultural values. Assumptions are a dangerous mistake to make."

"Noted."

Xandria angled her head, staring down her nose at me through the crack in the doorway. "What would you poison me with, if not apricots?"

"If I had to pick—" I pursed my lips, "—deadly nightshade is fairly prominent in the Western Territories. But I would never choose such a cowardly weapon to take a life. It's tactless."

Xandria eyed me. "I suppose that's good to know."

I took a step towards the doorway. The armed guards on either side didn't move to stop me.

"Despite what you might've heard, I do not drink the blood of children." I held up my hands. "I also do not have claws. Though sometimes I wish I did. Might be nice to have a weapon at hand all the time." My hands fell to my sides. "I want to help you, Xandria. I want to find who did this to you."

White eyelashes fluttered over her eyes. "The High King said you wanted to help me yesterday. I didn't believe him. I suppose I made an assumption about you that I should not have."

I pressed my lips together. "May I come in?"

There was a moment of slight hesitation on her part, but the door creaked open not a second later. Xandria stood in the doorway, cloaked in silver satin. Her height was similar to mine, as was her lithe form. Her broad, muscular shoulders and tapered waist were reminiscent of the shape of selkies that used to frequent the cliffs at the edge of the Western Territories. It'd been a while since I'd seen such a creature, though. They tended to scare off when they discovered they were being watched.

I entered the room, and she closed the door behind me with a click. Her room, unlike my own sterling silver, was a rich velveteen purple. It mirrored mine in layout, however. I meandered over to the pair of lounge chairs seated on either side of the window and sat, crossing my legs. I motioned for Xandria to take the seat opposite me. She cautiously obliged, sinking into the chair as one might a scalding bath.

She was the first to speak. "How do you think you'll be able to find who did this to me?"

"Forest Druids can feel what others feel. I'm hoping I'll be able to narrow in on whoever wanted to hurt you," I explained.

Her eyes widened a little. "You can feel what I feel? Even if I don't want you to?"

"I'm not sure if you can prevent me from feeling your emotions. I *can* say that the more you control them, the less I feel."

I thought back to Rhea, and the night we were attacked, how her barrage of emotions had me struggling to walk straight, let alone breathe. Perhaps Xandria would be more like her cousin, who I hardly felt unless I paid attention.

Xandria folded her hands in her lap. "My people tend to conceal their emotions, anyway. Llyr demands it of us."

"Let's hope your attacker is not one of your own, then. The more volatile the emotions, the more likely I can pick them out from a crowd," I replied. "Do you know of anyone who would want to hurt you?"

She shook her head, her hair shimmering as it splayed gracefully in the air. "I do not have any enemies."

I leaned back in the chair. "Do you know anything about my people?"

Her brows pinched together, wrinkling a seam between her eyes. "What does that have to do with my attack?"

I blinked. "Humor me."

She heaved a sigh, glancing out the window. "I know very little about your kind. I know they are extinct. I know they have been for quite some time. I know you're the first we have seen in a century. Anything else I've heard can only be regarded as hearsay. It's not backed by evidence."

Frustration bubbled in my chest. If she knew nothing about my father or my people, why would my attacker also want to target her? Perhaps it had something to do with Salem's father—the last person to see what may have been my father—alive.

"Do you know anything about Salem's father?" I asked.

She began to shake her head but paused as if remembering something. "I did—I did come across something a little peculiar in my readings the other day. Kyro allows me to spend my free time in the library here. I was combing the archives, and I found some journals that used to belong to High King Salar. Many were missing pages or had been entirely blotched out by ink. On one of the pages, though, I managed to trace over with a pencil to get the indents. It said something, but it didn't make any sense, really. I didn't know what to make of it, nor did my handmaidens."

That caught my attention. I leaned forward, placing my elbows on my knees. "What did it say?"

"I believe it read, 'should divine die, from death, divine will be,'" Xandria recited. "But again, I haven't the slightest clue what it means. I just found it peculiar. Most of the pages in his journals I couldn't trace. They'd been scribbled out over whatever writing had been there before. That sentence, though, appeared to have been written in there over and over and over again. I don't think anyone could've scribbled it out if they had tried. That paper was practically tattooed with it."

I scowled. "I don't know what that means either. You said you asked your handmaidens about it?"

She nodded slowly. "Yes. But they said they'd never heard that saying before, either. I wondered if perhaps it was a royal decree or something—some sort of addendum to a law—but it wasn't mentioned elsewhere in any of Arastya's books on laws or regulations."

"You said it was in his journal?" I asked.

Again, she nodded.

I sighed. "I suppose it could've just been rambles of a High King if it was in his personal journal. Random thoughts or something."

She frowned. "Do you think that could have something to do with why I was attacked?"

"I'm not sure. You wouldn't consider Zora an enemy? She seemed fairly confrontational before the challenge," I said.

Xandria's eyes softened, and a breath escaped her parted lips. "No. Zora would not harm me. I loved her very deeply. And I know she still loves me despite what you saw. She's a difficult person to understand. Even I struggle with it sometimes. But no, she would not harm me. Ever."

"And you get along with your handmaidens? Guards?"

"Perfectly," she replied. "If I ever sensed any irritation from someone else, I'd make a point to rectify it immediately. I hate conflict."

I sighed, shaking my head. "Well, this hasn't exactly narrowed down my list of suspects. I'll let you know if I feel anything concerning."

I stood from my seat. Xandria remained in her chair. "I appreciate your willingness to help me, Lady Quinn. I apologize for making any assumptions about you. I won't do it again."

I offered her a faint smile, then strode over to the door. I knocked thrice, alerting the guards outside to send for Kyro. The door opened a few minutes later, a hopeful-looking Kyro meeting my stare. As I exited Xandria's room, Kyro leaned forward.

"Anything?" He asked in a whisper.

I shook my head. "Nothing."

23

The week inched on without further contact with Salem. Kyro had come daily to check on me and informed me late yesterday that I'd be dining with Salem's court this evening. I had half-expected Salem to be the one making that announcement, but he'd been rather scarce. I hadn't so much as seen him in the halls. Perhaps the other females had been keeping him too occupied, not that it was a bad thing. It had given me a chance to take Orion out to the forest Salem had shown me, even if I did have to alert Kyro when I was leaving and when I'd return. Orion seemed glad to escape the pristine garden. One afternoon earlier this week had been spent lounging around the meadow, with Orion munching on the grass and I napping on his flank. It had been so peaceful I could've forgotten that I'd have to return.

As I stared at my forlorn expression in the mirror, this was what I thought of—the meadow, the crisp dusk air, and the chirp of the birds as they bid farewell to the sky for the evening and settled into their nests. However, even those pretty memories did little to lift the frown on my lips. Eyla had asked if that frown had been directed at her when she'd done my makeup, and I had to assure her it was my troubled mind, not her beautiful artwork. Beautiful it was, indeed.

She'd drawn out fierce black ink from my eyes and applied an odd shimmery material to the height of my cheekbones, which glittered like little stars in the golden candlelight. Ryz had forced my hair into a tight bun at the back of my head, insisting that any intricate hairstyle would detract from the gown. It hurt. The skin on my face felt absurdly tight.

The gown she'd chosen was black, embedded with crystals that swept up the bodice and down the sleeves to my fingertips. It glimmered and swirled like galaxies against a midnight sky. Clearly, Ryz had sought to make a good impression.

After they'd finished getting me ready, I'd thanked them and allowed them to leave early. Sometimes, I wished they'd offer to stay. But I knew they had their own lives that didn't involve humoring me while I remained locked in a castle. My mornings with Rhea were the only reprieve, but my inability to tell her about Xandria and my search for our attacker made conversation difficult. Orion wasn't any different. Though I shared in his emotions, he didn't seem to understand my situation—why I was so desperate to find a connection between Xandria's attack and my own. At this point, I was straining to find any lead to follow with my father. According to Salem, he was likely dead. I couldn't stomach the thought. He had to be alive. Somewhere.

Someone cleared their throat behind me, and my stomach leaped into my throat.

Kyro inclined his head. "Apologies, Lady Quinn. I had knocked."

I swallowed, steadying my heart. "Are they ready for me?"

Kyro's brilliant gaze examined the gown as I stood from my armchair. "Yes. I will take you to them now."

Knowing better now than to invite me to take his arm, he swiveled and headed out the door. My heels clicked as I followed. The more I wore the cursed contraptions, the easier walking seemed to become. Though, I still stumbled every now and then.

Kyro's gaze traveled to me through the corner of his eye. "Due to a last-minute change of plans, High King Salem will be dining with you tonight."

Irritation pricked at the underside of my skin. "I wasn't aware he hadn't been planning to."

"It was the High Queen who requested to dine with you. High King Salem was not involved," he clarified.

I smoldered. "It's *his* court and *his* mother."

"I wasn't aware you felt so strongly about him dining with you. I will make sure to convey this to him."

"Please don't," I grumbled, unsure whether he'd heard me.

We turned down another corridor, and my eyes fell on a familiar tapestry—two deities in an embrace. Kyro led me to the same room where Salem had infiltrated my mind. Questions burned in the back of my throat, a need to know why the potion hadn't worked on me—but I swallowed them down to my aching chest. Kyro wasn't aware that I was immune. Neither did anyone else. Just Salem.

Kyro knocked thrice on the oak door, my skin prickling. The tight gown strained against my rib cage, despite the High King removing all corsets from my wardrobe. He had kept his word in that regard, but it didn't mean the gowns were any less form-fitting.

"Come in," a gentle voice said.

Kyro sucked in a breath, turning the doorknob and pushing it open.

The room was just as I'd remembered; a long wooden table down its center and a crackling fireplace to my left. Various paintings and tapestries hung on the dimly lit walls, and a chandelier I hadn't noticed before dangled from the arched ceiling. The air smelled of wood smoke and tallow. Four Druids stood on their feet, chair legs groaning against the stone as they rose.

The first gaze I met was his. Cavernous eyes drank me in as if he were an alcoholic and I a stiff drink. Tonight he also wore black, a satin suit stitched with filaments of silver.

Next to him stood the High Queen, regal as ever in a deep indigo gown painted like winter dusk. A friendly smile had etched itself on her wrinkled lips, the skin folding around her brilliant eyes as she acknowledged me. My lips pulled into a similar grin without hesitation.

Beside the High Queen stood a female no older than me. Her dark hair and eyes mirrored Salem's, but the tips of her short hair were stained pink. Her lips were painted burgundy, striking against her brilliant teeth as she beamed. It was a smile I'd seen before.

"Stella. It's nice to meet you, Lady Quinn of the Wild," she said.

She glided over to me and outstretched her hand, her onyx nails as pointed as the edge of a blade. I eyed her palm for a moment before taking it and giving it a squeeze.

"Sister?" I asked.

"What gave it away? The eyes?"

I shook my head. "You have the same smile."

A wry brow rose in surprise. "Interesting. That's a new one."

One man stood on the other side of the table between two empty seats. He was in the room when my mind was torn open —the one with the crossbow. His thick arms were littered with gnarled scars, and keen amber eyes glared back at me as if I were an imposition. Dark skin rippled as he outstretched a hand toward me. My gaze, however, remained trained on the weapon he had slung across his back. It would be difficult to steal it from him should he aim it at me again.

"Iryx. Nice to meet you," he said in a gruff tone, his hand swallowing mine and squeezing it.

I didn't respond. I made my way over to the vacant seat between him and Salem, massaging the bruising joints of my knuckle. Iryx didn't trust me. I didn't have to utilize my powers to realize that.

"Please be seated," Salem said.

Everyone sank into the plush chairs, which groaned again beneath the sudden weight. In front of me sat a glass of water and a goblet of dark wine, glowing like melted gold beneath the chandelier light.

"It's been a while," I whispered to Salem.

He took a long drink from his silver chalice. "I've been busy," he replied, lowering the cup from his stained lips. "Dates. With the other Ladies."

"I see." I swirled the wine around my glass and took a sip. It was dry and bitter, with subtle notes of elderberry and oak.

"I wasn't aware my presence mattered to you so much."

"It doesn't. I thought you'd have interest in my conversation with Xandria, though."

His lips twitched. "Not now."

"Lady Quinn, is it true you grew up with only an elk?" Stella asked from across the table. Her dark eyes fixated on me for only a moment before flitting to her brother and narrowing.

"Yes, Orion is currently staying in your garden. My father was taken from me when I was young, and it has been Orion and me ever since," I replied.

She propped her chin on the palm of her hand. "How did you manage to train an Arastyan elk? I've heard stories of them killing Druids for wandering too close."

I gave her a tight smile. "Animals and I . . . we get along well."

"So you were never afraid? Living alone in the forest?" Iryx cut in with his deep voice. His muscles remained tight, hands never lingering too far from the crossbow slung around his shoulders. He eyed me, jaw flexed as his brows sank into a scowl.

"Why would I be afraid when I know I'm the deadliest thing there?" I replied.

I held the male's glare, allowing a grin to twist my lips and tell him that, *yes*—I was the deadliest thing in *this room* as well. Iryx looked away with a low grunt.

"As I mentioned earlier this week, I wanted you to meet with my son's court. I'm not sure you're aware of why," the High Queen said. "I wanted you to have a position in his court. As the last of your people, you alone represent the Western Territories. My son, however, believes your aptitude for telling the emotions of others may provide a certain... advantage in dealing with the issues that arise between the Realms."

I tried to appear surprised. "What exactly would this position entail?"

The High Queen smiled. "Accompanying my son to other Realms when necessary. Assisting in negotiations. Protecting our court from any malevolence."

I felt Salem's stare on me as I raised my chin. "What would be in it for me?"

Iryx leaned forward, his forearms pressed against the table. "I'll be sending some of my elite troops to rotate guarding the Western border against Mortal trespassers."

No wonder Iryx had the crossbow. He was in charge of Salem's military.

I waited for someone to bring up Orion's garden, but they remained silent. So I pressed on. "What else?"

The High Queen straightened her back. "Is that not enough? Protection of your homeland?"

"Your deer will have his garden, *wildling*. I've alerted the landscapers already," Salem said before I could respond. The obsidian ring atop his head glowed aureate beneath the tallow candlelight—less like a ring of stone and more like a halo of fire.

I nodded, pretending to mull it over in my head. "I suppose I can accept. But I would encourage your forces to avoid the Forest's edge. It's hunted by cu siths."

The High Queen clapped her hands together and beamed. "Excellent! I'll have the contract drawn up in a few days and have you sign it as soon as possible. I'm glad to have you with us, dear," the Queen beamed as she raised her chalice. "To Lady Quinn of the Wild and Western Territories, Mediator of Arastya."

The table murmured in agreement, drinking to my name. As everyone's lips met their chalice, my eyes met Salem's. His were already on me, expression as unreadable as the stars in an overcast sky. His gaze did not move as he drank from the goblet, the dark wine staining the tongue that swept across his bottom lip.

"This doesn't disqualify you from the competition, you know," he murmured as the conversation at the table shifted away from me.

"How is it fair for me to compete for your hand when I'm already in your court?"

"You may have your foot in the door, but *I* held it open for you," he replied, leaning towards me. "This advantage was given to you because of your abilities. I would hardly say it's a debate of fairness."

"The other Ladies won't like it."

"The other Ladies won't hear of it," he said. "Besides, we have more important matters at hand than the moodiness of high-born Druids. Have you heard anything around the castle—anything suspicious? Did you learn anything from your conversation with Xandria? Any enemies she might have?"

I shook my head. "No. Even she and Zora seem to be on good terms. Not entirely sure how that's possible given Zora's demeanor."

His lips twisted. "I can't think that any of the Ladies have a motive greater than the others. They're all equally capable, I suppose, but none would stand to gain anything other than my hand by eliminating other competitors. Perhaps it's not one of the Ladies; maybe it's one of my staff members."

It seemed an odd way to eliminate suspects—concluding that they all had equal motives and therefore, it was likely *not* one of them. To me, it seemed they all had the potential to be behind Xandria's attack, save for maybe Zora. But if the attacks were isolated to Xandria and me, it potentially placed her back in the running. I didn't even know if I could eliminate Rhea, given she knew who I was after. Ingrid had the most battle experience; she probably had access to multiple armed Druids capable of attacking the competitors. Aria seemed the least competent, given her demeanor and history, but she did come from a fair-eyed Realm. There was also the potential that the attack on Xandria came from her own Realm, orchestrated by a political rival or something of the sort.

I pondered Salem's proposal about those that worked in the castle. "Why would someone in your staff try to hurt Xandria?"

A calloused hand ran across the stubble dotting his jawline as his brows knotted in thought. "I have absolutely no idea. I'll think on it—try to figure some stuff out. In the meantime, let me know if you feel anything . . . off."

"Did you have a chance to speak to your sister?" I asked, turning away from the table as I spoke.

Salem's eyes flared. "Yes. I'll come to your room later and speak with you. Now is not the time."

That was what he'd said about Xandria, too, only to bring it up a few moments later.

I huffed in frustration and reclined into my chair, downing the bitter wine. Dark little tendrils coiled inside me, blossoming into gilded light in the pit of my stomach. My skin flushed as servants pushed through the creaking doors with silver trolleys and steaming platters. One by one, they were placed in front of us, and the lids were removed. A once silent hunger now gnawed at my gut. At Salem's word, we dug into our meals, the room falling quiet once more.

24

100 YEARS AGO . . .

ollowing my encounter with the dobhar chu, I found myself stumbling less and less over the Forest floor. The trees almost seemed to guide me through their labyrinthine limbs as I ran, pointing me in the right direction. Other than that, however, whatever Druid magic my father had hoped would manifest from the experience did not surface. He had been surprised that the beast was so gentle with me— allowing me to stroke it without ripping my arm from my shoulder. He'd mentioned that he'd only encountered a dobhar chu once as a child. It had chased him up a tree and circled him for a day and a half before moving on to easier prey. He'd never seen one be so docile, domesticated, even. But still, not a word of praise. Just surprise.

I hadn't told him about seeing myself through the beast's eyes. I hadn't explained that I felt its apprehension, fear, and agitation at us coming so close to its home. I hadn't mentioned how I knew we were close to its den. He hadn't asked. I wondered if he'd even heard me when I spoke to the creature. It hadn't felt right to me at the time. It was like I was intruding on something I shouldn't, crossing a boundary that ought to be left alone.

I loosed another arrow towards the red pigment staining the bark of my aiming tree. The golden rays of the morning seeped in through the dense foliage above me, the air appearing to glisten with gilded specks in the breeze that had somehow broken through the trees. The mountain air was cold, only reluctantly warming when dawn's fingertips brushed the horizon.

My father leaned against a tree behind me, watching my progress. I'd hardly improved in the last several weeks, but I refused to let my lack of success phase me. I wanted to learn how to defend myself in as many ways as possible. If I wasn't meant to be a Forest Druid, then I needed to be able to protect myself in other ways. While I was skilled at hand-to-hand combat and with a blade, I was still lacking in archery and a spear. I'd asked my father to look for one on his trading routes, but he'd scoffed and told me to figure out how to shoot an arrow first.

He usually went for a week or so on one of his trading routes, either to the west or the south. To the west, he'd meet with mortal men who dared to venture near Druid lands in exchange for healing potions and salves, which he was quite adept at making. The mortals were few and far between, the last remnants of the human world before the Druids reclaimed their territories. They were often crude and disrespectful, according to my father.

To the south, he would trade with the Light Druids, and Fire Druids, who he'd said were artisans and craftsmen. Sometimes, he brought back baked goods or a new tunic. He didn't really understand the Light Druids or their appreciation for creating new things. To him, everything needed was provided by the earth, and anything else was unnecessary. However, it didn't stop him from obliging in the trade route for my sake. I enjoyed their woven cloth tunics and trousers, even though they hung so loosely on me I had to tie them up with woven bark threads. He didn't understand the Fire Druids either, with whom he traded wood and dried fish for steel, silver trinkets, or blades.

The head of my arrow sunk into the base of the tree, my heart singing as I turned back towards my father. Unsurprisingly, he remained expressionless as if he hadn't seen the shot.

"I hit the tree!" I said, hoping he'd been daydreaming or something of the sort, not realizing my achievement. I was thrilled. Maybe I *was* improving.

"Off mark, Quinn," he countered, utterly disinterested.

I swallowed, the moment of pride sinking low in my belly and dissolving into frustration. He was right. I still hadn't hit the target. Near was not good enough to celebrate. It would not protect me.

But it was almost as if the trees had moved out of my arrows' path. Months, and I could still barely hit the tree. Perhaps my father was right; the earth didn't want me to wield a bow. Unfortunately for Danu, I was a poor listener.

A tight breath pushed past my lips as I raised the bow again, pulling the arrow shaft taut against the bowstring. Though my lithe arms strained against the stubborn bow, I pulled the arrow tighter. I closed one eye, angling the tip of my arrow just above the target. This one would hit. This one would.

A slow breath in, a steady breath out. Release.

The arrow sang in the air as it flew towards my mark, sinking into the red pigment of the outer circle on the target. A grin curled on my lips, yet another surge of pride and excitement flooding my veins. I was improving. I glanced back toward my father.

He remained impassive. "Again."

My soaring heart fell audibly to the pit of my stomach. I

waited for him to acknowledge the tears as they welled in my eyes, but he did not. My throat burned as I swallowed my pride and raised the bow once more.

Arrow after arrow, I shot into the tree until I could no longer lift the weapon from the ground. My arms ached as if the muscles had been shredded, my back so tight I wondered how I would climb the tree to safety tonight. Though my father had encouraged me to stop after a while, my success this morning had been enough to fuel me throughout the day. Several more arrows had sunk into the target, each a little closer than the last. One day, I hoped to hit the center. I *would* hit the center.

However, my father seemed discouraged by my successes, as if each arrow landing true made me less of a Forest Druid. Perhaps in a way, he was right, given that our kind did not typically wield weapons. However, I did not want to depend on a frugal goddess to save me should I need saving. I wanted to save myself, *by myself*. I didn't know if the incident with the dobhar chu was a fluke, but I hadn't felt anything similar since. Though it had made me wonder at the time if Danu had finally chosen to reveal herself, the lingering silence all but destroyed that thought.

After a long day of training, we ran back into the southern areas of the Forest, where we hoisted our supplies up a large pine tree for the night. Though my muscles screamed in protest, I was able to swing myself up its thick and sappy branches.

"Tomorrow, I will be going west to trade for a new water pack before we head further north at the season's change," my father said as I nestled against the tree trunk atop my branch. He handed me a woven blanket, watching me as I wound it around my shoulders. My muscles burned with every movement.

"When will you be back?" I asked, brushing stray hairs from my face.

"Several nights. I'm only trading for one thing, so I'm hoping it won't take too long, but with the mortals, you never know," he replied, the distaste evident in his voice.

Personally, I didn't have as much of an issue with them. There were so few of them left; they seemed like a futile thing to waste time hating. They'd lost the war long ago when the Druids rose against them and had since faded into a tiny population just past the western edge of the Forest. I had no doubt they'd be gone within the next few centuries, perhaps during my lifetime. The age of man was over, and the time of Druids had come.

"I expect you to stay close to this tree so I can find you when I return," my father said. "If you wander too far, I may not be able to find you, Quinn."

"Can I go to my aiming tree?"

"If you do, you must leave before the sun falls," he replied. "If you stay too late, you may not be able to find your way back, and staying in the northern Forest could make you easy prey. It gets dark very quickly."

I nodded, curling my own body to match my father's. This would likely be my last night of semi-restful sleep until he returned. I always worried if he was safe, and I knew I could not survive the Forest alone. Still young and inexperienced, I made easy prey for any one of the beasts calling the wild home. I tried not to think about it, however, and allowed my eyes to rest— for now.

25

100 YEARS AGO . . .

Several nights passed since my father left for the edge of the forest. Since then, I'd gone to my aiming tree daily, reveling in my newfound success. Nearly every arrow landed at the center of the bullseye, and the poor tree bark was taking quite a beating. I'd made a new bullseye on a nearby redwood to give the other tree a chance to heal. I made a red paste with some poppies I'd found in a nearby meadow, dried and ground into a powder. I smeared it across two of my fingers, drawing three concentric circles into the bark of the redwood. The red pigment wasn't as visible against this bark, but perhaps that would help my aiming. Real targets wouldn't have bullseyes painted on them, after all.

After a full day of firing arrows, I pulled my aching body up the same tree, hoping my father could find his way back to it. I knew he wouldn't risk venturing out at night, but if he saw our supplies up in the branches while I was off shooting, he would know to stick around until I returned.

After waiting for my father to return for five nights, I grew anxious. He was only trading one item, and he'd said it wouldn't take long. That day, I'd decided not to go to my aiming tree— that I would sit and wait for my father to return home safely. If he didn't by tonight, I would head out towards the mortal lands tomorrow at dawn.

I sat perched on a high branch in the tree, the sticky sap practically gluing me still. My quill of arrows hung off a branch in front of me. I held an arrow and a river rock, sharpening the arrow's tip. I was onto my third arrow, grinding the stone against the arrowhead when a few branches snapped nearby. My head whipped up in the direction of the sound. It was broad daylight, so I didn't suspect any beasts to be out roaming if they could help it. If it wasn't my father, then perhaps another forest creature.

Only when I saw a hunched-over figure emerging from the thicket did I allow myself to breathe again, peeling myself from the branches and swinging down the tree. My feet planted on the mossy floor with a thud. I spun around to race towards my father but paused when I took in the state of him.

One of his eyes was swollen shut, and a dark bruise formed in a circle around his eye socket. His cheek and upper lip had thick lacerations that oozed blood. The tip of his ear appeared to have been chopped off; the entire side of his head was caked with dark red. He cradled his arm, which was set at an unnatural angle, and walked with a limp, his foot trailing behind him in an odd direction. His clothes were torn and caked with blood and grime. A gut-wrenching cry escaped my lips when my father fell to his knees at the meadow's edge.

My throat burned as I raced towards my father, crumpling to my knees before him and taking his head into my lap. I could already feel the scalding tears brimming my eyes, threatening to spill over onto my cheeks. I could hardly breathe.

"What happened?" I croaked out.

My father's one working eye could hardly focus on me as he struggled to stay conscious.

"Men . . . always want . . . more," he said, spurts of blood trailing out of the corners of his mouth and down his chin.

A sob wrenched itself from my chest as I gingerly took hold of my father's torso and tried to pull him upright. He struggled against me. My muscles strained to bear his weight as he leaned into my side. I wrapped an arm around his waist and slowly walked him over to the tree, setting him down gently between two roots as thick as his body.

"I'm not going anywhere, father. I just need to get supplies, okay?" I whispered.

He couldn't even nod his head in response. I flung myself up the tree, grabbed one of our supply bags, and searched its contents. Satisfied that I'd gotten the right one, I quickly lowered myself to the forest floor, where my father's limp body lay unmoving.

"Did they kick your stomach?"

I thumbed through the contents of the bag again. I pulled out some woven cloth bandages, bottled herbs, and a mortar and pestle. My father said nothing but wheezed and coughed up chunks of blood. How had he made it to me without being attacked by any beasts?

A name rang in my ear—as if whispered by the wind.

I searched through the stored herb bottles, grabbing yarrow, nettle, and pyrola. I sprinkled nettle and pyrola leaves into the mortar and ground them into a powder with the pestle. I poured water from my pouch onto the grindings until it was a liquid, then gave the bowl to my father.

"Drink. Nettle and pyrola will help stop internal bleeding. I'm going to need to make a cut to drain the blood," I explained, hoping my father was conscious enough to understand some of what I was saying.

I held the bowl to my father's lips, tilting it back as the liquid trickled back into his throat. He could keep it down without choking, so I moved on to find his internal bleeding. I lifted the corner of his tunic, grimacing at the dark red and purple swell on the side of his belly.

"I have to release the blood," I said. "It'll kill you if I don't. Bite down on this."

I placed a cloth bandage between his lips and pulled an arrow from my quill. Luckily, they were sharp now. I hoped to be able to do this without causing him too much pain.

"One, two, three."

I pressed the tip of the arrow into my father's side. A blood-curdling scream wrenched itself from my father's chest as he bit into the bandage.

"I know—I'm so sorry. I have to—I'm so sorry," I whispered, tears flowing freely now down my cheeks. I swiped them away with the back of my blood-soaked hand. My eyes needed to be clear, so I didn't hit anything vital.

Blood rushed out from the wound like a river run high with snowmelt, and I grabbed another bandage, drenching it as I tried to soak it up. Luckily for my father, the internal bleeding seemed isolated to a smaller part of his stomach. Once the wound was opened, it didn't bleed as much. I cleaned it as best I could, then cursed my impulsiveness. I had no way to close it and prevent infection. I gritted my teeth together so hard I thought they might shatter.

"Fire," came my father's croaking voice. It was weak and shaky, and that terrified me. I was too young to live without my father in the wild. I couldn't lose him yet.

"Fire? What am I supposed to do with—"

"Melt . . . together."

My eyes widened, and I reached into the bag for my sharpening stones. Around the tree's base, I grabbed a few dead twigs and began scraping the rocks together to start a fire.

What I would give to be a Fire Druid right now.

After what seemed like forever, sparks splattered the dead twigs, and they erupted in gold. I grabbed a blade from the supply bag and held it over the flame until the steel tip glowed red. With a deep breath, I glanced at my nearly unconscious father. He was going to hate this.

I gingerly opened the gaping wound in his belly and removed the bandage from the open cut on one of his organs. I bit down on my bottom lip and sucked in a breath before pressing the blade's tip to the cut, melting the tissue shut. A gut-wrenching shriek echoed from my father's lips as I continued murmuring apologies through salty tears.

He shook his head, blood spattering his teeth. "Again."

I winced. His screams turned raw as I sealed the wound shut, hoarse until his consciousness finally gave way. His breathing became steady, and the bleeding stopped.

With him unconscious, I hurried to reset his broken arm and ankle, using nearby branches as splints that I bound to him with a spare cloth. If he survived this, we'd need to trade again soon for more gauze. I just hoped I had enough to keep him alive.

I made the yarrow leaves into a paste and applied it generously over his open wounds to clot any residual bleeding and prevent infection, but I knew it was a gamble. I was no healer, and everything I'd been able to do today had been because of his previous instruction. If he hadn't been teaching me herbal remedies from a young age, I didn't want to think about what could've happened today.

If I'd taken a day off, the world would've devoured me whole.

I swallowed bitterly.

When I was finally satisfied with my work, I fastened a twine rope beneath his arms and knees, tossing the end across a stout branch above me. Gripping the other end, I urged my sore arms to pull and hoisted my father up into the tree. With more twine, I secured him onto a branch as thick as his body, knotting the rope around the tree trunk for safe measure. Once he was safe, I checked his wounds once again.

Only then did I swing myself onto an adjacent branch, bow, and arrows in hand, preparing for a long night of hungry beasts who could smell my father's blood.

26

oimét daur.

I awoke with a start when the mattress underneath me shifted. My eyes flicked open, and my blood ran cold. The cool blade of a knife was flush against my throat, the hot breath of a masked assailant fanning my cheeks. I could only see their eyes—a pale blue. I only had a split second before their muscles flexed, and the blade began to slice through thin skin.

Whoever sent them was a dumbass. I slept with knives in my sleeves.

Quicker than they could move, I gripped the handle of one of my knives and drove it between their shoulder and neck. The blade dropped from their hand, and they let out a blood-curdling scream. I'd hit the bundle of nerves that ran down the shoulder and controlled their arm. Without it, they were paralyzed from the shoulder down. My father would've been proud.

My lips twisted as I bared my teeth, wrapping a leg around their waist and flinging them underneath me. I ripped the cloth tied around their mouth downwards, the fabric catching on the stubble of a trimmed beard. I then pulled the other throwing knife out of my other sleeve and held it against his throat.

"Who sent you?" I demanded, his skin dimpling under the blade.

"What did you do to my arm?" He gritted his teeth in discomfort. "I can't feel it, I can't move it—what did you do?"

"Severed the nerve supply. Your right arm is paralyzed. Congratulations." I grinned, angling my head as I pressed the knife deeper. *"Who sent you?"*

The man snarled and threw his left arm toward my throat, but he wasn't quick enough. I drove my other blade into his left shoulder. His arm went limp, and he heaved a scream.

"Let's try this again. Your leg is next. *Who* sent you?" I demanded, ripping the knife from his right shoulder and holding it above his pelvis. I thought back to Salem's statement about my father's likely fate. "Why are you trying to stop me if he's dead?"

Was it possible this was the same culprit behind Xandria's assassination attempt? If it was, he could lead us to whoever organized these attacks. It was now clear that this was not the estranged will of one Druid. This male was smaller than the guard who attacked me the night of the Announcement Ceremony.

"Because he's not dead, *Forest swine*," he spat. "And you won't find him."

I hissed, clenching my fist around his neck. His blood fluttered beneath my fingertips like a bird's wings beneath a predator's claw. I saw myself in his eyes. Bared teeth, furious mane, and wild eyes—every bit the monster they claimed I was.

An animalistic growl coiled in the back of my throat, almost a confirmation of the stereotype. "Let's go visit the High King, then, shall we?"

I rolled off of him, the soles of my feet bare against the frigid marble floor. Knife still in hand with blood dripping audibly onto the pristine floors, I yanked the male to his feet by the collar of his shirt. It was a thick material on his torso, possibly some sort of woven armor. Unfortunately for him, I stabbed hard.

With a groan and a plea to not go to Salem, I dragged him across the floor. His legs fumbled to stand underneath him as I yanked him onwards.

"You either walk, or I drag your body," I said. "You choose."

He shook his head, steadying himself on his feet as I yanked the door open and tugged him out into the hallway.

The bitter ferric stench of blood had my nose burning the moment I opened the door. To the right and left sides of my door, my guards' slumped, bleeding bodies lay in dark pools, disemboweled, and throats slit. A roar of raging guilt hollowed my chest. Bitter. Empty. *Cold*.

I yanked the assassin's collar, jerking his feet out from underneath him. "I changed my mind. You don't deserve to walk."

A yelp wrenched itself from his lips as I dragged his wriggling body across the floor.

I marched towards Salem's reading room. Given the late hour, I didn't know if he'd be there, but it was the best I could manage. The assassin moaned and groaned and pleaded the entire way. With a flick of my foot, I could've easily shattered his jaw and shut him up. But Salem would need him to speak. We needed answers.

Vile hatred boiled in my blood like wildfire.

This male *dared* to try and kill me? The beast inside my skin frothed at the mouth and thrashed against iron chains. It roared, echoing in my head until I could hear nothing but its screams. This male murdered the Druids who had been assigned to protect me. Their death was on my hands as much as his. I could've—*should've* protected them. My father would have.

I rounded a corner, slamming the male's shoulder into the

edge as I dragged him. He whimpered in pain. I felt it—a numbing, scorching ache. But I smiled.

Two guards were stationed outside the door next to Salem's reading room. Perhaps it was his bedroom. Regardless, it was *somebody*. Someone who could find the High King and take this murderous *cladhaire* off my hands.

"Is he in there?" I demanded.

The guards swiveled to me, eyes wide. "Lady Quinn, what did you—"

"Is Salem in there? *Yes or no?*"

"I'm afraid I cannot—"

I had no time for this nonsense. I flicked my wrist impatiently, knife still in hand. The floor rippled around the guards' feet and flung them to either side with a clang of metal armor. I gripped the hilt of the blade in my fist and pounded three times on the door.

The silence that followed was overtaken by the deafening roar of fury billowing in my head. My body yearned to crush this male beneath my feet, bury him alive inside the earth and watch the stones swallow him whole. I wanted to strangle him with vines, rip him limb from limb with branches, and allow the monsters in the Forest to feast on his body. My mind echoed with promises of cruel fate as I glared plainly at the door, desperate for it to open and interrupt the madness ensuing inside my head.

The door creaked open. For a moment, a very sleep-deprived-looking Salem appeared shocked at my presence. His hair was disheveled and dark circles formed rings around his midnight eyes. They swept to the male writhing in my left hand.

"Assassin, meet High King Salem." I grimaced in disgust, throwing the male at Salem's feet.

The look of shock that graced Salem's sharp features was something I thought I'd never see from him—genuine, unfiltered emotion.

"Guards," Salem said, his voice low and breathy.

He'd just woken up, it seemed. The guards clambered to their feet and rushed towards the door, armor clanging. "Yes, sire?"

"Take him to the dungeon for interrogation. Station more forces outside my room and alert Iryx of a break-in. Lady Quinn will be staying with me for the rest of the night, so there's no need for extra guards at her room. Station those guards at the rooms of Lady Rhea, Lady Aria, Lady Ingrid, and Lady Zora. I want as many as you can manage outside Lady Xandria's room."

I didn't argue with him. The guards yanked the male from the floor before me, dragging him away amidst a chorus of screams.

"He killed the guards at my door," I said through gritted teeth, a tide of shame cresting as a silver-capped wave before drowning me in a briny sea. I sputtered, my lungs filling—but not with air—with what any Forest Druid would've done, what my father would've done, what I *should've* done. I wrung my hands. Though my palms were dry, the bloodstains had sunk into my skin, etched into my very soul.

Salem didn't speak. He merely stepped forward and pressed the pad of his thumb to the underside of my chin, lifting it. "You're hurt."

I winced. "He killed them."

"Did he hurt you anywhere else?" A slight snarl curled on Salem's lips as he spoke, fixated on the beaded line etched into my throat.

"I don't understand how he could just—"

I gritted my teeth so hard I thought they'd shatter, my lungs burning. If I allowed a breath, what would come with it? My body shook.

"Breathe, *wildling*. Breathe."

Suddenly his tumultuous gaze was in front of my eyes, cool

breath fanning my lips. I couldn't, though—I couldn't let it out. If I held it in, it would go away. If I held it in, the monster inside me would devour it, just as it devoured everything else.

"He *killed them* to get to *me*."

"Quinn. Breathe."

Those dark eyes flicked back and forth between mine. I shivered when his calloused hands engulfed my right hand, wrestling the bloody knife from my fingers and dropping it with a clang. Both his hands then swallowed mine, the mere touch a sort of anchor to reality. I was just so angry, and I felt so *guilty*—

"Breathe," he said again, even softer this time. His thumbs grazed my knuckles. "You did well. *Breathe*."

I couldn't resist it anymore. With an audible shatter, my walls crumbled as the air fled my lungs. The world darkened as air hurdled into my chest, swallowing my shame and grief. Though numb and disoriented, I still felt a pair of arms wrap around me. All my muscles seemed to give out at once, and I fell into him, completely and utterly exhausted. *My fault my fault my fault my fault*—

It's not your fault someone wanted to kill you, a voice echoed in my mind.

I didn't allow my mind to protest the vulnerability I had shown when my emotions had devoured me; that this male who I'd despised now held me as I'd come undone.

The forest wasn't like this. Nobody tried to kill me. The beasts in the trees revered me as I did them, protected me as their kin. I was safe there. I'd been wholly destroyed after my father was taken from me, but the Forest had held me close and told me I was safe. I couldn't understand how someone could be so evil as to kill innocent Druids, so *cowardly* as to attack one while they slept.

Those guards had been at *my* door, protecting *me*. They had given their lives for mine. I had never asked them to; I'd never even known their names. How could I be so cruel as to let someone die for me without knowing their name?

"Nhaeve Korosa and Ivor Kade," Salem said.

"What?" I asked, pulling back from his embrace to meet his eyes.

"Those were the names of your guards," he clarified gently as if saying something the wrong way might shatter me.

"Thank you."

I didn't argue—didn't protest his presence in my mind. For whatever reason, that presence brought now me solace.

27

*M*y father woke the next day surprised to be alive. He was in immense pain, as to be expected, so I gave him white willow bark to chew on while I collected more herbs for our depleted supply. At least, that's what I *told* him I was doing. He hadn't seen me pack a bag with nuts and berries, sling my bow, and quiver across my back. I didn't know how long the trek to the Mortal lands would take me, but I hoped to return to the tree by tomorrow. Even if he worried about me, he couldn't do anything about it in this state. He would have to wait for me to return—once I'd given the men a taste of justice.

I paced myself as I ran through the trees, crisp morning air filling my lungs with each heavy breath and urging my muscles faster. I told myself I would run until I couldn't anymore and hadn't reached that point yet. I might make it to the mortal lands by sunset.

Rage simmered in my veins, fueling me onwards. It infuriated me to think that men, who are lucky enough to be allowed to *live* following the rise of the Druids, dared to attack a peaceful Forest Druid out to trade. My father was gentle and kind, patient and wise. How anyone could be so vile as to hurt *him*—to hurt him like *that*—made me feel sick. Those men tried to take my father from me, and they would pay for it.

I pushed myself faster, allowing anger to motivate me. I ducked under twisting branches and leaped over gnarled roots, paying little attention to my surroundings otherwise. Only at midday, when my stomach began to grumble, did I slow and set my bag beside me. Thumbing through the contents, I grabbed some berries and gulped them down for fast energy. I would save the nuts for tonight—when I'd need my strength the most.

After I was satiated, I slung the bag over my shoulder and picked up my pace again, charging towards the Mortal lands. The gnarled underbrush did little to slow me down. My pacing was quite effective, as the trees began to thin by the time the sun dipped towards the horizon. With bronze skies ahead and lilac skies at my back, I continued towards the cluster of settlements just beyond the thinning woods. I reached into the bag, pulled out a small sword, and fisted the hilt. Regardless of how badly I wanted to, I couldn't use my bow. I wasn't nearly as skilled as I needed to be, and I needed to determine *who* caused my father harm. I didn't want my rage to extend past justice. The only way to do that was to charge straight in and start threatening people.

My heart seized with fury as my feet carried me into the human settlement. I did not attempt to conceal my presence. A few men stood around a hearth at the center of the encampment. When their beady eyes landed on me, their thick hands flew to the swords sheathed at their sides. I hadn't realized until now how much taller my kind was. When I'd seen mortals from afar in the Forest, they appeared similar in size and appearance. I now realized that wasn't the case. I stood at least a foot taller than each of these men. I wondered if these men had seen a female Druid before, let alone one holding a blade.

"Crossing into the mortal lands is a death sentence, lil' miss," came the sneering voice from a pudgy man covered in ash and grime. His hair was unkempt and greasy, dark like oil, and fell in patches just below his ears. A beard severely needing a trim and a still-red jagged scar sat etched across one of his eyes. His eyes were equal in darkness to the black tar pits my father had found at the Forest's southern border when he was young. Animals and Druids used to wander into them, only to discover they could not escape. That is what his eyes reminded me of, what men's eyes reminded me of. Inescapable death.

"Exactly what I came here for. Have any of you humans come across a Druid male looking to trade? Dark skin and hair, green eyes? Left *bleeding and dying?*"

When the corner of the pudgy man's lips curled in a fiendish grin, I knew I'd somehow found the right place.

"Find his body, didja? Shoulda brought more goods to trade with if he's hopin' to return with his life," the man taunted.

Blood boiled in my veins. So much rage flooded my heart that I wondered if I'd remain corporeal or transform into a manifestation of it.

I ran my finger across the edge of my blade, hilt to tip. "Once, I might've pitied you, humans," I said. "I've come to remind you of your mortality."

"A *female* Druid is going to remind us of mortality? I didn't know yer' kind had a sense o' humor," the man next to the pudgy one cackled. The bones poking through his grimy clothes shuddered with the sudden movement. His face was gaunt and pale—as if his mortality walked with him hand-in-hand. Even if his life were spared by me, it would be taken, nonetheless.

"Let's find out how weak I am, then, shall we?" I challenged, swinging my blade once around my wrist and dropping my bag to the side. Everything inside of me ached for battle, ached to see their blood spraying—bodies lifeless on the earth.

It was too late that I realized the men's eyes had drifted behind me, too late when I spun around, only to be met with steel ripping straight through my stomach and out my front. The air paused in my lungs. My heart stuttered. My blood ran cold. I looked down.

Silver—covered in red and viscera.

A cough welled in my throat, gurgling. Hot blood spilled from my lips instead of air. But I felt no pain. I felt only anguish for my father, who now knew neither vengeance nor of his daughter's death.

28

*S*alem's room was massive. At almost twice the size of mine, his held a shelved collection of numerous liquors and a roaring marble fireplace. Atop the stone mantle sat various vintage pieces—an empty, dusty vase, a bejeweled sword held by two prongs, and a miniature wooden chest with a bronze lock. My gaze didn't linger on the three items but instead on the roaring fire that illuminated the room with a gilded glow. It drowned in silver as it crossed the room, meeting with moonlight that poured in from windows overlooking the mountains to the north. He had quite a view.

"Here," he said.

I tugged my gaze to Salem, who stood as I sat on the sofa. A glass of amber liquid was cradled in deft fingers, the singe of alcohol prickling my nose even from here. I took the glass from him and held it to my lips, taking a long swig. The burning bite hit the back of my throat, pulling my lips thin as I swallowed. The smoky oaken flavor warmed to a soft glow in my belly.

The sofa cushion sunk underneath him as he sat beside me, taking a drink as he stared into the fireplace. The skin of his bare chest shimmered like molten bronze in the firelight, crested against the dark shadows that brimmed the harsh lines of sinewy muscles. I had known from our skirmishes that he held a decent amount underneath the delicately embroidered suits that he wore daily, but I hadn't imagined how much. What captured my attention the most, however, was the silver chain strung neatly around his bare neck. It glittered, almost tauntingly, in the firelight.

I tightened my jaw and pulled my robe tighter around my body as if the plush cloth could somehow conceal my thoughts from his prying mind. Luckily, I think Salem decided to give me some mental space after my breakdown in his doorway. No talons grazed my subconscious now.

Without the Forest to comfort me, it was as if I'd been without an anchor. I felt like a tiny boat, and my emotions were a tumultuous sea, insisting on battering me until I drowned in them. Even now, the stench of blood seemed to cling to my nose, to my throat. It was as if my mind refused to rid me of the guilt and shame.

"I'm sorry you had to see me like that," I said. I kept my voice steady as if impassiveness could regather my abandoned dignity.

The weight of Salem's gaze settled low on my chest. "Why would you apologize for that?"

"Because how I acted was extremely inappropriate," I replied, fixating on the dancing flames as I took a swig of the liquor.

"Hardly," he replied. "I also have trouble managing my emotions when I'm far from my Realm. In the Southern Territories, the sun lingers at its high point in the sky for far too long. There are hardly any shadows, and if they're there, they're wisps of smoke. I can't feel them. I feel lost, and it's suffocating."

"I should've been able to control myself."

"You have a right to be angry, Quinn. I am familiar with the beliefs of your people. Killing those guards directly disrespects your heritage and the life your people hold so dear. You don't have to disregard your emotions for the sake of pride. Not with me."

I scowled. "Not with you? What's that supposed to mean? That because you're High King, I'm supposed to be completely and utterly vulnerable to you upon your command?"

"Is that all you see me as?"

I paused, words audibly dying on the tip of my tongue. "I'm not interested in seeing you as anything else."

Salem paused for a moment, lips parted and dry. A little breath escaped them as his jaw clenched shut, and he turned away from me, pinching his eyes. He heaved a sigh and looked back at me, throat bobbing as he inched closer.

"Let me see your neck."

"It's fine, *ciarán*. You don't have to do this whole thing." I took another long drink from my glass and let the burn sizzle in my throat before swallowing.

He set his glass on the stone table at our feet. "Do what, exactly?"

I glared into the fire until my vision went red. "Play the caring High King. I know you must be exhausted. You're more than welcome to go to bed. I'm fine here."

"You're infuriating, you know that?" He chuckled, and the cushion beneath me shifted. I leaned against the sofa's arm as if it could protect me from him. Calloused fingertips grazed my jaw, angling it to the side.

"Does that hurt?" he asked, frosted breath kissing the vulnerable skin on my neck.

"No." I swallowed thickly. His fingers delicately danced down my throat to the cut, and I hissed as they grazed the damaged skin.

"It needs to be disinfected before it heals over," he said with a sigh, leaning back.

"I can do it myself."

"For the love of gods," he grumbled, ripping a corner of fabric off my robe. I began to protest, but he stood and walked over to his bar, pouring a clear liquid onto the shredded cloth. I struggled to maintain eye contact as he sauntered back over, the firelight flickering across his body.

"Come here," he said, gently gripping my jaw as he sat beside me.

I swallowed, my eyelids wincing shut as he pressed the damp fabric to my wound. It was as if a hot blade had been pressed to it. My eyes clamped shut against budding tears. He set the cloth aside, examining his work and nodding in satisfaction. The cut did ache a little less now. Not that I'd admit it.

"I don't need you to take care of me," I said. "I'm fine."

"Tell me about your father. Did he take care of you? Or did you yell at him the way you yell at me?" Salem teased, resting an arm on the back of the sofa as he angled himself toward me.

"I told you before you don't have to do that."

His eyes narrowed. "Has it crossed your mind yet that perhaps I do care? That I'm genuinely curious about you?"

"Just because I work for you now doesn't mean you have a right to know everything about me," I replied.

I couldn't understand why he was so insistent on asking me questions, why he felt like he had to keep me company instead of getting the sleep I'd interrupted. I was fine now—he had an entire legion stationed outside his door.

"Quinn," he pressed. I turned to look at him. The hard-set lines of his jaw told me he would not be wavering anytime soon. "Tell me about your father."

I sighed, then reclined into the sofa, relenting. "We took care of each other. From the time I could walk, he taught me how to protect myself—take care of myself. Whenever one of us got injured or fell ill, the other would pick up the slack. When I was old enough, I took care of us both. Until he was taken from me."

"Was he like you? Furiously stubborn and a show-off?"

"Stubborn, yes. We argued almost daily. But I'm not a show-off, and neither was he. He taught me to keep the majority of myself hidden. The most powerful creatures in the Forest are the ones you never see coming," I replied, my heart beginning to ache with grief. I missed him terribly. I often wondered what he'd think if he saw me now—if he'd even recognize me, let alone be proud of who I'd become. My throat coiled and burned as I struggled to keep that anguish at bay. I glanced at the necklace hanging just below his collarbone. "You wear that all the time."

He glanced down at the pendant. "Yes."

"What is it?"

His jaw flexed, a moment of hesitation perhaps. "It's called the Silver Bough. It's sacred to Arawn. I got it from my father after his death."

So Salem's *father* had stolen it from my father, and then Salem had inherited it. However, why my father would have a necklace sacred to Arawn—the god of the Otherworld—I hadn't the faintest idea. Sure, every culture had its own relationship with the fabled god of death, but we didn't worship him like the Dark Druids did. He was not our patron deity. What could my father have wanted with a piece like that? And how did he manage to get it?

I couldn't press on about the necklace. Salem would see my interest in it and grow suspicious. I looked over to the fireplace. "What's in the box?"

He chuckled. "So you can ask questions, but I can't?"

"I'm asking questions about *things*, not about you."

A smirk twisted his lips. "I was only teasing you, *wildling*. You may not have sharp teeth, but your tongue is another matter entirely." He stood and walked over to the fireplace, taking the box down. He blew the dust from it and set it on the table in front of me. With a click, it opened, revealing several small cylindrical vials filled with a shimmering, silver liquid that appeared to glow all on its own. "This is known as Diaverita."

My breath stilled in my throat. "What is it?"

He closed the chest shut with a click, gingerly placing it back on his mantle. "It's believed to be the blood of a star. With each new generation of rulers, a vial is drunk. It's believed to grant us prosperity and peace. When the war against the Mortals was won, my great-great-grandfather received it as a blessing from the gods. Our bloodline's divine right to rule. Or so it's been told."

I resisted the urge to laugh. "You think a vial of that stuff grants you the divine right to rule?"

He shook his head. "No. It's a symbol of the Kalystan blood-line's divine right to rule. What it grants us are peace and prosperity."

"Doesn't seem very peaceful to me."

In the silence that followed, he finished his drink and walked the empty glasses back to the bar. He heaved a sigh as he spun to face me. "Take the bed. I'll stay on the couch."

"*Ciarán*, I'm really quite comfortable—"

He shook his head. "You need it more than I. I insist," he said. I swallowed, unsure of what to say. "I suspect you'll have trouble sleeping regardless, given what happened tonight," he continued. "The least I can do is make you comfortable."

I huffed and stood up, walking past him as I approached his bed. I clambered into the luxurious satin sheets, sinking into the soft mattress.

"Thank you," I said. He didn't respond.

29

100 YEARS AGO . . .

*Y*our death will not come at the hand of men, Quinn. They do not deserve that honor.

$\mathcal{M}$y eyes fluttered open to gilded sunlight on my face, pouring in through the paned glass. The bed was plusher than I'd remembered it, and my mind willed me to go back to sleep. However, when it registered that there was a figure standing in front of those aureate windows, my eyes shot open again.

I was in Salem's room.

I'd almost forgotten. I'd been attacked last night, and he'd given me his bed. Now he stood before the windows, buttoning up a loose-fitted white shirt. His tanned skin glimmered like gold, his dark hair like lapis lazuli in the sunlight. The Silver Bough hung loosely around his neck, glittering. *Taunting.*

"Good morning," he said, finishing up the final few buttons on his shirt before plodding over to the bedside and sitting. The mattress sunk under his weight, and my legs fell against his back.

"I should be getting back to my room," I said. "How late is it?"

"Relax. It's a little past dawn," he replied, the depths of his dark eyes dragging me in. Looking into them, I could see thousands of dying stars falling into his abyss. I felt unsettled by his intense gaze and tightened my jaw, breaking eye contact to look around the room. We were alone.

"I should go before anybody else wakes."

"No one will know," he said. "The guards from last night are sworn to secrecy."

"How will I get back to my room?" I asked.

"I will escort you," he replied. "After assuring the halls between my room and yours are completely empty."

Beneath his eyes hung circles of indigo, more apparent today than in the last few weeks. I should never have accepted the bed; he'd needed it more than I. He had a kingdom to run, and I could've napped all day if I desired.

He appeared to shift uncomfortably beneath my gaze. "I'd like to talk to you about my conversation with my sister—the Potions Master."

That caught my attention. I sat upright, earning a look of amusement from the High King.

"She said that the only cases of immunity she'd ever heard of involved the individual being of other blood," he said."

"I'm not sure I understand," I replied.

"One can only be immune to a potion if they're not a full-blooded Druid."

My heart stuttered. I was not a full Druid?

My father was a Forest Druid—that I knew for sure. He'd taught me how to feel the life around me, speak to it, and plead for it to answer my calls. My mother . . . I'd never known her. I'd once thought she could've been something else—when my bond with the earth was far from tangible. But mortals seldom wandered into the Realm, and more often than not, they were men, but I suppose it was possible. It would explain her untimely death.

"So you're saying I'm a demi-Druid? That my mother was a mortal woman?"

I tried to steady my traitorous heart. How could my father not have told me who she was—that I wasn't made of the same ancient magic as everyone else?

"I believe so," he replied. "It's unusual, though, for a few reasons. First, it's been a century since I saw the last Mortal on these lands. My father killed them immediately after they'd arrived. It's odd that your father, a nomadic Forest Druid in the most sparsely populated region of the kingdom, would somehow find a human woman. However, given that the border to the Mortal Realms is on the edge of the Western Territories, and I haven't the slightest clue how long it's been unguarded, it remains a possibility."

I swallowed. "And the other reasons?"

"I have known few demi-Druids in my lifetime. But the ones I knew had little control over the small portion of magic they had," Salem countered. "Your power, Quinn, is far from diminutive." His eyes met mine. "They also died fairly young."

I froze. "How young?"

"Around a century and a half."

If that was true, then I was nearing my life's end. Perhaps I was supposed to have died in the Mortal Lands when I'd attacked those men. Perhaps my century of solitude was nothing more than a gift of extra time from Danu.

"I'll be 126 this Alder Moon," I said.

My father explained that once the Druids regained control, we reverted the calendar to the ancient ways. Our calendar was divided into moon periods rather than the old mortal months, in which my birthday would have fallen at the beginning of April. If only he'd thought to also include the fact that I wouldn't make it to my 150th birthday when he'd decided to ramble off fun facts.

"You haven't begun to age yet, Quinn. All of the demi-Druids I had known appeared to be nearing 700 when they'd only been a few years past a century. Perhaps you have longer than you think."

His lips thinned into a gentle smile, but his sympathetic words did little to comfort me. I was a mortal in an immortal world and spent most of my life basking in the trees. What sort of a life was that? I would be gone soon, and nothing would be left to show for my life. No one would remember me; nothing had changed from the moment I was born to the moment I died. I would have come and gone from the world, and it would be as if I never existed at all.

"Perhaps I should've let the damn assassin kill me," I hissed. "He would've only been two decades early."

"You can't be serious," Salem retorted. "You came into my castle breathing fire, making the earth tremble beneath your feet and life yearn to please your every whim. Of every Druid I've ever met, you're the only one who's ever seemed so ridiculously determined to be heard—to be seen. You were meant for more than to become a memory. You were meant to have the earth herself bow at your feet. If you've truly forgotten who that Druid was, who pranced in here like she owned the place and brought me to my knees more than once, I'd recommend you leave now. If you're truly that convinced by what a Potions Master has to say about you, then you're not the *Queen* I thought you were."

He stood from the bed and stalked across the room to the fireplace. A cascade of shadows followed behind him like a dark cloak, clinging to him like moss to a tree.

"You don't know me at all, *ciarán*."

"I know you enough," he said.

I paused, glaring at those eyes that dared hold mine. His heart echoed in my ears like thunder charging down the foothills in torrential rain. Disbelief and anger pounded in his veins and fueled that raging heart, kindling a wildfire. Such inferno was hidden behind those dark eyes. Such *rage*. I almost wondered how I could've missed such a brilliant flame, even if it were hidden behind smoke and shadow.

I tightened my jaw. "So what exactly do you propose I do? Act in denial? Like I don't know that I will likely die within the next two decades?"

"I hardly think death would stand a chance against you," Salem said. "But regardless, it's been added to a term of your employment contract that I will help you search for a cure to your mortality. You will not die if I have any say in it."

"Why do you care if I'm alive or not?"

He stared back. "I just do." He turned, watching the sun begin its trek across the sky. "I should take you back to your room. Before the castle wakes."

I nodded silently and pulled myself from the sheets. My robe was drenched in dried blood. The cloth stuck to my skin. A bitter taste rose in the back of my throat. I realized there were multiple reasons he didn't want to be seen with me leaving his room. First, it would raise questions about our relationship. Questions he didn't want. Second, I was covered in blood. It would be difficult to talk my way out of that one.

Salem strode over to the door and cracked it open, whispering with the guard on the opposite side. After a moment, he pulled the door ajar and looked at me. "Let's go. We're clear."

My feet touched the cold stone, and I shivered, plodding over to him. His gaze wandered down to my bloodstained robe.

"I'll have a new one made for you," he said, then ushered me through the doorway. "There should be a second one hanging in your washroom that will do for now."

The walk to my room was silent. Whether that was to avoid attracting attention from anyone else wandering the halls at this hour or because neither of us knew what to say—I didn't know. Before I knew it, we'd reached my doorway. The guards' bodies had been removed already. Not even their pooled blood stained the floor. It was as if it had never happened at all.

"I had your sheets changed as well. And the locks on your window," Salem said. "You'll have more guards stationed outside your door tonight. More than two." He glanced back and forth down the hall.

I gave a single nod. The next moment, Salem was gone, hurrying down the hallway as quickly as we'd come.

I pushed the door open. The hinges creaked, deafening in the silence. As I entered, I was relieved to find that nothing remained from the skirmish from last night. Nothing to remind me of what had occurred. Relief bloomed in my stomach. I walked over to the bathroom, avoiding the mirrors and heading straight for the replacement robe Salem had mentioned. I peeled the bloodied one from my skin, bathed in scalding water, and scrubbed my skin raw, then put the new robe on.

But I still couldn't bear to meet my reflection's stare—one that had allowed another to give their lives for hers.

A wave of nausea roiled through me, and I grabbed the waste bucket beneath the washroom counter, heaving. But my stomach was empty. Nothing came up but bile.

Once my stomach settled, I cleaned myself up, hoping my handmaidens wouldn't notice the state I was in. I didn't want *anyone* to know what had happened last night. That I'd been unable to save my guards—that I hadn't even *noticed* they were dead until I opened my door. Some might say I did it. That no one had attacked me at all. That I'd murdered my guards because I was nothing more than a savage beast in a cage.

My breath tasted like acid.

A knock resounded at my door. I plastered the most impassive expression I could muster on my face. "Come in," I said.

To my surprise, it was not my handmaidens. It was Kyro.

The first thing I noticed was the smell. One I could not remove from my skin regardless of how I scrubbed. Metallic. Warm. Salty.

He was covered in it. The opulent suit he wore—it might've been blue once. But all I could see was red. *So much red.*

And then he spoke. "Xandria is dead."

31

100 YEARS AGO . . .

*M*y body burned with scorching pain. I could feel every shredded flap of skin, every splintered bone. A wound gaped in my belly, hot blood flowing from me like a scalding river. An ache throbbed between my legs, and shards of shattered bone burrowed into my thighs. The stabbing pain in my shoulders told me my arms had been dislocated from their sockets, though I didn't know if the arms themselves remained. My face stung as if the skin had been flayed, raw muscle exposed to the sickly cold air of the mortal world. I could not see, could not hear a thing—only smell the reeking ferric blood coalescing around my discarded body.

Forest Druids believed that with death came the journey to the Otherworld, an idyllic place my father saw only in intense meditations. We thought that upon our demise, a beautiful female cloaked in gauzy white and silver would receive us at the bay atop a wooden raft. If we had been true to our god and goddess, she would help us aboard. We would then travel west to the Otherworld, crossing the sea and joining our ancestors atop the island. This, however, could *only* be accomplished upon rejoining nature in this world. We believed that to pass to the Otherworld, our life force had to be transferred onto something else in nature, lest it anchors us back. So, we buried our kind and planted trees above them, allowing the body and the life force to unite again with the goddess that created us.

I concluded that because my body was above ground rather than cradled by the roots of an evergreen, I would *not* be traveling to the Otherworld in my death. It felt rather unfair to remain within my dead body while it decomposed. For the rest of eternity, I'd be bound to these bones even as they turned to dust. The concept was a bit upsetting.

Only when I felt the earth tremble slightly did I realize that something wasn't right. If I *was* indeed dead, I shouldn't be able to feel anything at all. The tremble only happened for a second but repeated, alternating with a moment of silence. I allowed my mind to wander, to wonder what the cause of the trembling could be.

Feet. Footsteps.

A loud *thud-thud* pounded in my head. It was steady and calm—but drenched in malevolence and cruelty that radiated from it like the smell of my corpse. It was evil, vile, and wicked —positively wicked.

A heart.

Then, more footsteps, more heartbeats, more vile sensations trickled down my spine like droplets of water. If I could move, I would cringe—recoil from it.

My mind pushed past the repugnant creatures on toward the slow inhale and exhale from the ancient trees guarding the forest. The sun peered through the clouds and bathed their leaves in golden light. Little feet scurried through their branches with a rapid heartbeat. *Hungry.* Those little feet belonged to a creature that needed food—and fast. The weather was growing colder.

Buried in the foliage were several tinier heartbeats, just as hungry as the other creature. I swore I felt tangible relief when a flutter of wings resounded around them, that their excitement was my own when their mother returned to fill their bellies. Today, they would survive.

Back through the tree branches, I spiraled down the swirling bark of the tree and into the cool dark earth below, where roots stretched into the ground. Deeper and deeper they went, growing ever smaller as if desperately reaching toward something.

Something. Something ancient. Something very much alive, with a heart that pumped once a millennium, a soul that bled through the trees, thicket, and grasses into the creatures and beasts in the Forest. Something that had its gaze fixated solely on me, watching—waiting for me to do something, *anything*.

Then, there was silver. It seeped into my skin as if it were nothing but water.

My mind reeled backward, back through the infinitesimally small roots to the trunks of trees, to the grass between the Forest's edge and the settlement, to the men that wandered aimlessly in a drunken stupor, and finally to my broken body, where I heard my heart—my faintly beating heart. My suspicions were correct. I was still alive. Barely, yes. But *alive*.

A scream lodged in my throat when my skin stretched, frantically pulling itself back together. It was as if my body had liquefied, had melted, and decided to become something new. My bones, already shattered, shredded again through tissue and muscle as they stitched themselves together. So badly, I wanted to wail and cry at the pain, but I couldn't move. My heartbeat grew stronger in my head, louder and louder, until it was the only thing I could hear, drowning out even my thoughts.

And when I opened my eyes, I felt no more pain.

32

*T*he armchair beneath me groaned as I shot to my feet. "That's—*what?*"

Tears fell silently down Kyro's cheeks. "Do not make me say it again, Lady Quinn. I beg of you."

"You're absolutely positive she's dead? I could—I know some healing—"

"She's dead. There's nothing you can do. Even Stella could not save her. She's been gone for hours." His chest trembled as he heaved a shaky breath. "High King Salem will spend the remainder of the day with you. He believes you are the next target."

I stilled. I'd just been attacked; they wouldn't come for me again, and so soon- would they? *Unless . . .*

Unless my attacker last night was *intended* to be caught. And my attack had only served as a distraction so another might sneak in and murder Xandria. Which meant I *hadn't* been the target last night. They'd be sending someone else to finish the job. Someone who was likely *much more capable* than the Druid I'd fought last night. Even my first attacker had been more skilled than him. He was *meant* to be captured.

I cursed under my breath. How could I have been so blind?

My feet vibrated with the sensation of dozens of footsteps approaching my door. As if on cue, guards clad in obsidian and cobalt armor lined up just outside my doorway. Kyro held the door ajar, his eyes fixated on the stone floor.

My nose burned with the smell of Xandria's blood. He'd tried to save her. *Frantically.* It's why he was covered in it. His emotions were no longer muted, as they had been thus far. He now drowned in them. Nothing I could say would make him come up for air.

A heartbeat I recognized marched through the open door-way, side-stepping Kyro. The High King placed a hand on Kyro's shoulder. Slowly, the Water Druid raised his head to meet Salem's eyes.

"Go to Neptan, Ky. Your family needs you," Salem said.

"You need me."

"I need you to do what's best for you right now." Salem inclined his head until his brow met Kyro's. "Go to your family."

Kyro's jaw flexed. As Salem stepped back from his advisor, Kyro gave a single nod, then fled the room. The moment he left, the weight of his grief did as well. Air flooded my lungs as the High King turned to me.

"You could not have anticipated this," he said, stepping toward me. "Just as I couldn't have."

I shook my head. "I should've known better. The first person who'd attacked me was far more skilled than the one from last night. I should've realized that multiple people were involved—and what that meant for Xandria as well."

Salem's lips twitched downwards as the door creaked shut behind him. "They think it was you."

Rage billowed inside of me. "What?"

"Only my council knows you have an alibi, that you were also attacked. But when news of Xandria's death broke, the villagers began to accuse you. They're calling for your execution."

My heart was pounding. "I didn't do this. I couldn't. I *wouldn't*."

Salem nodded. "I know it wasn't you. Kyro knows it wasn't you."

"What're you going to do about your *people*, then?"

His jaw flexed. "I could issue a statement of your innocence, but that won't do anything unless the real perpetrators are caught. The one who'd attacked you last night had ingested a particularly potent memory potion prior to his crimes. He does not remember a single thing about himself. Name, birth date, where he's from, his patron god—absolutely gone. Nothing remains in his head but fear."

"I should've forced an answer from him the moment I woke," I said. "The potion wasn't in effect then, or he wouldn't have remembered to attack me at all."

Salem nodded. The ring atop his head glinted in the morning sunlight that seeped in through the paned windows behind me. His shirt was buttoned to his neck, hiding what I knew rested there.

He ran his hand across his jaw. "The memory potion didn't go into effect until the early hours of the morning. Iryx had started questioning him before then, but he wouldn't budge. When the potion went into effect, your attacker lost it. Was absolutely terrified. Had no recollection of anything. Iryx said he even pissed himself." Salem shook his head in disappointment. "I won't let anyone else get hurt for the sake of my hand."

Of course, he was delusional enough to think this was all about him. That *he* was the reason Xandria was dead, that I'd been attacked twice now, and possibly even behind the death of Rhea's mother.

Rhea. I paused. "Rhea needs to be guarded too. Her mother was attacked."

"Already done. Stella and Iryx are with her, as are dozens of my best guards."

"And the others? We can't leave them unprotected either," I said.

"Yes, I agree," he replied. "But I'm convinced you're the next target."

I stilled. "Are you sure?"

He stole a cautious step toward me, as if afraid I'd flee.

"I think someone wants to control who wins the crown. Maybe someone thought with Kyro as my advisor and Xandria as High Queen, the Seas and Eastern Territories would have too much power. If this is all connected, you've been attacked twice. They probably don't want you to have the crown either. My guess is that they'll try to stab you too."

I swallowed. "She was *stabbed*?"

He nodded. "My sister is calling that the cause of death, despite her blue fingertips and lips. Exposure to some metallic salts can do that, as well as cyanide. But it also could've been due to her stab wound. Stella said the blade went right through the book she was holding and hit one of her lungs."

My hands wound themselves into white-knuckled fists. Whoever was after us clearly had very little regard for life. They believed themselves divine—able to decide who lives and who dies. It was *blasphemous*. The entire reason behind the rise of Druidry in the first place was regaining the lost connection to the earth and her elements. Believing yourself worthy of deciding the fates of others stood in complete opposition to that belief. It disregarded the delicate balance of life and death—of give and take. It shunned our beliefs. It trivialized our gods.

It pained me that I had no idea why Xandria and I were being targeted. There was no connection. Those who wanted me dead were doing so to prevent me from finding my father. Xandria knew absolutely nothing about Forest Druids, let alone my father. But she *had* known something about Salem's father.

And my father might've been captured by Salem's father. Perhaps High King Salar was the connection.

But it still didn't explain *why*.

I grimaced. "What exactly is your plan here? Do you think the assassin will come for me at some point today? And we're just going to *wait* here for them?"

Salem sat on the edge of my bed, his hands clasped together at his waist. "Unless you have a better idea."

I clearly hadn't been able to find the assassin in time using my power. Perhaps he was right, and the best solution was to use me as bait. Though part of me thought it would be quite foolish for any assassin to attack its targets two nights in a row, another part of me wondered if that's *exactly* why they would do it. Because it wouldn't be expected. I had no doubt I'd remain bait until we caught them, anyways.

"Does anyone else know about your plan?" I asked.

Salem shook his head. "No. If I'm correct in assuming the assassin has infiltrated the castle, releasing news of our high-alert status might scare them off. I want them to think they're safe. That they've escaped."

I sat back down in my armchair. "Let's hope I'm an enticing target, then."

33

I lay flat on my bed, a book in hand. One of my fingers pinched around the next page as if I was entranced by the novel—but I'd been reading the same sentence over and over again for the last ten minutes. I was bored out of my mind, and Salem wasn't any help. He stood in the corner of the room, cloaked in shadow, cradling a glass of whiskey. Such *angst*.

I sighed, closing the book cover and setting it beside me. "How are you so sure anybody is coming?"

"I'm not," he replied. "I'm hoping whoever is after you are bold enough to attack two nights in a row. Otherwise, I may have to cancel the competition. Send everyone home."

"That's not the worst idea," I said. "I abhorred the idea of a competition for your hand in the first place."

"Yes, you've made your opinion on the competition quite clear," he said with a tick of his jaw. "And yet you remain."

I shrugged. "I like the bed."

His gaze rose from the glass in his hands to me. "So *that's* why you've stayed. Not because of the threats made against your Forest. It all makes sense now." His lips twitched. "I always knew you had good taste. They're filled with feathers."

I recoiled. "From birds?"

Salem's eyes twinkled. "No, turtles." I leveled a steely glare in his direction, and he snickered. "Yes, birds."

My lips twisted into a sour grimace. "I hate the bed."

He swirled the ice around his glass, lips curled in a satisfied smirk. "Then I suppose you'll need to find a new reason to stay."

I rolled over onto my back and stared at the ceiling, hands clasped over my chest. "Are you planning on hiding in that corner until someone arrives?"

"I don't want to be caught by surprise," he replied. "Whenever they come, we'll be ready."

Guards had been knocking every half hour on his door and whispering updates in his ear. The last update, I suppose, wasn't a good one. He'd been brooding in the corner since then. Shadows cloaked half his face, the other half lit solely by the dimming sun through the paned window. Ryz and Eyla hadn't been in yet to light the candles. My guess was that they were being detained outside the room by the unnecessary amount of security stationed outside the door. It was all a little excessive. There had never been more than one attacker, at least when they'd come for me. Salem and I could undoubtedly handle them.

"You can see through the shadows," I said, rolling back onto my stomach. "I hardly think anyone could catch you unawares."

"I can't watch all the shadows at once," he replied, slowly stepping out of the darkness and into the dusk-lit air.

We'd been stuck in his room for hours now, and the sunlight outside had given way to twilight. Hardly any light entered through the paned glass, and the light that did was a pale lavender. Every aspect of him appeared darker. Sharper.

"Do you not think the *savage* Forest Druid could handle a single assassin alone?" I asked.

He chuckled dryly. "*The savage Forest Druid.*"

"I saw how your citizens looked at me when I first arrived.

They feared me. Hated me. They do even more now that I'm a suspected murderer."

The moment I'd arrived, the citizens of Kalys had decided who I was. Of course, my appearance had done little to challenge their opinions—with my tangled mane, muddied clothes, and unmanicured features. But despite doing nothing to them, they'd concluded that I was a feral beast. That I only *looked* like a Druid. That what lay within was nothing more than a savage creature out for blood.

Salem grimaced and swallowed the rest of his whiskey in a single gulp. "That is entirely my father's doing."

"What do you mean?"

"My father hated Forest Druids," he replied. "Spread rumors about them to encourage fear of them. Any prejudice that still exists is a result of that."

My jaw ticked. "Why did he hate us?"

We had no military, no Lords or Ladies, and no formal governing system. We just existed in tandem with nature. There was no political angle to gain from vilifying us. And there certainly wasn't an ethical one. My people had *embodied* morality.

A deep sigh heaved from Salem's chest. "Because they were different. They didn't collect taxes, didn't plead for his good favor. Just wanted to be left alone. He didn't like that." He set his glass down on a desk. "At least, that's what I believed his issue was. He never actually told me."

"And no one questioned him? His rumors?"

Salem shook his head. "When someone in a position of power says something, even if it's grossly untrue, people listen." His gaze fixated on his feet. "It's why I'm relieved you exist."

"I don't follow," I said.

"The fact that you're alive, that you survived the Plague, means there's a possibility that others did as well. For a long time, we believed Forest Druids to be extinct."

"What I've seen of your people thus far leads me to believe they didn't exactly *mourn* the idea," I retorted.

"I desperately want to mend the bridges that my father burned. You are not who my father made you to be; your people did not deserve what my father did to them. They didn't deserve to be vilified. We are all Druids borne of the same magic. Your heritage does not change that, nor does it warrant any disrespect," he replied. "When the Plague began, no one wanted to stop it. No one tried to. Your people were turned away from healers and apothecaries. My father refused to send aid to people who refused to pay taxes—to bend to his will. I will not forget what he did, the damage he caused to an entire race of Druids."

There was a moment of silence as his words registered. Perhaps he wasn't the High King I had decided he was. He wanted to change the kingdom, to make it better for my people —if any were left, that is. He had signed a treaty to help protect my Forest so long as I served him. While the latter benefited him, the first did not. He was trying to make a change simply because he thought it was wrong.

I sat upright. "I appreciate that."

His lips pursed slightly. "You look surprised."

"I am."

"Why?"

"After seeing how your people reacted to my presence, I'd expected you to act the same, if not worse," I replied. "I don't know the rumors your father spread about my people—but they must've been potent if they affected an entire kingdom."

Salem stepped back into the shadows that cloaked the corner of my room. The darkness there appeared to welcome him home, tendrils curling around him like arms in an embrace. He leaned against the wall, arms crossed, and faced me once more.

"My father told the kingdom that your people were no more

advanced than the animals you lived with. He claimed that Forest Druids had been a mistake of the gods, that you had all been created not in their image—but in the image of the monsters that dwelled in the Wild. He claimed you were all feral beasts and would sooner rip their heads off than maintain a civil conversation. To my people, you are a bloodthirsty, rabid animal. They believe the gods have disowned you."

It was truly despicable. The Forest Druids were among the most spiritual of Druidkind. My father had taught me how to pray to the gods, taught me of the sanctity of life, and that anything the gods created must be *protected*. We maintained close relationships with the gods. In addition, we were far from bloodthirsty. Forest Druids saw no difference in the values of life. The life of a Druid was worth nothing more than the life of any other creature.

"How could no one see that whatever your father told was untrue?" I asked. "My father told me Forest Druids sometimes traded with members of the other Realms, that the Southern Territories often would trade cloth and fruit for fish and timber. If anyone had ever interacted with a Forest Druid, they would know that we are far from bloodthirsty."

"As the Plague continued, and the numbers of Earth Druids dwindled, trade essentially ceased between the other Realms and the Wild," he replied. "By the time Forest Druids were the last remaining race, very few ever came into contact with them. Those that did were few and far between, and one voice could not stand against a kingdom. We feared what we did not know, and no one knew a Forest Druid."

"The Plague."

It never made sense to my father how it had happened. The less nomadic Earth Druids had died off first. As the most nomadic of them all, Forest Druids were the last to go. He'd suspected it had something to do with genetics, some sort of blood disease that had been passed down a long line of Earth

Druids and had randomly decided to become active at that point. He'd said we'd been lucky—that we'd been blessed by Danu with good fortune and good health.

Salem swallowed. "Yes. The Plague."

"Were any other Realms—"

I paused the moment I heard it, a faint heartbeat on the other side of the castle wall, approaching the window from the outside. It fluttered like a hummingbird, rapid and gentle. Anxiety twisted her stomach as lithe fingers curled around the frosted stone parapet.

We were no longer alone.

I glanced at Salem, but it seemed his shadows had given him the same foresight my abilities gave me. He lifted a finger to his lips, and my breath stilled at the height of my throat. His cheek glowed blue as he turned towards the window, every movement silent as he pulled a blade from the inside of his jacket. The weapon was cloaked in shadow, only the very tip of it twinkling silver in the moon's rays.

I flicked my wrist downward and snatched a throwing knife from my sleeve. It remained flush against my skin as I reached for my book. I set it in my lap, thumbing the page. The tip of my blade dimpled the paper. I pretended to furrow my brow as if I were confused by the subject matter. I couldn't alert whomever it was that I knew they were coming. Truthfully, I think the book was upside down this entire time. It was no wonder the sentence I'd been rereading made absolutely zero sense.

A soft click pierced the air as the latch of the window unhooked. A bracing breath of night air curled against my cheek, smelling of frost and pine. Now, I turned. I feigned surprise when the petite dark figure leaped in through the window, a gasp fleeing my lips.

Metal sang through the air as Salem flung his blade at the female's right shoulder, pinning her body into the wall. She loosed a blood-curdling screech as the weapon hit home, her fingers clawing at the hilt. However, Salem had perfect aim and a strong throw. She was stuck, essentially nailed to the wall.

I couldn't imagine a worse place to be stuck than between Salem and me. She seemed to acknowledge this as I met her fearful gaze. Tears budded between her pale lashes like frozen dew droplets on aspen branches. Glacial eyes held mine for a moment, trembling, then rolled back in her head as her body slumped against the wall.

34

Salem tore the fabric covering her face and flung it to the ground. He took a step back, and my jaw fell slack. Blonde tendrils of hair fell loosely around her heart-shaped face, a pink tinge to her pale cheeks. I could hardly believe my eyes. It seemed Salem was just as shocked as I was.

Aria sat slumped against the wall, eyes closed in a peaceful slumber as if she hadn't just passed out in fear.

"I never sensed any sort of malevolence from her," I whispered in disbelief, kneeling in front of her.

I never would have believed this. Timid Aria—trembling from the moment she walked in the doors—an assassin. She played her part so well; even her *heart* had pretended she was a soft little creature. If I hadn't seen her with my own eyes, I wouldn't believe it.

"She was shaking from the moment she walked through those doors. Every encounter I've ever had with her, she's been the same meek female," Salem said. "Someone else has to be behind this, forcing her to do this. Perhaps they sent the other assassins as well."

"Why do you think that?"

"Last week, she jumped at her own shadow," Salem replied with a sideways glance. "I find it hard to believe all these attacks aren't connected. It's too coincidental. No attacks at all. Then, the moment the competition begins, the Ladies are attacked."

I fought the urge to spill what I knew. That my attackers were trying to keep me from finding my father. That Xandria had discovered some weird phrase in High King Salar's journal. That if this were truly to stop someone from winning the competition, other Ladies would've been targeted, not just Xandria and me.

I swallowed my words. "So you think this all has to do with the competition? With you? With the crown?"

"I thought so, but now, I'm not sure. Aria has less motive than anyone else," Salem said, heaving a deep sigh and running his fingers through his already disheveled hair.

I stood. "What do you mean?"

"Regardless of who won, she would've been among the wealthiest Ladies in the Arastya. Her parents are ridiculously greedy and have amassed a wealth that exceeds my own. Luckily for me, they're too stingy to spend even a single penny," he explained, taking long strides as he walked over to the door and cracked it open. I heard him murmur something to the guards outside, resulting in footsteps running down the hallway.

"Her parents withdrew her Aavali birthright," I said. "Perhaps marriage to you was her only opportunity to earn her parent's favor and stay in high society."

He pursed his lips. "Even without her birthright and marriage to me, she's the eldest daughter of the Lord and Lady of the Arastyan Highlands. Finding her another suitable match wouldn't be difficult by any means," he replied. "And, she'd still be considered a Matron beneath her sister should she remain unmarried. It's an honorable position in Aavali culture. She'd still have wealth far beyond my own. She has no motive to become High Queen other than to be with me, and I think she finds me more frightening than anything else."

"Perhaps her fright was all part of the act."

Salem shook his head. "No, I don't think so. You saw the fear in her eyes. I don't think she expected me to be here."

He closed the oak door with a creak and leaned against it. His intricate suit jacket was now wrinkled and unbuttoned, revealing tanned skin still beaded with sweat and a glittering necklace I couldn't shake from my mind.

"So she was afraid of you, not of me?" Her miscalculation was amusing.

The corners of his lips quirked upwards. "Like I said, everything Arastya knows about Forest Druids is largely based on rumor. She probably thought you were all bark and no bite."

I glared down my nose at her slumped form. "She's lucky she passed out before she got to see my bite."

I still was in utter disbelief that out of everyone here—it was *her*. But what did she know about my father? Why would she want to keep me from him? I didn't think I'd ever even spoken to her. How could she have such a vendetta against me when I'd never interacted with her?

"I'm lucky as well. We need to interrogate her. Your bite, I know all too well."

A knock resounded at the door, and Salem swung it open. Three guards hurried inside handcuffs and a strip of cloth, which they tied across her eyes. They snapped the cuffs around her wrists and tossed her willowy frame over one of their shoulders.

My jaw flexed as the guards carried her from the room. "You think somebody from another Realm is making her do this?"

"I think that's where we need to start. I will send word to my mother that you and I will leave for Hypnos Keep tomorrow morning," Salem said with finality, once again opening the door and sticking his head outside to speak with a guard.

"Hypnos Keep?"

The door closed, and Salem's chest heaved with a deep sigh. "Hypnos Keep is the capital of the Air Realm. It's where Lady Aria's parents, Lord Typhon and Lady Thetis, live. It's a fortress built into the heart of a mountain."

I tilted my head to the side. "I hardly think they'll enjoy hearing that their daughter has been arrested for attempted murder and treason."

Salem chuckled. "That's what I'm counting on," he replied. "They'll likely try to bargain her way out of the charges, and I'll take whatever information they can give me."

"Do you think they orchestrated this?"

He meandered over to my side. "I don't want to believe they would do something so immoral and foolish. Like you said, Lady Aria didn't have any malevolent intentions that you could see. And I haven't the faintest idea why Typhon and Thetis would move against myself and the other Realms."

Could the Air Realm have something to do with my father's disappearance? Perhaps they were holding him hostage somewhere and wanted to keep him hidden for whatever reason. It would then make sense why I would be targeted. They could've seen me as a threat to that. But what Xandria had to do with any of it still had me confused. All I had between my father and her was High King Salar, and even that was a flimsy connection at best.

"Does the Air Realm have any connection to Xandria?" I asked.

Salem shook his head, deft fingers undoing one of the buttons on his jacket. "Not that I know of. Xandria was familiar with Ingrid, Zora, and Rhea. I don't think she met Aria prior to this competition. I hadn't."

"Rhea mentioned this was the first time her parents allowed her to leave their palace," I said.

Salem nodded. "That's what I had heard as well. It's just odd.

No motive, no connections of any sort—and yet *she* was the one climbing through your window."

I wandered over to the window that Aria had crept through. The chilled mountain air crept up my spine as it flowed past me, just as silent as Aria had been. I couldn't help but feel that the wind itself was teasing me as if it had also longed for Aria's success. I suppose I couldn't blame it—what stands in the way of wind but the earth?

"What will happen to Lady Aria?" I asked, my breath misting in the chilled air.

"I'll hold her here and interrogate her," he replied. "I won't be able to use the same tactics I normally do when I interrogate traitors to the crown, primarily because I don't know that she's the only one at fault. I will likely have to use her subconscious against her once more, see what I can gather from her head."

I turned around to face him. He leaned against the bed, his head hung between his shoulders. He looked defeated. I suppose I would be as well if I believed multiple people had been assassinated due to a situation I'd forced them into. His chest was tight with anxiety, his heart a tempestuous sky.

"Do you truly believe these could all be connected? Including Lady Vara?"

Salem's empty eyes rose from the floor to meet mine. His impassive expression did little to hide the weariness in his eyes.

"I suppose it's possible," he said. "For now, I want to wait and see what Lord Typhon and Lady Thetis have to say about their daughter. About what happened tonight."

Despite the gnawing suspicion that grew with every moment I stared at the ajar window, I knew he was likely right. I had to wait.

35

$\mathcal{T}$he sun didn't want to rise today. Regardless of how much I pleaded with the horizon to let the gilded eye of Lugh peer above the eastern skyline, the heavens remained dim. After staring at my ceiling for what felt like hours, I relented and pulled myself from my sheets. Last night, I'd told Ryz and Eyla that I'd be gone for a while on an errand and that they weren't to tell a soul about it. I'd also asked that one of them deliver a message to Rhea, asking her to meet me in the gardens at dawn. I didn't know if she'd received it or not. But I'd head there anyway.

Ryz and Eyla brought the clothes I would wear on my journey late last night. To my surprise and total elation, the High King had finally provided me with pants.

They were fitted trousers—much more restrictive than the ones I'd worn in the Forest. He'd also supplied me with boots that rose just below my knees, as well as a tunic and a thick silver cloak as tall as I was. With my handmaidens gone, I fought with my mane for quite some time until I'd managed to pull it into a thick braid. My hair would not fit beneath the hood of the cloak otherwise. But given the way the braid tugged at my head, I'd likely be forced to abandon it relatively soon.

Just as gold began to line the eastern sky, I made my way down to the gardens. Orion was already awake, grazing. His head reared upright when he heard me approach. Relief fluttered in his chest when he realized who I was.

I gave him a tender smile. "Good morning, Orion."

The massive elk lumbered towards me, jaw flexing as he continued chewing. He came to a stop mere inches from me, nuzzling against my shoulder. His cumbersome antlers nearly hit my head several times, and I laughed.

"I missed you too, my friend," I said. "I'm afraid I'll be gone for a short while."

At this, he stopped nuzzling me and glared into my eyes. He didn't want me to go. He didn't like it here; I was the only reason he remained.

I frowned. "I know. But you know how badly I want to find my father. And this could lead me to him. I promise I'll return as quickly as I can. And I'll make sure Rhea brings you some of those apple cakes the kitchens made the other day. Okay?"

The beast heaved a sigh, then began to graze at my feet. He liked Rhea more than Salem, that much he'd made clear. I felt I could trust Rhea to give him some attention while I was away. She seemed to enjoy him as much as he did her.

Footsteps pressed the grass behind me, and I spun around. *Rhea.*

"I must admit, it's a little early for me, Lady Quinn," she said. "Can we not arrange for secret meetings at midday? Or at least allow the sun to rise a little?"

I smiled. "Normally, I'd say yes. But today, I'm afraid it had to be now."

Her brows swept low. "What's the matter?"

She stepped forward, the grass bending beneath the flat soles of her shoes. She wore a white dress that appeared to have been made of a sort of linen. It was much less opulent than the other pieces I'd seen her wear. Perhaps it was just something she had slipped on to meet with me.

My breath stilled in my throat, but I forced the bitter words from my lips. "Xandria was assassinated, and someone is trying to kill me too."

Rhea blanched, her steps faltering. "*What?*"

I swallowed hard. "She was murdered two nights ago. I was attacked the same night. And nearly attacked last night as well. I'm supposed to be going with the High King to try to put a stop to these attacks. He knows about my ability to feel others' emotions and thinks I can help figure out who is orchestrating all of this."

Rhea's expression was unreadable. "Do you think it could have something to do with my mom as well?"

My jaw flexed. "We're not sure."

Her throat bobbed. "And I assume the other Ladies do not know of this? About you?"

I shook my head. "I don't think so. Please do not tell them. I'm only telling you because I trust you. And I was hoping you would check in on Orion while I was away. He loves those apple cakes the kitchens make if you ever have the inclination to sneak him one," I said. "I also wanted to ask you some questions about your mother before we left. I'm trying to figure out how all of these attacks could be linked."

Rhea clasped her hands together at her waist. "Of course. Anything I can do to help."

"Does your mother know anything about Forest Druids?" I asked.

Rhea frowned. "No more than anyone else. As far as I knew, anyways."

I grimaced. "Did she have anything to do with Salem's father?"

Rhea pursed her lips in thought. "No. But she was extremely

close with the High Queen Regent, High Queen Soren. I don't think she ever interacted with High King Salar directly. Perhaps she saw him in passing at balls or something."

Again, a flimsy connection at best. I sighed in frustration. "Alright. Let me know when I return if you can think of anything else, alright?"

She pulled her lips into a thin line. "Of course," she said, glancing at Orion. "How long will you be away?"

"I'm not sure. Hopefully, only a day or so," I replied.

My feet trembled with the sensation of more footsteps approaching around a hedge. I turned in their direction just as the High King stepped past the shrubs. He wore all black, with a billowing cloak that appeared partially made of shadow. The crown sat atop his head, the same onyx shade as his hair. Again, I could not see the necklace that I knew hung around his neck. But the idea of it being so close taunted me.

Salem's brow furrowed. "Lady Rhea? Why are you awake at this hour?"

"Lady Quinn has asked me to care for her companion while she's away," she said with a smile.

Salem stared at me. "You told her?"

"I trust her," I replied. "And I needed someone to care for Orion."

Salem's jaw flexed, but he nodded, relenting. "I see. Very well. Lady Rhea, should I arrange for an escort to show you back to your rooms?"

Rhea's lips twitched into a semblance of amusement. "No, Your Highness. I'm perfectly capable of finding my way back." She turned to face me. "I will pray to Lugh for your safe return, Lady Quinn. Rest assured, Orion is in good hands."

A sigh of relief escaped my lips. "Thank you, Rhea."

She nodded and turned back to Salem, starting to walk past him and pausing. "High King Salem?"

He stilled, his eyes meeting hers. "Yes?"

Rhea's jaw ticked. "Keep her safe."

A moment of silence followed, so thick it hung in the air like smoke. Even Orion seemed perturbed by it as he stopped grazing and looked up at the High King.

"Yes, my Lady," he replied in a voice so soft, I hardly heard it at all.

Rhea, now satisfied, continued on her way back to the castle. The High King turned to me, expression unreadable. However, the apprehension that had sunk its claws into his chest, thinning his every breath, was all too apparent.

I turned to Orion, running a hand along his neck. "I'll be back soon, my friend. Stay safe."

He nibbled at my shoulder in solemn acknowledgment. I knew he understood why I had to leave him, but it didn't make it any easier. I swallowed the guilt and stepped away from my companion, following Salem out of the garden.

When we reached the courtyard, a single carriage drawn by two black steeds stood at its center. A male Druid, willowy and short in stature, leaped from the front when he noticed our approach. Skin wrinkled around his eyes as he smiled up at Salem, but his expression faltered when he looked at me. The black suit he wore hung loosely off his frame as he swept into a low bow.

"Your Majesty," he said in deference to Salem. He then hesitantly bowed again to me. "Uh—Lady Quinn."

"Good morning, Mr. Aven. I apologize for the short notice," Salem replied.

The male chuckled. "It's no matter, sire. I hardly sleep these days. My children are old enough to wander—it keeps me awake. I had your bags stowed in the back already. The horses are watered and fed. We're ready to leave at your earliest convenience."

"Thank you, Mr. Aven," Salem said.

My boots clicked across the stone as we approached the

carriage. Various silver adornments covered the luxurious ebony wood, the same shade as the horses pulling the coach. Mr. Aven hopped back up to the front of the carriage as Salem and I clambered into the carriage. Velvet cushions sat on either side of the interior, a deep shade of blue.

Once Salem and I were seated, he knocked on the wood behind his head. "All set, Mr. Aven."

"Yes, sir!"

With a crack of his whip, we were off.

"Is this really necessary? Couldn't we have just ridden there?" I asked, suppressing a smile as I leaned against the seat.

"Since we will be there on official Arastyan business, I had to ensure we looked as formal as possible. And I don't particularly want my people to massacre you on our way out," he replied, eyes examining my body. "Nice outfit."

I folded my legs with a huff. "I believe that's complimenting yourself, seeing as you picked it out."

"Would you have preferred it if I put you in another glittering gown?"

My attention was drawn outside the little window to my side, and I held the short velvet curtain back. Druids were just starting their days—arranging fruits and vegetables in the stalls lining the Kalystan streets, setting hats that were far too extravagant to be sensible atop ceramic models. I wondered if they knew their High King sat in the carriage idly rolling past them. If they did, they didn't seem to care too much.

"Not particularly. What will the other Ladies think when both you and I are gone?" I asked, turning my attention back to the High King.

"I had word sent to them that I had official business that had taken me away from the castle and would be back soon. If anyone asks about you, the handmaidens and guards have been instructed to tell whomever that you have fallen ill and are sick in bed. Kyro will return back to Kalys shortly and keep every-thing under control."

"Why not just tell them the truth?" I asked. "That you're going to investigate the motives behind the assassination of Xandria and Rhea's mom and the attempts on my life?"

"They don't need that much information. They're guests at my castle. Not members of my court," he said, expression tight-ening. "My people are already calling for your death. If the Ladies knew that I'd allied with you to prove your innocence, I scarcely think it would end well for either of us."

"They think I killed Xandria too?" I asked.

Salem shrugged. "It's just a rumor. I'd rather fix the issue before I address it."

As we traversed a little stone bridge, the carriage thumped, and I held my hands against the seat to steady myself.

"I just don't see the point in lying," I said.

His ashen eyes glimmered with silver embers as they gazed into mine, muscles taut as he leaned forward in the seat. "It's good you didn't have to lie then."

I shifted uncomfortably. "Why are you looking at me like that?"

"Like what?"

"Like you're waiting for me to do something."

"Well, we *are* in a carriage, alone, for the next few hours." He beamed, the insinuation making my blood boil.

"You're despicable," I retorted, breaking his gaze to look again at the passing countryside. The gilded light of dawn rained on yellow fields of wheat that rolled like waves in a breeze, only interrupted by sparse cottages dotting the landscape.

"You're easily agitated," he replied, adjusting the lapels of his gilded jacket.

"You say that as if your insinuation was baseless."

He shrugged. "That's for you to decide."

I could feel his gaze burning into my head, claws curling at the recesses of my mind with a click.

"Stay out of my head, *ciarán*." I resisted the urge to bare my teeth. "If I'm supposed to sit next to you for the next few hours and not commit regicide, I'd keep those claws to yourself."

"Unfortunately, Lady Quinn, I've begun to quite enjoy your threats." He grinned. "Upping your resume from assassinations to regicide is quite ambitious, I must say."

I glowered at the High King, his amused expression only tightening my wound fists. I swallowed and looked back outside. Very faintly, in the distance, I could see massive trees darkening the hillsides beneath the Arastyan mountains. I knew immediately what I was looking at. *Home.*

"Do you think there's more Forest Druids out there?" I wasn't entirely sure I'd said it aloud until I heard the deep sigh escape Salem's chest.

"I doubt it. I had doubted we would even find you," he replied.

"You think I'm the last one?"

I suppose I had been thinking the same thing for quite a while now, but saying it aloud made it all the more possible. I hadn't seen another Forest Druid since my father had been taken from me. But then again, I hadn't seen any Druid since then. And given the amount of traveling I'd done during the century I guarded the Forest, the chances there was another out there that I'd somehow missed seemed very slim.

"It's hard to know for sure," he said. "The Western Territories is so vast and unmapped, it'd be impossible to scour the entire forest and come back alive. I hope that there's more. I hope the Plague didn't wipe your people out entirely."

My jaw tightened, and I looked back out the window, watching my home pass us by in the distance. My chest grew heavy with each breath, a tangible ache ever-present within its walls. Neither Orion nor I belonged in a city.

My throat tightened to the point of pain. I missed home desperately. Salem didn't need to see how much. We remained silent for a while, neither of us sure what to say following such a depressing topic. Once dusk had begun its descent upon the sky, I looked outside the windows and saw a jagged horizon. The rapidly approaching foothills grew larger by the second. Behind them, the serrated faces of the Arastyan mountains stretched up towards the darkening sky. Mist swirled around their peaks like Druids in prayer dance around a fire.

"How are we getting to Hypnos Keep?" I asked.

"Zephyr Pass. It's a winding road through the mountains to the Arastyan Highlands."

"Is it well traveled?"

"Not particularly. Air Druids prefer to fly over the mountains as opposed to passing through them. Most everyone else opts to take the ferry from Hera in the Southern Territories to the port just outside the keep."

"So why didn't we take the ferry?" I scowled, though I was rather content staying on solid ground.

"Would've added two days to our trip. We should be there by nightfall taking the pass."

"When will we be coming back?" My voice was far more eager than I'd intended it to be.

I was met with a withering glare and a monotonous response. "That depends on what we're able to figure out."

After a few moments of silence, I figured we were probably done talking, so I leaned my head against the thumping side of the carriage and watched the hills pass us by.

As night began to fall, we began to climb through the pass. One side of the trail was met with a steep cliff face that fell thousands of feet into a ravine, the other with the sloping, jagged side of a mountain. The path was just wide enough for the carriage, but it might as well not have been with the way the horses were acting. Their racing hearts were audible, their curdling stomachs sending waves of adrenaline surging through my veins. The carriage driver tried to urge them faster with a crack of his whip, but it only agitated them further.

"Will you stop that? They're scared to death, and you're only making it worse!" I called out the window to the driver.

"At this rate, we won't make it to Hypnos Keep by sunrise, milady," the driver replied.

I began to yell at him further, but Salem placed his hand on my knee and shook his head.

"Those horses are going to bolt and get us killed," I said. "They're petrified. It's dark, and the path is narrow. The stone beneath their hooves is loose."

"They'll be fine," Salem insisted. "I trust Mr. Aven. He will navigate them through. We must get to Hypnos Keep before word of Aria's arrest reaches her parents. Otherwise, we could be facing a less than peaceful protest."

"What would they do?"

"Hopefully, nothing too drastic. If we are the ones to deliver the news, with you present to attest to the attempt, we should be able to sway them in our favor," he replied.

I leaned back, brows pinched, and arms folded. I wasn't exactly keen on trusting Druids over animals, but I could see Salem's point. We had to reach Hypnos Keep before any messenger did.

36

*D*espite what Salem had said about making it to the keep by nightfall, the stars were now in full bloom, and we were still in Zephyr Pass. The horses remained unsteady, and the carriage driver continued to whip them despite my protests. Something gnawed at their minds, gripping their hearts in an unyielding clutch. Their heads swung from left to right, eyes frantic as they searched the darkened mountainsides. Even as I'd told Salem this, he'd mumbled about me being overdramatic and needing to listen to Druids rather than horses. I'd scoffed and ignored him for the next half an hour. I prayed that nothing was indeed watching us, but something told me that Salem would eat his words.

"Still giving me the silent treatment?" he asked, forehead pressed against the glass as indigo shafts of moonlight cascaded across his face. His hands were clasped in his lap, two long fingers fiddling with a chunky silver ring.

I continued to look out the window. A snarl lodged itself firmly in my throat. I wasn't fond of being called overdramatic when I was here to *help him*.

"Shame. I felt like maybe I'd share a secret with you, but

seeing as you're not speaking with me," he hummed, pressing his lips together in feigned thought.

As much as I didn't want to play into his little game, I had to take any information he was offering. There was always the potential it could lead me to my father.

My will faltered. "Take back what you said, and I'll speak to you."

"The overdramatic part? Or the part about only listening to animals and never the people who actually know what they're doing?"

I shot him a fierce glare, a chuckle rumbling in his chest. He leaned forward and placed his elbows on his knees, hands dangling between his legs.

"Fine. I take back what I said," he relented. His arrogant smirk made me feel less like he'd conceded and more like I'd lost a fight. "Now, would you like to hear a secret?"

"Whatever, *Your Highness.*"

"Zora is not who you think she is," he said. "She acted as my eyes and ears on the inside. She was there for your protection as well as mine. I knew none of the Ladies personally and wasn't about to trust them roaming around my castle freely. Zora was my spy. She has been for a while."

My jaw popped open. "Then why has she acted so . . . vile?"

He snickered. "It's been her tactic for a while. Vilify herself, so anyone angling against the Ladies might see her as a potential ally. It's why she singled you out in particular. She thought you were at the most risk."

I couldn't hide my shock. Zora played her part as well as Aria had—it seemed. But I'd chosen the wrong one to create into a villain.

"Why Zora?" I asked.

He leaned back into the seat cushions, adjusting the ring atop his head. Silver glittered for a brief moment just beneath his tunic. "She's my cousin from my father's side. She's been involved in politics since she was a child. Sometimes I believed she'd make a better ruler than I ever would. Her dedication to the crown is remarkable."

I grimaced. "Given what I've seen of her, it's hard to imagine her on a throne."

His lips twitched. "She's given up everything for me. She broke up with Xandria because of me—because *I* asked her to. Because I believed it would make Xandria a target if someone discovered her. Because I thought a relationship might make her a weaker asset to the crown. She never stopped loving Xandria. And I'm sure she blames me for her death. For her dying without knowing how Zora truly feels about her."

My chest hollowed. "Xandria knew."

Salem's eyes fixated on mine. "What?"

"When I spoke to Xandria before her death, I asked if she had issues with any of the Ladies and specifically mentioned Zora to her. Xandria knew how Zora felt about her," I replied.

Salem's expression was as stiff as the silence that followed. I couldn't tell if he was furious with me for keeping this information from him or relieved that he hadn't done as much damage as he thought he had. Before I could reach through the earth to feel for him, to try to understand, he spoke.

"You should tell her. When we return. Zora," he said. "I've completely isolated her from the world. The amount of pain and guilt she feels after Xandria . . . she hasn't moved since I told her, just keeps staring at the book Xandria died with. Hasn't eaten, hasn't bathed—I don't even think she's blinked. And I know that this was my fault, that I put her in this position. But maybe telling her that Xandria died knowing that Zora still loved her would ease some of that pain."

"I suppose I can," I replied. "If she'll let me. She and Rhea got into it at the first challenge, and I became involved. I'm *positive* she despises me."

Salem's cheek dimpled as he pursed his lips. "Again, Zora was playing a role."

What she'd said to Rhea—both at the Announcement Ceremony and the first challenge—made me wince. If it was truly just a role she had to play, Salem was correct about her remarkable dedication. *Rhea.*

"Do you think Aria also assassinated Rhea's mother?" I asked.

"I'm not sure what reason she would have to assassinate Lady Vara. I'm unsure why anyone would have any reason to assassinate Lady Vara. She was a martyr; she had a massive garden that she would harvest and give to the hungry for free. As of a few years ago, the Southern Territories eradicated all hunger thanks to her dedication. They also solved their unemployment problem by creating the ferry system out of Hera. Lady Vara was adored by everyone, probably most of all by my mother. They were very close. She was devastated when I told her what had happened."

"And Lady Vara's body made it back to the Southern Territories in time?"

Salem's expression softened. "Yes. Her rites were given before she could turn into a sluagh. As were Xandria's. Kyro made sure of it."

The horses outside whinnied, and my blood ran cold. Frosted fear coiled around their hearts, sending my own into a frenzy. They stomped their feet as Mr. Aven urged them onwards. Something was *very* wrong. Salem protested as I clambered out of the now-stopped carriage, marching around the front to see the horses. They were both frightened out of their wits. Their thunderous hearts were beating far too fast, icy adrenaline stinging as it surged through their blood. I placed my hand on one of their flanks, trying to steady them. But it was no good. They knew something was wrong. And they were trying to tell us.

"Lady Quinn, I must insist you get back in the carriage or—"

Mr. Aven's voice was cut off by the whipping of an arrow and a gargle.

I spun around. Blood seeped from the corner of his mouth. An arrow had lodged itself in his gut. His eyes bulged as he wheezed, chunks of ferrous blood spluttering on his shirt. Another gurgle and then silence as his body slumped.

By Danu, the horses were right. We *were* being watched.

Another arrow whizzed past me, and I ducked just in time, scrambling back to the carriage and flinging the door open. Salem's eyes went wide.

"Aven's dead," I said. "We're being attacked."

He cursed under his breath and flew out the carriage door. A sickening sensation settled into the pit of my stomach. Wisps of shadows coiled around Salem's feet, poised to attack. We peered through the dark for any movement, but only the stomping horses seemed to catch my eye.

Then, he turned to me. His eyes were glazed over—like a gauzy blanket had been thrown across his darkened irises. "There are four Druids perched on the mountainside," he said.

I had to remind myself that he could see through the darkness and wasn't just omnipotent.

"I can't feel them," I replied. "Wherever they are, they're out of my reach."

"Two of them are coming down. You handle them, and I'll go get the other two," he said, climbing up the side of the mountain without so much as a second thought.

I widened my stance and scanned the area, but I couldn't see a thing, let alone feel any heartbeats. The horses were the only thing I could recognize.

Gravel shifted to my left, and I swiveled, my hand clutching the still twitching shaft of an arrow mere inches from my face. The tip would've hit my right eye had I not caught it.

Now, I was irritated.

My gaze shifted in the direction from which the arrow flew, honing my senses until I could feel the faint beating of two hearts. My lips pulled back in a feral smile. *This* is exactly why Druids hardly made it out of the Forest alive. If I hadn't stopped Salem and Kyro from attacking the nuckelavee that night, they wouldn't have made it out either. So quick to attack—never smart enough to yield.

The earth rippled beneath my feet in excitement—*far* too eager. My wrists snapped outwards, and the trembling soil raced towards my targets. My soles shook the moment it found them, then stopped the moment it swallowed them whole. Heartbeats thundered in my ears as the two Druids struggled for breath beneath the earth. I strolled towards where they had once stood, standing above where they writhed mere inches below the surface. As those heartbeats began to falter, I flicked my wrists again, and the earth parted, allowing their heads to breach the surface.

A male and a female, both blonde-haired, inhaled frantically. Their heads lolled to either side, jaws slack. Unconscious.

Aria also had blonde hair. Perhaps these were Air Druids sent by the Hypnos Keep to intercept us. A hiss crested in the back of my throat but soon fell silent as the air fled my lungs.

My eyes opened wide in shock as I gasped for air. Though I willed my lungs to open, they remained tight within my chest—the air just out of reach. My hands clawed at my throat, and my vision began to blur. Someone held the air from my lungs. Sharp gravel bit into my knees as gravity took hold.

"Arrogant little *soith*," a voice seethed from behind me.

The cool bite of a blade pressed against my neck. I couldn't think straight. I couldn't even lift a finger to defend myself. The corners of my vision began to darken, the numbness in my fingers spreading up my hands. A little too familiar a sensation. Something deep inside me—something I had kept as far within me as possible—slowly opened its eyes.

A scream filled the silence. A growl, deafening at first, then as soft as a whisper. Air flooded my chest. The euphoria was overwhelming. I fell onto all fours, my lungs searing with pain as I began to breathe again. My eyesight began to clear, the tingling in my fingertips fading as quickly as it had arrived. I wheeled around in search of the source of the scream.

A single white hound stood, haunches raised, between myself and my attacker. The creature was the same size as a stag.

I did not hesitate. My magic flexed, and the earth beneath the Air Druid gaped open like the jaws of an ellen trechend. Then, there was silence.

The hound turned to face me, teeth bared. The pointed ears atop its muscular head were as red as blood. It stood there for a moment, watching me with silver eyes like the moon. I reached through the earth, feeling for its heartbeat—for its emotions. There was nothing but silence. As if the creature weren't there at all. Saliva dripped down its muzzle as it panted. I'd never seen a beast like this before. The only hounds I'd ever encountered in the Forest were the cu sith, and those wily creatures had nothing on this animal.

Where had it come from? It must've climbed down the sloping mountain or further up the pass. The hound began to walk towards me—a slow gait, given its long limbs. I held my breath, daring not to move. I could feel all creatures of the Forest. But I could not feel this one. And *that* was terrifying.

My chest screamed, but I refused to inhale, even as the creature came within inches of my face. It smelled like my homeland—like pine and rain and absolute wilderness. The hound raised its head, its snout sniffing my face. My heart thundered in my ears. Those silver eyes were unlike anything I'd ever seen before. The closest that came to them was Salem's, but only when he was emotionally charged.

The hound stepped back from me, its piercing stare holding

me captive. It licked its chops, then loped off down the pass. The horses screamed as the creature blew past them, faster than I'd ever seen a canine run.

"Quinn!"

I spun around as Salem scrambled down the side of the mountain. Darkness pulsated around him like a living, breathing monster. His heart was racing. Concern etched into his features as he hurried over to me.

"Salem?" My voice was weak—breathless.

His chest heaved in deep breaths. "Are you alright? I saw you fall to the ground. It looked like you were choking."

My lips parted. "Did you see that creature?"

His brows swept low, wrinkling between his eyes. "What creature?"

"The white hound."

He swiveled his head, scanning the area around us. "I don't see any animals aside from our horses. Perhaps you were right. We should've listened to them."

My mouth went dry. "You didn't see that creature?" I asked again. "It was right here. Stood right in front of my face."

He pursed his lips and shook his head. "No. But given your powers, I suppose it doesn't matter all too much. Did you tell it to attack that Air Druid for you?"

Blood pounded in my ears. I hadn't even felt the creature. There was no way I could've asked for its help in saving my life. The revelation sunk in my gut like a rock.

That hound had saved my life. And I hadn't asked it to.

Salem continued on as if I wasn't internally panicking. "When I got up there, there was only one. The other had come down to attack you. I think you were the target. Not us. *You*," he explained, turning to face me.

That ornate jacket of his was covered in dark blood. Silver threads glinted in the moonlight, just like the eyes of that creature. Unyielding. Fearless. Foreign.

"Did you hear me?" Salem asked, his voice ripping me from my thoughts. "This means Aria wasn't acting alone. That other Air Druids were helping her."

I could still smell blood as I swallowed. "You think they were all Air Druids? All of the attackers?"

He shook his head, a snarl dripping from his lips as he stalked toward me. I had to admit, I was shocked when he knelt down in front of me.

"It's appearing that way," he said. "Did they hurt you?"

He tilted the base of my chin up with his thumb, examining my throat.

"No," I replied.

I could still smell blood. I blinked, realizing there was some on his cheek. Without hesitation, I ran my thumb across the crimson-stained skin. His eyes watched the movement, then met my gaze.

"Don't do that," he whispered, his voice breaking.

Those thunderous irises cleared as if I'd found the eye of a storm.

"I thought it was yours," I said, motioning to the blood on my thumb.

His stern expression loosened, the wrinkles disappearing between his brows. "They didn't even touch me," he replied, pulling a black handkerchief from his pocket and wiping my thumb clean. "But I appreciate the concern."

Salem stood and strolled over to the carriage. Mr. Aven's eyes were glazed over with grey, staring straight ahead as if he had seen the arrow coming. "We're going to have to leave him and the carriage. Travel by horseback. We can't risk moving any slower, or we might be attacked again."

"What about the whole 'formality' thing?" I asked, standing to my feet. I knew we should've traveled on horseback from the beginning. Perhaps he should've listened to me.

"I have a feeling we're not going to be welcomed either way."

He walked over to the horses and unhooked them from the carriage. They were still a little spooked, but it seemed like they had calmed down since the Druids had been dealt with. And after the hound had left. Its image flashed in my mind. Silver eyes. Red ears. White fur.

"Why would the Air Realm assassinate the Ladies?" I asked, walking over to him and running my hands down the horses' necks. Their hearts were beginning to steady, taut muscles unraveling. But was it the Air Druids they feared—or the creature who'd saved me?

"At this point, you know as much as I do."

He gripped the withers of one of the horses and swung onto its back. I followed suit, mounting the other horse and meeting his gaze. There was a moment of silence as we looked at each other, our gazes locked in absolution.

He knew we might be walking right into a trap. He didn't know that I knew far more than he did.

37

*I*t was still dark when the looming white stone castle of Hypnos Keep came into view between the mountain ridges. The fortress was alight with silver torch fire, glimmering like sunlit snow against a wall of black granite. My stomach churned as we raced onwards. Though we were still deep in the Highlands, the horses seemed more than pleased to be through the pass. I wish I could've said the same.

We slowed to a trot in front of gargantuan quartz walls nestled into the base of an imposing peak that rose several thousand feet into the indigo sky. Stars appeared to flutter down from the heavens, dusting the tops of our hoods. A dark ravine stood between us and the entrance, which, almost teasingly, sat wide open. There were several guards stationed there, clad in silver and white armor.

"Who goes there?" one of them called out, hand on the hilt of his sword.

"High King Salem of Arastya and Lady Quinn, Advisor to the King," Salem yelled back. Immediately, the guards straightened their postures and looked at each other as if unsure what to do.

"This is taking too long." My impatience earned a snicker from Salem.

"I will alert Lord Typhon and Lady Thetis of your arrival. Lower the bridge!" The guard's voice was thinned by the falling snow.

I watched in astonishment as the other guards reached toward the sky and lowered a huge piece of stone across the ravine. Salem and I urged our horses onwards. The granite beneath their hooves was coated in ice. I tried to calm them as they slid across the bridge, but the cold silence was interrupted by frantic whinnies until we reached the other side.

"I will request to see Typhon and Thetis immediately," Salem said. "Any delay, and we might be trapped here."

We approached the guards in silence.

"I will take your horses to the stable. Levi will show you into the castle," one of the guards explained.

We slid from our horses' backs, my legs aching as they trembled beneath my weight. My boots slipped on the slick rock, and I gripped the saddle to regain my balance. The guard took the reins from our horses, tugging them off to the south side of the castle. The guard behind him, who I assumed was Levi, inclined his head in acknowledgment.

"Your Highness. My Lady." Levi did not meet our eyes as he turned on his heel and beckoned us to follow.

My boots clicked against the frosted stone as we approached the castle. Each step was a cautious one. I felt like a fawn learning how to walk. Though my eyes struggled to stray from my feet, my gaze lifted to the fortress. It appeared to be a similar quartz to the wall, veins of rose and lavender slicing through an otherwise infallible white.

I listened more closely to Levi's thundering heart, taking note of his tightly wound fists and stiff posture. I gave Salem a sideways glance, and his jaw flexed in acknowledgment.

Levi pushed one of the massive silver doors open and led us

into what appeared to be a smaller version of the Kalystan ball-room. However, while Salem's boasted a pair of giant obsidian thrones at one end, this one did not. Instead, it featured ethereal paintings of soaring Druids amidst lavender clouds and billowing snow. A chandelier composed of thousands of delicate tear-drop crystals hung from the center of the ceiling. Thick quartz pillars with bases drenched in silver lined the length of the glittering hall.

"I will show you to your room," Levi tossed over his shoulder. Straw-colored hair cut to his jaw framed his cherubic face, free of wrinkles and imperfection.

"We see Typhon and Thetis now," Salem said.

His power cascaded across the room, slamming into me with the force of a thundering wind. My knees shook on impact. Levi trembled as he swiveled around, facing us.

"I'm not sure they're available at the moment, your High-ness." His voice shuddered.

Salem shook his head, his expression uncompromising. "I wasn't asking. Tell them I'm here and need to speak with them immediately."

His voice was all too calm for the rage simmering beneath his skin. If we hadn't been attacked on our way here, perhaps the High King would be in a better mood.

Levi's body quivered. He reluctantly bowed his head in concession and hurried off down a corridor.

"Was that necessary?" I eyed Salem, who huffed and straight-ened his bloodstained jacket. I wondered if the guards had noticed—if that had added to their fear.

"I don't think they respect me. The only way to get them to listen was to make them fear what would happen if they didn't," he grumbled.

I recalled him mentioning that he preferred *not* to have his constituents bend a knee out of fear, but it seemed he wasn't entirely averse to it either.

"Do you think Thetis and Typhon will be receptive?" I asked.

Salem adjusted the obsidian crown atop his head as if he'd forgotten it was there. "I have no idea. If it's them behind these plots, then we might get less talking and more fighting," he replied.

"Why would they want me dead?"

Salem's lips fell open as he began to respond but paused when the crack of heels on stone echoed down an adjacent hall. Heels—and *many* footsteps.

The male had slicked white hair and a trimmed beard, eyes like glacial ice glowing against olive skin. His attire was similar to Salem's in style but was as pale as his hair. A cloak billowed behind him as he marched, the only dramatic feature of his otherwise simple attire. The female had hair the color of ash. Her lips were set in a frown, pale eyes fixated on Salem and me. She, too, dressed modestly; a collared white gown swirling with filamentous silver.

Behind them trailed a dozen guards clad in white armor. Pale swords glittering with opaque jewels clanged in their sheaths as they marched obediently after the Aavali Lord and Lady. It seems the High King was right. We were not being greeted on the grounds of negotiation and compromise—but on the grounds of battle.

The Aavali Lord's lips peeled back in a stiff smile. "High King Salem. To what do we owe this *honor?*" he sneered.

A low snarl pushed past my lips, and I grimaced, my jaw clenching tight. This was already going south. Disrespecting the High King was a favorite pastime of mine but doing it in front of others who shared the ill sentiment seemed to border on outright treason.

"Lord Typhon, if you speak to me in that manner again, I'll remove your tongue. Are we clear?" Salem said, his voice deceptively calm. "Dismiss your guard. We speak alone."

Thetis looked to her husband, but the Lord of the Air Realm did not budge. "I will not until I know your intentions."

Salem's heart thundered in my ears, no longer a steady beat. Now, it raged with the fury of a tempest. I tried to center myself, to drown out that fury, but it was difficult when the emotion was shared by everyone else in the room. My breath remained shallow in my throat.

"We were attacked on our way here. Surely you had nothing to do with that?"

Lord Typhon pursed his lips. "No, my King."

The Lord of the Air Realm glanced at me, his eyes a disarming blue. A slow heart stuttered within his chest, the smell of his unease and fury sulfurous in the air. I grimaced. His heart was far too slow—too steady. As if it were *trained* to be that way. Given his anger, his heart should mirror the High King's. But it did not.

He lies.

The words echoed in my mind until Salem stiffened beside me. Lord Typhon's attention shifted back to the High King.

"Have you decided to provide us aid with the Blight?" Lord Typhon asked.

Salem frowned. "Blight?"

Typhon stiffened. "I've sent multiple messengers to Kalys over the last year asking for aid, and they've all returned empty-handed. Our glacier leeks and spinach have stopped growing. Many of my people have died because of you."

This wasn't a lie. Salem swallowed. The guards in the room reeked of a similar fury to Typhon. This was not looking good.

"I haven't received any messages, Typhon. Your messengers never delivered anything to Kalys. I hadn't seen an Air Realm Druid in Kalys until a few weeks ago when Lady Aria was brought in," Salem explained. "But given the opulence throughout your home, I'd think you have more than enough resources to handle the issue."

Typhon clasped his bejeweled knuckles at his waist. "I've heard news that my eldest daughter is being detained within your castle, High King Salem. If you're not here to help my people, I assume you're here to discuss the terms of her release? However, I must confess, I haven't the faintest idea *why* she was detained in the first place."

Again, the smell of anxiety saturated the air and burned in my throat. Despite this, his heart remained slow, his demeanor infallible.

Lies. My lips curled in distaste—though I did not speak. Salem's jaw tightened.

"You lie to me, Lord Typhon. Perhaps you're not as attached to your tongue as I thought." Salem's voice was venomous. "I watched your daughter attempt to assassinate Lady Quinn. I suspect Lady Xandria's death may be her doing as well."

Typhon's jaw fell slightly ajar as he appeared to struggle for words. The smell of his fear in the air was becoming nearly intolerable. Though, given his disrespect for the High King, it was odd that he was so afraid. He blinked, looking around the room, before settling his glacial eyes on me. His gaze did not budge, though his lips spread in a sickly smile.

"Is this her? The beast you plucked from the trees? The one your people accused of murder?" Typhon paused as if savoring the words. "Some of my contacts would pay a pretty price for your head. Attacking the castle and murdering a Lady—though I wouldn't expect less of a Forest Druid."

I did not speak. Neither did Salem.

"Tell me, beast—do you feel lucky to be alive after your people are gone? Or do you wish you'd died like the rest of them—like bloated, plague-ridden pigs?" Typhon's pale eyes glimmered with hate.

The guards behind him laughed.

My throat tightened to the point of pain. The earth stuttered briefly beneath my feet, a barely noticeable nudge. Still, Salem's eyes shifted to me in acknowledgment. He'd felt it.

I gritted my teeth. "Do not disrespect the memory of my people in my presence."

Typhon snorted. "There's nothing to disrespect."

"If the High King does not remove your tongue, I will. Do not test me, Typhon."

The Aavali Lord's lips twisted as he bared his teeth. "You dare call me by my first name? Your lips do not even deserve to speak my name in *prayer*—"

Wind billowed in the hall as he stepped towards me, hands balled into fists at his side. His face was twisted—gnarled like tree bark. He moved to take another step, my heart thundering. My vision bled red as I tugged at the stone beneath me, waiting for him to lunge. I'd seen it before. In the Forest, animals would attempt to intimidate each other in a standoff, a claim for dominance. This disrespectful Aavali male thought he could force *me* into submission. I fumed at the mere prospect.

I blinked when the High King stepped in front of me. His back flexed as power flooded from his skin, shuddering as it swept across the room. Typhon's stance faltered, and he stepped back, narrowing his eyes at Salem and me.

"A Forest Druid—really?" Typhon sneered. "*That's* who you choose to protect? Rather than the people who pay your taxes, who bend to your crown? She is accused of *treason*. She is accused of *murder*."

"If I had received your request for aid, I would have sent it immediately, Typhon," Salem replied. "Your people are also my constituents. Their pain does not give me pleasure. However, you overestimate my mercy when it comes to disrespect. It would be wise of you to apologize to myself and Lady Quinn."

The Aavali Lord scoffed. "I'd die a thousand deaths before you could make me apologize to a Forest Druid. I'd die a thousand and one before you could make me apologize to you."

My chest tightened. I could feel Salem's torrential fury battering the underside of his skin, a tempest roaring in his ears and clouding his mind. The disrespect—*had he been his father, he would've beheaded the male the moment he'd walked in. But he couldn't be his father. He couldn't be so merciless and cruel, despite how much this male deserved it. He couldn't—*

"Dismiss. Your. Guard. Typhon." Salem spoke in deadly calm.

"Or what? What will you do?"

"Dismiss them. Now."

My stomach leaped into my throat when Typhon continued to speak. "I suppose I'm not at all surprised at your treason, Salem. Your father always did say his son was cursed by the gods—a spineless, disgraceful twit. I had encouraged him to disown you, claim that your whoring mother slept with a commoner, and you were born of that union. He, of course, would've done so if it wouldn't have reflected poorly on his choice of wife. It's a shame your father passed. I, and all of my people, wish it had been *you* in that coffin instead. Your *father* was a better High King than *you'll ever be.*"

For a moment, everything was still. Everything was silent, save for the heavy beats of Salem's twisting heart. Nausea coiled in my belly as his pain—*so many years of pain*—battered into me. My knees shook, and bile crept up my throat. What on earth had the High King been through?

Shadows exploded from the corners of the room, blanketing the hall in pitch darkness. I held up my hands but could not make out the fingers. Bile crept up the back of my throat. I knew that smell. Salty, like the ocean, but as warm as a body.

Gurgling noises echoed across the room. Hearts, once thundering and enraged, fell silent and cold. My stomach bottomed out.

And when the darkness fled, revealing the scene before us, I nearly hurled.

Pools of blood, as dark as garnets, reflected the glittering chandelier lights above. None of the guards remained standing. None of the guards remained *breathing*. They all lay mutilated on the floor, their white armor drenched in scarlet as if it were ink spilled across a page. My stomach lurched.

He'd killed them. Salem had killed *every single one* of those guards.

He'd said he'd understood the beliefs of my people—why I was so affected by the bodies of my own guards slaughtered outside my bedroom door—but he clearly did not. Or perhaps he did. And still chose to completely disregard them.

I nearly gasped for breath when Salem finally spoke. "You are correct in one matter, Aavali. *I am not my father.* Though my mercy isn't endless, it is more than he would've given you."

Salem's heart roared with fury. Thetis screamed. Typhon began to shout at Salem, but I could not make out the words. Everything in my mind began to quiet.

Coimét daur.

My breath stilled in my throat. That was my father's voice. Was he here? Were they keeping him captive here?

A female's scream echoed through the hall, pulling me from my mind. Dark tendrils swarmed from the shadows, constricting around the Aavali Lord's body. They swirled as they lifted him from his feet and pried his jaw ajar. The world was suddenly deafening. Every heartbeat thundered, shaking my very bones. The scent of blood soured the air. I could not breathe. I could not—

The female screaming was Thetis—her opulent gown billowed as a gust of wind exploded from her fingertips toward Salem. I did not think. My foot twisted, and a slab of granite erupted from the floor, blocking the assault. Thetis turned to me, her pale eyes absolutely feral.

Still, the tendrils pulled Typhon's lips open.

Then, the Aavali Lady charged. Brisk blasts of ice-laden

wind slammed into me. My feet skidded across the slick floor as I struggled to remain standing. I could not tell if the wind was screaming or if it was her.

A fist slammed into my cheek. Blood coated my teeth.

Quite a right hook for a Lady.

My eyes peeled open, fixating on her. I could see it now—muscles defined beneath the thick cloth of her gown sleeves. She knew how to fight. How or why, I hadn't a clue, but I would not underestimate her again.

This time, when she attacked, I was ready. I used my height to my advantage and swung at her head. When she ducked, my foot connected with the side of her head. She fell sideways, grasping at her balance. I leaped into the air and spun, slamming my foot into her skull. She crumpled, sobbing.

I could not tell if the heart raging in my ears was my own. My body shook. I thought it was the adrenaline. But perhaps it was the screaming that echoed across the room.

Typhon writhed and howled incomprehensibly as Salem stepped towards him, pulling a little blade from the inside of his jacket. It sparkled in the chandelier light like freshly fallen snow. I swallowed. It tasted like blood.

Should I have told Salem to stop? Should I have played the part of a merciful Mediator and pleaded for peace? My father would've. My father would've offered his own tongue in Typhon's stead, regardless of how he'd spoken of our people. Any Forest Druid would've. And I should've. I should've told the High King that too much blood had been spilled already—that suffering could not be dealt with by adding to it. I should've spoken. I should've said something.

But I didn't.

Thetis screamed beside me, frantically clambering to her feet. Her head was bleeding. She fell sideways again, disoriented.

My mind fell to a deafening silence as Salem slid the steel between Typhon's teeth, a dark tendril pulling his tongue out. And I did not blink when Salem's blade sliced cleanly through the pink flesh, as blood splattered his hand and poured from Typhon's lips like drool. I stared at the appendage on the quartz floor—at the growing pool of red that it continued to twitch in. Then, at all of the red Salem had painted in this white room.

My stomach lurched, but no bile came up.

"I will not force a thousand deaths on you. But perhaps now you will understand the power of words, now that it has been taken from you." Salem's voice was soft, almost apologetic.

Thetis's screams seemed to grow quiet, as did Typhon's gurgling cries. All I heard was the blood in my ears, the whisper of a voice in my head that seemed to grow louder by the second. *You're no Forest Druid. Not by blood. Not by heart. Not by choice.*

Salem turned to face me, his hand and sleeve drenched in red. His eyes searched mine. My gaze shifted as he wiped his blade on the hem of his jacket, then slid it back into a pocket on the interior lining. Typhon was crumpled on the floor behind him in a pool of vomit and blood. Thetis appeared to be trying to comfort him. Still, their sobs remained quiet. But I could not tell if they were actually that way or if the absolute chaos in my head had drowned them out.

"I'm sorry you had to see that," Salem murmured.

All I could manage was a nod.

He looked at me for a moment, then loosed a breath. "We should go. Now."

I glanced back at the Aavali Lord, his back arched as he heaved more vomit onto the floor, screaming in agony as bile soaked his wound. Thetis's white gown was splattered in red and brown as she knelt next to her husband. Her once olive skin now matched her hair. She looked about ready to faint.

Salem adjusted the crown atop his head as he strode quietly

past the Lord and Lady. I followed, eyeing the twitching appendage soaked in vomit. *If this was merciful—*

Lady Thetis cried out after us, her voice raw and frail. "You traitor! How could you do this to him? We've tried to reach you, and you couldn't even send us a response! We're not even the ones orchestrating all of this!"

Salem paused. He swiveled, meeting her accusatory glare. "If it isn't you in charge of these attacks, then who is?"

Lady Thetis sobbed. "I have no idea. Typhon was the only one who ever corresponded with them. And now you've taken away his ability to speak." Her tear-stained cheeks glowed beneath the chandelier light. "Guards!" she shouted over her husband's gurgling sobs. "Seize the Traitor King!"

My heart lurched. Cool adrenaline flooded my veins. Salem looked back at me, his eyes wide.

"Now, *wildling!*"

The world fell silent once more.

Coimét daur.

My father. Is it possible he was being kept here? What if this was my only chance to save him?

I could not abandon my mission now. I would not abandon my father. If there was any chance he was here, if this was why the assassins wanted to keep me from him—I had to find him. I had to save him.

I looked to Salem. The earth vibrated beneath my feet as dozens of boots thundered against the granite floor. They would be here any moment.

I swallowed.

I will buy you time—go. I thought as loud as the voice in my head could manage.

Salem's eyes widened. "What?"

I couldn't give up the chance to find my father. If he was here, and I let this opportunity go, I'd never forgive myself.

Guards in polished white armor charged into the room. Salem looked at me frantically. Silently, I raised my arms above my head in surrender.

Leave me, ciarán. It's alright.

His jaw flexed. "You've lost your mind."

And then he bolted.

38

$\mathcal{M}$y hands were bound with silver chains. The links rubbed against my skin as I walked down the corridor, a guard on either side of me. Each had a firm grip on my arm, undoubtedly bruising it. Their fear was palpable. Which meant they weren't completely incompetent. They knew I could've escaped if I'd wanted to. And they were afraid now because they wondered *why* I chose not to.

I'm sure Typhon thought differently. He was not afraid, just in pain. The arrogant male, his lips drooling with blood, thought he'd outwitted me. Captured me. He believed me nothing more than a wild beast with no rational thought. Perhaps he now planned to have me executed—to finalize what *all of his assassins* could not accomplish.

I shuffled along the hall, which was truthfully nothing more than a long tunnel through the mountain. Cold granite surrounded us, doing very little to keep the temperature above freezing. My skin was prickled with goosebumps. Little lanterns lit the tunnel, struggling to remain aflame.

The tunnel fell into a set of stairs, which we descended. At its base was a series of long halls that diverged from this one. A labyrinth. Heartbeats thrummed through the stone, vibrating against the soles of my feet.

We'd arrived at the dungeons.

"This way, Forest Druid," one of the guards said.

They tugged me down one of the tunnels. It grew darker and darker as we walked until I strained to see my own feet. Heartbeats, frail and quiet, fluttered as we passed them by. Each rose and fell in a crescendo. I could not see what held the prisoners, let alone what they looked like, so I had to rely on memory alone. The memory of what my father's heart sounded like. But thus far, none of the ones we'd passed had flared any recognition.

The guards came to a stop, yanking me backward. I fought the urge to unleash myself.

Patience.

The sound of metal creaking as it skidded over stone echoed down the tunnel. I could not see them or what they were doing. A pair of hands shoved my back, and I fell forward, landing on my side. The stone bit into my hip and my shoulder.

"Not going to uncuff me?" I asked into the darkness.

I could still feel the guards there, despite being unable to see them. One of them chuckled dryly. "What's the point? You'll be dead soon enough."

He made a spitting sound, and a glob of wet landed on my cheek. I grimaced. Disgusting.

"*Forest swine.* Your kind should've stayed dead," the other said.

A foot slammed into my stomach, and my body coiled in response. Sharp pain shot through me, crackling every nerve ending. I sputtered. My lips still tasted of blood, but I could not see if it was fresh.

The earth tensed beneath me, poised to strike should I will it.

Another kick landed into my ribcage, and it splintered, my

vision bleeding white. I grunted, gasping for breath. That one—they would pay for. *After* I searched the dungeons. *After* I knew if my father was here or not. I had to stay focused.

Laughter ricocheted from cavern walls, echoing around my head like the searing pain. I coughed. This time, the blood tasted fresh.

Metal creaked again. The stone beneath me vibrated with the movement. One of them fumbled with the metal as if locking the door shut. I clambered forward, struggling on my knees to move. My hands wrapped around frigid metal bars. The silver around my wrists was unfathomably cold.

More laughter echoed down the tunnel, footsteps growing quieter and quieter until I was met with complete silence. Aside from the heartbeats.

There were hundreds. Each beating at a slightly different pace.

How was I to find my father out of all of these heartbeats? There were so many. With my sight gone, it was as if my other senses had taken over. Each heart thrummed in my ears, louder and louder. But my pain was louder than them all. Deafening.

No. I couldn't allow myself to become overwhelmed by this. This was my chance to find my father and free him.

I choked as I pulled myself into a seated position. My body crumbled beneath me, straining beneath its own weight. I folded my legs and sat still. My fingertips pressed into the biting stone. Each breath felt wet against my lips. In and out. In and out.

Ignore the taste of blood.

My mind raced down through the granite, deep into the mountain. Too deep. I wheeled back, focusing on the fluttering life around me. The first was far too slow and felt full of soured greed. I moved to the next, a quick-paced heart stained by pride. Definitely not. The next was inconsistent, skipping every other beat. It drowned in fear. Fear so corporeal, I could nearly taste it. But it was not him. It was not the melodic hum of my father's heart, an ever-steady beat like the tick of a clock. It did not feel like his did—like a drizzling rain as you nestled into branches of thick pine. Calm. Free. Home.

I knew what he would say to me at this moment—if he sat in front of me now like he did those days in the meadow. If I silenced my mind just enough, I could almost see him. Legs folded, eyes closed, forehead momentarily free of wrinkles. His calloused fingers pressed into the soil, chest inhaling and exhaling like the rhythms of the tide.

You were impulsive, he would say. *You did not think.*

I did, I would reply. *I thought about you.*

Did you think about what you would do if you found me? he would ask.

I would rip the world in two for you, I would say. *I'd bring the castle down if it meant you were here. Alive. If it meant I could see you again.*

Then, his eyes would open—the most enviable green. *You see me.* He might touch my hand in comfort. *But now, you must do what you would for me, for yourself.*

One by one, I listened to each heartbeat, felt their pain, and moved on when I realized they were not him. With each passing heart, my own seemed to falter. After a while, my chest hollowed in desperation. I must've gone through hundreds.

My father was not here.

I could've sworn I'd heard his voice, but perhaps it was nothing more than a memory—something brought to the forefront by the adrenaline. Regardless of the reason, my father was not in Hypnos Keep.

I was wrong. I'd been captured—and for nothing.

My throat tightened to the point of pain. I was trembling from the cold. I could not feel my toes anymore. My feet were beginning to grow numb.

Is this how they executed people here—by letting them freeze to death?

It was almost as far from humane as Salem's execution of those guards. I swallowed bitterly. Perhaps he hadn't had a choice. And it might've been a small mercy that he'd cloaked the room in darkness before doing it. But it did not erase the gore from my mind—the smell, the taste, the guilt that coiled in my stomach tighter and tighter until I could hardly manage a breath.

I had to escape. Hopefully, the High King escaped but remained nearby. I might be able to find him yet. How long had I been down here? Minutes? *Hours?*

I cursed under my breath, muscles aching as I pulled myself to my feet. My wrists stung from the chains—biting cold against my now raw skin. If I was going to escape, I needed these off.

I reached down into the earth—to the slumbering presence that lay there. *Please,* I thought. *Give me the strength to escape.*

The earth peered a single eye open, annoyed by my request. *Please,* I thought again.

You know the rules. No death without permission.

I bowed my head. *Of course.*

I stomped my foot into the stone. The earth grumbled as a pillar rose from the ground beneath my wrists. I placed my hands on either side of it, the chain directly in its center. I stomped again. Another pillar sunk from the stone ceiling, slamming into the chain between my wrists. The metal squeaked for a moment, then clinked as it snapped.

My hands dropped to my sides. I rubbed my aching wrists, wincing at the raw skin.

Time to get out of here.

I flicked my hand, flinching at the sharp pain from the movement. A chunk of stone rose from the earth, then slammed into the cell bars. The metal groaned as it yielded to the rock. I did this over and over, bending a hole large enough for me to walk through. I didn't have long. If guards were listening, they *definitely* heard that.

I felt around for the hole I had made, my fingertips nearly numb from the cold. Still, I squeezed between the bent metal bars and into the tunnel. At one end, a faint light glimmered.

My unfeeling feet stumbled beneath me as I broke into a run, charging for the exit. My ribs screamed in pain at the pace, lungs aching for breath. But I pushed on. For the first time, I realized I was using my powers to guide me more than my sight. I felt and swerved around every divot or rock on the ground. My heart raced. Other prisoners groaned as they heard me run past their cells, but I couldn't free them all. I had to free myself. I had to get out of here before the Air Druids tried to finish what Typhon's assassins could not.

I thought I'd remembered the way we'd come, but after several minutes of blind sprinting through the dark, I realized I hadn't the faintest clue where I was. Every corner I'd approached, thinking it would lead towards the light, remained drenched in the pitch dark. I still could not see past my nose. The world was nothing more than black.

Around me, I felt nothing but cold granite and faint heartbeats. I couldn't even feel the guards. Wouldn't I have felt them if I were getting closer? Was it possible I was going in the entirely wrong direction?

I cursed silently under my breath.

What was I going to do?

I peered around the pitch black as if somewhere, a light would beckon me in its direction. My hands clung to the frigid rock wall, gripping every crevice in the stone.

Wait. That was something.

My eyes strained, aching. A faint white light glowed in the dark. Nothing more than a pinprick.

But that was enough.

I charged, ignoring the screaming of my ribs as I ran. The taste of iron clung to my lips like the cool air.

But as I approached the light, it became apparent it was no hallway. It was not even a lantern. And there were two of them. Each no bigger than a pebble. But they stared back at me.

I slowed to a limp. Whatever it was that watched me, I could not feel it.

The sound of panting met my ears. Was it—could it be the same creature from Zephyr Pass? Little more than a meter off the ground, two steel eyes looked back at me through the pitch darkness.

And so I knelt.

The panting got closer. The eyes grew larger.

And though I could not see the creature before me, I knew I was right when it too knelt and pressed a wet nose into my hand. This was the same animal. Though I wasn't quite sure 'animal' was the correct term for what it was.

How had it gotten into Hypnos Keep?

"I'm lost," I whispered to the creature.

I couldn't feel it. I had no way of knowing if it understood me—if it even saw me as a kindred spirit rather than a potential predator or prey.

I winced as teeth latched around my hand. Thick, carnassial teeth. But they did not bite down. Instead, they *tugged*. Gently, like a wolf carrying her pups.

Hesitantly, I stood, allowing the creature to lead me down the hall. As we walked, I couldn't feel its steps or its heart. It was almost as if it weren't there at all. As if I'd made it up entirely. Perhaps Salem was right, and I had gone mad. Though the sensation of teeth and breath against my palm felt too real to be a figment of my imagination.

Its strides were long. I could only tell by the echoing scrape of its claws against the stone floor. It was much larger than any wolf I'd seen and at least double the size of any cu sith I'd ever encountered. All other canines I knew of were diminutive in comparison.

And I could feel those creatures. This one was like a ghost.

We rounded a corner and broke into the light. The sheer brightness of it stunned me, and I raised my other hand to cover my eyes, which struggled to adjust. My eyelids pinched shut, straining.

A staircase came into view, blurry at best. My feet wavered beneath me as I gripped the wall, stumbling up the first few. The creature to my side released my hand, and I grabbed its fur, stabilizing myself as we clambered up the steps. Now, I could get a good look at it.

I was correct—it *was* the creature from the pass.

Its fur was white as snow, a large canine beast that rose to the height of my ribs. Its coat was not matted or coated with grime but was instead as infallible as the clothes worn by Typhon and Thetis. A pair of pointed ears were perked towards the top of the stairs, the tips of each stained crimson. I blinked. It was not blood. The creature's fur was that color, but *only* at the peaks of the ears. Its jaws were massive, framed by pearly teeth, each as sharp as Salem's dagger. It glanced up at me as if it sensed my studying it. Silver irises stared back at me.

My breath stilled in my throat. But the creature returned its attention to the staircase and continued leading me upwards.

My eyes began to adjust to the light, though my head was now pounding. As we neared the top of the stairs, the smell of warm iron stung in my nose. Blood. And lots of it. But there were no heartbeats. We passed through the archway at the top, and I paused. Blood pooled across the floor. But there were no bodies. Perhaps Salem had come this way. Was it possible he stayed in the castle, waiting for me?

I looked back down to the creature who had gently led me from the darkness. But all that remained was a wisp of white smoke, curling like the last breath of a dying candle.

I blinked, my jaw falling slightly ajar. If I was indeed hallucinating, that could pose a problem. But it was a problem I could deal with later. There were more pressing matters at hand. Namely, how to get the *ifreann* out of this place.

Even if I managed to escape the castle, how was I to get back to Kalys without going through the pass? While Salem could still be here, the rational part of me was more inclined to think he'd fled. It was possible he'd left with both horses, leaving me relatively stranded. Perhaps I could steal another horse.

Sensation began to work itself back into my feet. They ached as I ran down the corridor, which was far longer than was probably necessary. I tried to ignore the stabbing in my chest, the inability to take a full breath. After what felt like forever, I finally breached the tunnel exit into the keep.

My chest stung, as did my feet and my wrists. The sudden temperature change was startling. My skin felt hot—as if I'd walked into a desert. My shoes clicked against the quartz floor as I walked, trying to remember which way I'd come from. Grandiose white pillars rose from the ground to the ceiling, which was painted in a similar style to the one I'd seen upon entering the keep. Opulent chandeliers hung down every ten feet or so, glittering like water droplets frozen mid-fall.

No wonder the Aavali were so intent on guarding their mountains. From the looks of it, they were brimming with wealth.

I snuck down the corridor, hugging the walls as I crept along. I hadn't come across anyone else yet. Perhaps they'd all left, going after Salem after my surrender. I peered around a corner, a breath of relief escaping my lips.

The doors. They were right there—right on the other side of this obscenely large ballroom.

A servant was mopping the floor, grunting to himself as he worked. Red smeared around the head of the mop. I swallowed when I realized it was *Typhon's* blood that he was cleaning up. And his vomit.

I had to somehow sneak past him to escape. Or, I could just attack him and run.

But he was only one Druid. And given the lack of furniture in the room, I opted for the latter option.

I rose from my crouched position and strode into the ballroom. The servant looked at me, eyes widening. His heart fluttered in his chest. Pale hair framed his cherubic features.

"You're the—the—"

"Hello." I bared my teeth in a savage grin. "That's the exit just there, isn't it?"

The servant gulped. His legs were shaking. "Don't—don't come closer. I will—I'll fight you."

I raised an eyebrow. "You could. *Or* you could hand me that mop and run for your life."

I took a step to prove my point. The ground trembled, bracing beneath me. The servant jumped. His heart raced faster and faster. I took another step towards the servant, the ground shaking.

That was all it took. He scurried off, dropping the mop to the floor with a thud.

Perhaps being seen as a monster wasn't all that bad.

I hurried over to the mop, gripping the wood shaft and snapping it just above the head. It wasn't sharp, but it would do.

With my makeshift weapon in hand, I ran for the doors.

39

100 YEARS AGO . . .

I grunted as my muscles strained to pull me to my feet. I could vaguely hear men's voices shouting in the distance. Men who had *tried* to kill me. Men that had *tried* to kill my father. Men who very nearly succeeded.

Far too quickly, I turned in their direction, the motion sending me off-balance as the world spun. I may have survived by some miracle, but my body was far from functioning properly. My eyes strained to focus on the humans, which appeared only as dark, blurry figures swaying back and forth, growing larger by the second. By the time I could see them clearly, I realized I was *yet again* in imminent danger. I might've survived them once, but I doubted I'd do it again when I was so weak.

I glanced over to the bag I'd discarded upon my arrival. It looked empty. My treasured bow and quiver were gone, as were the sacks of food I'd stashed. The men had likely ruffled through my bag for any items of use to them. I'd spent *ages* working on making that bow and all of those arrows, even more time perfecting my skill in shooting them. I wondered if I'd ever see it again or if I had to start from scratch. But that all depended on if I could somehow make it out of here alive.

My gaze drifted back towards the rapidly approaching men, throwing vile curses my way. My heart thrummed. I was unarmed and weak, barely conscious as it was. I was severely outnumbered. And the men had *swords*.

Was there any realm of possibility that this ended well for me?

I thought back to the meadow, where I'd felt the dobhar chu through the earth. I remembered how it had stopped mere inches from my face. It could've easily ripped me to shreds had it so desired. But it didn't. I remembered how my father knelt down afterward and continued meditating, yielding himself to the earth. Despite knowing a deadly creature lingered nearby, he *yielded*.

At that moment, every stubborn wall I'd built came crumbling down.

I knelt to the ground and sat, folding my legs. The dry soil cracked and powdered around my fingertips as I dug them into the earth. This land was barren. My eyes landed on the men one last time in resolution. I then pinched them shut, allowing my mind to sink into the earth.

Please. Help me.

For a moment, there was nothing, only the trembling of the earth beneath the men's approaching footsteps and their gruff voices shouting names at me. *Witch. Demon. Monster.*

Something ancient opened its eyes.

The earth shook.

Then, I opened mine.

Chunks of earth the size of wolves swirled around me in midair like moons in orbit, powdered dirt raining to the ground as they flew. I looked at the men, who had stopped their charge and now stared at me in horror.

Monster indeed, I thought. As if he heard me, the pudgy man gulped.

The earth beneath his feet split, a well of darkness gaping beneath him. He screamed for a moment as he fell down into the pit, the earth herself swallowing him whole. My gaze shifted to the other men, who appeared frozen in terror. Their heartbeats raced within their chests, their fear as tangible as a bracing midwinter breeze.

"Run while you can or suffer the same fate as your friend. Your choice."

The voice that came from my chest was one I hardly recognized. Deep. Powerful. Utterly terrifying.

They glanced at each other, each too afraid to make the first move. They didn't want to seem weak in front of their brothers, surrendering to a female—a female Druid, no less. I sensed their resolution before they made the first step toward me.

Wrong decision.

The chunks of rock orbiting me soared towards them. The sickening sound of bones crunching and blood splattering filled the air upon impact. Each stone had hit true, crushing the bodies of the men into puddles of blood, viscera, and splintered bone. The smell of iron was thick in the air, and I fought the bile that crested in the back of my throat.

Killing was against everything my people believed in. By some grace, I lived, but who I was now, I had no idea.

The thought of my father had tears springing to my eyes, blurring the world around me. I held my breath, forcing the tears back down. I would not mourn his inevitable disappointment. I was alive. The earth had saved me. *Danu* had saved me.

Slowly, she returned to her slumber. Though my body now felt vacant, my mind did not.

The realization dawned on me like the sun suddenly peering out above the clouds.

I could feel it. I could feel *everything*.

The trees groaned and stretched at the edge of the forest as if settling into a deep slumber. Squirrels scurried around their branches, frantic as they searched for food to survive the coming winter. Birds nested in the thick leaves, relieved they'd been able to provide for their young today. Grass and moss furrowed their lithe roots into damp soil, desperate for water between the monstrous tree limbs that gnarled the ground. A spider spun its web between two elm branches, annoyed with the droplets of dew that had settled onto its masterpiece.

It was all there, within me, like it always should've been. I felt so wholly myself, like I'd been searching for fulfillment my whole life and finally found it.

With a heave, I pulled my aching body up to my feet. The massive chunks of earth still swirled around me but slowed as they sank back to the ground. Once they touched the soil, they powdered into piles of dirt as if they'd never existed.

"Thank you," I croaked.

Unsurprisingly, I got no response.

I limped over to my bag. As I suspected, it was completely empty. The men had stolen my food as well. I'd have to scavenge the entire way home, and at a limping pace, it would take me ages. I groaned and swung the bag over my shoulder. My feet dragged as I hobbled toward the obliterated bodies of the men. I grimaced at the gory scene, the mere smell making my stomach lurch. I went from man to man, hoping by some small miracle by bow and quiver had escaped unscathed.

To my complete surprise, the last man had his arm outstretched. It remained untouched by the boulder. In his fist, he clutched the shaft of my bow, still intact, as well as my quiver, full of arrows. My cheeks ached as my lips pulled into an elated smile. I ignored the screams of my muscles as I bent down and wrested my prized possession from his hand. I bit my lip to keep from groaning and hung the bow across my chest, the quiver around my shoulder. *Now*, I was whole.

I did not look back as I limped toward the Forest. For the first time in my life, it welcomed me with open arms.

40

rigid air and blustering snow slammed into my skin when I stepped through the doorway. Once again, the world around me was pitch black. My eyes strained against the dark.

"*By Danu*, what is it with these people?" I cursed under my breath.

A hand gripped my arm, and I jumped. Heartbeat. *Salem's* heartbeat.

"You're still here?" I asked, my heart thundering.

"I've kept the entire Keep in shadow since they took you. They're looking for me. We have to go. Now. Which way did the guard take our horses?"

I struggled to remember which direction the stables were. "I think the southern side of the keep."

"Once I release the darkness, they'll come after us. Are you ready to run?"

I heaved a breath. My feet ached. But I had no choice. "Yes."

The world exploded into being around us. Thankfully, it was still dark. I didn't know if I could adjust my eyes to sunlight after all they'd been through.

My cheeks burned in the icy wind, and my fingertips already beginning to numb. We wouldn't last long out here like this. Our feet slipped on the frosted stone as we ran across the courtyard, lit only by the light seeping from the Keep. My heart roared in my ears as bells began to chime.

Salem cursed loudly. "They found us."

"No shit."

We rounded a corner to the southern end of Hypnos Keep, darkened in mountain shadow. The stables were dug into the granite mountain face, with a warmly lit entrance guarded by several armed Druids. I groaned in irritation. Why couldn't this be easy for once?

I dug into the earth and wrenched up stone bricks from the courtyard, flinging them at the guards with a heave. Two of them dodged my assault, charging at us with swords unsheathed.

"Your aim sucks," the High King said beside me.

I shot him a glare, and he laughed—he *laughed*—as if this situation was at all amusing. Dark limbs materialized from thin air, gripping the guards by their necks and discarding them over the ravine.

My stomach churned. My bricks wouldn't have killed them. I should've aimed better. Then they could've been spared.

I pushed those thoughts aside as we shoved the stable doors open. The stalls were lit with an orange glow, each housing a white steed. There were only two black horses in the hall; of course, they were at the opposite end. A single stable hand, a boy, stood shaking in front of their stalls, a dribbling water bucket held in each fist. The buckets fell to the floor, water splashing onto the stone as he held his hands up in surrender.

"They're right here." The boy pointed at the two black horses.

"Thanks." I gave him a grin, and he shuddered.

Salem and I hurried down to their stalls and opened their

gates. They hadn't been unsaddled. My bow and quiver remained hooked on the side of my horse. I sighed in relief.

We clambered onto their backs, gripping their thick manes. The High King glanced at me once before digging his heel into his steed's flank, charging down the stable with a whinny. I followed suit, pleading with my beast to move faster.

Through the stable doors, guards had begun filing into the courtyard. Bows and swords were drawn, prepared to strike us down. My breath caught. I reached down into the earth, eyes widening as an archer adjusted his footing. He was going to fire.

"Salem!" I screamed above the wind.

Then, it all went dark. Again.

I could still see Salem, his horse, my own, and the path before us. We charged on through the courtyard. Earth shifted beneath my horse's feet. We were on the bridge. And they were trying to raise it.

I slammed all of my willpower into the earth. Rock splintered around us, forcing the bridge to stay put. Screams echoed above the deafening wind.

Salem and I charged through the mountain pass, cloaked in darkness. He'd blanketed all of Hypnos Keep in an impenetrable shadow. It swirled around us in a thick, undulating cloud. By the time they saw us, we'd be too far gone—I hoped.

Winds whipped around us as the horse's hooves clacked against gravel and stone. I could only make out the edge of the path beside us; a steep drop, I'm sure. It was jagged, much like the edge of Typhon's severed tongue. Salem charged in front of me as if he could see where we were going through the dark. He probably could, come to think of it. I could feel the pass through the earth, where it began to level into a plain blanketed in permafrost. We were almost there.

The air around us seemed to struggle against us as we ran, every now and again gusting with enough power to blow us off the pass. Our horses faltered, shifting closer and closer to the edge with every gust. The Aavali were trying to kill us. And they'd nearly succeeded several times.

As we approached the plains, Salem's darkness shuddered. Almost as if his hold on it had slipped a little. Was he getting tired?

"Salem?" I yelled over the wind. He didn't look back. "Salem, are you okay?"

Again, no response. I gritted my teeth. The pass leveled, eventually drowning into a sea of ice-drenched grass. I urged my horse faster, though he shook his head in protest. We surged up to Salem's side. He was hunched over, cradling his left shoulder, where an arrow had pierced his chest and remained embedded.

I cursed and reached over, pulling back on his horse's reins and slowing us to a stop. The sphere of shadow encircling us fluttered, and light from the night sky seeped through. The High King's head lolled to the side, his eyes weak as he looked back at me.

"That's a slight issue," he said, voice raw.

Only then did I notice he wasn't looking *at* me. He was looking *behind* me.

I turned. A swirling mass of white clouds dipped down from the sky at the mountains' base. The ground shuddered as it pierced the earth. The wind roared around us, pulling us towards the funnel. My stomach flipped.

The ground continued to shake as it charged toward us. The horses whinnied in fear, stomping their feet. They wanted to flee. I looked back to the High King, his skin pallid and eyes half-lidded.

"We need to run," he heaved out.

I scarcely believed we could. I didn't even know if he could stay in the saddle like this.

I hesitated. "Do you really think—"

"Now! Go!"

Salem winced as he reached over and slapped my horse's flank. The horse whinnied and fled, his feet thundering like my heart in my throat. Hair whipped across my face as I looked back at Salem charging after us. He was hunched over on the creature's back, careening to one side. He was going to slip.

I cursed under my breath and pulled on my horse's reins, turning us around and charging back toward the High King. My steed came to a rearing stop right in front of his, forcing his horse to skid to a halt.

"What in *ifreann* are you doing? I told you to run!" Salem shouted as I slid off my horse.

The ground trembled beneath my feet. I didn't look back as I began walking toward the tornado.

I didn't have a choice. I had to.

We couldn't outrun it, not with Salem in this state. I doubted his power could halt the tornado even if he wanted to. Even darkness has its limits. This was up to me.

"Quinn!" He shouted again, his voice ripped from his mouth as soon as it left his lips. I reached into the earth and felt him adjust atop his horse as if moving to dismount.

My lips twisted as I turned to look back at him. "Do *not* move."

Whatever he saw in my eyes had him frozen. He didn't say another word.

I spun back around, the wind roaring in my ears louder than my own thoughts. It was jarring—how the air around me seemed to vibrate with energy and power. It almost felt alive.

I stretched my mind down into the earth, relishing in the warmth that filled my chest. The world around me fell silent.

What do you need? Her voice echoed in my head, thudding in my chest like a war drum.

I knelt down and pressed my fingertips against the hard earth, frozen solid with permafrost. The earth hummed in acknowledgment, bowing her mighty head and granting me access. My eyes rose from the soil to the swirling mass of white clouds. Wisps of wind accelerated as the twister barreled towards us, fixated like an ellen trechend on a lone doe. Salem's heart raced in his chest, echoing in the back of my mind. That ever-steady heart; now I knew what it took to make it falter.

I stood and stepped forward, digging my heels into the stiff soil. My arms stretched in front of me. The earth tensed under my instruction. I lifted my hands to the sky, my muscles meeting firm resistance as the ground yielded.

The earth groaned. Massive mounds of stone and earth flew into the sky with a deafening roar as the ground gave way. The land continued to shake in protest as I pushed the mountain higher and higher. It shuddered as the whirlwind hastened, speeding towards its new challenge.

My body screamed in agony, blood roaring in my ears as I fought to hold the peak. Gravity tugged and tugged on my creation, begging it to collapse back into the planet's heart. Icy sweat beaded on my brow as a groan wrenched itself from my chest, my legs trembling beneath the mountain's weight.

But perhaps that's the greatest thing about mountains—they move for no one.

No one except *me*.

Pain seared in my arms as the tornado slammed into its side, gouging out boulders from its face and flinging them in its whirling limbs. The earth shook as massive chunks of rock rained down on either side of the peak, the body of the mountain shielding us from the twister's fury. The horses whinnied in fear but did not bolt.

With a thunderous boom, the tornado exploded into thin air. White wisps evaporated up into the sky above. My ears rang in the sudden silence, screaming muscles finally giving in to gravity's temptation. My knees shook as my hands fell to my sides.

With them, the mountain I had built crumbled. As quickly as it had grown, it was now gone.

I heaved an aching breath, turning to face the High King. His eyes were vast and empty—dark as the sky above us. That sharp jaw was set tightly as if he were afraid to open his mouth. His eyes followed me as I hobbled over to him and mounted my horse. My body shook as I heaved myself onto its back, somewhat surprised I'd been able to get up at all.

It seemed I was making a habit of rendering Salem speechless. Or he had a habit of underestimating me. To be fair, however, I wasn't sure if any Forest Druids had ever had the power to make mountains. My father hadn't.

"We should get going," I said. "Can you keep riding, or should I see to that?" I motioned to the arrow in his shoulder.

Salem merely looked at me as if he were seeing me for the first time. The monster he'd let inside was much more than a beast with claws and teeth. I had something much worse than that, something far more deadly.

Power.

41

*S*alem's stance faltered. "How did you do that?"

Something bitter and cold and *far* too akin to fear clutched his chest. It wouldn't surprise me if he did fear me. He certainly wouldn't be the first. Even I sometimes gawked at the energy held within my fingertips. Though the powerful creature inside me seemed endless, my body was far from it. Every inch of my body ached in pain. My muscles screamed in an effort to keep me on my feet.

I held his stare—one so impassive I couldn't tell if it was from fear or reverence. "Aren't you glad I didn't do *that* at the Announcement Ceremony?" I chuckled dryly.

Salem didn't laugh. "You never—I wasn't aware you had that sort of power."

"I wouldn't have shown you if I didn't have to," I replied. "We could not have outrun that with how you were riding."

"I'm sorry I forced your hand," he said. He shifted uncomfortably under the weight of my stare. "Are you going to tell me why you let the Air Druids take you? You were there for two hours. I thought they were going to kill you."

I glanced down at my raw wrists. "No reason," I lied. "Just felt like it."

The High King glared at me. When I met his gaze, he looked away. "You're a poor liar."

The smell of the blood drenching his tunic burned in my nose, and I winced. "You stink." I looked at the arrow bolt in his shoulder. "That'll need to be cleaned."

His expression softened a little. "Yes. I'll have to find a new shirt once we reach the ferry port. And a bandage."

"We're not taking the pass back?"

"If I ever see that pass again, it'll be too soon," he replied.

"Is there no other way back? Preferably on land and not through paths riddled with assassins?"

I didn't like the idea of being on the water for an extended period of time. I couldn't very well use my power atop an ocean. I would be at the mercy of a different god—one that I did not worship. That unsettled me.

He shook his head. "The ferry is very safe."

His posture remained stiff, his heart unsteady. The way he struggled to meet my gaze was a little concerning. Perhaps he was wrestling with the wound more than he was letting on. Or perhaps I really had scared him.

"Were most Forest Druids not able to do that?" I asked.

I walked over to him and offered him my hand. He eyed it for a moment, then took it. I helped him up into his saddle.

"Some could make the earth rumble, but none could do what you just did. None that I ever saw, anyway," he replied. "I'll be fine to ride for a bit. We should get going if we're going to make it to the ferry station by sunrise."

I clambered onto my horse's back, every muscle screaming as if it were about to snap in two. As I settled into the saddle, my aching body slumped forward and gripped my steed's withers. It would be difficult to stay balanced, given what I'd just put myself through.

Salem eyed me for a moment, waiting for my go-ahead. I nodded in his direction, and he clicked his heels against the horse's flank. Despite my weak state, we galloped off towards the flat horizon, a glimmer of gold shimmering on the skyline. My body burned with pain at every jolt from the horse's gait. I watched Salem's form as he ran in front of me—watched him flinch every time he readjusted on the beast's back. The horses were exhausted as well, so we didn't push them very hard. I did my best to reassure my steed that soon he would be able to rest for days, but he didn't like the sound of a boat either. I'd only seen the ocean from a high-up cliff in the Western Territories, watching the selkies on the rocks below. All I'd seen from the sea was tumultuous waves slamming into a rocky shoreline, carving at the cliff face. My gut coiled in apprehension.

However, I was more than happy to be out of the Air Realm's reach. If they sent another tornado thundering our way, I wasn't sure if I had it in me to stop it. I wasn't even sure if the earth would oblige again. She had a notoriously stubborn predisposition and preferred to stay asleep.

Sleep.

The mere thought had my body aching for a bed. Not only was my power drained, but my energy was as well. I couldn't even remember when I'd eaten last. Was it yesterday afternoon or morning? It was difficult to tell if the gnawing sensation in the pit of my stomach was from hunger or anxiety.

As we rode on through the early morning, the shimmering gold on the horizon erupted into fiery oranges and pinks that spread in tendrils across the deep blue sky. Even the waning crescent moon seemed slightly startled by the vibrant display, as it opted to hide behind silvery-white clouds rather than face the dawn.

The closer we got to the horizon, the more I realized that the skyline was not land but water. It reflected all those brilliant colors, glowing like embers underneath the sunrise. I'd never seen anything so vast. It stretched from one end of the horizon to the other, seemingly as endless as the sky. I could make out a faint structure dotted next to the water, which Salem turned us towards. I assumed that was the ferry station.

I looked over my shoulder, loose tendrils of my hair whipping around my face. The snow-capped Arastyan peaks were now a faint dusky blue against the dawn-lit sky. However, I could no longer see Hypnos Keep, which was a relief. The further we were from them, the better.

I knew Salem had been telling the truth when he said he had never heard of whatever Blight Lord Typhon had insisted his people were suffering from. However, it also seemed like Typhon was telling the truth when he said his messengers had returned empty-handed after requesting aid. I didn't begin to know what to make of that situation, let alone the fact that Salem had removed his tongue on my behalf. Sure, he'd threatened to do it when we'd walked in, but it was Typhon's disrespect of me that had the High King reaching for his blade.

Part of me hoped Typhon had seen when I'd yanked that mountain from the earth. That fear had found a home in his heart. That he feared the day he'd see me again. Because wherever they were keeping my father, it wasn't here. And I wouldn't give up until I found him.

The horses began to slow as we approached the small red cabin on the beach next to a long wooden pier. A relatively large boat sat at the end of the dock, dark waves lapping up against its silver sides.

Salem dismounted his horse, and I followed suit. The moment my feet hit the earth, I nearly collapsed. My muscles struggled beneath my weight. Salem cradled his shoulder, the bolt still sticking out of it.

I limped over to him. "Let me fix that."

He glanced down at the arrow jutting out of his shoulder.

"What? You think the ferrymen will know we're fugitives?" He chuckled, but the smile didn't meet his eyes.

I rolled my eyes and stepped towards him. "This is going to hurt."

He snorted as if he didn't believe me. I reached forward and yanked the bolt from his chest, earning a grunt of pain from the High King. I smirked, moving his tattered jacket and tunic out of the way of his bare skin. The Silver Bough hung just beneath his collarbone. It was so close I could touch it.

His breath fanned my cheek as I examined the wound. I swallowed, sucking in a breath. I had to heal him, not steal from him. Even though I wanted to—*badly*.

I stepped back. "When we get wherever we're going, you'll need actual medical attention, or it'll get infected. I don't have any herbs on me. Could you ask the ferryman for some yarrow leaves? Maybe also some liquor."

Salem's throat bobbed, but he nodded. "Yeah. Stay here with the horses until I return."

He hurried off towards the cabin and tugged his dark hood over his head, wrapping the cloak around his tattered and bloodstained clothes. A weight lifted from my shoulders as his power receded from the air, just like he had done in Kalys. I wondered why he didn't just prance around telling everyone who he was. I'm sure we could've gotten tickets for free if he had.

Perhaps he was worried that Lord Typhon and Lady Thetis had put a bounty on our heads. Still, though, he was the High King. Surely the people in the Air Realm would remain loyal to him, even if their local governance was not.

I kept the horses calm as I waited for Salem to return. It took him a few minutes, but he finally did with four slips of paper, a glass vial, and a flask.

"Four?" I asked as he handed me two of the slips.

His calloused fingertips grazed over mine, though I wasn't sure if it was done consciously or not. "One for you, one for your horse," he said.

I hummed and took the glass vial of yarrow leaves and the liquor flask from him. "Bite down on your sleeve," I said, lifting his other arm to his mouth.

He rolled his eyes but obliged, taking the fabric between his brilliant teeth. When I poured the liquor onto his wound, he stiffened, his eyes pinched shut as a groan pushed past his gritted teeth. I tapped some of the yarrow leaf paste onto my finger and dabbed it over the wound, his body flinching with every touch. When I was satisfied, I gingerly pulled his tunic and jacket back over the skin.

"Don't touch it until we can see a healer," I said. To my surprise, he nodded. "Any chance you could barter with the ferryman for new clothes too?"

Salem shot me a glare. His cloak would have to do. I prayed other Druids weren't as sensitive to the smell of blood as I was. The yarrow paste did seem to disguise the metallic odor a little bit. Hopefully, that was enough.

Keeping his head low as he tugged his horse onward, Salem approached the ship. I followed, leading my horse into the pier. His hooves clicked against the rackety wood, and his ears perked as his head swung from side to side, nostrils flaring. I couldn't calm him, though- I felt just as anxious.

I followed Salem aboard, allowing the stable hand to halter the horses. He explained he would take them downstairs to be housed with the rest of the cattle for the journey. I'd frowned, unsure of what conditions the cattle would be kept in, but Salem assured me it would be fine and led me onto the upper deck. There weren't many people aboard- perhaps because it was so early in the morning. Regardless, I appreciated it.

I leaned against the railing, watching the dark ocean waves

beneath us. I couldn't help but feel that whatever had just happened in Hypnos Keep wouldn't be left behind so easily. Just as these ocean waves would grow, so too would the ones we made in the Keep. All we could do now was hope to weather the storm.

42

I woke to burning cheeks and gilded light tugging at my eyelids. The deck radiated warmth like a fire, my skin tender as my calloused fingertips brushed its surface. My eyes adjusted to the brilliant light, straining to focus on the pale sky above, dotted with wispy cirrus clouds high in the atmosphere. The ocean sparkled gold and silver. The domineering waves of yesterday's dusk seemed to have given way to a docile sea. The outline of land jutted from the horizon, a shade darker than the sky around it.

I'd fallen asleep atop one of the wooden benches on the ferry deck, my cloak wound tightly around me. Salem had done the same on an adjacent bench. We were exhausted after Hypnos Keep, and the boat's gentle rocking had lulled me to sleep despite it being dawn when we boarded. I must've slept for quite some time, given it was dawn yet again.

The Western Territories were never this warm. I didn't think I'd ever experienced a day like this one. The forests were cold and dreary; each day met with low clouds skimming the treetops and an occasional drizzle of rain or snow, depending on the season. I had grown accustomed to the ever-lingering wet chill that would ache in my bones, and the lack of its presence was almost uncomfortable.

I let my head hang slack backward as I reveled in the golden sunshine. I felt I now understood why Rhea missed her home so dearly—why her people felt those in the north had no right to rule over them. They lived in an entirely different world, one of warmth, gilded light, and deep breaths of fresh air.

I squinted as I walked over to the side of the deck, watching the gentle waves below nudge against the metal hull. As if on cue, a breathy horn blew from the helm, no doubt a signal from the captain that we would soon be arriving.

Glancing around me, I saw no sight of the High King. He must've risen before me. Maybe he went to check on the horses. I stood still in the sun, closing my eyes and basking in its warmth. The gentle swaying of the boat threatened to put me back to sleep.

A gentle creak of wooden floorboards behind me and a brisk chill trailed across my bare neck, despite the heat. I swallowed, my heart stilling.

"It's nice, isn't it?" Salem's voice broke the silence.

He, too, had his neck craned back, eyes closed as he basked in the sun. I suppose I'd expected him to cower in the sunlight, being the High King of Darkness.

"We don't have sun like this in the north," I replied, returning my attention to the glimmering waves.

"No. No, we don't. It drains me. But it feels so nice; sometimes I can't help myself," he said. "We can't stay in the Southern Isles for long. It's been a while since I was last here, given its distance from Kalys. My object of coming was primarily to check on the territory following the assassination of their Lady. While the reports from Lord Hellas have been good, I need to see for myself."

"So, we weren't just running from the Air Realm? This was

your plan all along?" I asked, a little perturbed that he hadn't initially told me this was also an errand run.

"No, it just worked out that way. However, as a member of my court, this is part of your duties," he replied, raven-winged eyes glinting silver as they squinted through the bright rays.

"I just hadn't expected this to be a long trip," I said. "I hadn't expected much of what's happened thus far."

Salem motioned with an upward tilt of his chin towards the golden land fading into view from the horizon. "There they are. Welcome to Hera, the capital city of the Southern Territories."

Slabs of rock rose from the sea like towers of sand. Some of the islands that passed us by were small and uninhabited by anything other than nesting birds. Hardly anything appeared to grow on them. The soil was as yellow as the sunlight. A large cliff rose from the crashing waves, stretching across the northern horizon beyond the small isles. Slowly, it grew larger and larger until sandstone cliffs jutted into the cerulean sky above us.

I was beyond thrilled at the prospect of being on solid ground again. I hated feeling absolutely powerless out here. I couldn't feel the earth beneath me and hardly felt any life around me. Even the Druids on the ferry seemed blurry.

"That's odd," Salem grumbled as we approached the docks.

Waves crested against the rickety wood, creaking in rhythm with the rise and fall of the ocean. The only other boats docked were coated in rust and grime, tattered sails flapping in the salty breeze. Sour-faced Druids scrubbed away on their docks, blistered skin peeling as they tied filthy ropes into intricate knots and tugged away at the sails. Their skin, though tanned as Rhea's, was pink and peeled across their cheeks and noses. We received a few pinched glares as the ferry floated by—a few snarls of disgust as they saw the fabric of our hoods and the lack of dirt and sweat on our skin.

"What's odd?" I asked, holding the guardrail as the ferry

rocked back and forth, docking alongside the wooden pier with a deep groan.

"This dock used to be a lot nicer," he replied. "Seems to have fallen into disrepair."

He pulled his hood over his head and motioned for me to do the same. I obliged, tugging the fabric over my hair. The braid had fallen out while I was asleep, and the hood refused to stay put over my furious mane. I grappled with it, fighting to keep it in place.

"I thought you said Lord Hellas had everything in order," I said.

Salem's silent glare burned into the side of my face as we walked across the deck toward the lowering loading ramp. "He said he did. Whenever I offered him aid, he refused and insisted they were doing well."

He examined the surroundings as we approached the ramp. As inconspicuous as possible, we left the ferry, our eyes trained low. It was only when we stood on the rickety dock that Salem paused.

"Your horses, sir," a voice grumbled from behind me.

I fixed my eyes on the island as Salem slipped the leathery reins into my hand. The velvety nose of my horse brushed against the back of my arm, letting me know he was there. I smiled and turned to him, running my fingers down his snout. He heaved a breath, perhaps in relief at the sight of land.

I followed Salem and his horse as they walked across the dock toward solid ground. Silvery waves lapped against the golden bluff, dried salt clinging to the rock several feet above the water level. A winding road ascended from the dock through rows of sandstone houses with orange roof tiles. They slithered back and forth across the jagged cliffside like a serpent, higher and higher up the island. Each house was decorated with hundreds of pink and white flowers sprouting from vines across their walls. The distant mumble of village chatter filled the salty air, only muted by the cresting waves.

The moment my feet touched solid earth, I nearly collapsed in relief. I could feel everything again so clearly, from the steady heart of my horse to the silent push of the flowers reaching for the sun. I hated boats, I decided.

I turned to face Salem as he climbed atop his steed, steadying the reins. His face was impassive, brow set in a stiff line. "Lord Hellas will not be expecting us. When we reach his palace, stand behind me and don't say a word. If he discovers you are a contestant, he will be furious, and I'm trying to maintain good relationships with my realms. No one can know who you truly are."

"When do we go back to Kalys?" I huffed and climbed atop my horse. A briny wind tugged on my hood, and I gripped the fabric, holding it still.

"That depends on how well our arrival is received. If we are asked to leave, we will leave tonight. If not, I would like to stay until morning and talk with Lord Hellas about the state of his Realm. Given how poorly the Air Realm treated us, we need as many allies as we can get," he replied, nudging his horse onward. I pressed my heels into my horse's flank as he followed suit.

The horses' hooves clacked against the sandstone bricks that lined the curved road up to town. Though the road had begun as sand at the docks, it hardened into stone the higher we ascended. Waves lapped at the cliffside below us, interrupted only by the mumbling of Druids exiting the ferry. Druids in threadbare cloth, bleached by the sun, filed around us as they descended towards the docks. We were met with curious stares and noses upturned in distaste at our steeds and fine clothing. Though we were draped in hooded cloaks, the quality of the cloth was unmistakable.

The higher we went, the more Druids bustled around us.

Salem's heart stuttered, knuckles white on his reins, when huddled Druids begged us for change. Carts lined the streets, their owners shouting with the bargaining shoppers who tried to swindle more products. Very few of them contained any food. The ones that did carried very little, and I could tell they weren't of high quality. If the Southern Territories were doing as well as Lord Hellas had insisted, why did there appear to be a food shortage and quite a few impoverished Druids roaming his streets? Didn't Salem say that Lady Vara's policies had eradicated homelessness, hunger, and poverty?

Salem nudged his horse into a trot, and I followed, bustling Druids parting for us like a winding river around a rock. We continued uphill through town, approaching what appeared to be a castle composed entirely of sandstone. It, too, was draped in flowers and vines, surrounded by shale walls and a pair of gates guarded by two Druids in gilded armor. As we approached the gate, I watched their eyes fall on Salem and me.

"State your name and your business," one of the armored Druids said, tightening his grip around his golden-plated spear.

"High King Salem of Arastya, I wish to speak with Lord Hellas as a matter of urgency," Salem grunted from beneath his hood. There was a resounding silence following his statement, the two guards seeming almost bewildered.

"Do you have any identification, sir? For you and your companion?" The other guard asked.

Salem angled his head towards the guard and reached up, pulling back his hood. The bitter smell of fear thickened in the briny air, the guard's hearts thundering within their chests. I grimaced.

"A-and your companion, your Majesty?" One of them stuttered.

Salem's jaw tightened, and I could've sworn the temperature dropped. "None of your concern. Open the gates and alert Lord

Hellas of my arrival. The steeds will need food and water as well. See them taken care of."

The guards couldn't seem to move fast enough. They unlatched the gilded gates and swung them open, allowing us through.

The gardens were magnificent. Leading up to the palace was a pathway made of sandstone brick, lined with manicured shrubs budding with white and pink flowers. Palm trees swayed in the breeze above us, and behind the pruned shrubbery sat thriving flower bushels. The flowers in my forest were small and inconspicuous, dotted amongst fields of long grass and thorny bushes. These were proud and bold, saturated in color and velvety petals.

I followed Salem's lead and gripped my horse's withers as I slid off his back. I patted the side of his neck and thanked him for his service. He whinnied a little in response but didn't protest when the guards took him and Salem's steed away. I'd bet they were even more exhausted than we were.

"Keep your hood up for the time being. I don't want Hellas to know who you are if he doesn't already. We can't have a repeat of Hypnos Keep," Salem said under his breath.

"How am I supposed to help then?"

"You're to watch and not say a word," he replied. "If you sense malevolence from him—if you can tell if he's lying—we will discuss it in private later on. For now, I need to keep your identity a secret. I trust you can do that."

My lips fell open, a witty retort on the tip of my tongue. With a grimace, I bit back my words and tugged on my hood. Now wasn't the time to argue with him. I was here as a member of his court and had a duty to fulfill. I was not here for myself, as difficult as that was for me to swallow.

Salem's boots clicked against the sandstone as we approached the gargantuan palace doors, ornately painted turquoise and terra cotta. When the doors swung open, I was surprised to see a male nearly identical to Rhea facing us. Aside from a few smile lines around his eyes and the stubble of hair across his jaw, he was almost her twin. His braided hair glimmered gold with strands of metallic filament, the same shade as his aureate eyes. His sandals flopped against the sandstone as he approached us, turquoise tunic and trousers stark against his dark skin. The rather large grin on his face seemed to be a good sign.

"High King Salem, it's a pleasure to have you at my home." He bowed low, offering Salem his hand. Salem gave him a firm shake, and the male beamed, glancing in my direction. "And who is this?"

Salem flinched. "Miss Isbeth is Lord Kyro's assistant. She's been helping me while my advisor is away." The Lord of the Southern Territories seemed satisfied with this answer, so Salem continued. "You're looking well, Lord Hellas."

"The weather's been good this year, and we've had a plentiful harvest. I feel well, my King. How is my daughter? Is she doing well? Her mother's passing was—it was devastating to her especially." Hellas's face fell. "I appreciate your haste in sending Vara's body back to Hera in time. She was laid to rest and received her rites without any issue."

Salem's throat bobbed for a moment. "I'm relieved to hear that Lady Vara was laid to rest. May Lugh preside over her soul with Arawn," he replied. "As for Lady Rhea, she is well. She has been readjusting to life in Kalys comfortably, and I've ensured she has access to anything she could want."

"Good. Well, as much of a pleasure as it is to see you, my King, I must say I am surprised at your arrival. What brings you this far south?" Hellas asked.

Curiosity burned off his skin like sweat. While he gave the appearance of a calm demeanor, his thundering heart and tight posture gave him away. Something seemed wrong here, as well.

Salem's jaw flexed. "Perhaps we should discuss this sitting down."

43

100 YEARS AGO . . .

*T*wo nights passed as I trekked through the forest, my aching body restricting me to a snail's pace through the gnarled roots and branches. I couldn't pull myself up a tree at night, so I slept at the base of them—or I tried to. Every sound of a heartbeat, every tremble of the earth set me off. Yet, the most I'd come across was a doe munching on some moss. For whatever reason, it seemed the beasts had left me alone.

My newfound connection with the earth had me stopping at every sound of a heartbeat in the bushes. It was impossible to stay focused. It seemed my prior apprehension was warranted, as my mind was now occupied with the sounds of all the life around me. I could easily drown in it.

By the third day, my body seemed to have gotten a little kick of energy, so I moved a little faster. I still wasn't sure how I'd been able to heal from the surplus of wounds I'd received at the hands of those men. I'd *felt* that blade pierce through my stomach, the unmistakable pain between my legs, and all the bones shattered throughout my body. I *knew* what had happened to me was real. I wondered if I'd ever forget that pain. Yet, I was somehow alive, and the only thing I had to show for it was a white scar running down my belly.

Part of me wanted to know what had happened—if I'd been blessed by Danu or if it was a form of Forest Druid magic my father had never mentioned. I doubted the second. If my father had a mysterious healing power, I suspected he would've used it. He *did* say that some Druids were blessed by the gods with magic beyond what others had. Perhaps I'd been given magic over healing. I'd have to ask him when I returned home—if he didn't disown me first.

I tried not to think about the punishment I knew awaited me upon my return. I'd disobeyed the cardinal rule of Forest Druid magic. I wondered if my father would still look at me the same way—if after I told him what they did to me, he would still see me as his daughter. At the same time, I wasn't the same Druid who'd left him. Trauma weighed heavily on my shoulders. Every time I closed my eyes, they were there—grimy hands gripping my skin, dull blades stabbing through muscle and flesh. I flinched.

No—I wasn't the same. Perhaps it was foolish to think my father wouldn't see that.

Even though I was healing, the thick underbrush was difficult to get through. Branches reached across the thicket, forming impenetrable webs I had to work around. It was full of thorns and sharp twigs that stabbed at my already vulnerable skin, protesting my journey. Even as I pleaded with the earth to move them out of my way, they stubbornly remained. I suppose my powers had a limit.

The closer I got to my home, the more I realized I was no longer alone. More and more heartbeats echoed in my head as I pushed on, as if a growing number of creatures had decided to follow me. But as I looked around, they were nowhere to be seen.

It was easy to see how Druids and mortals could get lost in these woods. Every direction looked the same, thick with gnarled branches and underbrush. Dappled light bled through the leaves and branches above me, the air heavy with humidity and blossoming flowers. The Forest's floor was soft beneath my aching feet, damp with recent snow melt.

My head roared with a multiplicity of thrumming hearts. The sheer number of creatures around me made me wonder if they could somehow sense my power and were warned off. They took no issue in approaching me prior to developing my magic. I wondered if it was different for others—if the beasts devoured the ones that didn't scare them. If that was the case, I wondered what those beasts saw within me. Maybe they saw something I didn't.

After days of limping through the Forest, I broke through the trees into the meadow at the base of the tree I'd left my father at. When I saw his figure, hunched over a mortar and pestle, I couldn't stop the heart-wrenching whimper that escaped my lips.

Immediately, he spun around, emerald eyes wide as he stared at me.

"Quinn," he whispered, voice breaking as he spoke my name.

I dropped my bag and the bow from my shoulder, ignoring the protests from my body as I ran towards him and felt his arms wrap around me. I couldn't stop the sobs that wracked my body as he held me, his hands holding my head as if it were the most precious thing in the world.

I was home. Finally, I was home.

When I pulled back from his embrace and looked up at him, he frowned as he wiped the tears from my cheeks.

"There is shame in your heart, Quinn. Why?"

I knew he would be able to tell. I never could've hidden it

from him, even if I had tried. For some reason, it didn't surprise me that the first question he asked was not about where I'd been or what I'd been doing but why my heart was upset. That was who my father was.

"I went after those men that hurt you. They nearly killed me. I thought I was dead, but I—and then the earth, she helped me, and I—"

"You killed them," he said in absolution.

I swallowed. Then I nodded.

44

I sat next to Salem's chair in the Great Hall, a massive room with golden archways and gigantic windows overlooking the sea. Hellas sat at the opposite end of the long table from Salem, munching on some strange fruit I'd never seen before. The Lord of the Southern Territories made no further comment on my accompanying Salem, which was to our benefit. Any malevolence from Hellas I could report immediately.

"So, Sire," Lord Hellas said. "What is it you would like to discuss?" He raised a golden chalice to his lips and gulped down the liquid.

"Your docks seem to be in quite the state of disrepair," Salem began. "I understand your late wife, may she Rest in Peace, had eradicated all hunger and unemployment in recent years. Yet, when I rode through your streets, it was apparent that that wasn't true. Why not ask for financial aid? That is the purpose of the crown, Lord Hellas."

I munched on some baked pastry I'd never seen before. It was filled with an odd fruit paste that stuck to the roof of my mouth.

Hellas adjusted his posture in his seat. "Your Highness, I don't quite understand, I'm afraid. Lady Vara had made it her mission to eradicate those afflictions of our Realm, yes, but she hadn't succeeded yet. Not to call into question your intel, Sire, but we had never sent anything that would convey that. Also, we sent you numerous letters asking for aid after we were hit by a severe storm this past summer. We have received no response."

Salem's heart lurched. A cold claw tapped against my mind, scratching at the surface of my consciousness. Nausea coiled in the pit of my gut at the sudden presence.

I have not received a single letter from them, nor did I receive any from the Air Realm.

I looked back up at Hellas. He had stopped chewing and maintained eye contact with Salem as he drank from his goblet.

"I have not received a single message from you within the last half year, Hellas," Salem replied. "The last message I received had explained Lady Vara's eradication of your societal afflictions."

Hellas leaned back in his gilded chair and drummed his fingers against his arm. His metallic hair, albeit braided, shimmered in the daylight like the refractions of light beneath a river. It was identical in shade to Rhea's.

"How could that be the case?" Hellas asked. "My messengers returned empty-handed every time I sent them." The room was silent for a moment before he spoke again. "Let's ask them, shall we? I would love to resolve this misunderstanding now that you're here in person. It's much easier than corresponding through the written word."

"I agree," Salem said.

Hellas clapped his hands, and a dark-skinned, golden-haired male hurried out from an adjacent hallway. "Elias, find Aro and Kahlia for me, will you?" Hellas asked. The male gave a quick nod before scurrying off as quickly as he had come.

Once again, a sharp claw trailed across my consciousness. Bile crawled up the back of my throat. *You tell me if they're lying.*

Despite how much I despised obeying his orders, it was odd that the Air Realm *and* the Light Realm had tried asking Salem for aid but received none. Typhon wanted help with the Blight, and now Hellas wanted help repairing Hera after a storm. Salem wasn't lying when he said he hadn't received messages from either Realm. Someone *had* to be interfering. Whether that was on a broad scale, encompassing both Realms, or if someone close to Salem was betraying him—remained to be seen.

Elias scurried back into the room, followed by a male and a female. The male's skin was similar in shade to Salem's, but his hair was the color of spun gold. His heart wavered, throat bobbing as his tawny eyes fell upon the High King. The female kept her head bowed, eyes fixated on the bricks her graceful feet skirted across. Her iridescent hair drifted in a nonexistent wind, stark against her dark skin. While her features were as cherubic as Aria's, she appeared as ethereal as Xandria. When both had approached Lord Hellas sufficiently, they hinged at their hips and swept into bows.

"Aro and Kahlia, High King Salem insists he never received the messages I sent you to deliver to Kalys over the last several months. Care to explain why he believes this to be the case?" Hellas asked, popping a small, round fruit in his mouth.

The male spoke first, and I honed my focus on his heart. It thumped calmly in his chest to start but sped as his lips fell open. "Each message was delivered to the guards at the gate to the Kalystan Royal Palace, Lord Hellas," he replied. "I haven't the faintest idea why His Highness believes otherwise."

I nudged Salem's leg with my own. *Lie,* I thought as loudly as I could.

Salem's jaw flexed, but otherwise, his expression remained impassive. I didn't have to feel through the earth to recognize his budding fury. The High King's gaze shifted to the female next to the male. Her gaze lifted, a pair of crystalline eyes settling on the High King. The resemblance to Xandria was jarring.

"What Aro says is true, my Lord," she said.

Her heart stuttered a moment, throat tight as she swallowed. The acrid smell of fear seeped into the air though no ill intent had laid claim to their hearts. Lying to the High King, I'm sure it was classified as a sort of treason. But still, whatever their reason—*it was not malevolent.*

I nudged Salem's leg again. He swallowed.

"High King Salem, perhaps you should question members of your own court," Lord Hellas said, folding his hands atop the table. His gilded eyes flicked to me. "You never know when someone you trust is lying to you."

Did he mean me? Did he know about my father? Was Hellas the one behind all of this? Had he orchestrated the Air Realm's treason?

Salem slowly turned back to the messengers. "Describe their uniform. The guards you claim you gave the messages to." I could taste the venom in the air the second the words left his lips.

The female parted her lips as if to speak, but nothing came out. The male filled in for her when he noticed she was struggling.

"Dark. Swirling designs on the metal." His voice wavered, sweat beading on his brow.

Salem's lips twitched. "Name the color of the tunic they wear beneath the armor. You would've been able to see it."

Goosebumps pricked at the surface of my skin as the gilded light in the room darkened ever so slightly.

"Black," the female replied.

Her male counterpart glared in her direction. Lord Hellas's gaze turned back to Salem. The High King's heart rate slowed as if he were trying to keep calm. And failing. Miserably.

Salem leaned back, hands resting on the armrests to either side of him. "Your messengers are liars. My guards wear blue tunics, all of them. They have for the last year. My sister decided to implement a new uniform policy."

Though the High King's stature might portray nonchalance, the white knuckles hidden beneath the table told me all I needed to know about his true feelings.

Hellas's throat bobbed. "Is there not a chance some of your guards decided to wear black tunics instead?"

"No."

The Lord of the Southern Territories turned to the male standing next to the messengers. "Elias, take Aro and Kahlia to the dungeons to await trial for treason." He looked directly at Aro and Kahlia. "I entrusted the well-being of my Realm in your hands. You both have failed me. You have failed my people."

"Wait." Salem held up a single hand, and Elias froze. "You will tell me why you chose not to deliver the messages."

The male glanced at the female, who turned and met Salem's fierce gaze. "From death—divine will be," she replied.

Xandria.

Xandria had mentioned that before. When she was reading through the archives. But she didn't know what it meant. Is it possible that *that* is why she was killed?

Salem's heart lurched in his chest, thundering as Elias escorted the two Druids from the room. The Lord of the Light Realm paused, his throat tight as he waited for the echoing of footsteps to fade. Then, when we were met once more with silence, he spoke.

"Is he referring to the prophecy, sire? No common Druids have had access to that prophecy since its conception."

"You know nothing of sharing the prophecy with your people?" Salem's knuckles blanched as he gripped the ornate wooden armrests.

"It would promote civil unrest, Your Majesty," Hellas replied.

"I swore an oath, like every noble, to keep it hidden from the public."

His heartbeat remained steady, albeit furious. I had no idea what prophecy they were referring to, or why the statement about death was so reactive. Was what Xandria had read a prophecy? Why would they want to keep it hidden?

Salem glanced at me, and I gave him a slight nod—barely noticeable. His grip on the chair relaxed. He knew Hellas was telling the truth.

"Very well. It seems someone has been spreading anti-monarchy propaganda to your people. I would see to it that the prophecy is explained away as a falsehood—something that does not exist," Salem replied, interlocking his fingers in his lap. "In the meantime, I shall send you whatever funds and support you need to help your people. Put your requests in writing, and I will leave with them today; send aid likely later this week."

"I'll release a statement today, Your Highness," Hellas said. "I appreciate your assistance. I can assure you that any correspondence from this point forth will be ensured to reach you."

Salem was furious—that much I could tell. The rage in his chest swelled like a tempest, battering his ribs with every labored breath. His hands balled into fists beneath the table. Tendons flexed as he clenched and unclenched them.

The Air Realm's messages about a Blight had never reached Kalys, and neither had the messages about the storm hitting the Southern Territories. Someone had, however, sent a message to Salem, falsifying the drastic changes Lady Vara had imposed on society. Perhaps it had been made to ease Salem's worries about a lack of correspondence between the Realms. Whatever the reasoning, the forged message had apparently done its job.

Salem stood up from the table, dusting off his clothes. "Very well. If that is all, Lord Hellas, I shall be on my way momentarily. Write down your requests. I will leave as soon as you're finished."

Lord Hellas did the same, bowing his head low before hurrying off down the hallway Elias had taken the messengers.

Salem's eyes remained fixated on the corridor Hellas had scurried down. "We'll ride home today," he said under his breath. "With tensions rising in the Realms and one Lady already assassinated, I must send the Ladies home. It is wrong to keep them in a cage when these misunderstandings could cause an outright war."

My heart skipped a beat for a moment. Would he be sending me home as well? I hadn't uncovered the truth about what had happened to my father yet. I had no idea where he was. If he wasn't being kept in the Air Realm, despite the Air Druids acting as the assassins, and Hellas did not know anything about the messages being interrupted before today—I was at a dead end. But my father had to have gone *somewhere*. I could not return to my Forest without knowing where—and there was a chance he still lived.

"You're sending us home?" I asked.

"Not you. I must insist you stay. I know I'd said before you could return home whenever you wished, but you're far too useful to me right now."

It was as if he'd read my mind, though I'd felt no claws against my subconscious.

Hellas hurried back into the room, his sandals scuffing against the sandstone floor. "Here you are, Your Highness," he said. "Once again, I sincerely appreciate your assistance, and I will eradicate the propaganda as soon as possible." His heart thumped like a rabbit's foot against the earth.

Salem appeared completely calm despite his rage. "I will speak to you again soon, Hellas."

Salem shook Hellas's hand before heading back down the way we had first come. While I was content with the fact we were heading back to Kalys—back to Orion and Rhea—it was becoming all too clear to me that whatever mess I'd found myself at the center of was not going away anytime soon. But what did my father have to do with any of it?

45

*O*nce we were out of Hera's city limits, I yanked the godforsaken hood from my head, relishing in the breeze that blew through my curls. Salem hadn't said a word since we'd left. I suspected he was distracted by the prospect of treason rampant throughout the kingdom. The self-loathing radiated off of him in thick syrupy waves. I shuddered when they'd crash into me, leaving a bitter taste on my lips and an ache in my bones.

Still, I understood where he was coming from. I, too, might've blamed myself if I were in his position. People needed his help, and it was his responsibility to provide that. However, it wasn't his fault that the messages requesting aid were never received. That fault belonged to someone else entirely—but who, we had little idea.

The horses were getting tired in the hot sun, and we'd been riding for hours, just now able to see the faint outlines of trees dotting the skyline ahead. We were heading along the Southern Road towards Kalys. Despite being fairly manicured and appearing well-traveled, we hardly saw any other Druids. Salem attributed the lack of travel to the blistering heat.

"Do you think the Ladies will be upset with my sending them home?" Salem asked, his gaze fixated on the horizon ahead.

Darkness hung heavily in the air like the damp cold of midwinter in the forest. Shadows seemed to pulsate around the High King and his steed, thumping in sync with his slow heart. The tight leash he usually maintained on his power seemed to have slipped. He sat slumped atop his saddle, fingers loosely gripped around the reins.

"Perhaps. But it's for their best interest," I replied. "They're most likely going to ask when they can return and continue to compete. I'd be prepared with an answer for that."

"I don't *have* an answer for that. Tensions are rising now. I don't feel comfortable keeping the daughters of my Lords hostage in my home when *their* homes are in turmoil. I cannot rule selfishly. *I won't.*" He bit out the last two words as if they were acid on his tongue.

"I would abolish the competition altogether if we're being frank," I replied. "There's no place for it now, nor was there ever. You should be free to choose if you should marry or not, just as I should. Just as everyone should."

I placed my hand alongside the powerful neck of my steed. Though he appeared to be the same breed as Salem's Nuin, his coat was a charred grey rather than pitch black. Speckles of silver hair bunched between tufts of black were evident now in the beating sun. He was much quieter than Scáth had been, and I'd yet to get his name, despite having been on his back for the last six hours.

"It's not that simple, Lady Quinn. There must always be someone of Kalystan descent on the throne."

"Why?"

"It was a condition of the blessing given to my great-great grandfather when he received the Diaverita. The peace and prosperity of the potion will only last as long as Kalystan blood remains on the throne. Perhaps that's why all of this is happening—because I've waited too long to take the potion, to take a wife. I have to bear heirs to continue the line. It's why there are only females competing for my hand, despite the fact I'm attracted to all genders."

"What about Stella? Should you not marry and bear an heir, she could," I replied.

Salem shook his head. "Stella is in love with a female Druid. She will not bear a child. And I will not force the crown *or* the bloodline on her."

Violet rings hung beneath his eyes, stark against the yellow pallor of his skin. It appeared the consistency of worn leather, hanging loose from his angular bones as he stared blankly ahead. Salem did say that too much time in the South was hard for him, and that was without the unity of a kingdom hanging over his shoulders.

"What makes your blood so special?" I retorted.

My horse's graceful ears flicked back towards me, a snort heaving from his chest in amusement.

"We are the only ones permitted to drink the potion. If another tries to drink it without being wed to us or having Kalystan blood, they will die. Diaverita is the *Kalystan* divine right to rule. It cannot be taken by a different bloodline. Arastya would fall." Salem fought to speak clearly, but some of his words slurred as if he were drunk.

"What about Zora? Or do you have another cousin?"

"Zora is from my mother's side. Not my father's, which is the Kalystan side," he replied. "She is my only cousin."

I narrowed my eyes at him and tugged on my horse's reins, his head rearing back as we trotted to Salem's side. I reached over and pulled back on his reins, earning an icy, albeit exhausted, glare.

"What are you doing?" he asked, baritone voice raw.

The male that pranced through my Forest with such disrespect now appeared nothing of the sort. He looked weak and feeble—on the verge of crumbling.

"You're going to pass out if we keep riding," I replied. "I'll get us some shade until nightfall. Then we can ride through the dark when you're coherent."

If Salem had tried to protest, I couldn't tell. His breaths grew quieter by the second. I slid off my horse's back and pressed my fingertips into the dry earth. *I need your help.*

The earth groaned beneath my feet for a moment, and I stepped back, pushing the horses with me. Salem wilted like a flower in his saddle. Such dramatics.

A crack resounded as a massive oak tree sprung from the dry ground where I'd only stood a moment ago. Its leaves were a brilliant green, glimmering like gemstones in the golden light. The foliage was thick, providing cool shade over the parched earth. I tugged the horses' reins, pulling them beneath the shadow.

"Please stay," I whispered to the horses.

They huffed in agreement, lowering their heads in much-needed rest. I approached the side of Salem's steed, reaching up and peeling him from the hot saddle. As his weight shifted to me, my nimble muscles struggled to hold him, and I haphazardly set him on the ground with a huff.

"How did you—the—green?" Salem slurred, lazily pointing at the dense leaves above us.

I heaved a deep breath and sat beside him, resting my head against the oak's gnarled bark. "I asked."

I'd never confessed that to anyone. Even my father didn't know I spoke to the earth, let alone the fact she sometimes listened. I'd only felt comfortable telling Salem now because I doubted he'd remember anything I said. Sure enough, when I glanced over at him, his eyes were shut, chest heaving up and down in steady, deep breaths. Fast asleep.

Glancing across the horizons around us, I could only make

out the faint hills and trees of the Western Territories to our north. Everything else was flat grassland, void of any defining features. It was no wonder there was hunger in Hera. It surprised me that anything grew out here at all in the barren soil. Even as the earth had willed it, the tree struggled to take root beneath me. It had protested, hesitating before reaching up from the ground. I knew the tree would likely starve and die in the following weeks, but it was my hope that earth would simply take what she had given when I no longer needed it. She'd done that with the mountain when I'd wrenched it from the ground; why shouldn't she now?

I pulled myself from the ground and reached into the saddle bag on Salem's horse, pulling out a water jug. I poured a little into my palm and gave it to each horse. It was only a tiny amount, but their throats were as dry as the land around us. The grass was dry and brittle, and they hated it but munched anyways to satiate the gnawing in their stomach.

"We should be home by tomorrow. I appreciate your hard work." I said to them, running my hands up and down their noses.

They both closed their eyes as if to thank me for being kind to them. They were overheated, and their muscles ached beneath them. They'd needed the shade as much as Salem, it'd seemed. I hoped that once we reached the Western Territories, we might find a creek for them, maybe some lush grass.

Hours passed as I sat beneath the oak tree, waiting for Salem to wake. Only when the sun kissed the horizon did he shift, eyes flickering open.

"What happened?" He groaned, holding a hand to his forehead and wincing in pain. "I feel like I've had too much wine."

"The light was draining you. You passed out for a few hours. I was hoping you'd be ready to ride again by sunset so we could go through the night," I replied, patting the side of my stallion.

Salem's brows pinched together in thought as he heaved

himself from the ground. Then he turned to me, eyes once again swirling with smoke. His skin had regained its usual vitality, violet rings absent for the first time in weeks.

"Thank you. I don't even remember seeing this tree. You must've searched for quite some time," he said. "I should be ready to ride through the night if you are."

I pressed my lips together and gave a quick nod, clambering into the saddle once again. Salem did the same, his body no longer wilting beneath him. As we rode to the north, I glanced back at the tree, noting how it shimmered silver beneath the dark. It stood for a moment longer, then shook as the ground swallowed it whole.

46

100 YEARS AGO . . .

$\mathcal{M}$y father sent me to the Arastyan mountains after I confessed. When I'd asked if he was disappointed, he'd shaken his head.

"It is not for me to be disappointed in you," he'd said. "You're a Forest Druid now, and you must make peace with the earth. I do not have an opinion on your actions, and I do not get one. But you are my daughter, and your heart's truth is always safe with mine."

So, he'd sent me, alone, to the mountains for two weeks.

He told me to make peace with Danu, ask her for forgiveness, and meditate on what I could've done differently. He was worried that the earth would not forgive my transgressions and could infect me with the same Plague that killed off other Forest Druids. I hadn't argued with him. I knew I'd done something terrible, even if it was in self-defense. Killing was against everything I now stood for, everything I'd suddenly become.

I'd gone up into the high peaks of the Arastyan mountains

with nothing more than my bag, bow, and quiver. A shallow cave hollowed the mountain's face near its peak, protecting me from the blustering snow and screaming winds. My thin tunic and trousers did little to shield me from the frigid cold. As far north as I was, I could've been close to the western border of the Northern Territories, where darkness swallowed the day. When the sun hesitantly broke the horizon, I drilled holes into the ice and shot arrows tied to string at fish that swam by. With each one, I thanked them for their sacrifice, as was customary for my people.

The remainder of my time there was spent alone in the dark of my cave, meditating. I'd sat cross-legged for hours upon hours, never sleeping. When the sun rose, I'd go fish. When it set, I meditated until it rose once more. By the end of the two weeks, my body was weak and thin, but I'd developed a keen awareness of the earth. The meditation allowed me to seek forgiveness from the gods and the earth and ask them how to avoid making the same mistake in the future.

You must only kill with our permission, was the sanction I'd been told. The principle tenant—one that must be obeyed at risk of alienating Danu entirely.

I do not want to kill at all, I'd replied.

That is not your future. You will take life, and life will be given for yours. There is no avoiding it. There is only asking permission.

I hadn't questioned further. I was lucky enough to be alive and unpunished by the gods. I wasn't about to push them. They'd done far more than enough for me, providing me with the power to protect myself, and, I suspect, allowing me to heal when I'd faced death. I promised them that, in return, I'd defend their forest fiercely, protecting all that dwelled within it. Though I'd received no response, I suspected that it pleased them.

After two weeks of solitude, I descended the mountains to the river banks my father had told me to meet him at. He'd migrated further north with the turn of the seasons. It'd gotten progressively warmer as I went, the sun seeming to linger in the sky a little longer with every step south. When I arrived, the high-altitude flowers of spring were in bloom. Late spring. My father had been thrilled to see me, to hear of my conversation with the gods and the earth, that they had forgiven me, and that I wasn't about to die from the Plague. He said we would go berry picking that night to celebrate, as it was a full moon. With the cool breeze following me down from the peaks, my father said the beasts were unlikely to be out. They despised the cold, and the moonlight made them easier to see. Tonight, we would be safe.

a cool breeze billowed through the pines from the moonlit Arastyan mountains, carrying with it the smell of blooming wildflowers and frosted dew. We were hunting for berries tonight when the predators remained in their dens under the full moon. After spending weeks in the mountains living on only fish, I was thrilled to eat something sweet. The forest seemed to buzz with life around me, welcoming me back home.

I'd just picked a strawberry from a thick bush when we heard a twig snap from several meters away. My father held a finger to his lips, silencing me.

That had been when we saw them. Men—riding on the backs of massive draft horses shredded their way through our forest. With every slash of their sword, I winced as if I had lost a limb each time a tree did.

My father demanded I stay back in case they attacked, commanded I remain unseen until he returned. And I listened. I climbed a pine tree and perched on a thick branch, watching through the needles as my dad approached the pack of men.

"—Forest Druids might still be 'round these parts. Keep 'yer wits 'bout ye," one of the brawny men hollered over his shoulder at his companions. The others mumbled in response.

They were hideous creatures. They all had thick, stout bodies and burly beards that seemed as unrefined as their voices. Their beady eyes peered through the thicket as they sliced through it with abandon, carving through my home. Hideous creatures—inside and out.

The forest was our home. These trees had seen kingdoms rise and fall, men wander aimlessly through them, never to return, and wars waged by ancient races that no longer existed. Even before my connection with the earth had formed, these trees were my teachers, my shelter, and my ground. Seeing these men shear through them like they were nothing wounded me.

My father inched closer to them, his footsteps as quiet as a doe across a field of moss. He had taught me well, my movements just as silent as I readjusted on my branch.

Snap.

A twig gave way underneath my father's foot, and my heart stuttered. The mighty draft horses beneath the burly men paused, stamping their hooves in protest as the men yanked back on their reins.

I could do nothing but watch as one of them, olive-skinned with a black beard speckled with grey, clambered off his mount and yanked my dad from the bushes.

"Hopin' to catch us while we slept, didja? Scavenge for food or money? Worthless tree lover, 'yer kind don't have no power no more," the oafish man heckled. "Hidin' 'mongst the bushes and eatin' nothin' but berries and leaves. Let's see what the king has t'say 'bout 'yer wretched self."

He easily tossed the willowy body of my father over his shoulder.

Tears budded my eyes as I began to scramble down from my tree. My father looked up at me one last time, meeting my gaze through the pine needles and shaking his head once, telling me not to follow. I hesitated but began to descend again.

No.

A deep voice rumbled through my bones. I trembled against the bark. That voice had not belonged to me, my father, or the men. It was the same voice as the goddess in the mountains. Unyielding.

Still, I moved to clamber down again.

No.

Louder this time, if it were even possible. Branches began to coil around my legs and arms, pinning me to the tree. I wriggled against them, but they remained intact. I wanted to scream. I wanted to tear my body apart. I wanted to shred the world into pieces. Anything—anything to get to my father.

But I didn't. I remained silent.

And the world remained whole.

My chest heaved as I took a wavering breath in, then shook as I let it out. My father's eyes glistened with tears—glowed as he mouthed, "*coimét daur.*"

A weight slammed into my chest. Tears stung in my eyes, carving scalding rivers down my cheeks. My father's face blurred as those brutes carried him off into the trees, as my muscles strained and pulled against the taut tree limbs. When I could no longer see him through the foliage, I listened for the hooves of the men's steeds. When the hooves faded into silence, the tree released me from its grip, and I tumbled to the ground. My skin was raw and bleeding from where the vines had held me, where branches had grasped at me during my fall.

My throat seared as I struggled to breathe in. Tears blurred the world around me. I heard only the thundering of my heart and ragged gasps for air as I heaved myself to trembling feet.

They couldn't take him from me. Not when I'd fought so hard to get back to him. To be the daughter he wanted me to be. The daughter I *finally* was.

I stumbled to the horses' tracks, still pressed into the soft earth. And I followed.

Despite the burn of my lungs, my raw skin, and the inability to stop crying—I ran faster than I ever had before. The trees blurred around me. Even as a voice screamed in my ears and rattled my bones with a resounding *"no,"* I didn't falter. The Forest itself grabbed at me, trying to force me to stop. I didn't. Branches and vines scraped at my skin and drew blood, but I didn't wince. Even as my vision began to darken, my lungs unable to keep up with my body, I kept running.

I would not hesitate to give the mortal men another taste of my power. Not after this. My wrath had become its own entity inside my chest—a living, breathing, furious thing with claws and teeth and the power to level mountains. I had not known any feeling like this before. I had not known I was capable. But now, it seemed to be the only thing keeping me alive.

I clung to it. Faster and faster, I ran.

The trees thinned, giving way to a vast dark sky and thousands of stars. Past the trunks and foliage, the land beyond came into view. What I had expected to be an expanse of barren, flat land was instead rolling hills and jagged mountain peaks to one side and undulating grasslands to the other. I had not been here before.

This was not the Mortal Realm.

The revelation struck me to the core, and I stumbled, crashing into the earth just at the Forest's edge. My chest ached as if I'd completely shredded my lungs, an unreleased sob still held tight in my throat. I glanced behind me, hoping that I'd somehow left their trail. But my father had taught me all too well, and the hoofprints led right beneath me and toward the looming mountains to the north. Though night had swallowed the sky, the peaks were easily discernible from how they blotted out the stars. A glow of golden light sat at their base, alone in the dark.

Perhaps he was taken there. I could not rest.

I moved to stand but was immediately tugged back down by thick roots that had tangled themselves around my legs. I tugged at them, grunting in frustration.

No.

The world around me seemed to tremble as if it had heard her voice too. My jaw was clenched so tight I thought my teeth might shatter.

"Why won't you let me save my father?" I screamed out in desperation. "He is all that I have. Please. Please let me save him. I can do it. I understand how to protect myself now. I can do it."

You will be slaughtered. I cannot let that happen.

My head throbbed as I struggled against the roots. My fingers bled as I tried to tear them off, but they grew back faster than I could remove them. "My death should be my own choice," I replied.

Not anymore.

"You can't stop me," I seethed.

I can. And I will. You swore an Oath. Guard the Forest.

"From who?"

From those that stole from you. Their greed will destroy us all. You mustn't allow it.

I looked back towards the lights in the distance, towards where my father could be headed. Alone. Helpless. "How long must I stay?" My voice became hollow.

When you see the mark of your father on another, your journey will begin. And I will follow.

48

*W*e rode through the night without anything eventful happening, which was new for us. Far off in the distance, the tops of trees rose into the sky. I could practically hear her calling to me through the thicket. *Home*. The trees groaned and stretched, heaving a slow breath as we passed them by. The beasts stirred ever so slightly in their caves, heavy hearts beating soundly within their chests. I wondered if they missed me like I'd missed them. To them, I was little more than a fellow creature of the wild, but I wondered if they thought of me—if I'd ever return.

If Salem could hear my thoughts, somehow sense my heartache, he didn't show it. We remained silent throughout the night, only speaking when I'd suggested we let the horses drink from a creek that trickled beneath a bridge in the Southern Road. He'd obliged, finally admitting to himself that I knew the animals best.

Treason still weighed heavily on the High King's chest. Every breath he took seemed labored as if the crown atop his head had grown in weight overnight. Even if I hadn't sensed his pain, the way the stars screamed down at us from the abyss echoed

Salem's misery. Cool darkness seemed to swirl around him as we rode, wisps of dark smoke billowing like his cloak in the wind. I couldn't tell if the drop in temperature was due to our venture north or if it was his doing.

From what my father had told me, treason was a common occurrence, especially in the times of the mortal world. When humans had reigned, they often betrayed one another, thinking their own beliefs best. Why should we believe ourselves any more advanced? Perhaps Forest Druids were, but the other Realms seemed content engaging in the niceties of polite conversation, all with a blade poised to stab another in the back. I'd known from the moment I'd entered that castle that I was no longer dealing with wild beasts, motivated only by a means to survive. The monsters within the castle were far more terrifying.

As dawn's rosy fingertips danced across the skyline, I began to discern the jagged edges of the Arastyan mountains before us. The glow of sunrise illuminated their faces in brilliant pinks and violets, luminescent against the pale sky behind them. Before the mountains stood the shadowy city of Kalys, the stonework of the royal castle now painted in the same hues as the peaks behind it.

Upon seeing their home, the horses seemed to find another burst of energy and began to gallop up toward Kalys. Their hooves clopped against the road, which had transitioned from dry dirt to cobblestone. It was only when we approached the wall around Kalys that Salem slowed his horse to a halt.

"Something's wrong," he said, more to himself than to me.

The horse beneath him stomped his foot twice in impatience. Salem turned to face me, his eyes swirling with something indiscernible.

"What?"

His jaw set in a stiff line as his fingers gripped the hilt of the blade at his side. "The guards aren't at their posts," he whispered.

The main gate was wide open. Crimson stained the stone up on the parapets of the wall, running down its side in rivulets. Something was very wrong, indeed.

My stomach lurched, my heart thundering in my chest as I pulled a single arrow from my quiver and notched it against the shaft of my bow. I gave Salem a single nod, and he urged his horse forward. We inched through the open gates into the lower village. Even the horses seemed to quiet their hooves as we moved through the lower levels of Kalys, the streets deserted. No lights were lit in the cottages. The animals weren't out grazing in their pastures.

My heart skipped a beat as movement caught my attention at the end of the road. My breath stilled. The horses began to pant, stomping their hooves. Salem steadied the reins of his steed, but I could not move.

A white hound with red ears and silver eyes stalked down the street, fixated on me. I swallowed, my heart thundering. But the creature continued towards us. And though it stared at me as it passed us by, it did not stop.

"Did you—did you see that?" I whispered.

"See what?" Salem asked.

I was hallucinating. What a terrible time to be hallucinating.

As we passed through to the upper villages, my blood ran cold.

The bodies of mutilated guards sat to my left and right, dark blood splattering the grey stone beneath them. The metallic scent of death hung in the air like Salem's darkness, coiling around his arms like vipers waiting to strike. The horses were petrified. The steed beneath me eyed the scene, his heart thundering. They needed to get out of here. I wouldn't allow them to become victims as well.

Quietly, I dismounted my horse and placed my hand on his

neck. "You and your friend must leave at once. Do not return until it is safe, or you may be killed," I whispered.

He nickered in response and nudged the other horse. Salem slid off its back, landing silently on the balls of his feet. Together, the horses strode quietly out of the courtyard, leaving to what I prayed would be safety.

I glanced toward the High King—at the dark tempest swirling around him. I was glad I had been able to offer him shade yesterday. He would need whatever energy he had left, it seemed.

"Stay close," Salem said, crooking his finger.

Though my lip curled in distaste at his instruction, I inched to his side. My arrow remained taut in my bow. I peered around the courtyard for any signs of movement, any stutter of a heart-beat- but felt nothing. As we approached the massive doors on the castle's face, my hand flew out and yanked Salem back by his cloak.

He gave me a nasty glare, but I shook my head, pointing to the door. There were heartbeats on the other side of it, waiting. There were many.

"They're waiting for us," I mouthed, motioning to the door with an upwards tilt of my chin.

Salem's jaw tightened as he sucked in a deep breath, shadows coiling tighter around his body. He swung his sword around his wrist once, then looked back at me. "If you're going to run, I'd suggest you do it now," he grunted.

I did not need to reach through the earth to know he wanted to beg me to stay.

There was a part of me that recoiled at the thought of saving those who wanted me dead. They'd accused me of treason and of murder, then called for my execution. If Salem hadn't believed my innocence, they might've succeeded. Was it really my responsibility to save them? Would it be unjust for me to turn from them as they did from me—from my people?

My father flashed in my mind. His kind eyes—his gentle hands. Humans had tried to kill him, but he did not seek revenge. I did, and it nearly killed me.

I shook my head. "I'm staying."

A loss of life is a terrible thing, and those who killed without mercy, without restraint or dignity—they needed to be brought down. *That* was my duty. I may have been the last of my kind, but I would never let those beliefs die. To kill another was akin to blasphemy—to taking Dagda's prophecies and rewriting them yourself. My father would not sit idly by. Nor would any of my people, were they still alive.

The High King turned back towards the door. Dark tendrils uncoiled from his taut arms and slithered away from his body toward the door. Night curled around the door handles, awaiting instruction. Salem glanced at me from the corner of his eye, and I nodded, my stomach churning.

I held my breath tight in my throat until it began to burn in my chest. Adrenaline sang through my veins, coating them with ice. But my muscles—oh, how they *burned*.

The doors swung open.

Hundreds of Druids rushed out, screaming. White armor clanged as they ran, their faces obscured in pale masks. The Air Realm sigil stood carved into each and every breastplate—a triangle with a jewel at its center, surrounded by whorls painted the color of salmon flesh. Nausea coiled in my stomach.

The Air Druids had come to take Kalys. It seemed we had started a war.

They obviously had little respect for life if they'd not only sent a Druid to assassinate me—but their own Lady for the same task. It was likely they'd killed Xandria as well. Salem had mentioned her lips and nails were blue. Was it possible she was suffocated? That perhaps when she didn't die immediately from her wound, the assassin pulled the air from her lungs as they had done with me?

And Lady Vara. Her overturned carriage flashed through my mind—the curtains covering the windows and the single shot by an arrow. Whoever killed her might not have been able to see her to get a straight shot. But if they had been able to alter the direction of their arrow, so it didn't require a perfect angle...

I knelt on the ground, cold slate biting into my knees as my fingertips flattened to the stone. *I cannot stop lives from being lost if I do not take them. Do I have your permission?*

The earth rumbled beneath my feet in acknowledgment. *I am with you.*

I notched my arrow against the shaft of my bow and pulled on the string. In and out. In and out.

Release.

I do not miss.

The arrow tip sunk between the cerulean eyes of an Air Druid. He stilled, blinking as rivulets of crimson dripped between his brows. The spine of the arrow protruded from his skull. As he fell, I loosed another.

The Druid behind him clawed at his neck in agony. The arrow stuck out at an angle from his throat, a pulsing artery spraying blood into the air like mist. He heaved through his scarlet-stained mask, frantically trying to breathe. The whites of his eyes were the color of garnets. With a clang of his armor, at last, he fell. And he did not move again.

Danu, forgive me.

The smell was all too familiar, the pitted hole in my chest exactly the same as when I'd first taken a life. Bile crested in my throat, and I bitterly swallowed it. The gods had told me I would have no choice, only sanctions. I could only listen. And beg for forgiveness when it was done.

A sword came down on me, and I rolled out of its arc. I scrambled to my knees just in time to dodge it as its master swung it again. I had no time to fire another arrow.

"The world will take advantage of that day. And it will swallow you whole."

Rage billowed in my chest. Again the Air Druid swung.

"Stay close. Do not give them a chance to breathe."

My father's voice was nearly corporeal. As if he stood by me through this battle. As if he'd never left.

My leg swung, and I kicked the hilt from the Air Druid's wrist. The sword flew through the air. The first rays of dawn glinted off it like the sun on an icefall. The Air Druid screamed, charging for the blade. And I took the opportunity, pulling an arrow from my quiver and slamming it into his neck. He quivered, thrashing as blood spurted from his wound. Droplets splattered my face and clothes, drenching me in hot, metallic-smelling red. The Air Druid fell, writhing in a pool of scarlet. The hilt of the blade descended simultaneously, landing unceremoniously in my hand.

My lips parted to apologize, to ask for forgiveness.

"Do not apologize for your successes, Quinn. No one else will."

Tears stung in my eyes. Or blood. One of the two.

Another Druid charged me. Her blade met mine, steel ringing in the air. She was much more skilled than the last Druid. Every arc of my sword, she countered.

"Good. Again."

I aimed for her head. She blocked, and I swung low, slicing across her stomach. A squelching sound filled the air as her guts spilled onto the stone. Her eyes rolled back, and she crumpled on top of her insides.

Definitely tears. This was not what I wanted to do. I ground my teeth together, trying to swallow the acrid smell of blood that stained the inside of my nose. I could not shake this. What I'd done. What I had to do.

"As quickly as you breathe in and out."

I swung the sword around my wrist.

"Blades."

I battled my way to the door, my father's voice ringing in my ear as loud as my own heartbeat. I wanted them to die immediately. There needn't be more pain in this world than they'd already caused. Inflicting more of it would make me no better than them. With every blink, I saw my father sparring with me in a meadow beneath an overcast sky.

"Again."

"Again."

"Again."

I turned to look at Salem. Bodies littered the courtyard in his wake. Every Druid he'd come across had been cut down, and the ones that hadn't were strangled by the raging dark that swirled and pulsated around him. Could the Air Druids feel his breath? They hadn't noticed me in Hypnos Keep, but they fought him as if they could see him through the shadow. I sensed where he stood, but only through the earth—the thumping of his mighty heart. The less I focused on that, the blurrier he became.

We forced our way towards the castle doors, cutting down soldiers as we went. I fought the urge to apologize for each life I took, but the voice in my ears telling me not to apologize for my successes kept me moving.

There was so much death. So many souls that could become sluagh. This would be a nightmare to fix if we even survived it.

"Quinn!" Salem called from behind me. I spun and met his stare. "Go make sure the Ladies are safe. I can handle this," he said.

My breath lodged in my throat, and I paused, hesitating. Could he?

Fury blazed in his eyes. "Go!" He shouted again.

This time, I listened. It seemed most of the forces had stayed at the front doors. My boots clicked across the stone floors as I sprinted through the corridor and up the stairs, only meeting battle a few times. When I turned down the hall that led to Rhea's room, my body collided with another's. We both fell. I coiled myself into a crouched stance, arrow notched in my bow, and aimed between their eyes.

It was only when I saw the eyes that I lowered my weapon. Irises like hearth-flame. Skin like embers.

Ingrid.

"Lady Quinn?" She breathed out, her pained expression crumbling in relief. "Thank Brighid, you're alive. Where is the High King?"

"He's in the ballroom. He wants me to find and protect the other Ladies," I replied, pulling myself upright.

Ingrid rose to her feet, twin blades gripped in either hand. The swords glowed gold in the candlelight as if lit aflame. Crimson stained her cheeks, her satin gown in tatters. A narrow cut had etched itself into her bare arm. It appeared shallow.

"I had the chance to fight alongside a Forest Druid before and did not take it," she said. "I will not make the same mistake twice. I have your back."

My mind whirled at her response. She'd fought alongside my people before?

I parted my lips in response, but she cut me off. "Rhea's room is down the hall. Let's go."

I needed little more encouragement than that and hurried down the hallway alongside her. Doors we passed by were unhinged, some covered in crimson. I struggled to restrain my thundering heart. By the time we reached Rhea's room, the door was already ajar. My stomach lurched into my throat when I took in the state of the room.

Everything was in shreds, torn down, or simply obliterated. Blood splatters fanned the swirling wallpapers, and one of the windows was shattered. The gilded light of dawn spilled in through the cracked, bloodstained glass, turning the pools of blood into melted gold.

I paused in the doorway, flinging my arm out in front of

Ingrid before she could plow into the room. My heart pulsed in my throat.

Stella was unconscious on the floor, her ebony dress in tatters. Crimson blood splattered her tanned skin, a blade still clutched in her hand. Luckily, her heartbeat still fluttered in her chest, but the lifeless guards strewn haphazardly around her were not as fortunate. As upsetting as it was, that wasn't what concerned me.

What concerned me was the much louder heartbeats hiding on the other side of the open door. This was a trap.

49

J held my breath as my mind began to race. I didn't know what to do. I didn't know if Rhea was in here, but even if she wasn't, I was still obligated to save Stella.

I turned to face Ingrid, giving a disapproving gesture before looking back through the doorway. Stella's heart was weakening by the minute. If I was going to act, I had to do it now- consequences be damned.

I notched an arrow against the shaft of my bow, closing my eyes as I fixated on the locations of the hearts behind the open door. Each had a slightly different pace. They weren't touching the ground, which made the task incredibly difficult.

"Channel your thoughts away from yourself. You have to allow yourself to become one with the earth, Quinn. You're far too determined to remain separate."

My mind soared through the stone, down further and further, until I was met with an unblinking stare. Ancient. Unyielding. A mirror to the presence inside me. *You see me.*

Four hearts pumped on the other side of the door. One directly behind its edge, two on either side of that one, and the other lingering in the back corner.

"Being able to sense all life around you—it is what makes us who we are."

I angled my bow to the right, the wooden shaft biting into my shoulder. I heaved a breath, slow and steady.

I sprinted through the door and fell to one knee, kicking the other leg out behind me. My shins skidded across the marble floor as I let my arrow fly. One arrow sunk deep into the cheek of the foremost Druid, crumbling to the floor with a sickening crunch. I loosed another at the Druid behind him. It hit just below his collarbone, but he continued towards me, sword raised. Two others came from behind him, both wielding swords as well. Their feet touched the ground not a meter before me, blades singing in a metallic chorus as they arced through the air toward me.

"As quickly as you breathe in and out."

I dropped the bow and pulled the sword from my belt.

Steel sang in the air as I met the first blow. My heel rammed into his knee, snapping the tendons with a pop. The Air Druid grunted in pain, sword arcing towards my side. I met his sword with my own, then gripped an arrow from my quiver and slammed the tip into a chink in his armor. He squealed as hot blood spurted from the wound, and he fell back, clutching his side. The armor clanged as it hit the ground.

"Ready?"

The other two were right behind him. I slammed my foot into the ground, a shockwave of rock rippling towards them like a riptide. It knocked them from their feet, allowing me enough time to recollect myself. I stabbed the blade into the heart of the one closest to me. Tears blurred my sight as I watched the light fade from their pale irises.

The one to my right rose to their feet.

"Your attacker is going to aim for your head repeatedly, Quinn."

A silent sob ached in the back of my throat. Then they swung at my head. I pulled a rock from the earth as a shield, deflecting the sword, and stabbed an arrow into their jugular. Their eyes rolled back in their head as hot blood soaked my arm, seeping through the tunic sleeve and drowning my skin. I swallowed back bile, the ferric smell of blood singing my nose and coating my throat. Maybe I shouldn't have aimed for the jugular.

I picked up my bow from the floor and peered around the room, waiting for another attacker. None came. My eyes slid over to Ingrid. She watched me with an unreadable expression, almost as if she, too, were on the verge of tears.

I hurried over to Stella's side, pressing two fingers against her neck and lowering my ear to her lips. A gentle nudge against my finger pad and a faint breath of air against my ear had my shoulders sagging in relief. I leaned back, and my heart lurched—a blade was lodged in her thigh. It looked like it had sliced through the main artery supplying her leg, and dark blood pooled beneath her. Druids could heal quickly, yes—but not fast enough to stop her from bleeding out.

I looked back to Ingrid. "I need yarrow leaves. The room where the healing supplies are is just down the hall. Once you leave here, head right and take your next left. The third door," I said.

"I shouldn't leave you alone here, Quinn," Ingrid replied, motioning to my arm. "You're hurt too."

I glanced down at the slice through my forearm. I hadn't even noticed it. Blood beaded from the wound—my skin already red and inflamed. It would definitely scar, regardless of whether I could stitch it up later.

But my will only hardened when I looked back down at Stella. Her tanned skin had begun to turn grey, her pitch hair appearing to do the same. "If you don't, she will die," I said quietly.

"Watch your back, Forest Druid," Ingrid grunted, gripping

her dual blades in white-knuckled fists and hurrying out of the room.

The shouting of Druids and odd gurgling noises seemed to follow her as her footsteps sprinted through the hallways, echoing through the floor. Clearly, she'd earned her title as Morrigan.

I ripped a shred of cloth from Stella's torn gown and wound it tight around her thigh, shoving the body of a dead guard beneath it to elevate it.

Footsteps filed in through the doorway, light and graceful. Could Ingrid already be back with the yarrow?

"Quinn!" A scream echoed from behind me.

As I turned around, a blinding flash of light hit my eyes. I winced and pinched them shut. It did me little good. Gilded light seared through them as if I were staring into the face of a star. Pain exploded in my skull.

Two things hit the floor with a thud, the ground trembling through the soles of my feet. The brilliant glow began to fade, and I peeled my eyelids open. Everything was fuzzy and far too dim to discern anything with definition. I closed my eyes again and focused on the earth, honing on the single heartbeat I could still feel aside from Stella's. It was familiar. I knew this heartbeat. Ingrid? No—not Ingrid.

"Rhea?" I asked, my eyelids fluttering open.

I still couldn't make out anything that well, but I could see the glowing outline of a female on the floor beside me. I crawled across the floor over to her side, blinking as I tried to regain the use of my eyes. Golden light bled through her skin, her irises akin to the very sun. Her hair shimmered as if sunlight had been woven through every strand. It was hard to believe *Lugh* could hold a candle to her.

"You couldn't feel him—he—Air Druid—flying towards you —about to kill you," she stuttered out through labored breaths.

My gaze, albeit still fuzzy, drifted down to the hands folded across her waist. A growing pool of darkness had begun to expand beneath her glowing fingertips like a solar eclipse.

"Rhea—Rhea, what did you do?" I stammered, placing my hands atop hers and looking back toward the doorway. "Ingrid!" I screamed, my voice raw.

The metallic scent of her blood stung my nose, my vision still blurry from her explosion of power. Rage coiled inside of me like a feral animal ready to pounce. *How could they do this to her? How could they?*

My hands shook as I lifted her fingertips from her wound. A tiny blade had stuck itself deep in her abdomen. There was no way it had missed vital organs. My father flashed before my eyes, bleeding out from the wounds dealt to him by mortal men—

"There is shame in your heart, Quinn. Why?"

"No. No, no, no!" I placed my hands over the gaping hole, blood pulsing through my fingertips. "Ingrid!" I screamed as loud as I could. My throat burned. "Ingrid!"

They sent assassins to kill Xandria, their own Lady to kill me. They killed Lady Vara. They killed my guards, they killed Mr. Aven from my carriage. They tried to kill Salem and me. Now, they'd laid siege upon Kalys, killing countless innocents and fatally wounding perhaps the only Druid friend I'd ever known.

My rage was endless—insatiable.

Rhea's blood-soaked fingertips brushed my cheek, interrupting the scalding tears that streamed down them. "You—you can't save me now. This is my time." She smiled weakly up at me.

"No, no, it's not. Please, Rhea. Please stay with me," I sobbed freely now.

Her light was dimming from the waist out. She was dying. *She was dying, and there was nothing I could do—she saved me, and there was nothing I could do—*

This wasn't how this was supposed to be. I was supposed to protect others. *That* was my duty. No one was supposed to protect me. Despite what the gods had said—I never wanted anyone to give their life for me. I'd hoped they were wrong, that my fate was not what they believed. I didn't even want to be here—I wanted to be in my forest, away from all of this- why had she given her life for me? If I hadn't been here, she would be okay. She wouldn't have done that. She wouldn't have needed to.

As I gazed down at her, I could see my father. My father's green eyes looking up at me, his hands coated in his blood. I watched him being carried off into the Forest while I did nothing, while I stood there, hiding—

"Why?" My voice was hoarse through my sobs. "Why?"

Tears budded in her eyes now. "I told you. I would not let them hurt anyone—anyone I loved again."

I screamed. Gods, I screamed.

The floor shook as Ingrid stumbled through the door.

"By the gods—"

"Ingrid, yarrow!"

The Morrigan hurried to my side, shoving the vial of yarrow paste into my hand. I uncorked it. Blood-soaked fingertips covered mine, stopping me.

"No, not me." Rhea shook her head weakly, turning to look at the still-fading Stella.

A faint smile tugged on her lips. Only Rhea could manage a smile in the face of Death.

"I can't lose you. Please. Don't leave me here. Please." My voice shook.

"You are meant for so much, Quinn of the Wild," she labored. "You—you will not lose me. I am with you."

Crimson beaded the corners of her lips. The glowing beneath her skin had faded up to her neck and fingertips.

Scalding tears budded the corners of my eyes. I'd survived worse than this. Maybe I could heal her.

I reached down into the earth, pleading for the gods to give her what they'd once given me. When I'd been disemboweled, ravaged, and on the edge of Death, the gods had brought me back. Surely they could do the same for Rhea. Rhea deserved more than this. This world needed her. I needed her.

No. The word resounded through my body with an echo, loud enough to prove a point. *The Otherworld awaits her.*

My throat tightened to the point of pain, scalding tears carving down my cheeks. I choked on the air that welled in my chest, a weak sob shaking my body to the core. Rhea's dimmed fingertips, now ashen and cold, gripped my hand in hers. Blood trickled from the corner of her mouth as he heaved a rattling breath.

The fading light reached her chin—her blazing irises beginning to dim. My body shook with sobs.

"I should—I should've told you—sooner," she croaked, her voice weak. "I need—need you to remem-ember." There was a pause as a breath crackled in her throat. Blood trickled down her chin. "From death, divine will be."

And then her eyes went dark.

The prophecy. She was referring to the prophecy.

As the light left her body, I watched my father being carried off into the woods, saw him shaking his head and telling me to stay put. Another life, another soul given for me.

I shut my eyes as tightly as I could, scalding tears streaming down my cheeks as I held my breath within my chest. I knew if I let it escape, it wouldn't make any difference.

I turned back to Stella and yanked the serrated blade from her thigh, scalding blood splattering my blood-soaked tunic. I pulled the skin together and looked at Ingrid.

"Melt it."

Ingrid's eyes went wide. "Are you sure—"

"Now."

Fire blazed at Ingrid's fingertips as she pressed them to Stella's wound. The smell of burning flesh seared the inside of my nose. Blackened skin covered the serrated line. I piled the yarrow leaves over her wound, binding them to her skin with shreds of cloth. The yarrow would help her blood clot, hopefully keeping her alive. I was no healer, though, and she needed one. I glanced at Ingrid. She stared back at me.

"I'm sorry," she said quietly.

I shook my head, biting my lip to keep the tears from streaming again. "Stella needs a healer," I replied. "She will live if you can find one."

She nodded. "What will you do?"

I swallowed, standing upright and walking over my sword. "Put an end to this."

Ingrid watched me for a moment, her expression yet again unreadable. Then she stood and ran off down the hall.

I reached down to the earth, the slow heart thudding beneath me. *I need power.*

I could feel her rumble beneath my fingertips in response. *This is a dangerous path. You are acting out of vengeance, not protection.*

The feral animal within me bared its teeth. *Her blood is on my hands.*

The earth groaned. *You were warned of your fate. Vengeance is not the answer.*

If they ask for mercy, I shall give it.

Silence. Then the ground shook. *Mercy, and it will be done.*

That was all I needed. I rose to my feet, my veins surging with power and fury. Stone shuddered beneath me, every brick of the castle leaning an ear to my voice. The earth beneath Kalys tensed, waiting for instruction. Slabs of marble rippled like a pond beneath the soles of my feet as I padded toward the doorway. The steady heart of the earth slowed, gaze fixated solely on me.

Mercy.

Where was mercy when they baselessly accused me of murder? Where was mercy when they wanted me dead? Where was mercy when my people died of Plague, but no healer would treat them? Where was mercy when the High King demonized an entire race and they chose to believe it?

Where was *my* mercy?

I was enraged. If fear was a kindled flame, then rage was an untethered forest fire. How *dare* they steal the life of another? How *dare* they mutilate without so much as a bat of an eye? This was not what life was supposed to be—this was not civilized. How could any Realm call itself civilized when it engaged in this sort of destruction?

Druids were supposed to be a higher race, gifted by the gods. This was so far from that purpose, I wasn't entirely sure if it had been that way, to begin with.

Stones liquefied beneath my feet, swirling around me as if gravity had become nonexistent—as if the only thing tying them to this earth was me. The castle walls began to shake as I reached the door. Dust and small rocks fell from the walls and the arched ceiling above, flinging themselves into orbit around me. The candelabras on the walls flickered, swaying as the castle did.

I hoped none of the Druids asked for mercy. I so badly wanted to deprive them of it.

50

I was rage incarnate. Wilderness, herself. Ruthless. Feral. Every bit the monster they said I was. Every bit the monster they'd *forced me* to become.

Too many lives had been ripped away—all for some trivial disagreement between Druids. Killing for the sake of politics was barbaric. It was reminiscent of human wars, of the mortal men desperate for power and glory. I used to believe that it caused the downfall of mankind and that Druidkind's spirituality allowed us to rise above them.

It was now blatantly obvious that the lust for power and glory had merely shifted hosts.

I exited Lady Rhea's room into the hallway. Stone and brick orbited around me like moons, tethered only by Danu's sanction of mercy.

However, these stones were not meant to maim. I would not be drinking the pleasure of death. The suffering had to end. Regardless of how the bloodlust and vengeance pounded furiously within my veins, I would not act on it.

I couldn't.

Suffering would not end with more suffering. It had to be

snuffed from this world like a fire. I could not put it out by adding to the flame.

A dozen Druids rounded a corner before me, the white Air Realm sigil emblazoned on their chests. Sickening delight bloomed in the pit of my stomach as horror dawned on their faces, jaws slack and eyes wide.

Is this what gods and goddesses saw when they chose to smite a mortal? The awe-stricken terror and trembling knees— even I found myself enjoying it.

"You're no Druid," one of them whispered beneath their helmet.

Tears shimmered under the metal, trembling breaths tentative as they inched past their lips. They knew their fate before it had even been dealt.

Through their eyes, I saw the beast I'd become. Drenched in blood and weaponless, with massive rocks orbiting around me on varying axes and eyes vacant and cruel—I was the feral creature they had been taught to fear. It trickled down their spines like droplets of cold water, goosebumps blossoming across their skin and hearts thundering in their ears. It tasted acrid on their tongue, breaths held tight in their chest—afraid to move.

I wondered if this was what I looked like to the men who had first tried to kill me. I hoped it was. But I would not allow them to label me as just a monster—because I was *so much more* than the savage creature they made me out to be.

I was *one of them*. And that was *so much worse.*

"Yes," I said. "I am."

Their first words were not for mercy, I was thankful for that. I didn't know if, after Rhea's death, I would've been able to follow through on that vow. The suffering needed to be eradicated, and the demise of those who had inflicted it would suffice.

My power stretched through the earth, flexing its muscles and hurdling towards them- yet they could not see it. I crept towards them, the stone floor rippling beneath me like the surface of a pond. The castle walls shuddered with every step, making the tallow candlelight flicker with raining dust and debris.

And I watched with delight as, one by one, their eyes rolled back in their heads, and their legs crumbled beneath them like loose stones.

I strode past them, not needing to look down beside me to know they were dead. Their corpses were cold and limp, leaden on the stone's surface. With every life that bled down into the earth, the air grew a little bit fresher—the colors a little bit brighter. They would cause no more suffering. Not even in their death did they suffer—only in the moments before, when they knew what was coming. That, I suppose, was my mercy.

My heel sunk into the marble as I turned the corner, my boots echoing down the corridor. Only Zora and Aria's rooms remained. Aria was likely still in the dungeon, and Xandria's room had been vacant since her assassination. So, I would save Zora, despite my dislike of her.

Shouts boomed down the hall as I approached, feet shuffling and armor clanging. Air Realm soldiers clambered into formation, blades trembling as the front line aimed them toward me. Silence fell across them as a grin tugged at my lips.

"If you—if you want to live to see another day, I—I'd suggest you start running, Lady!" A male Druid shouted from a few lines back.

One by one, bodies thumped as they fell to the stone floor. The male who spoke shuffled a few steps back, blade shuddering in his fist. I approached him slowly, allowing his fear to bloom as his companions collapsed around him. Only when he was the last soldier breathing did I speak.

"For the last time," I said. "*I am no Lady.*"

My arm flew out, and my fingers clenched around his throat. With surprising ease, I lifted him off the ground. His blood pounded beneath the pads of my fingertips, the acrid smell of fear burning in the back of my throat. His body shook, cool sweat beading on his brow as pale blue irises trembled in blood-shot eyes.

"What are you?" He wheezed, fingers clawing at my hand as his body writhed. "Are you a god?"

Rhea did not writhe. Rhea did not have a chance to. They *took* that from her.

And so I did not smile. I did not snarl. I did not breathe as the words breached my lips.

"I'm worse."

Euphoria flooded my fingertips, up my arms, and swelled in my chest like a rising tide. Goosebumps blossomed across my skin as his pale irises lolled back in his head, arms falling limply to either side. His once thundering heart slowed to a faint thud in my ears, then went silent. Energy surged, and my blood raged in my ears, every cell in my body thrumming with life and power. A swallow lodged in my throat, the metallic taste of blood lingering on my tongue.

I grimaced and dropped his corpse to the floor with a sick-ening thud, heaving a sigh as I stepped over his body and continued on. Just as I strolled past what was Aria's room—I paused.

There was a heartbeat coming from inside.

The wooden door sat closed, gilded light bleeding out from beneath it. I gripped the aureate doorknob, wincing and yanking my hand away. It was freezing. I hissed and grabbed it again, shoving the door open.

To my surprise, a sobbing female sat on the edge of her bed, cloaked in tattered brown clothes. Matted silver hair hung loosely from her scalp, her skin the color of freshly fallen snow. When her blue eyes rose to meet mine, her heart flut-tered in her chest, her stomach lurching as bile rose in her throat.

"Lady Quinn," she gasped, clambering towards the back of her bed as if she'd somehow escape me.

She'd climbed through a window to kill me. She'd likely orchestrated Xandria's murder as well as the first attempt on my life. And yet, her heart thundered in fear, and her throat burned as she held her breath. She was petrified. Malevolence hadn't sunk its teeth into her just yet. She didn't want to kill me —she didn't even want to lay a finger on me.

While it did little to satiate my bloodlust, my footsteps faltered as I entered the room. The dead flowers held in various vases around the room stretched their decomposing vines toward me, scraping across the floor and swirling up each of my legs. The brittle vines broke and regrew with every step, climbing my legs and swirling around my waist. Flowers were always desperate for attention, even in death.

"Lady Aria," I seethed through gritted teeth. These soldiers were here because of her. "You tried to kill me."

"Please—please have mercy. I didn't—I didn't want to hurt anybody," she pleaded with bloodshot eyes. Her cheeks were covered in grime, cleared only by the trails of tears etched through them.

I paused. She'd asked for mercy. As badly as I wanted to rip into her, I could not. My power tensed in my blood, frozen. A hiss crested in my throat, fury bubbling beneath my skin.

"Stay. Put." I bared my teeth.

With a flick of my wrists, the desperate dead vines flew from my skin. They hit the walls with a crunch and crumbled to the floor like ashes.

Lady Aria watched me like a fawn watching a wolf, eyes wide and heart fluttering. But I knew what lay inside was no doe. She was the ellen trechend, hiding behind angelic features and a soft persona. She was every bit the monster I was, if not more. As badly as I'd wanted to exact revenge on her, now was not that time.

I let my powers flare again beneath my skin, the relaxed stones flinging into action once more. The earth flexed beneath my feet, rippling with every step. I left Lady Aria's room and went next door, tiptoeing over the bodies that scattered the hallway floor. The musty smell of death hung in the air as potent as the iron tang of blood.

I entered Lady Zora's room. To my complete surprise, it was pitch black. If it hadn't been for the earth, I wouldn't have been able to see a thing. I could faintly make out the bed to my right, the thudding heartbeat of a female perched against the headboard.

"Zora?" I asked.

The moment my voice left my lips, the darkness around me began to fade. Lady Zora appeared in the shadows, her legs folded and fingers interlaced neatly in her lap.

"Lady Quinn," she mused, unfolding her legs as she climbed off the bed and strode over to me.

Her gown remained unwrinkled, a black satin that shimmered in the daylight now reluctantly peering through her paned windows. Her makeup was pristine, not so much as a scratch touching her infallible skin. I could only smell her bergamot perfume—no acrid smell of fear seeped from her as it had with Aria. Dark irises followed the swirling chunks of stone that orbited me, pausing only to glare at the patches of drying blood splattered across my tunic and trousers. A grimace twisted on her lips. Only then did her eyes meet mine.

"You're wondering how I'm still alive," she posited, lifting her arm to motion to the opposite side of the room. I turned to look where she had gestured.

Piles of bodies lay neatly stacked against the wall. Blood drenched the stonework around them. I didn't want to know how she'd gotten their mangled corpses into an ordered pile. Still, the monster inside me silently admired her handiwork.

I turned back to her, staring like I would at my own reflection.

I could see her so clearly now. She was a spider—she'd spun a beautiful web of shadow and allowed her prey to wander inside of its own accord, only then inflicting her savagery. She was as much a monster as I was. The feral beast inside me yielded, seemingly amazed to have been met with an equal.

"I know. I know who you are," I said quietly. The stones around me stilled in midair.

She swallowed. "I don't know what you mean."

"Xandria knew you loved her. She told me. She knew, Zora."

Tears budded in her dark eyes, her bottom lip trembling. Her shoulders heaved as a silent sob shook her body. "Thank you," she whispered.

My lips pressed together. "I'm sorry you lost her. I'll make sure you don't lose anyone else."

Her jaw flexed as she hastily wiped away her tears. "Try not to destroy the castle, Lady Quinn. I'm rather fond of it," she said.

I hesitated, holding Zora's stare before giving a brief nod. Satisfied, she clambered back towards her headboard, folding her legs and allowing the shadows to spin again. Darkness followed me out the door.

I beelined straight for the grand staircase. The few Air Realm soldiers that crossed my path did not ask for mercy—did not hesitate before drawing their swords. Bodies littered the floor behind me as I strode through the halls, the castle trembling with every step. Though fury still sang in my chest, I was exhausted. My muscles ached. The wound on my arm throbbed with pain now. Every step was a challenge—a weight that I struggled to bear.

My feet stalled at the top of the staircase. There were hundreds of Air Druids below. Several guards fought alongside Salem. We were severely outnumbered, even after all we'd done. And I was just one Druid. The power I'd been given put serious strain on my body. My legs shook. If I tried to fight them all, I would die.

"I promise you, my daughter. If you open yourself to the earth, she will listen."

I swallowed my tears. Then I reached deep down inside me, where something ancient lay in wait. *Please. Help me.*

All at once, endless power slammed into me.

White flowering vines slithered from the banisters, desperately reaching for me. Thorns pricked my skin as they coiled around my legs, up my waist, down my arms. Budding blossoms exploded into full bloom across my body. The floral smell cleansed my throat of the ferric stench that lingered with the drying blood.

Beneath me in the ballroom, Salem's darkness erratically swung from soldier to soldier, strangling them as he fought with a drenched blade. He was a raging tempest of oblivion and shadow. Malevolence's claws trailed across his heart, the tips of her talons digging into the soft flesh. I didn't know if he would stop.

A female screamed as she charged up the staircase towards me, the shaft of a wooden spear gripped in her hands. My eyes met hers, and she paused. Her heart lurched one last time in her chest before it fell silent. Only when her body hit the floor, tumbling down several steps, did the High King look in my direction. His starless eyes met mine, his breath lodging in his throat. The hilt of his sword slipped from his hand. With an echo, the blade hit the stone floor and clattered still.

The Air Druid soldiers around him paused, turning to see what he was looking at. Hundreds of eyes fell on me. I recalled my first descent down these stairs when I'd made the High King's constituents shudder in fear at a mere taste of my power. That paled in comparison to what happened now.

A predatory grin settled on my lips as their knees began to tremble. The sunlight pouring in through the stained glass windows behind me stained the air a myriad of different colors. For a brief second, that light felt less like a radiating heat and more like a comforting hand. A hand I had held before.

I clenched my jaw tight and swallowed the grief that shattered me, allowing fury to hone those shards into a blade.

Then, I began to descend. The staircase quivered beneath the soles of my feet, the earth beneath the castle shaking with my power. It flexed and huffed like a feral beast, reaching through the ground and tugging on every stone until they trembled, waiting for instruction. The rocks orbiting around me spun faster and faster until they glowed orange with heat, as bright as the day's light at my back.

My hands coiled into white-knuckled fists. "Enough." The voice that escaped my lips was deep. Powerful. Irresistible.

"If you want mercy," I began, dark vines furling around my waist and across my arms. They stretched up the sides of my neck, thorns digging into my skin. Tendrils entangled in my hair, twisting to the top of my head. They coiled like a serpent into a ring of vines and thorns. "Bow."

The world shook.

Chandeliers flickered, and windows shattered. Pillars of solid stone quivered as if they, too, contemplated obeying my order. Screams erupted, almost as loud as the thundering heartbeats that echoed in my head. The acrid smell of fear burned in the back of my throat as I swallowed. My eyes remained glued to Salem, unwavering as he held my stare.

A little breath escaped my lips as the High King, clad in smoke and a starless sky, fell to his knees. His heart stuttered as malevolence released him from her clutches. His chest heaved as he inhaled—slow, as if in resolution.

His obsidian gaze only split from mine when he lowered his head to the floor. Darkness ebbed and flowed out from him in waves like the night-kissed sea. It spread outwards across the ballroom, an ocean of stars hitting every corner of the room.

Salem sat like a moon in the night sky, surrounded by an abyss. The surviving Kalystan guards followed suit, collapsing to their knees. Only the heads of the Air Realm shoulders remained above his shadows.

I paused, waiting. But no one else chose to bow.

A snarl tugged at my lips. "I said *bow*."

Like a crescendo of violins, the wails and screams of fallen shoulders echoed around the room. The glowing stones orbiting me exploded into sparks and dust, falling like snow. The ground quaked as my power frothed at the mouth.

The metallic stench of blood coated my lips now. Hot blood pooled across the stone floor, though I could not see it. The soldiers were given the choice to bow, and they hadn't. With their femurs shattered, they no longer had that choice.

I heaved a deep breath, fixated on Salem's bowed figure, as my feet stalled at the bottom of the staircase. The heartbeats echoing in my head faded into silence as I walked through the lines of soldiers toward the High King. Only the Kalystan guards and the High King were spared.

Vines cracked and coiled behind me in a blanket of white blossoms and thorns, having swallowed the staircase and half the ballroom whole. Salem's darkness ebbed in gentle waves against the vines—his tempest now calmed to a clear sky.

And as I stood before the bowed High King, the earth quieted once more.

51

*M*y body felt hollow. My voice was raspy as I said, "I was not expecting you to be among those that bowed, Salem."

His head rose from the floor. His eyes, dark like the night sky, were swirling with stars and smoke. Not moments ago, they had been eternally dark and deep, unrelenting to any sort of light that might try to pass through them. Now, they glimmered with the light of galaxies and moons.

"I wasn't either," he replied.

His heart thundered in his chest. I could taste bitterness in the air—something I knew all too well.

"So, why did you?"

I never thought I'd see him on his knees willingly, let alone with his forehead to the earth. Of course, I'd been able to throw him to his knees before, but this was different. This was his choice. He *chose* to bow. To *me*.

"I saw you, and I—," he paused as if the words had escaped him.

My throat constricted. "You were afraid."

He paused, blinking.

I swallowed bitterly. His gaze lingered on the field of thorns and blooming flowers behind me, my chest heaving as I willed them back to the banisters. They groaned and protested but relented as they coiled and snapped back to the staircase.

My eyes were still locked on his as he peeled himself from the ground. As he did so, the darkness that had stretched throughout the room shrunk back towards him as if it were the seas and Salem, the moon.

His wary eyes surveyed the room, the hundreds of corpses scattered in pools of blood that glimmered like gold in the daylight. Their skin had turned grey, eyes glazed over and cast towards the staircase, wide with a terror that would never fade. Their souls had gone to the earth, back from whence they came.

"How did you do this?" The High King asked, his hoarse voice not more than a whisper.

Silence filled the castle like the stench of blood. It had not been that way since I'd first arrived. There had seemed to be a constant buzz about the castle, with the various servants and handmaidens running about. Now, Salem's breath was shallow against his lips, a slow drip of blood dribbling onto the floor from the sleeves of his jacket.

I should not have had to take as many lives as I did today. There should not have been as much bloodshed as there was. There might not have been had I not angered Lord Typhon and Lady Thetis when we'd gone to the Air Realm. This battle had been my doing. If I had been home, where I belonged with the other savage beasts, none of this might've happened. Perhaps Rhea would still be alive.

I stilled for a moment before I spoke, choosing my words carefully.

"My father once told me a story about the Mortals. That they stood in a cave with their backs to the sun, refusing to turn around and look into the light. All they learned from the world was by watching the shadows the light would make on the cave wall," I explained. "I once warned you that you knew nothing of the monsters that dwelled beneath my skin. You still do not, but you have now seen their shadows."

I should not be here. I should not be where I could easily cause so much damage—so much death. I was a danger to us all.

If I had been in the Forest, Rhea would still be alive. She'd have no reason to give her life for another. When would I ever learn? When would I stop allowing others to sacrifice themselves for me? First, my father, then the guards outside my door when the assassin came, and now Rhea. I was weak, cowardly even, for allowing such a thing. Perhaps all of Arastya was right about me. Perhaps I was nothing more than the furious creature that crawled beneath my skin.

"Quinn," Salem said, his brow furrowed as he took a cautious step toward me.

Claws curled against the recesses of my mind, a low whisper deep in my head. Nausea bubbled in the pit of my stomach. *What happened?*

"Get out of my head, *ciarán*," I snarled, my hands balling into fists as my chest swirled with empty rage.

I remembered Rhea's last moments, how the darkness had enveloped her golden light like the night swallowing a star whole. What struck me now were the last words that left her lips as they grew cold. *From death, divine will be.* It was the same thing the messenger had said in the Southern Territories, something of a forbidden prophecy that Salem had dismissed when I'd brought it up. It was the last line to the phrase Xandria had found in the archives, something that might've led to her assassination. Clearly, more people knew of it than he thought, and apparently, some of them were of high status.

"From death, divine will be," I whispered through gritted teeth, my nails biting into the skin on the palms of my hands.

What did that mean? What was the prophecy? Why would

she say that to me? Was she involved in all of these assassinations? Did I know her at all?

"What did you say?" A growl erupted from Salem's lips, and my eyes met his intense glare. His eyes, once brimming with the light of a thousand moons, were now as void and dark as the night-kissed sea.

"The last words that left Rhea's lips after she gave her life for mine," I replied, my lip curling in warning.

Salem's eyes widened briefly before he quickly averted them from mine. A frustrated growl wrenched itself from his sharp lips as he ran a hand through his midnight hair. He swiveled back to me, eyes flaring.

"It was a prophecy foretold long ago, during the time of my great grandfather, the first High King of Arastya. Some Druid claimed to have had contact with Dagda and was told a single message. *If death's door should find its key, the sky shall fall to earth's rising, and light will reign from eclipsed peaks. Should divine die, from death, divine will be.* It's a treasonous prophecy that those who stand against the Kalystan rule preach. They think 'the sky shall fall' refers to the end of the Kalystan reign," he explained.

My brows pinched together. Why would Rhea say that to me? Why would *those* be her last words?

Seeing my frustration, Salem continued. "It's forbidden to speak aloud. Kalystans have suppressed the spread of the prophecy since it's telling, but it's obviously still whispered in the shadows. Apparently, even in high places," he grumbled. "I would've never believed Lady Rhea to partake in such a treasonous philosophy."

I felt my stomach coil like a viper being attacked. I knew the Southern Territories had opposed Northern rule, and that was why Rhea had come, to extinguish any fears from the crown regarding some sort of separatist movement. But what if she had been a part of that very movement? What if her coming here was not to satiate any concerns from the North but to prove to the South that the Kalystan rule was flawed? That Salem forced her to leave her people and compete for his hand?

What if this had all been a tactic on her part, a ploy to infuriate the people even further? Had Rhea been protecting her people at all, or had she simply been trying to get a crown of her own?

Did I know Rhea at all?

Fingertips grazed my chin, turning me away from the mass of bodies I continued to glare blankly at. Despite my instinct to swing for his gut, I allowed my gaze to turn towards Salem, who looked at me with furrowed brows and solemn eyes.

"Let her rest, wildling," he said, placing his hand on my shoulder.

"But she—"

Salem merely shook his head, a few locks of dark hair falling loose across his forehead.

"Was a friend to you and gave her life for yours. Let her rest. What's done is done," he said.

"I did not find your mother or Iryx," I said.

Salem nodded. "My mother is probably in the safe room, and Iryx is probably guarding her. Stella should be there as well. That's protocol."

I swallowed. "No, I found Stella. Ingrid went to find her a healer. She looks—she was injured in battle. I did what I could and I think she'll be okay but—"

Salem held up his hand. "You saved my kingdom today. And my family."

I shook my head, the metallic scent of blood still heavy in the air. So much death, so much pain, and suffering.

I did not do enough.

"So many lives are gone, and what will you do with the Air Realm? They've blatantly disrespected you now and have launched a full-blown attack on the capitol—," I began to ramble, but Salem stopped me once more.

"You saved my kingdom today."

He reached up to his neck, where the necklace I'd stared at for so long dangled. His fingers looped around the chain as he pulled it from his throat, then draped it over my head. A surge of power, cool and ethereal, thrummed from the necklace into my skin. Any words I might've once said died then on my lips.

"What—"

"As a sign of my loyalty to you, my debt to you for what you have done. My kingdom lives because of you. I will figure out what to do with the Air Realm. In the meantime, we will rest, and we will heal. There is much to be done."

He was right. What was done was done, and there was much to do. But for now, we would rest and we would heal.

52

The forest welcomed me into its dark embrace. Droplets of dew clung to the thicket, dampening the sleeves of my tunic. Above Orion and I, silver clouds stained violet with dusk sifted through treetops that stretched into the overcast sky like alpine peaks. The smell of damp earth and bark clung to the moisture in the air. Despite this, every breath from my chest was labored. The hollowness there—the unrelenting ache—had yet to subside.

The ground was soft beneath my feet, bending beneath each step as if the earth herself wanted to ease my path. Orion kept his head low as he followed after me into the thicket. My companion had remained in the gardens throughout the attack, and thankfully the only Air Druid who'd thought to search them he'd quickly trampled. I didn't know if I'd recover if something had happened to him. My throat tightened. Orion pressed his nose against the back of my leg, perhaps to remind me he was with me. That I wasn't alone. That the battle was over.

But it didn't feel like it. It felt like we now teetered on the edge of a precipice. A sudden gust of wind is all it would take to send us into freefall.

Kyro told me that Rhea would be sent to the Eternal Lands today. Following the battle, her body had been sent on a carriage home to Hera, where her father had been waiting. He had now lost not only his wife but his eldest child. I didn't think I would've been able to see him following her death. Not only did he resemble her in more ways than one, but I couldn't bear more agony than I already felt. I suspected that his grief would send me to my knees.

I did not have words to describe my heartache. After a century alone in the woods, I think I'd forgotten what it felt like to have someone that cared for me. That saw you not for what others said you were, what you could be or might have once been—but who you are. Someone that cared if you made it home safe. Someone that would give their life so that you may live on.

And yet, someone that I hardly seemed to know at all.

I pinched my eyes shut, swallowing the grief that seared in my throat. Orion nudged my leg again. I turned back to him. His dark eyes looked up at me, wide and concerned. He was right. I did still have him.

I told Kyro I was going to the woods today. The castle was stifling. The air still smelled of blood, regardless of how much the chambermaids scrubbed. I'd wounded the castle in my fury —gashes in the marble, chunks of stone gauged into the floor, shards of glass from shattered chandeliers- I had damaged it more than the Air Druids had. I'd half hoped that Salem, now that he'd seen my power, would send me away. It was apparent now that I was as much a danger to his people as the Air Druids —perhaps even more so.

But I still didn't know what had happened to my father. If he was still alive, or if he'd been killed and Salem's father had something to do with it.

And now, part of me yearned to know who Rhea truly was— if the person I'd known was only a facade. I trusted her, and she could've been working to separate the Northern and Southern Territories this entire time. Salem told me to let her rest, and I tried, but my mind continued to obsess over the prophecy—why so many people found it so important. I couldn't understand why someone with as high of standing as Lady Rhea would've believed in a prophecy depicting the downfall of the monarchy. She benefitted as much as any other Lord or Lady from its existence. If the Southern Territories had delivered their messages to Kalys, Salem would've sent aid and there would've been no reason for anti-monarchy sentiments to begin with.

My mind often went round and round with these thoughts, and I kept coming back to the messages. Why hadn't Salem received the messages from the South or the Arastyan Highlands? Hypnos Keep was a shorter ride than Hera, so it would've been very difficult for an experienced rider to get lost along the way, even if they had taken Zephyr Pass.

Someone had to be interfering. But who? And why?

I came to a stop when we breached the meadow. Larks chirped around me in the twilight and rodents scurried through the grass, little claws grasping at the earth as they scrambled back to their dens. A babbling brook wound its way through tangled roots at the meadow edge, its water as clear as ice. I stepped over it and glanced back as Orion crossed the stream as well. He raised his head into the air, stretching out his neck now that we'd broken through the thicket. Breath misted around his nose. He took a step closer to me and pressed his forehead against mine. Tears welled behind my eyes. I still had him.

"Let's go sit." My voice was weak.

He heaved a breath in acknowledgment. We walked over to where Salem and I had lain in the grass, watching the stars. I knelt down to the earth, pressing my fingertips into the cool soil. Life hummed around me, buzzing in the vacant space behind my ribs.

Though this wasn't the Western Territories—my home—it was close enough.

Orion began to graze beside me, his steady heart keeping me centered as I allowed the earth's hymn to fill the aching silence, the wound that Rhea had left. My eyelids fell shut, and they did not open until a jolt went through my fingertips.

Footsteps. I opened my eyes. Through the thicket, the High King approached. He was clad in his usual glittering attire, the obsidian ring perched atop waves of dark hair. His skin appeared lavender in the overcast dusk.

He stopped a few paces in front of me. His posture was stiff —uncomfortable. His lips parted as if to speak, but he paused as if second-guessing himself. Then he tried again.

"I thought you might be here."

I pressed my lips together. "Was Rhea laid to rest?"

Salem stiffened. "Yes. I just received word. She was placed on a raft and lit ablaze before sailing off to the Eternal Lands. May Lugh see her soul to Arawn and the lands beyond." he bowed his head.

I nodded, my teeth gritted. I prayed that whoever Rhea truly was, her intentions were benevolent enough to reach the Eternal Lands. Perhaps Arawn would be merciful with her given her sacrifice. It was honorable, at the very least. But the God of the Dead was known for being particularly difficult to please. It was believed that the specific funeral rituals performed for different Druid types appeased Arawn some-what, making it easier for him to judge the souls and pass them on to the Eternal Lands. It ached me to think that my father would not have made it, given his lack of a proper funeral. I wondered how many of my people hadn't made it either during the Plague.

Salem shifted under the weight of my gaze. "I cannot keep you here against your will, Quinn. Not after what you've done for me. For Arastya. I'm granting you clemency in regard to the competition. I cannot continue to keep you from your home when you saved mine," Salem said. "I will continue to uphold my end of our agreement and have guards on regular patrol around the outskirts of the Forest, both on the Arastyan edge and the Mortal one. I've also released a statement of your innocence, as well as the debt owed to you by the kingdom."

I waited for him to laugh, to imply some condition to his terms, but none came. He was serious.

"The competition is set to continue? Even after all that has happened?" I asked.

He nodded stiffly. "I spoke to the Lords and Ladies across Arastya and it seems they still want to compete for the crown. Air Realm excluded of course. They will be dealt with separately. My mother and I have drafted amendments to the Decree for Royal Arastyan Bloodline Mediation for times of war and in special circumstances, like your own."

Orion shifted beside me. I knew how badly he wanted to return home. The gardens in Kalys, despite their lushness and grandeur, were no place for a mountain elk. Kalys was no place for a Forest Druid either. But I suppose that's only half of what I was anyways.

If the Forest would continue to be protected under Salem's reign, then what use did it have for me? I missed my home—I missed it desperately, but there was so much I had yet to accomplish. I still hadn't found my father. I did not know if he lived. I didn't know what he had to do with Salem's father and the Air Druids, why the messages between Realms were interrupted, and why someone didn't want me to find him.

It seemed there was so much left to be done, too many unanswered questions for me to return home.

"I will stay," I concluded.

Salem blinked in obvious confusion. Tendrils of night began to darken the undulating clouds above us.

"You—what?" He asked.

"My Forest does not need me now. Your people do. I will return to Kalys by morning."

The High King stared at me, dumbfounded. "You're going to stay *here* the entire night?"

I glared back. "I am not the same Druid you found in the Forest, Your Highness. But I am just as wild as I was then."

He swallowed, nodding slowly. "I—I'll await your return then, Lady Quinn."

He watched me for a moment longer, then disappeared back into the thicket. Only when his footsteps receded into silence did I allow my mind to wander back through the earth beneath me, to the ancient roots gnarled deep into the soul of the world.

The sky darkened to a pitch black as if a veil were drawn across the world, cloaking it in shadow. The ocean of clouds parted, revealing blossoms of silver starlight in the dark. But it was not the sky that had me entranced, but the shadow-drenched forest just beyond the meadow. There were no creatures there that I could feel, no beasts or fauna. But there was something familiar about the lovely depth of darkness between the trees--- as if when I stared into the abyss, it stared back.

Only when I felt Orion's heart lurch did I pause. I spun around. The sounds of the other animals fell silent.

Orion's head was held high, eyes wide and alert. Breath clouded his nose in the cool night air. His eyes looked about frantically. Something was wrong.

But I didn't feel anything unusual. I sensed no beasts greater than a doe nearby. But the doe fled. A warren of rabbits nestled into the thicket, trembling in the shadow. The meadowlarks silenced their song. Even the trees seemed to pause mid-breath as if bracing themselves for what was to come.

Then, I heard it.

"Coimét daur."

My father. That was my father's voice.

My stomach lurched into my chest. Orion didn't move. Was

that voice merely in my head or had he heard it too? I peered through the shadows. I couldn't seem to stop the hope that swelled in my chest. I'd heard his voice in the battle, I thought, as well as the night I'd been attacked. Was it possible he was alive? Had he been in the Northern Territories this entire time? Had this been where those mortals took him?

A twig snapped nearby. I looked in its direction. Two silver irises stared back at me from the shadows. A pair of crimson ears. A beast with silver fur.

Shadows swirled at the edge of a small clearing next to me, but what I felt was not Salem. It was something—someone—I did not recognize. Which meant this was another Dark Druid or something else entirely.

Someone stepped through the smoke, into the dappled starlight. My first instinct was a Druid, but the moment I felt the weight of his power on my chest, I realized I was wrong. This power—this power rivaled my own. Perhaps even greater. My stomach flipped and my lips pulled back in a snarl. I yanked an arrow from my quiver and aimed.

He was massive. Perhaps as tall as Orion. A cloak of heavy black fur hung over his back and shoulders. At the back of his neck sat a hundred short black branches—a high collar that remained open at the front. A massive crow perched atop his right shoulder, its head cocked to the side as it stared at me. In his right hand was a blade the color of ink, a silver handle glinting stubbornly against its master's dark attire. In his left hand, he held a gnarled wooden staff braided with blackthorns. The male raised his head, meeting my glare.

Silver stared back at me. A moon shrouded by clouds. A veil. Another world. Something I'd seen before. Something I'd tried to forget.

Though he didn't appear much older than I, most of his hair was the color of starlight. It fell in loose waves to his shoulders, where the silver became a deep, blood-red. Fine dark hair dotted his jawline and around his lips, which pulled back to reveal brilliantly white teeth. The air turned cold and thrummed around me.

I was in the presence of something that made me want to run. Something that—when I reached through the earth—*I could not feel.*

"*Coimét daur,*" he spoke, his voice like a dobhar chu's growl, "—I see you've found my necklace."

ACKNOWLEDGMENTS

First and foremost, thank you to my readers. Some of you have been with me since I first started writing on Wattpad, following the many iterations of this story over the last decade. Your support, patience, and belief in my work mean the world to me. To my new readers, thank you for giving a debut indie author a chance. In a world dominated by major publishers, it means everything that you took the time to read this strange creation I somehow brought to life.

A heartfelt thank you to my editor, Chersti Nieveen, for guiding me through the complexities of this world and its characters. Your invaluable feedback and encouragement helped shape this story into something magical and meaningful.

To the Celtic nations of Ireland, Scotland, Wales, Brittany, Cornwall, and the Isle of Man—your rich and beautiful lore, powerful history, and patience as I learned from and about you have shaped not only this book but also the person I am today. Thank you for reminding me of the proud heritage I come from and for proving that magic has always existed in some form.

To the National Park Service, thank you for providing me with my sanctuary and teaching me from a young age the importance of respecting and protecting nature. To Colorado State University, thank you for supporting me throughout my undergraduate career and for providing countless beautiful places to write.

To Taylor Kassel and Hannah Lardinois—your friendship and loyalty have meant everything to me. Each of you has inspired my characters in some way, and I could not have written this book without you.

To my beautiful dog, Oslo—thank you for being my unwavering companion, for loving me at my worst, and for making me smile when nothing else could. Though you may not live forever, I hope that Orion immortalizes your sassy, protective spirit and the beautiful soul that you are.

To my incredible parents, thank you for always supporting me in every venture I've pursued. You raised me to never quiet my voice, to stand up for what I believe in, and to see every challenge as an opportunity to rise. As lucky as I am to have been raised by you, I am luckier still to call you my closest friends and confidantes.

Finally, to my beautiful fiancé—thank you for loving me in the way I thought only existed in books. Thank you for indulging my obsession with Greek mythology, for taking me to the forest when I feel overwhelmed, for climbing (and jumping off) mountains with me, and for showing me a love so immense, it could never be encapsulated by words alone—but I will continue to try.

With all of my gratitude and love, thank you.

ABOUT THE AUTHOR

TJ Tristan is a debut fantasy author, and *Lovely, Dark, and Deep* is her first published work. Writing under a pseudonym, she weaves stories that blend mythology, magic, and the untamed beauty of nature.

Beyond her passion for storytelling, TJ Tristan is a dedicated medical student with a Bachelor of Science in Biomedical Sciences from Colorado State University. Born in the Pacific Northwest and raised in the rugged landscapes of the Rocky Mountains, she has always felt a deep and abiding connection to nature.

instagram.com/authortjtristan

tiktok.com/@authortjtristan